forgotten desires

WHITLOCK
F A R M S

Forbidden Hearts

Broken Dreams

Tempting Promises

Forgotten Desires

forgotten desires

NEW YORK TIMES BESTSELLING AUTHOR
CORINNE MICHAELS

Forgotten Desires

Cover Design: Sommer Stein, Perfect Pear Creative
Editing: Nancy Smay
Proofreading: Julia Griffis & Michele Ficht
Cover Art drawing: Samaiya Beaumont

Dear Reader,

It is always my goal to write a beautiful love story that will capture your heart and leave a lasting impression. However, I want all readers to be comfortable. Therefore, if you want to be aware of any possible CW please click the link below to take you to the book page where there is a link that will dropdown. If you do not need this, please go forth and I hope you love this book filled with all the pieces of my heart.

https://corinnemichaels.com/books/forgotten-desires/

dedication

To the women who put everyone before themselves and find some solace in reading. I hope this one reminds you that you're worthy of being someone else's priority.
Because you're amazing.

author's note

Thank you for purchasing Forgotten Desires. I truly hope you enjoy this book as much as I enjoyed writing it.

Forgotten Desires utilizes American Sign Language through the story. For better ease of reading, it is not written in proper ASL format. ASL is different from written English with it's own rules and structure. Most of the time, my characters will speak aloud at the same time as they sign. There are no clear rules on how to format sign language and I went back and forth with how to do it. In the end, I chose quote marks and italic.

ASL has its own dialect, which is called glossing. You may notice words not contracted, this is because there is not a contraction form for each word. This is mostly done when we are signing.

As always, I do my best to write situations and characters the best possible. Any discrepancies are mine alone and based on my experiences or those who I consulted with.

I want to address the d/Deaf writing in regards to Olivia specifically. The D/DHH community is so diverse and it is honestly a spectrum - no deaf/hard of hearing individual is the same. Everyone has a different experience, whether it's the medical diagnosis/aspect or the community aspect. I consulted with many people and there was diversity among those people to which I used my best judgment in writing. Olivia was born deaf, therefore, she would identify as Deaf (capitalized). I use this several times even though we are not in her point of view. Some members of the D/DHH do not choose to capitalize the word, some do. I am always striving to learn and do better, and hope that the Deaf representation is seen with compassion and under-standing as well as bringing awareness to what some may experience.

one

"I now pronounce you husband and wife. You may kiss the bride," the reverend says as all the guests erupt in applause. The youngest of my older brothers is now officially married and I can barely contain myself.

Rowan and Charlotte—once his mortal enemy, now his wife —turn to face us, lifting their entwined hands and then heading down the aisle of the beautiful barn with white gossamer lining the rows.

The wedding party follows them. I'm paired up with Micah, Rowan's very handsome ranch manager, and together we move outside where I hug and kiss my new sister and my brother.

"Congrats, you guys," I say, feeling so much joy for them that I can barely contain myself.

"Thanks, Brynn. We couldn't have done this without your help," Charlotte says with a smile.

I scoff. "It was nothing. I love weddings and we had fun planning."

Addison, my brother Grady's fiancée, myself, and Faye, who is Charlotte's best friend, worked tirelessly to get this wedding planned in a month. Since Asher and Phoebe are getting married

1

next month, they were super preoccupied and couldn't help much. Not to mention they have a baby and she's in grad school.

It's been nonstop with the Whitlock men finding women who were kind enough to take on their ridiculousness. As much as I joke, I love my brothers. They have been more like father figures to me than anything, since I'm so much younger than them.

Asher is the oldest, he's the one who dropped everything in his life to come move to Sugarloaf after our mom died. He took custody of me, raised me, and has been my rock. "You did good, kid," Asher says, moving to my side and grinning down at me.

I exhale and smile up at him. "I'm really not a kid anymore."

"You'll always be a kid to me."

I glance over at his fiancée, who is younger than me. "What do you call Phoebe then? Infant?" He grumbles under his breath and I fight back a laugh. "I'm kidding. I'm glad you approve."

"When have I ever disapproved of you?" he asks.

"When have I ever done anything to make you?"

He grins. "Never."

And that's because I'm a genuinely happy person. I love. I laugh. I forgive. I live my life with a cautious but open optimism. Bad things happen to good people and it's up to each of us how we handle it. Lord knows I've had enough bad to last me a lifetime, but I choose not to let it define me.

I thank my brothers for that.

Each of them has shown what strength in the face of turmoil looks like.

"I learned from you fools what not to do," I tell Asher, and he chuckles.

Where Asher was more of a parent, Grady was already enlisted in the navy, so he couldn't be here as much, but he was always checking in. He lost his wife almost four years ago and found love again, despite initially refusing to even consider it.

Rowan was the opposite of them. He is my fun brother. The one who snuck me alcohol, took me to parties that I definitely shouldn't have gone to, and encouraged me to make bad choices whenever I could get away with them.

Lord knows he made enough bad choices.

However, Charlotte was not a bad choice. She was the right one, and they were dealing with so many changes to their businesses, it was just easier to have a quick and small wedding.

"Pelt him in the face," Grady says as he hands me the bag of birdseed.

"Or not," I warn. "Because neither of you have good aim and you'll end up hitting Charlotte."

Seriously, what is wrong with men?

Grady gives me the stink eye. "You're no fun."

I swear, it doesn't matter how old they are, they're all still immature.

Rowan and Charlotte exit the barn with all of us waiting in rows for them outside. They stop at the doors, kiss, and we all clap and toss the birdseed up in the air. Thankfully my brothers behave and don't use the seeds as projectiles. The guests move around to the standing tables where there is food and champagne. Meanwhile, the bridal party marches back inside to arrange the barn into a reception.

Rowan and Charlotte will spend the next hour taking photos while the guests stay in the outside area around the barn for a more laid-back, cocktail party. It's beautiful and honestly the perfect setup.

However, this part inside the barn isn't fun.

Asher and Grady are setting up the tables and I'm making sure the chairs are correct based on the seating chart.

"Remind me again why we didn't hire a company to do this?" Grady asks as he's heaving another table over.

"Because it's expensive and we're free labor," I remind him.

"That's right."

We both smile and get back to it. It takes a good thirty minutes of us working together to get things put in the right spots. Phoebe and Addison are hanging more gossamer and my niece, Olivia, is throwing flower petals everywhere.

I let out a long sigh, surveying the room. It's really pretty. So perfect for them.

"Can you help me put the rest of these nameplates out?" Phoebe asks.

"Of course."

We go around setting up the nameplates. I take the bridal table and then do a little rearranging of where Charlotte put the town troublemakers—everyone knows you can't put Mr. Cooke next to Albert. There always needs to be a buffer.

"Who is Carson Knight?" Asher asks, looking at one of the nameplates.

Grady walks over. "Oh, that's Rowan's new boss and the guy I work for in New York. Good guy. I bet he gives great gifts."

I roll my eyes. "Yes, because either of them is the slightest bit materialistic. I'm sure they just want a good working relationship with him."

"Speaking of work, how is it going with your new company?" Phoebe asks.

I'm currently in the final stages of starting my own crisis management PR company with Catherine Cole's friend Thea in New York City. I spent a month with Catherine in California and absolutely loved my job. She owns one of the biggest PR companies that handles mostly celebrities, but she started in the corporate sector. While living in Pennsylvania and working in Manhattan isn't ideal, I have a plan to make it work. I can head into the city when I need to while we're building and I'll move when I can afford it. Because last week we signed the papers, and yesterday I made the largest bank transfer I've ever made in my life. Which means I sure as hell can't afford to live anywhere but in my cottage that's free.

I'm so excited. Thea and I already have meetings set up with potential clients and I am ready to take this industry by storm.

"It's great, we are just waiting for the paperwork back from the state and then we're in business."

"Nothing like going to college for half your life to not use the degree," Asher says offhandedly.

I know he doesn't agree with me leaving law, but I really

didn't like it. "Would you rather I throw my life away and be unhappy?"

"Of course not!"

"Then, shut up. I invested my savings in something I'm passionate about. Which is what *you* would've told me to do."

Phoebe slaps his chest and then turns to me. "I'm so happy for you, Brynn. I know you wanted to stay with Catherine's PR company, but this is really great. Hey, maybe you can chat up this Carson Knight guy and get him as your first client. I know billionaires usually need crisis management."

I laugh and turn to my brother. "What table is he at?"

Asher's eyes narrow. "The one I'm standing at . . ."

"Right." Well, this is pure luck because it's my table.

"How about we put him next to you since he doesn't have a plus one, and . . . you're by far the nicest Whitlock, and will make him feel welcome," Addison suggests.

Yes, that's my role in life, to make everyone happy and comfortable. However, it's what I'm good at. I've always been this way and it's not bad to do nice things for others. It just sometimes gets my heart into trouble.

"All right," I agree, and hope to make a good impression.

Phoebe is right, maybe this will work in my favor. Lord knows I can't afford to screw around, since I drained my life savings to start up my company.

Not to mention, I've been sending my dad money to help with his medical appointments for the last six months without my brothers knowing, and I'm about to have a whole heap of them myself.

Which is something I want to address with them, but it needs to wait until after this wedding and then Asher's in a few weeks.

I just need to make sure they're happy before I have them all mad at me.

"This is as good as it's going to get," Grady says, looking around.

I smile because it's amazing. Charlotte and Rowan are going to be so happy. "We did good."

"We really did."

We open up the big barn doors and usher the guests in. They fill the room, taking their seats, and many ooh and aah as they see how beautiful it is now. You'd never believe this is the same room where Rowan and Charlotte just got married.

I say hello and make small talk with some of the people at my table. After a few minutes, I head to the bar and get a glass of wine while there's no line. Once I have my glass, I turn to head back and see the seat next to me is now taken. Good, I get to meet a stuffy billionaire and hopefully win him over.

I take a few deep breaths and get to my seat, and when a pair of ice blue eyes meet mine, my breath stops.

I can't think. I can't move. Everything inside of me is screaming that I need to leave. To get out of here.

Because it can't be him.

Crew.

No. Oh, God. No. No, this can't be.

My heart is pounding so hard in my chest I swear it'll bruise. I look at him, trying to piece together how this man is sitting at my brother's wedding in a chair next to me reserved for Carson Knight.

He stands. "Brynlee."

"Crew?"

This is not Carson Knight. This is Crew Knight.

"Actually, it's Carson."

And then it hits me.

He lied to me. He lied about everything, including his name.

For years I've dreamed of this man who I spent a week wrapped up with. A week where I bared my soul to him, allowing him to love me the way I loved him in the limited time we had.

I've clung to that feeling. The way he looked at me, touched me, made me feel as though I was everything in the world that mattered.

And then he left me.

I shake my head. No. No, I will not stand here. I turn, feeling sick, and move around the table, past my new sister-in-law,

Phoebe, and Addison. One of them calls my name, but I rush into the bathroom and close myself in a stall.

I'm shaking as the reality of my life crashes around me. Crew Knight is actually Carson Knight, who must've thought it was cute to change his name for a spring break trip. What an asshole.

I can't go back out there. I can't possibly see him, talk to him, *sit next to him*. Not happening. I'll just stay here the rest of the day. It's fine. No one will even notice.

"Brynn?" Charlotte calls and my plan is going to be thwarted, I can feel it.

"I'm not here."

"Well, since you answered, I know that's a lie. Are you sick?"

I rest my head on the wall. "No."

"Upset?"

"I'm not here anymore. I've left this earth."

She laughs at that. "And yet I hear your voice, are you a ghost?"

"I wish."

"Why?"

Why? Because Charlotte invited the man I thought was going to be my forever. I loved him. I really did. I dreamed of him asking me to marry him, and when he left me that morning, I wanted to die.

Dramatic? Sure.

Do I give a shit? Not a bit.

"Is she okay?" I hear Phoebe's voice.

"She's in the bathroom—dead, but talking," Charlotte calls back.

"You're all going to be dead if you don't let me wallow," I warn.

The door opens and Charlotte, Addison, and Phoebe are standing there, looking at me sitting on the toilet seat.

"What if I was peeing?" I ask.

"Then you would've locked the stall," Phoebe says back with one brow raised. "Do you want to explain why you ran into the bathroom?"

7

"Crew is here," I say, knowing they won't understand, but hoping it's enough of an answer.

Charlotte purses her lips and slowly shakes her head. "I don't know anyone here by that name and since it's my wedding and all, I know the guest list."

"Crew is Carson."

"What?"

I explain it all, because they're my family and they're not my brothers, so they're less likely to kill anyone or threaten to do that.

All these years and it took only one look in his eyes for everything to come flooding back. The day we met, the smiles, the kisses, the way he held me at night on the beach, telling me he would love me until the end of time. Falling in love in just days, looking forward to the years we'd have going forward.

But that was a lie too.

How can you love someone and then walk away without a goodbye?

"Wow," Phoebe says, knowing the entire story of my past, since it sort of entwines with hers. "Was he your first after . . . him?"

She doesn't need to explain who she means since I've only been with two men. The first one also ruined Phoebe's life. "Yes."

"Wow," she says again. "Okay, so what do you need?"

I look up, not sure what the hell she means. "Need?"

"Yeah, do we change and go dig a hole, or are we ignoring him? Hoping he leaves? Do we pretend we don't know your story? What do you need from us?" Charlotte answers.

"I always wanted sisters," I say, tears welling up.

My brothers are great. I love them, I really do, but more often than not, I'm cleaning up their messes. They mean well, but they're dumb boys and they fuck up—a lot. For the first time, I feel like I have people behind me, a squad that will have my back —and I'm so overwhelmed.

"Now you have them," Addison says with a smile. "However,

you have to get out there, you can't hide out in the bathroom if you want to not look like this bothers you."

I hear shouting from outside the bathroom and Rowan's voice cuts through our girl time.

"Charlotte?"

"Go away!" I yell to my brother.

He groans. "I didn't call for you! Everyone is waiting for us to have our first dance, wife."

Charlotte looks to me and then the other girls. With a sigh, she answers him. "I'll be out in a minute. Stall them!"

"Stall?" he asks, confusion in his voice. "How?"

Phoebe replies, "Tell jokes, dance, do a jig, we'll be out when we can."

I can't do this. I can't go out there. The idea of seeing Crew after I just ran away is horrifying. My stomach churns at the thought of seeing him again, and I break.

Tears start to roll down my face and the girls gather around me.

The door slams and then my brother is there, hands balled into fists as though he can fight the world. "What's going on? Who hurt you?"

But it's him I want to fight. He invited Crew and being mad at my brothers is much easier than the hurt I feel inside. "You did!"

"Me? What the hell did I do? I got married!" Rowan looks as though he's on the brink of losing his shit.

Charlotte steps in front of me, blocking my view and squaring off to her husband. "You invited Carson Knight?"

"You knew the guest list. He's our new boss. Of course, I invited him."

Charlotte huffs. "You didn't tell me he dated your sister!"

He looks around Charlotte, his blue eyes finding mine. "You dated him?"

"Yes, but I didn't know it was him!"

"Oh my God, can someone please explain what the hell is going on here?" The exasperation in his voice echoes in the small space.

I want to tell him the story, but he'll never understand. Not only that, he'll probably flip out because . . . brothers.

So, I need to pull my shit together and stop this crap. I'm stronger than this.

Addison and Phoebe help me to my feet and I shake out my pretty dress.

"I didn't know Carson Knight was the Carson Knight that you knew."

He looks like he's on the brink of losing it. "Brynn, I'm lost, and I really need you to dumb it down for me."

I move close to him, keeping my voice even. "Do you remember when I went to the Outer Banks in college?"

"I don't remember what I ate for breakfast."

Men. I roll my eyes and sigh heavily. "Okay, Row. I went to the Outer Banks every spring break during college. It was my favorite thing I did with my sorority sisters. We rented the house on the beach, and we'd party and whatnot. My junior year, we went and the house next to us was a frat from up north. We hung out, partied with them, and I met Crew."

"Who the fuck is Crew?"

"Carson."

He turns to his wife. "Is this some kind of wedding prank? Like, you get my sister to pretend she's lost her mind and then fuck with me to see if my head explodes?"

"If it was, I'd be having a lot more fun."

Yeah, we'd all be having fun if this was a joke, but it's not. Although sometimes it feels like my life is part of a comedy skit.

Rowan looks back to me. "So, again, who is Crew?"

"Crew is really Carson."

"As in, my new boss? The billionaire who owns Knight Food Distribution and those other companies?"

I nod. "The same one and I didn't know."

"I'm trying to keep calm and follow this, but can someone please tell me what has her crying?" Rowan asks us.

"She loved him," Addison explains.

"And he left her," Phoebe chimes in.

"And now she finds out that he lied to her about who he was. All this time, she's searched for him, thinking his name was really Crew, and now he's at our wedding because you invited him," Charlotte adds on.

"My fault, got it."

Charlotte smiles. "Learning early, husband."

"Do you want me to kick his ass?" Rowan asks.

"No!" all four of us yell.

"Then what the hell is the point of this? I'll throw him out, respectfully, so I can afford to live, and tell Crew/Carson he can't be here because he dated my sister however many years ago and she's crying in the bathroom."

Charlotte goes to him, rolling her eyes. "You need to go back out there, tell the DJ to cue up our song and play it in three minutes. We're going to get Brynn ready, and she's going to march out there being the badass woman she is, not even looking at him again."

Rowan huffs and leaves, then the girls move to help me. We clean up my face and fix my dress. I stand in front of the mirror, smoothing my long, reddish hair, and sigh. "I can do this."

"You absolutely can," Addison says and then kisses my cheek. "I'm going to check on Grady and make sure Elodie and Jett didn't destroy the cupcakes. Since these kids can find trouble anywhere they go."

She heads out, then Charlotte pulls me in for a hug. "I'm sorry he's here, but . . . let him look at what he walked away from and eat his heart out because you're beautiful, smart, and he should've seen that."

I grin. "Thank you."

Then it's just me and Phoebe.

Of everyone, she and I are closest. Phoebe is the only one outside my brothers who knows about my past. She knows about the man I loved when I was only sixteen, who told me he loved me, would always love me, and then took advantage of that trust.

Phoebe understands better than anyone else possibly could, since the same man did the same thing to her.

I didn't think I could ever trust a man again, give a part of my heart to another, until I met Crew.

Phoebe takes my hand. "We're all here for you, Brynn."

I squeeze it back. "I know."

"Do you want to sit with Asher? I'll totally sit next to Carson and drive him crazy," she proposes, and I laugh.

"No, but I love you for offering."

"You know, after Jonathan, I never thought I'd ever trust anyone again." A tremor runs up my spine at the mention of his name. "Asher showed me that it's okay to be vulnerable sometimes. He gave me a safe place to be who I am and he loves me, despite all my faults and insecurities. If he left me now, I'd be broken, but . . . I'd be so grateful for the healing he's helped me have too. Maybe that's what this guy gave you, a way to be stronger after the hell you endured."

Crew had been exactly that. Ours was an honest type of relationship. While it was only a week, it was seven days that felt like years. My cheeks would hurt at night from smiling so much because he just made me happy.

"It wasn't even hard to fall for him," I explain. "It was as though I conjured the perfect man and there was Crew. He was funny, sweet, talked to me about his fears and worries like we had endless time before us. I thought we'd at least try, not that he'd disappear in the middle of the night."

Phoebe gives me a soft smile. "He's here though. He had to know who you were."

"How? He knows Rowan Whitlock, but it's not like he knew he was my brother."

"Maybe not, but hiding in here isn't going to get your answers. I'm not exactly the authority on men, but I don't know many guys who come to weddings for their business contractors, you know? I kind of think he had another reason to come to Sugarloaf."

A flicker of hope starts to ignite, but I snuff it out quickly. If he does have another reason, I'm going to find out, and then I'm going to guard my heart.

two

CARSON

I'm torn between going to find her and leaving. I shouldn't have come. When I got the invite, I told my assistant to decline, but somehow, it slipped through the cracks and she forgot. Then, a few days ago, I had a meeting with Rowan about the increase in goods we'd like to move toward, and he mentioned the wedding, how he hoped I could make it. Then he said his sister, Brynlee, was driving him and Charlotte nuts.

The second I heard the name everything changed.

I knew I had to see her.

It's crazy, since it's been ten years and I wasn't exactly what you'd call a good guy the way I disappeared, but time has passed and she's never left my thoughts.

Not ever.

Not even when I married my ex-wife Jacqueline.

Our marriage wasn't exactly born of love, it was arranged through our families. A merging of assets. One where children of wealthy families have an understanding of what's expected and we were pawns who fell in line.

It was utter bullshit. The only good thing that came from that marriage was my daughter, Layla.

Fuck it. I should go. This was stupid.

As I move to stand, the DJ starts playing music and Charlotte and Rowan take the floor. Then, as if time never passed and we'd been connected all along, I feel her presence.

She pulls the chair out and sits beside me, her eyes just a little puffy and my heart aches at that.

"Brynn . . ."

"Crew, or should I call you Carson?"

I deserve the icy tone in her voice. Ten years ago, I was a fucking idiot. I was twenty-two, had a family breathing down my neck to prepare for my upcoming life, and then my life was flipped on its side because of Brynlee Whitlock.

"Crew is what my friends and family call me."

She nods. "So you just lied about your name?"

I sit up straight, hating the mistakes I made back then. Everything we shared for that week was real, other than my name. That was the only lie I told. However, I doubt she'll believe me. Not that I blame her.

"That was truly the only lie I told. Everything else was the truth. Probably more of the truth than I ever told anyone," I admit. "It kind of happened and then I couldn't walk it back. I'm sorry."

She exhales, clasps her hands in her lap and looks at me. Those big brown eyes are exactly like I remember. "All these years, Crew. All this time, and you appear now?"

"I wish I could explain it."

"Try."

Okay. I can do that. "Do you want to know why I left that night or why I'm here now?"

Brynn shakes her head with a small smile. "I guess both, but let's start with why you're here now."

"I was invited."

She huffs. "I walked into that one."

"I wanted to see you," I answer honestly. "I didn't realize Rowan was your brother until he mentioned it the other day, then before I knew it, I changed my entire schedule to be here."

"You changed your schedule?"

I feel a little stupid admitting that, but it's the truth. "Yes. To see you."

"Kind of an insult to the bride and groom."

I smile. "I'll make it up in the wedding gift."

The teasing—just a few seconds of it—and I'm taken back to when we met.

"Come on, Crew!" Ford yelled as I ran toward the football he'd purposely thrown at the sorority girls who were tanning next door.

It was definitely not a bad view. "Sorry, girls!"

A few giggled and the others rolled their eyes as they went back to sunning themselves.

I reached where the football landed, squatted down to look for it, and I saw a pair of long, tanned legs before me, with one foot tapping. Slowly, I let my gaze travel her body, up over her flat stomach, to where a very nice rack was waiting above.

"Hello there," I said, coming to my full height.

The little redhead looked up. "Hi. Did you lose something?"

"My ball."

She put her hand on her hip, extending the football with the other. "I figured. Be more careful, not every girl here grew up with a houseful of brothers who threw things."

"A houseful?" I asked, intrigued.

"Well, three, but if you factor in when they had friends around, the number grew."

"Crew!" Ford yelled and I lifted my hand up, not even turning to look at him. "Bro!"

The gorgeous girl raised one perfectly arched brow. "You're being paged."

"He can wait."

"He looks pissed."

I grinned. "Good. He threw the ball at you girls—this is his punishment. He can wait. Now, what's your name?"

She looked off to the side before meeting my gaze again. "What's it worth to you?"

"My life," I said rather dramatically.

"Your life? My name is worth that? Wow, I'm pretty damn important."

"You are."

She smiled. "Brynlee."

"Beautiful name for a beautiful girl."

That caused her eyes to roll. "Dear God. Does that work on girls at whatever college you go to?"

"Yale."

Her pouty lips pursed. "Yale? Wow. Smart guys."

"Goddamn it, Crew! We're playing a game!" Ford yelled again.

"Some of us were," I said to Brynlee and then turned to my best friend and threw the ball. "Here. Now fuck off." Ford flipped me off, I returned the gesture and then went back to the beautiful woman before me. "There. Where were we?"

"I think you were telling me how smart you are with all your cheesy pickup lines," Brynlee said with a tilt of her head.

The way she talked to me made me want to spend hours with her. She had no idea who I was, where I came from. That gave me a freedom I'd never felt before with a girl. In New York, my family name is known. My grandfather and father are multi-millionaires. Both built an empire that would one day be mine.

I didn't have the luxury of casual dating or meeting a girl on a beach at home, but here I did.

"How about we take a walk and I'll try a few of my favorites out on you?" I offered, hoping she'd take the chance.

Her lips pursed. "How do I know you're trustworthy?"

"You don't."

"So why should I go?"

I leaned in, my voice was low and husky. "Because that's the fun of spring break. You take a risk and hope it pays off." I extended my hand and waited. Brynlee looked at it, back at my face, and then placed her palm in mine, and that week got infinitely better.

. . .

"Do you remember when we met?" I ask, pulling myself from the memory.

"Of course I do. I also remember when you left." There's no anger in her tone, just sadness and hurt lingering there. "It was ten years ago. I've gotten past it, but I remember."

"I do too," I admit. "I was leaving in a day, and I wanted to spend every second with you. I never wanted what we had to end, Brynn. It was fucking incredible, but I didn't know how to walk away. How did I tell you that my life was already mapped out and we could never be more than just the time we'd spent?"

She lets out a long breath and then stands slowly. "I don't know, but the way you did it was wrong, and it broke my heart."

I get to my feet. "It broke mine too."

Her eyes fill with sorrow and then she forces a smile. "It was a long time ago. I hope you're doing well. It's clear you are, since you own the company my brother is doing business with."

It feels like she's dismissing me. Not that I blame her. Not that I thought I deserved anything more, but it isn't what I want. I would give anything to catch up, know more about her life, tell her about mine. To talk to her the way we did when we were kids.

"Do you want me to go, Bee?" I ask.

Her eyes flash at the nickname, but she recovers quickly. "No. You should stay, you were invited, after all. I just need to make my rounds. It was good to see you, Crew."

I take a step back, allowing her the space to leave. "I hope we can talk again."

Brynlee smiles again and nods once. "I'm sure we will, since we're seated next to each other."

Then she walks away, and I feel the same tear in my heart I did ten years ago.

three

BRYNLEE

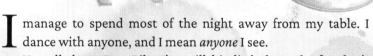

I manage to spend most of the night away from my table. I dance with anyone, and I mean *anyone* I see.

He called me Bee. Like I'm still his little honeybee? I don't think so. He's going to need a reminder that bees sting and right now I'd like nothing more than to cause him pain like he caused me.

I'm searching for a new dance partner when Asher approaches me, hand out. I take it eagerly. "You look beautiful, Brynn."

"You look quite handsome yourself."

"Are you okay?" he asks.

"I am now."

It's the truth. While this hasn't exactly been fun and stress free, I'm surviving better than I thought I would at the start of the night.

"Do you want to tell me about it?"

I smile up at my protective and loving older brother. "No."

He chuckles. "I figured."

"You're not exactly known for handling things well when it comes to the women in your life."

Asher jerks his head back. "Me? I'm completely rational."

Definitely not the word I'd use. "Correct me if I'm wrong, but didn't you drive twelve hours to punch a certain person in the face because he hurt Phoebe?"

Not that he didn't deserve it, but still, twelve hours is a long time to hang onto a bad decision. Knowing Asher, he probably just got angrier the farther he went instead of calming down like a normal person who might question whether something is a good idea.

"And you. Let's not forget that. But, yes, I did, and I'd do it again."

"Exactly my point," I laugh.

"Does this guy require an ass kicking?"

I roll my eyes. "What is with you Whitlock men? Are you just all itching to fight someone?"

He spins me around the dance floor and grins. "We'll fight for the things we love."

"As much as I appreciate it, I promise it's fine. He just took me by surprise, that's all."

"Can you give me a little more than that?"

Though telling Asher is at the bottom of my to-do list, I know that if I don't give him some of the story, he'll probably say or do something that will make things worse—like deck Crew.

"Carson and I met a long time ago on one of my spring break trips in college. Things didn't end great. He kind of ghosted me and I was really hurt by it. We haven't seen each other in ten years and really, the last place in the world I ever expected to see him again was at Rowan's wedding."

That should do it.

"Why would that upset you so much?" he pries further.

I should've known that with Asher, no amount of information is good enough. "I liked him. I loved him, really. I know you think that it's asinine falling for someone in a week, but I did. Instead of saying goodbye to me, he left, and we didn't even have each other's phone numbers, it was . . . sad."

"And you're sure you don't want me to kick his ass?"

I laugh a little. "No, Asher, I don't."

The song ends and he kisses my cheek. "I don't think falling for someone fast is asinine, Brynn. You have a very open heart, you always have, and it's what we all love about you. I fell for Phoebe fast, and let's not even talk about Rowan and Charlotte. What I think is asinine is that he could live his life after walking away from you."

Tears fill my eyes and I blink them back. "That was sweet."

"It was honest."

I give my big brother a hug, tell him how much I love him, and we part ways. As I'm going to find another dance partner, Crew steps in front of me.

I stop short and my pulse jumps. "Crew."

"Will you dance with me?"

Oh, no. That's so not a good idea. "I'm really tired," I try as an excuse.

"Okay, we'll sit at the table and talk."

Shit.

"Actually, I think I might have to help with my nieces or nephew. You know, kid duty," I try for another way out of this.

"I'll go with. I love kids."

That makes me pause. "You love kids? Since when?"

I remember a very in-depth conversation where he explicitly said he was never having kids.

"Dance with me and we'll talk . . ." He extends his hand.

There's no way the people of this town aren't paying attention to this. Not only because they're nosey as hell, but because he's new here and I'm sure people know he's Rowan's boss. So, I have no choice really.

I smile, place my hand in his, and let him lead me to the dance floor.

"I remember the first time we danced," Crew says with a smile.

"We didn't have music then."

"No, we had just our heartbeats and the ocean."

It was my favorite song.

I don't say it. I won't say it because that will make me sound ridiculous, and I'm pretty sure I've done that already.

"Well, we have music now at least."

Crew's blue eyes stay on mine. "I liked our song better."

My stomach tightens and I swear I could swoon as though I was in a regency novel. Lord help me.

I clear my throat, plaster on my smile, and decide we need to get off the topic of us and the past and focus on him. That will at least be easy. "So, it seems you're doing well?"

"I am. I work a lot, but . . . it goes with the territory of owning five companies."

"Five?" I ask with surprise.

"I have a new tech start-up that took off very quickly, Knight Food Distribution, and three companies that support both of those, which instantly doubles my profits and also provides help to other companies."

"Leaves very little time for a life."

He nods slowly and pulls me a little closer to avoid someone who was about to bump into me. His cologne fills my senses and I want to melt into him. He smells the same—tobacco with a hint of vanilla and bourbon. It's sexy and warm, and I remember wanting to bathe in it.

That scent that clung to my pillow after that night. I took that pillow home with me and slept on it until the scent disappeared, just like he did.

"A lot has changed in ten years," Crew says, pulling me away from my thoughts.

"Yes, I figured. And a lot's changed for me too."

And yet I'm here, like a ninny, remembering a spring break romance.

"Some things feel the same though, don't they?"

I nod. "Some."

He laughs softly. "So, any husband? Boyfriend? Kids?"

I shake my head. "Nope. I've been finishing up law school, helping my family get their lives together, and caring for the animals I have on my sanctuary. You?"

His body stiffens just a little and now I'm even more focused. "I got married, and divorced, she's a . . . well, it wasn't amicable, to say the least. The only good thing that came out of that mess was my daughter. She's four, her name is Layla."

I was prepared not to like his answer, but for some reason, I'm not as upset as I thought I'd be. "Layla is a beautiful name."

"She's literally the reason I exist anymore."

"I told you back then that kids are everything in this world."

He smiles. "You were right. Want to see a photo?"

I nod.

Crew pulls back a little, grabbing his phone out of his pocket. "Here, this is her."

The photo shows the most beautiful little girl I've ever seen. She has Crew's ice blue eyes and her hair is the softest blond. "Oh, she's gorgeous. I bet she's the most spoiled girl on the planet."

He inhales deeply. "She is. She's perfect and I love her. I'm actually starting a custody battle."

"You are?"

"Her mother is a raging alcoholic who is more focused on her own needs than Layla's. Layla cries when I have to take her home, and the nanny said the other day, after her day off, she found her wearing the same clothes she left her in."

My heart sinks. "Oh God. I'm so sorry."

Crew knows about my childhood. How my father, Howie, hit my mother and would rough me up a little, and that we left to escape his abuse. He, too, was an alcoholic and had no desire to get sober. It wasn't until I was an adult that he finally started to change. It's a daily battle for him, one that he lost again about a year ago. But he's sober again, and now, more than ever, he needs to stay that way.

The music ends and we step apart, not sure where to go from this point. As he opens his mouth, his phone rings. "Excuse me, I have to take this."

He steps over to the side of the room, and I make my way toward my seat. Crew gets there around the same time as me. "Is everything okay?"

25

"No, I have to go. I'm . . . I'd like to have coffee or something. Talk more."

There's a big part of me that wants to say yes. To fall back into that safe place where Crew and I existed, but there's no point. His life and mine are in completely different stratospheres.

"I don't know if . . ."

"Don't say no," he says quickly. "Here, this is my card. Call if you ever want to. I understand if not. But, fuck, I hope you call." Then he lifts his hand and brushes my cheek with his thumb. "I really want to see you again, Bee."

Then, just like he did ten years ago, he leaves, and I don't think I'll ever see him again.

four

CARSON

"Y ou're kidding! It was *her*?" Ford Warner, my best friend and right-hand man, asks as we're eating takeout in my office.

"It was her."

"So what happened?"

I lean back, dropping my fork and feeling like a hundred times the asshole I am. "I showed up, we danced, talked, and I gave her my card."

"Your card?" he asks with a laugh. "Smooth."

"I got a call from the nanny and needed to get to Layla. I didn't have time for much else."

He shakes his head. "You didn't ask for her number?"

This is what I regret most. Sure, I could have my security team find it for me, but that's not the route I'm going. She needs to come to me this time.

"I put the ball in her court."

He laughs. "Pussy."

"Fuck off. I didn't want to be too pushy. I hurt her and if she never wants to see me again, I get it. My life isn't exactly one that many women want to jump into. I have a crazy ex-wife, a kid, and I'm a workaholic who never seems to be satisfied no matter what my bank account says." I'm not exactly a catch outside of my net worth.

Ford tilts his head and smirks. "That's true. You also aren't much fun anymore. However, you know you've never stopped thinking of Brynn. Even after you married Digger."

My ex-wife, also known as Digger—short for gold digger—could never compare to what I felt when I met Brynlee. It was . . . indescribable and definitely not normal. But we were kids. I was a rich, asshole kid who was about to inherit my family's company and my grandfather's fortune when I graduated college.

I knew all we'd have was that week.

I couldn't have a future with some random hookup on spring break. My family never would've permitted it.

However, my heart didn't give two shits about any of that. It wanted her. She made me feel like a normal person for the first time in my life.

She cared about me, not the money, my family's last name, or what I could give her. Not like Jacqueline, where that was literally all she cared about.

"No, and Jacqueline never let me forget that. She hated the girl she could never be, even though she didn't even know Brynn's name."

"She hated humans with hearts too, but that's not the point."

"What *is* the point, Ford?" I ask.

"The point is that you found her after all these years. And she happens to be the sibling of the new contract you signed? Dude, that's like . . . fate or some shit."

I pick up my fork, taking a bite so I don't have to say anything back. I don't know that fate would be so goddamn cruel as to bring her into my life at a time when everything is falling apart.

"It would've been better if I went on with my fucked-up life never seeing her again. I never should've gone to that wedding, but I just couldn't stay away."

Ford shakes his head. "I've known you my whole life, Crew. Since we were what? Six? I've never seen you walk away from something you want."

"This isn't a fight I can win. I'm getting ready to start a goddamn custody battle. The last thing I can do is bring another woman into the mix, not while Jacqueline hired a bunch of fucking photographers so she can make me out to be a man-whore who cheated on her. Not when Layla is where my focus needs to be. I want my daughter to be away from her toxic, manipulative mother, and with me. That's what I can't walk away from."

My daughter needs me. Layla can't fight this fight, I have to. As her father, it's my job to protect her, even if it's from her own mother.

"And your companies," Ford tacks on.

"Always that."

Work has been the only thing I've excelled at since I graduated from college. My father is still a part of the daily running of the company, but I hold the control. When Dad was off doing what-ever model he was doing, I took this company from being a middle-of-the-road distribution company to being at the top. After that, I started four companies that feed the needs of this company and many others, which only further increased my wealth.

It's been what drives me. At least, until I had Layla.

Ford groans and raises his arms over his head. "Well, the lawyer you hired seems to be a shark. She'll get you more time with Layla."

"It's not about time, it's about protecting her. Layla is . . ." I don't have to explain it, everyone knows how Layla is. She's perfect.

No matter how she came into this world, I wouldn't change the fact that she's here and she's mine.

"I know, Crew. I know. She's the cutest freaking kid I've ever seen, even though the poor thing looks exactly like you."

I laugh at that. "It's the eyes."

"Yeah, your whole family has those freakishly light blue eyes. Everyone hates them."

"Kimberly never complained." A slow smile creeps over his

face at the mention of my sister, and I point at him. "Don't even think about it."

Ford has had feelings for Kimberly since we were kids. The thing is, my sister would never consider dating him. So, we all get to watch him pine after her and laugh as she turns him down repeatedly.

He stands, tossing our lunch in the garbage. "I'd never dream of it."

"That's all you dream of."

"Unlike you, who dreams of a woman who you just found again but are too much of a chicken shit to go after."

I roll my eyes. "She looked at me like I destroyed her."

"You walked out of her room that night and never went back. You probably did."

That's also what is keeping me from reaching out to her. Not to mention, it was ten years ago. What the hell am I going to say? *Sorry, I wasn't man enough to wake you and tell you the truth. I wanted to go back, give you my number, tell you the truth, but I thought it was better this way since we had no future. By the way, I loved you, even though I didn't know what love was then.*

Yeah, every girl's dream man right there.

"I needed to go. We already were in too deep, and my parents would've eaten her alive."

"Maybe, but you should've been honest with her," Ford reminds me.

I should've. I knew that then and I know it now.

"It never would've worked."

He shakes his head. "Maybe not, but your grandfather is dead now. Your father couldn't give two fucks about who you're dating or who you marry, since you did your duty. Let's cut the crap, Crew. You could be with her."

"Not now."

He shrugs. "Not with that attitude."

"It won't work, she wouldn't want this life."

He rolls his eyes. "Please, and Digger did? Sure, her family was all prestigious and whatnot, but they were never up to your family's caliber. Digger's family wanted to be, which is why they hitched their wagon to yours. Their pockets were never as deep as yours."

"Not many are as deep as mine now."

"Exactly!" he yells. "None of that matters now. Get the girl you want, not the one who was forced on you."

Yeah, all of that sounds great, but the one I was forced to take will never be out of my life.

My phone buzzes and my assistant, Ginny, speaks. "Mr. Knight, Ms. Banks is here to see you."

"Send her in." Ms. Banks is the lawyer I hoped would help me secure custody of my daughter.

I clean up my desk and stand as Ford shakes her hand before she makes her way to me. "Mr. Knight, it's a pleasure to meet you." Ms. Banks is nothing like I expected. She seems like she'd be a tall, broad woman with her deep voice. Instead, she's maybe five foot—with heels—has short hair, and dark skin with the most piercing eyes I've ever seen.

"You as well." I shake her extended hand.

"I received your email and the details sent over by Mr. Warner." She looks to Ford. "Everything looks to be in order, and I think we have a very good case against your ex-wife."

"You do?" I ask skeptically, gesturing for her to sit in the seat in front of my desk.

"Yes, I've worked with many fathers who want custody of their children with similar situations, and I have an excellent win record."

"So you believe we'll be able to get full custody of Layla?" I ask, leaning back in my chair.

She crosses her legs and nods. "I believe we have a very good chance, yes."

That isn't a yes. "You think there's just a chance?"

Ms. Banks smiles, but there's no humor there. "Mr. Knight, I'm not in the habit of making promises I can't keep. Do I think we can get custody? Of course I think that, or I wouldn't be sitting here. Do I have a good guess on the chances? No. It depends on the judge and the information your ex-wife is presenting. Do you do drugs?"

"No."

"Drink excessively?"

I shake my head. "No."

"Have you ever hit or abused your wife or child?"

"Not ever." My voice leaves no room for confusion on that.

"Cheated?" She continues her interrogation.

"No."

She shifts in her chair. "Good. And you have proof of a possible neglect situation?"

"I have the nanny, who is willing to testify. I have voicemails where Jacqueline is belligerent and can't remember where she is. The fact she doesn't come home some nights and Layla cries because Jacqueline is—unkind—when she's drunk."

"All of that is good, but I want to temper your expectations. It is very hard to get a judge to remove a child from her home to go into an unsteady household. She's the child's mother and they are going to consider the time that you spend with your daughter in comparison to the time she spends with your ex-wife."

"I've never missed a visitation," I inform her.

That's the one thing I am adamant about. I will always be there for Layla. If I can have time with her, I take it. Two weeks ago I flew sixteen hours to spend three with her. There's nothing I won't do for that little girl.

Ford clears his throat. "The issue is that Jacqueline claims two of the above things are true. That he cheated on her, and he was emotionally abusive. She's trying to get Carson's visitation reduced and an increase in child support and alimony."

"I imagine she is. Your net worth has grown and she signed a pretty iron-clad prenup," Ms. Banks replies, keeping her gaze on mine. "I've dealt with this before, Mr. Knight. Which is why I believe you contacted me. I know her lawyer well, and he's good, very good, but I believe I'm better. How long have you been divorced now?"

"Three years, three months."

Her brows rise. "So you were in the process of divorcing when your daughter was born?"

"Jacqueline thought if she could become pregnant, I'd drop the divorce. She got me incredibly drunk, and got herself pregnant when she stopped taking her birth control the day I filed the papers." Yeah, that's my ex-wife. A manipulative and calculating bitch who had a child just to keep her finances where she wanted them.

"I see," Ms. Banks says, pursing her lips. "And I'm assuming since the baby was born during the process, there were concessions on both ends?"

Ford laughs. "I think you mean on Carson's end."

"Yes, I agreed to a monthly amount for Layla's needs. I also fought for fifty-fifty custody, but since she was an infant, it was denied because I was living in a hotel and Jacqueline was going to breastfeed Layla."

"And did she breastfeed Layla?"

"No," I say, feeling a surge of anger that only comes when I think of her.

Ms. Banks nods once. "For a medical reason?"

"No. Because she didn't want her perfectly paid-for breasts to deflate and wanted to drink wine. Which is fine, I don't care about that, but it was what kept me from more time with Layla as a baby, and that's what I'm angry about."

Truly, I couldn't have given two shits why she didn't want to breastfeed. Her reasons weren't my concern, but Layla was. I wanted to be there with her. I wanted to hold her at night, be the father that mine wasn't because he was always gone.

I know she'll never remember that time—she was a baby—but I wanted it. Time is a luxury that you can't afford to give away. I could have all the money in the world, and it wouldn't matter because I can't buy that back.

"I understand." She clasps her hands, resting them in her lap. "Mr. Knight, I'm going to get to work, and do what I do best, which is dismantling every possible angle of defense that she is going to use. We'll start off filing a petition, which can take time to get through the courts. Then we'll have a preliminary hearing, where your ex-wife will have a chance to present her case, and then we will. It's not easy, it's not fast. I want you to be prepared for a long fight, and one that often shows sides of people we never wish to see. In the meantime, what I need from you is perfection."

I lean back in my seat, glancing at Ford who shakes his head. "Perfection?"

"Yes. You need to be the perfect father, businessman, friend, brother, son, I don't care whatever titles you hold, each one has to be perfect. You need to appear like the family man that every man aspires to be. If you're seen with a woman, you're marrying her. No dating, no casual sex, no hints of bachelor life. So, if you don't plan to marry the woman you could be linked to, don't be linked. I want you to continue your charity work, but do some . . . showboating, if possible. All of your life, every aspect, has to be meticulous. Do you understand?"

"So cancel the trip to Bali with my two model friends?" I ask, kidding.

She grins. "Cancel everything other than things for business or Layla." Ms. Banks stands and extends her hand, and I shake it. "I believe I can get a court date in a few weeks thanks to some friends. As I said before, be ready, because this is going to be a long process."

Ford walks her to the door and when it closes, he turns to me. "Guess now you have another reason not to talk to the small-town girl you boinked in college."

"Yeah, unless I plan to marry her."

~Two Weeks Later~

I have a fucking headache. That's what two hours of meetings with lawyers and Jacqueline gave me. That's all they gave me, in fact.

I'm no closer to having custody of Layla now than I was when we started. I'm fucking tired of this. My lawyer comes up behind me as I stand on the corner of Ninth and Fortieth, feeling so much anger it's not even normal.

"Mr. Knight." My lawyer's voice breaks through.

I turn to her, giving her the full weight of my displeasure. "I pay you an ungodly amount of money to get results. What the hell was that?"

"That was your ex-wife having her say. I told you that the first part of this was going to be stressful."

I point to the building. "That wasn't stressful, it was a goddamn massacre. Photos that aren't even real! I had to sit and listen to her paint me as some fucked-up playboy who has done nothing but dick around since I was a kid. When exactly was I going to have the time to do that when I built four companies and practically rebuilt the fifth? That was the whole reason she cheated on me!"

To my surprise, Ms. Banks doesn't flinch. "And in the next meeting, we get to discuss your ex's transgressions and the fact that she paid to have those photos taken. I warned you that trying to take custody from a perfectly sane—on paper—charitable woman was going to be hard. As much as you hate her, she has the exact look that a judge wants to see. She lives in a cozy brownstone that you bought, equipped with a room for a princess, a nanny, carpeted floors, and baby proofing. You're a bachelor, living in a penthouse that is made of marble, and you have your picture taken by her private investigator whenever you're seen with a woman. I warned you about that."

I run my fingers through my hair. "I have dinner meetings."

"Don't." The one word feels like a reprimand from my mother.

"You're telling me that I can't conduct my business life the way I have to?"

Ms. Banks picks at her nail. "I'm telling you that if you want custody of Layla, you need to be a saint. A family man. You want to do business? Fine. Find a woman who will go with you. One who is your steady girlfriend. Find a wife, Carson, not dinner dates. No models and no actresses. Find a down-home, wholesome girl who looks like an angel next to your ex-wife. I understand you're not doing anything wrong, but perception is what we're working with. Your ex painted that image because she knew it would garner sympathy. The billionaire who has everything he wants and would rather stick his daughter in the corner of a multimillion-dollar penthouse than pay the alimony to give her a stable home. That's the game she's playing, and she's playing it well. We have a month until the next meeting, where we'll present our side of this."

I shake my head. A month of Layla being with the nanny and Jacqueline doing God knows what.

"She's a raging alcoholic. Layla needs to be out of that home."

"I understand that, but being an alcoholic doesn't make her a bad mother in the eyes of the law."

Unreal. "Neglect does."

"And I'm building that case."

"Why is the judge extending this so much?" I ask.

"Because Layla isn't in apparent inherent danger. We'll have our day in court, Carson. Until then, please take what I say to heart. If you need to meet with women, appear to have a steady girlfriend who is beside you each time. Even better if you put a ring on it. I know it's not fair, it's often not in these cases."

I exhale deeply and straighten when Jacqueline walks out with her lawyers. She has her big, round sunglasses on, holding a tissue under her nose. She comes toward me. "I loved you with my whole heart, Carson. I wish you weren't trying to hurt me so much. Layla is my life. How could you try to take her from me? How could you be so cold? I always thought your abuse would end with me, not extend to Layla."

I bite down because anything I say at this point can be used against me. My lawyer maneuvers herself between us. "Please allow Mr. Knight some privacy. We'll communicate through your lawyers."

Jacqueline pulls her glasses off, dabbing at her eyes as though she's in line for an Emmy based on this performance. She definitely would've won one in the judge's chambers. "It doesn't need to be this way. I still love you, Crew. We can find a way through this and do what's best for Layla, which is having both her parents together."

Her lawyers come to her, pulling her away, and I stay silent. Once she's gone, Ms. Banks turns to me. "I'm going to continue working with our investigation team to build our case."

"Whatever it takes to get my daughter."

She nods once. "Understood."

My driver, Cliff, pulls up and exits the car to open my door. "I'm going to walk," I say before he can get near.

"Very well, sir."

My mind is spinning in a thousand directions, none of them leaving me feeling much optimism. I hoped, even thought, that maybe today would go somewhat well. I never thought we'd end up meeting again. Although, that's probably exactly what Jacqueline hoped for. She increased her request for more money, stating Layla needed better care.

What the hell a four-year-old needs sixty-thousand dollars a month for will never make sense to me.

But it's not the money. I'd give her every penny in my bank account if it meant I could have Layla with me. I don't get to kiss her goodnight or see her run to me when I walk in the door.

What my lawyer said is right, I work a lot. I do it because I have nothing to come home to. There's nothing forcing me to rush to my penthouse. It's cold there, and maybe that's something I need to think about. How to make it a home. Somewhere that Layla can feel comfortable, although she never seems unhappy with me when we're together.

Still, I can give her more.

I want to give her more.

I want to give her the life I dreamed of, the one I spoke of ten years ago, when I believed I could ever have something like I had with the woman I walked away from. The only woman I would consider having as someone steady in my life . . . but I can't do that to her again.

five

BRYNLEE

"We need to do a few more tests and if everything goes well, we'll be ready to go with the liver transplant." The doctor smiles warmly as she places her hands on her desk. "Do you have any questions?"

My father reaches over to take my hand. "My concern is my daughter. What is her recovery going to be like being a donor?"

"It really will depend on Brynlee's body, but she's young, very healthy, and seems to have a great support system. She'll spend about a week in the hospital, then after that it's a very slow ease back into normal life. I usually estimate around six to eight weeks until you feel back to normal, but I won't sugarcoat this. It can take six months before you are able to do strenuous activities."

"Does that mean caring for my animals? I have Second Chances Sanctuary and those animals mean the world to me."

She gives me a soft smile. "You'll need to find someone to help care for them."

"And how soon will we do the surgery since we know I'm a match now?" I ask.

"I'd say in the next four to six weeks. Your father's faring well, so this isn't a life-or-death situation, but I don't want to get to the point that he's in end-stage liver failure, and also we can't delay much past our eligibility date. You have a little over three weeks until you will have been sober for twelve months. As soon as we meet that date, I would like to move forward with the transplant."

I glance to my father, who inhales deeply. He's been trying hard and doing so well, but he relapsed a year ago, and I'm so afraid he'll do it again. "I'm so proud of you, Dad. We're so close."

He squeezes my hand. "It's a battle, but I won't lose this time."

I hope not. As much as my past with my father is tumultuous, he's still my father and I don't want to see him die. If I can do this, help him, then I'll at least know I did everything. However, the next few weeks are up to him.

"So, about a month or so?"

"Yes. Have you had a chance to speak with the financial team regarding the costs?"

Yeah, that part is a huge issue. Since I don't have a job, I don't have insurance. Howie definitely doesn't have insurance. His medical costs are being paid for by a charity and the transplant center, but mine can't be covered in full. I have to come up with almost $300,000 for my care and the surgery costs.

Which I don't have.

Not that I ever had that, but I spent my life's savings a few weeks ago when I started my company.

"I'm not sure what to do," I admit. "I'll find a way, but right now I don't have a clear idea where to get the money."

Howie coughs a little. "You shouldn't have to pay for this. If I didn't screw up last time and start drinking, everything would've been covered."

"Dad, it'll be fine. I'll figure out a way."

Dr. Carr writes something down. "There are a lot of charities that can help with your costs, Brynn. Normally, insurance will cover a living donor, but since you're both uninsured, it poses a new set of challenges. Still, I'm sure there's somewhere we can get some help."

I nod, praying she's right. I can't take out a loan, or I would. Right now, my company isn't even functioning, so I have no income. I would've told Thea that I couldn't start the company if I knew we were going to move on this now and that my part of the operation wasn't going to be covered by the hospital.

All of this is the worst timing possible.

"I don't want my daughter saddled with debt," Howie says, frustration seeping into his voice. "Not because she's trying to save me, someone who doesn't even deserve it."

"Dad, stop. You deserve to be saved, just as much as anyone else," I reassure him.

He struggles with his grief over what he put us all through. When he first tried to get sober, he came to me as part of his step program. I cried as my father professed his sorrow for the things he did, the abuse and fits of rage. For the fact that he abandoned me and my mother or that he ever drove us away. When I lost Mom, I thought for sure he would return and try to be a father in some way, but he didn't. I struggled with that for a long time, but I chose to forgive him because hate in my heart only weighs me down.

"Just promise me you're not going to borrow money or do anything that will affect your future."

I sigh, knowing there's no real way out of this fight. "I promise."

Which is a lie because I'll do whatever I have to. I can't let my father die. Not when I know that I can save him. I have to save him.

"All right. I'll have the billing team reach out to you and we'll get things moving. Just remember no changes in medications without talking to me first, no alcohol for either of you, and keep going with your rehabilitation, Howie. Reach out if you have any questions or concerns."

We both stand and shake her hand. My father and I make our way to the waiting area and he grabs my arm. "I mean it, Brynn. I'm not worth you putting yourself in trouble just for this. I did this to myself, do you hear?"

"I'm not going to let you die, Dad."

"You aren't going to ruin your life, either. I've done enough of that already and I can't handle being a cause for more of it."

I let out a breath through my nose, trying to find the right words. "Do you know what I remember most from my childhood?"

"I'm afraid to even ask."

"I remember when you built my dollhouse. You spent months on it, carving every detail, making sure the rooms were big enough to get my hands in there, making all the furniture. There was nothing in the world I owned that meant more to me than that dollhouse. I played with it every day for hours."

My father's eyes fill with tears. "And then I broke it."

"But that's not the memory I hold onto."

Before the night when my father hit my mother, he was angry about something, and he went after the dollhouse. He lifted it, throwing it to the ground as Rowan stood in front of me, shielding me from seeing it. I cried and cried until I finally fell asleep. It was a horrible night, and we didn't spend many more with him.

"I have ruined everything in your life, Brynlee. The fact that you even speak to me at this point is a miracle. You have to understand why I don't want you to do this. Not for me."

"I do understand, but I'm asking you to understand my side. You're my father. You're alive and I can help keep you that way. We lost a lot of time, Dad. For years I didn't have you there and now . . ." I inhale, my heart pounding as emotions flood me. "Now I don't want any more of those absent years. I'm asking you to understand that. I want my dad. I need you to be alive so we can continue to try to reconcile."

My dad pulls me into his arms, and I hold on to him. I keep the tears from falling, trying to focus on the fact that we're in a better place now and I can help.

After a minute, he pulls back and smiles at me. "I have an AA meeting I need to get to. You'll be okay getting to the train station?"

"Yes, Dad. I'll be totally fine."

Usually, when I'm in Manhattan, I meet up with Thea, but she's meeting with two potential clients in Connecticut. I had a client dinner as well, but they canceled on me yesterday, so I'll just take the train back into Jersey and drive back to Sugarloaf and maybe, finally, get the courage to tell my brothers about the transplant.

It's just so hard because I know they're going to flip out. Those three men are overprotective and they loathe my father. Not that I blame them. I was in their camp for a long time. While I may have forgiven Howie, I haven't forgotten.

My brothers haven't forgiven anything.

As I'm walking toward Penn Station, not watching where I'm going, I start to trip, but two strong arms grab me, keeping me from falling.

"I'm so sor—"

The words die on my lips as a pair of ice blue eyes that I'd know anywhere stare down at me.

"Brynn."

"Crew. Thank you for saving me," I say, noticing he's still holding me.

He steps back, clears his throat, and smiles. "I think you probably did a little of that right now for me."

"I did?"

Crew nods. "I just left my first custody hearing, and my head isn't exactly where it should be."

My chest tightens as I hear the ache in his voice. "It didn't go well?"

"No."

"I only did family law for a short time, and it was brutal. I can imagine it was difficult to sit through it as they discussed you."

I was co-counsel with Sydney Arrowood, my mentor in Sugarloaf, on one case, and I hated every moment. It was awful listening to the parents tear each other apart because the mother was getting remarried and he wanted to make her life miserable.

We won, thank God, because I don't think the kids would've been happy with their father, not from what we gathered at least.

45

"It was all lies. It was whatever Digger could do to make me look like a sex-crazed bachelor who didn't want to pay for Layla's care."

"I'm sorry, Crew. You seem to really love your daughter."

He sighs heavily, running his fingers through his dark brown hair. "You have no idea. Can I walk with you?"

My eyes widen. I'm stunned at that question. "Walk? Where?"

"Where are you going?"

Definitely not where he's headed. "To the train."

"Perfect, we'll walk together."

Seriously, this day is just going down the shitter.

"You're heading to the train station?" I ask.

"Yup."

Liar.

I decide to call him out on it. "Right, but you were walking toward me and slammed into me. So, I'm not really sure how that math adds up."

Crew smiles and I swear the sun brightens. Ugh. I need therapy. A smile does not make the world brighter and definitely not his. "Can you let me pretend that I'm going that way? I could use a win today."

I think we all can. If we had more wins in the world, maybe the losses wouldn't hurt so much. I sigh, giving in. "Fine. We can walk to the train together."

"Thank you."

We start to walk in silence, but I have things I want to know. Questions I couldn't ask at my brother's wedding. "So, your name is really Carson?"

"Carson Benjamin Knight. My nickname is Crew. Everyone outside of work calls me that."

"So not a total lie?"

"It wasn't a total lie. I was on the rowing team all through high school and college, so I was literally a member of the crew. It stuck and even my dad calls me Crew."

"I guess that makes sense. Still, probably why I could never find you. Not that I was looking."

Crap. I totally gave myself away with that.

"Of course not." His grin tells me he definitely isn't buying it.

I let out a breath that's more like a laugh. "Well, it's all water under the bridge. I'm glad to hear that you've done so well."

"Thanks. What brings you into the city? I never expected to run into you—literally."

Definitely not what I expected either.

I'm not sure if I should tell him, but there's something inside of me that wants to tell someone. To unburden myself of all this anxiety.

"I came into New York because"—I pause, unable to say the words right away—"well, I'm . . . going to be giving my father part of my liver. He's going to die without it and I'm a match, so I'm here for one of the last appointments I needed to have."

He coughs and then grabs my wrist, stopping me from going forward. "You're donating your liver?"

"Part of it. Yes."

"To your father?"

I shrug. "That's what I'm doing here."

"Brynn." Crew says my name, shakes his head, and finishes. "You told me your dad was a horrible man. That he hit your mother, was emotionally abusive to you and your brothers. I remember that story about you leaving and how it was the last time you saw him. I fucking hated him. I wanted to find him, beat the shit out of him for ever hurting you."

The memories are there for me too. I was snuggled up on his lap late after the sun had set. Instead of drinking with our friends, we'd find a quiet spot and talk for hours. We held each other together while we laid out the broken parts of our souls.

It was why I thought I loved him the way I did. He picked up each piece for me, held it in his hand, and mended me. Or at least it's what I told myself.

I stare up into his eyes. "People change and I can't just let him die. I have to find a way to help if I can. He gave me life and the least I can do is give him a part of my liver, so he has a chance to

47

maybe someday meet his grandchild, if I ever get married and have kids."

Crew shakes his head. "I don't know what to say, other than you are even more remarkable than I remember."

I don't think doing the right thing is remarkable, but I guess to some it is. "It's just what I think I should do."

"What do your brothers think? You talked about how incredibly overprotective they are, and after the wedding Asher looked like he wanted to kill me, so I'm guessing they still are."

Ah, the Achilles heel in my plan to help Howie. "Yes, they are. They don't know."

He grins. "I can imagine how that will go over."

"You and me both," I say with a sigh.

"Do you have plans?" Crew asks suddenly. "Tonight. Do you have dinner plans?"

My pulse quickens at the idea of spending more time with him and I'm not sure I can say yes, but I don't think I will walk away.

six

CARSON

S he should turn me down, but God, I pray she won't. I thought that the freedom I felt with Brynlee when we were kids was because she didn't know who I was. That it was just that the stigma and expectation of being wealthy and powerful was gone.

I was so fucking wrong.

It's her. Just her.

It's the sweet, kind, selfless person she is, and I'm selfish enough to want more of her warmth.

"Dinner?"

"We can go wherever you want. I know this great Sushi place. Or if you want steak, we can do that. I'll find anything."

She smiles, tucking her red hair behind her ear. "I'm not sure that's a good idea."

"Why? Do you not eat?" I tease.

"Stop. You know why I'm saying that."

I raise my hand. "I vow to be on my best behavior. I just really don't want to go back to my home and be alone. Also, I have no idea if we'll ever see each other again, so I'd like to have dinner and say a proper goodbye."

Brynn glances at her watch and sighs. "Well, I missed the train anyway, I guess dinner will work."

I fight back smiling. "What are you in the mood for?"

"This is going to be so cliché, but my area seriously lacks good Italian food. Any recommendations?"

The city is brimming with fantastic food, and we have no shortage of good, authentic Italian food. It's one of my favorite things about living here.

"I have several, but there's one that's really lowkey and close to where I live. It has the best burrata I've ever had, and I swear the owner will treat you like family."

Brynlee smiles. "That sounds perfect."

"Let me get the car."

I reach into my pocket, grab my phone, and text my location to my driver.

"Does your car drive itself here?" she asks playfully.

"Not the car, but the driver does."

"You have a driver?"

"I do. His name is Cliff and he's been with me for years."

She shakes her head in what looks like dismay. "I can't wrap my head around it. You were so normal when we met. You weren't flashy and didn't act like you were some rich asshole from New York. You were just . . . Crew."

"I'm still just Crew," I say, wanting her to believe that.

"You're Carson Knight. You're a CEO and a billionaire who has his own driver and plane and pilot on standby. I can't even begin to imagine your house or the cars you probably have."

I'm sure it can feel overwhelming to her, but I'm the same guy she met. I have more money, and yes, I have nice things, but at the heart of it, I just want the same shit every other person does.

"Those are all external, Bee. You might be the only person in the world who knows what lies beneath."

Her brown eyes find mine. "Is that true?"

"Every word."

Her lids lower and she tucks her hair behind her ear. "Well, that's a sweet thought."

Cliff pulls up in front of where we're standing and gets out of the car to open the door, but I raise my hand to stop him. "I got it, Cliff."

My hand rests on the small of her back as I lead Brynn into the back seat and follow, wishing I could find a way to keep touching her.

Cliff turns in his seat. "Where to, sir?"

I give him the address and we head out.

"Sir, there seems to be an accident up ahead, I'm going to take an alternate route."

"That's fine."

"Would the young lady like a water?" Cliff asks.

She shakes her head. "I'm good, thank you."

"Cliff, this is Brynlee Whitlock, an old friend from college." Cliff knows she's much more than that. When I came home from that trip, I confessed everything to him. He didn't hold back telling me how wrong I was, and how stupid I was for letting her go if I felt that strongly.

He was right, but at twenty-two, I didn't have enough sense to fix my error, and then a year later, I was with Jacqueline.

"Miss Brynlee, it's an absolute pleasure to meet you." I can see his eyes warm as he looks at her through the mirror.

"You as well, Cliff."

Through most of the ride uptown, Brynn stares out the window, seeing all that New York is at night.

"That's where I live." I point out the residence tower.

"You live in *that* building?"

I nod. "Yup. I'm the one with the huge balcony about eighty percent up. I have spectacular views."

She laughs once. "Of course you do. Isn't that the area of the city they call billionaire row?"

"It is."

"Well, I guess it's fitting you live there then."

When I left Jacqueline, I needed to move to a place that would piss her off. Petty as it is, I didn't care. She always wanted to live there. Instead, I bought a brownstone in Greenwich Village that was where I wanted to start a family. After that family dream imploded, I didn't give a shit and told Kimberly to find me a penthouse.

My sister, being the most ridiculous person in the world, found a three-floor penthouse as a joke and I bought it.

"I think Kimberly thought it would be funny and I wouldn't buy it."

Brynn grins. "Or she figured you were defiant by nature and knew you would."

I laugh and Cliff does too. "Sorry, sir."

I shake my head. "Don't apologize, you know me too well."

Brynn turns her attention to him. "How long have you worked for Crew?"

"Since he was a boy."

She turns to me, realization dawning on her. "You mentioned him. I remember you talked about someone who was like an uncle to you."

"That's him. Once I took over my companies and could afford it, I asked Cliff to come work for me. He lives in the penthouse as well."

Her eyes widen. "Lives with you?"

"We have staff quarters and Cliff stays there."

"Does he treat you well, Cliff? You can tell me, I'll beat him up."

Cliff laughs. "Mr. Knight knows I'd take him over my knee if he wasn't kind."

I sigh because I have no doubts. "Yeah, yeah."

Brynn laughs and I swear it goes straight to my heart. "You mentioned Kimberly, I remember you have two brothers too?"

"I do. Each of them has their own companies and Kimberly works for me while she prepares to take over my father's other business. She wants to learn as much as she can from me and what not to do."

Not that I have much to teach her. Kimberly is by far the most qualified and smartest out of all of us. Of course we'll never admit that.

She smiles. "I'm sure you're teaching her a lot."

"Not really. If anything, she's learning how not to be. I demand perfection at work and it's what makes me both ruthless and respected. It's a double-edged sword."

She purses her lips. "I can see why that works in business, but you can't be terrible, or your sister wouldn't stay."

"Well, Kimberly is terrifying."

"Most little sisters are," Brynn says with a laugh. "Lord knows I drive my brothers to the brink of insanity."

"Why?"

"Well, for one, I'm very intrusive in their lives, but it's only because I know what they need, when they're too afraid to do it. One of the many other reasons is Second Chances Animal Sanctuary."

"You mentioned that at the wedding, but I have no idea what it is."

She shrugs a little. "I save everything that needs to be saved. I have two horses, three goats—they are very mischievous—sheep, cows, two deer, a peacock, a donkey, and chickens, we have lots of chickens."

"At least you have eggs," I say, trying to process the fact that she basically has a damn petting zoo.

"Oh, they don't lay eggs, they all went through henopause, so they're no longer producing. They are just, as Asher says, a drain on the economy, but I love them. Each morning I go out, bring them treats, and give them love."

I'm really trying to picture it, but I can't, so I'll have to take her word for it.

Cliff clears his throat as he pulls up to the entrance. "I sent a text to the owner and a table is waiting for you."

"Thank you, Cliff."

He goes to exit the car, but I catch his eyes before he can get out and he understands it. I want to be the man who helps Brynn.

I go around the car, button my suit jacket, and open her door. Brynn's hand rests in mine and I tuck it in the crook of my arm as we walk in.

"You know the owner?"

I smile. "I do. I have a lot of dinner meetings here since it's close to my house and we get the view of Central Park. I like to impress possible clients."

Brynn laughs. "I bet you do."

We're shown in and taken to the back area where the owner, Antonio, always has tables available in case his top customers decide they need dinner. We order drinks and place food orders, and once the waiter is gone, I lean back and smile.

"What?"

"Just . . . glad you're here."

A blush paints her cheeks. "I am too."

"You're sure you don't want any wine?"

Brynn shakes her head. "I have to abstain from alcohol before the transplant."

Shit. Of course. "And when is that?"

Brynn looks to the side and shrugs. "In the next four to six weeks. My father was due for this about a year and a half ago. I got all the way through the testing, and he relapsed again. He'd been sober for four years and then he just . . . got close to the surgery and couldn't handle it. We're nearing one year of sobriety now, and as long as he keeps that up, then we can do it. He needs it."

"I'm sure this is a lot for you."

She lets out a nervous laugh. "You have no idea. I just started a new company, so I invested everything I saved to get that started. Plus, I still have all my student loans from college and law school, so now I wish I'd kept my savings for this surgery. My brothers, while they're amazing men, are not going to be okay with this, even though in the end they'll support me—begrudgingly. Since Howie had his setback a year and a half ago, he lost his job, and his insurance was paying for the transplant, but now he doesn't have that so it's all out of pocket, but he got a grant from the hospital for his portion. It's fine. I'll get everything figured out. But, my partner with the PR firm is amazing, and we're branching off an already established PR company so hopefully the growing pains won't be as severe."

I hate to tell her that most new companies all have growing pains, and they're usually way worse than expected. However, I'm not opening my mouth about any of that. She needs to stay positive, and it seems her excitement is great regarding her possible job. "I didn't realize you did PR."

"I do!" she says with a bounce in her seat. "I'm clearly a shitty business owner since I didn't even mention it and you're . . . well, you. We do crisis management for corporations, if you ever need someone to help, you know who to call."

I nod. "I do now. You're also a lawyer?"

"I was, but I hated it."

I can understand why she would. After spending two hours with my lawyer, I hated her and her damn job.

"And you love PR?"

She nods with a smile. "Yes, it's kind of similar in a way. I see a problem and in this job I can actually fix it. There's something really special about helping someone. It's why I thought I really wanted to do family law. I learned quickly that it's less about that and more about hating the broken system."

"I see that in action now."

"I wish I could give you some great advice, but, it always depends on the judge."

"Layla deserves more."

Brynn reaches her hand out, covering mine. "She has a father willing to fight for her and I think there's nothing a little girl needs more than that."

I cover hers, keeping the connection because I need to touch her. "And you're a girl saving her father, I can only hope to be deserving of that someday."

Brynn smiles softly. "You are, Crew, don't ever doubt that."

The sad part is that I've only ever felt secure about deserving love when I'm with Brynn, and I fucked up any chance of having that back.

seven

BRYNLEE

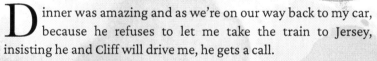

D inner was amazing and as we're on our way back to my car, because he refuses to let me take the train to Jersey, insisting he and Cliff will drive me, he gets a call.

"I understand. I'll be there in ten minutes." There's a pause as someone else speaks. "Don't worry about Jacqueline, I'll handle it." Crew hangs up the phone and speaks to Cliff. "Head to the brownstone."

"Yes, sir."

Crew looks to me. "I'm sorry, I have to go to Layla. I know you want to get back to your car, but I have to go."

"Of course! Is everything okay?" I ask.

"She's hysterically crying and the nanny can't get a hold of Jacqueline. She's crying about her stomach and won't let the nanny near her. I need to go to my daughter."

"I understand. It's fine," I say quickly, hoping there's nothing wrong.

Crew's leg bounces as we drive and I reach out, offering whatever support I can. "I'm sorry."

"Stop apologizing. This is what comes along with parenting. My brothers would do the same. Hell, I would as well."

"This just keeps happening." He runs his fingers through his

59

thick hair. "This is why I want her with me. I'm not running off to get drunk or God only knows what else she's doing while the nanny raises my daughter."

I wish I could say something, anything, but I can't fix this. I can just be a friend in this moment.

Soon, we're pulling up to a beautiful old brownstone with ornate wrought iron railings and detailed brickwork above the windows. He exits the car, waiting for me to get out, and places his hand on my back, ushering me up to the house. When we get to the door, it opens before he can knock or ring the bell and the nanny has tears in her eyes.

"Oh, Mr. Knight, I'm so sorry. I didn't know what to do. She just keeps crying and saying how she wants Jacqueline, but she got drunk, screamed at her, and left."

"Where is Layla?"

He doesn't even get an answer because we can hear Layla wailing. Crew barges in, with me behind him.

"Layla? Daddy's here!" he calls and a little girl rushes to him from the hallway.

His arms open, and like a scene from a movie, he cradles her in his embrace. Her little arms wrap around his neck, head tucked, and he protects her.

So many times in my life that was how it was with Asher, Grady, or Rowan. They'd hold me close, keeping all my worries away, while I could pretend that with them, I was safe. Howie couldn't hurt me when my brothers were shielding me.

Crew holds her, rubbing her back, murmuring soothing words as her cries quiet in the arms of her daddy.

She sniffles and then looks up at him. "Daddy, I miss you."

"I miss you too. Why were you crying, my love?"

Layla sniffles a few times and wipes at her tears with the back of her hand. "I didn't mean it."

"Didn't mean what, Ladybug?"

"I sorry, Daddy," she says, and her lip trembles.

"For what?" Crew asks patiently.

"Mommy was so mad."

"Did you do something wrong?" His voice is tempered, but I can hear the undercurrent of anger.

She shakes her head. "I just wanted a story."

He looks over at the nanny. "Were you present?"

"No, sir. I was downstairs and when I came up, she was huddled on the floor and Ms. Knight was screaming and leaving the home."

Layla wipes her nose with the back of her wrist. "I sorry! I didn't need a story. I sorry!"

"Baby, no," Crew says quickly. "You did nothing wrong."

"Mommy was so mad."

My hand covers my mouth and my heart breaks for this little girl. The first time Howie got in my face and screamed until I cried, my mother came in asking me what happened. I made up a story to protect him.

I don't know why I lied.

I just did.

I didn't want my mom to know he terrified me. I was maybe six, and even then, I had an instinct to protect him.

Sometimes I think children are born that way. To protect their parents because we're wired to need them, even when they can be horrible.

"Well, I'm here now."

He needs to be recording this. I reach into my purse to grab my phone and Layla notices me, her blue eyes get wide. "Who is that?"

Crew's eyes turn to me and he smiles. "That's my friend, Brynn."

I crouch down and wave. "Hi, Layla."

She waves back tentatively.

"I like your outfit. Your shirt is very pretty," I tell her.

"Do you like dolls?"

I grin. "I do! My niece and I play with dolls all the time."

"I love dolls," she informs me.

"Can you bring me your favorite?" I ask, hoping she'll grab one from the other room so I can tell Crew that he needs to document this, take photos and video of whatever Layla is saying.

She nods enthusiastically. As soon as she does what I hoped, I relay the info. "You need to record whatever she says. Video and photos," I tell him.

"Of course. I was just so . . ."

"I know. It's just important for your case against her, if you believe this is happening at her mother's hands. I'll record for you so that you can talk to Layla again, just make sure you aren't coercing anything. Let her tell you."

"Okay."

Layla returns a moment later with two dolls. "May I hold them while you talk to your daddy? After, maybe you can show me all your dolls?"

The crystal blue eyes that are exactly like her father's light up. "Daddy, will you play dolls?"

"Maybe, but I need to talk to you about why you were crying."

Layla and Crew go back and forth, her recounting how Jacqueline screamed and kept yelling at her. She holds her doll as Crew asks questions and Layla answers, the whole time tears fall down her little cheeks. After she's clearly done telling him, she moves over to the dolls and starts to play.

Crew sighs heavily as he sits beside me. "I need to take her now. She can't be here."

The lawyer in me immediately intervenes. "You can't do that; I know you want to. Hell, I want to, but you can't without risking your entire case. It could even be considered kidnapping if your ex-wife isn't aware of it." I drop my voice. "I would also be careful talking here."

He lets out a heavy sigh. "The walls have ears?"

I shrug. "They probably do."

He nods.

"Layla." He moves to the floor beside his daughter. "Daddy has to take Brynn home, but I'll be back in a few days, and we will have dinner, and you can sleep at my house this weekend."

"You promise?"

"I promise," he vows.

Her lip wobbles as the tears fill her beautiful eyes. "I want to go with you *now*, Daddy!"

"I know, and I want you to come with me always, but we can't do it now. But tomorrow, when you wake up, just know I'll be here as soon as I can, okay?"

Layla throws herself into Crew's arms and my chest is so tight, I worry it'll crack. This man is her hero and he's doing everything he can to protect her. I wish I could help, that I could do something so this sweet child never has to worry about being hurt again.

This is the pain I endured as a lawyer. Watching kids placed in situations they never should be in. The idea that one parent can do better, but for some reason, the other parent shows some bullshit and wins is heartbreaking.

Crew nods to the nanny who comes behind Layla and pulls her close. He stands, and I can see the rigidity in his stance as he moves to me. "Let's get you home."

I nod and as we exit the house, I slip my hand into his, lending him all the strength I have.

"Earth to Brynlee." Phoebe waves her hand in my face as my newest niece, Sienna, sleeps in her arms.

"Sorry, my head is a mess," I admit.

Last night was the most amazing and horrible night I've had in . . . forever. Dinner with Crew was like being a kid again. We laughed, talked, caught up on all the holes in our lives, and my cheeks hurt from smiling so much. We were able to be ourselves and I had fun.

Something I didn't know I was still capable of having with a man.

I've been with two men in my life. Both men hurt me in such different ways, leaving scars and pain in their wake.

CORINNE MICHAELS

With Jonathan, I was young and naïve. I wanted the fairytale —a man who was older and smarter and who saw me as a woman, not just a little girl who followed her brothers around. He gave me the illusion of that.

With Crew, it wasn't a game or manipulation to possess power over someone weaker. We were equal, or at least it felt that way. Then the week ended and what went from one of the most fantastic nights turned into a reminder that life isn't fair and men always leave.

"How was your meeting in New York?" she asks, her eyes probing as though she knows it wasn't for business.

"Fine."

"Fine?"

I nod. "It was fine."

At least the first part was. The meeting where I found out that giving part of my liver was coming much sooner than I expected. That I can save my dad or at least have a chance to.

"Okay, then. Who did you meet with?"

"A few people," I say, evading Phoebe's eyes. I hate lying. I'm actually the worst at it, which is why the whole "being a lawyer" thing wasn't exactly a good plan.

She sighs and laughs. "Brynn, you can tell me anything and I won't tell Asher. I'm your friend and your soon-to-be sister. You can trust me."

It's not that I don't trust her, it's that I'm honestly afraid of everything about this surgery. Giving voice to it kind of makes it worse. However, I can't lie to everyone. "I know I can. I want to tell you, I truly do, but . . ."

She reaches her hand out, gripping mine. "I won't judge. I promise I won't tell your brother."

I swallow and force the words out. "In four to six weeks, I'm going in for surgery."

Phoebe's eyes widen and she leans forward. "Surgery for what?"

"My father needs a liver transplant and I'm a match."

64

Phoebe, who is never without words, gapes at me. Her mouth opens and closes a few times. "Okay, then . . ."

"Not what you were expecting?"

"Not even a little. I thought it was going to be about Carson. Like, maybe you saw him and you guys reconnected."

"Oh, that happened too," I say with a shrug.

"Oh, sure it did. Okay, so, surgery and a billionaire."

I sigh heavily. "It's a lot."

"It is, but why haven't you told the guys? I know they're protective to a fault, but they love you more than anything."

"I know, but you guys have the wedding and school and a new baby. Grady and Addison are dealing with the merging of their families, and then we have Rowan, who just got married. Everyone is overwhelmed."

Phoebe rests her hand atop mine. "And? So are you. How about we start at the top and end up with the New York trip, okay?"

I nod and fill her in on everything. I literally unload and talk more than I ever have. Phoebe listens, squeezing my hands at different parts and fighting back her own tears as I talk about how I feel regarding Howie. It's such a hard thing to explain. To love someone who has hurt you so much, and to not know how to reconcile the two emotions.

It feels good to talk, though. Normally, I hold things in and let them fester, trying to battle the demons on my own, but Phoebe never interrupts, just lends me her support and asks questions along the way.

"What are you going to do about the money?" she asks after I explain the cost issue.

"I applied for charity funding. I have a good feeling it'll come through."

"Then I'll share in your good feelings," she says. Sienna starts to wake up, fussing as she does. "Sorry, she's sort of moody after a nap."

I laugh. "Aren't we all?"

She gets Sienna settled again, giving her a bottle, and then turns back to me. "Now, tell me the dirt about Carson."

I do, recounting the amazing dinner and how he absolutely refused to let me take the train, and about his daughter.

The car ride to my car just beyond the tunnel was silent, just the two of us in the back seat, holding hands as I could only imagine the pain he was feeling. I know the other side of it, what Layla must've been going through.

All of it so unfair.

When we got to my car, he opened my door, kissed my cheek, and said he hoped to hear from me soon. Then . . . he was gone.

"Why the hell didn't you kiss him?" Phoebe asks rather loudly.

I glance around the diner, hissing at my future sister-in-law. "Could you maybe not be so loud?"

She lifts one shoulder. "I'm sorry, but come on, Brynn. You are not a nun."

"No, but I make bad choices with men."

Her face softens. "That's not true. You were young and Jonathan took advantage of that. He was a liar and a manipulator. Carson seems like a nice guy who likes you enough to show up at a wedding to see you and then drove you back to your car parked in Jersey. I mean, if that's not chivalry, I don't know what is."

I laugh. "Yes, anyone willing to go into Jersey on their own accord is a hero."

"Don't tell Faye that, she'll probably try to kill us."

"Yes, our Jersey girl who loves to remind us how superior the state is."

Sienna fusses and Phoebe sits her on her lap. "Hello, beautiful girl," I say to her and she smiles so wide I swear her cheeks might crack. "Are you a happy girl now that you're all fed?"

"It's the only time she's happy. Or when her daddy is holding her. Then, she's nothing but joy and sunshine."

"Asher has that effect on women."

"Don't I know it."

I snort. "Anyway . . ."

"Did you at least give him your number?"

I shake my head.

"Brynlee!"

"What?"

"You like the guy. He's super hot. He's nice. He explained everything about when you guys were kids, and clearly there is something still there. Why are you being a dummy?" Phoebe asks with a huff.

Did he really explain anything about why he left? He said his life was mapped out, but so what? I don't understand how that excuses the way he did it. Maybe a part of me really isn't over it.

I know that hurt still lingers and I'm not sure I want to feel that again.

"Well, the night didn't exactly end well. I wasn't going to be like, hey, Crew, I know your daughter is home and you worry constantly, want my number?"

Seriously, it was not the right time. Not to mention, I'm not going to get into any kind of relationship now. I'm about to start my company and give part of my liver in a few weeks. I don't think any man in his right mind would be interested now.

"Call him."

"What?" I nearly screech.

"Right now. Pick up your phone and send him a text. Thank him for dinner and the ride back, and check on his daughter. Let him know you've arrived back in Sugarloaf without any issues, and you'd love to have his babies."

I nearly choke. "Phoebe. Jesus."

"Leave the last part out, but do it or I will."

Knowing her, she's not lying. She'll totally send some crazy text and I'll never be able to walk it back.

I grab my phone, out of fear more than anything, and pull out his business card.

"He has three numbers!" I say, looking over the card.

Phoebe snatches it out of my hand. "This one says personal. Go with that."

I huff and type the number in.

> Hey, Crew. It's Brynlee. I just wanted to thank you for last night. Dinner was great, and it was nice getting to catch up. Hope all is well with Layla. Let me know if I can help in any way.

I hit send and feel like a total jackass. Hope all is well? Really? We know it's not. *Ugh, I'm an idiot.*

Phoebe reads the message. "Better than what I would've said to Asher."

"Please, don't feel inclined to tell me what you'd have sent."

She laughs. "Now you've put the ball in his court."

The phone rings and I look down at it, sure enough, it's him.

"He's calling."

"Answer it!"

"And say what?" I nearly yell.

"Hello would be a good start," Phoebe says, shoving the phone at me. "Dude!"

I grab it and hit the green button.

Play it cool, Brynn.

"Hey, Crew," I say much calmer than I feel inside.

"You texted."

"I did."

"I wasn't sure I'd ever hear from you again. I hoped, but I wasn't sure."

I shift in my seat, my cheeks burning. "I guess it's a good thing I did."

He laughs softly. "In more ways than one it's a good thing you reached out. I was actually going to be that asshole who went to Grady to get your number this evening if I had to. I need to talk to you."

"About?"

"It's rather delicate and really needs to be discussed in private."

"Is everything okay?" I ask.

He hesitates. "Not really, but I'm hoping you can help. Can I come to you tonight to talk about it?"

My jaw drops and I start to panic. "Come here? To Sugarloaf?"

"Yeah."

He says it as though it's the most natural thing in the world. "Umm, I mean, sure. You can come here today. To talk about what I can help with."

Phoebe is practically vibrating in her seat.

"Great. I'll fly in later tonight. I have a meeting and a call with my lawyer again. I'll see you around seven."

"Seven is great."

"Perfect. I'll call once I land, and you can tell me where to meet you."

"Sounds good."

"Bye, Brynn." His voice is deep and washes over me.

"Bye, Crew."

When I hang up, I lift my gaze to see Phoebe smiling wide. "Well, dinner tonight?"

"It seems so. He said he had to talk to me and was going to get my info from Grady, but then I texted. Said he wants to talk about something."

"Oh, I bet I can guess what he wants help with." She wiggles her brows.

I shake my head. "You're ridiculous, it could be about business. Maybe he wants to buy my part of the land for Rowan?"

"Or maybe he's in love with you, has dreamed of you for the last ten years, and can't spend another moment without you."

She really needs to be brought back to reality. "I know you love romance and all things that end happily, but this is real life. I am going to have dinner with him, let him tell me whatever it is he needs to, and watch him walk back out of my life."

"Whatever. I think you should get going and prep," she suggests.

"Prep?"

"Shave, scrub, buff, polish, you know ... prep."

I roll my eyes. "None of that is necessary."

"Famous last words."

Yeah, no shit.

I'm going to get my daily steps in just from all the pacing I've done the last hour.

I went out to the sanctuary, fed the animals, spent time with the chickens, and then came in to prep, as Phoebe called it. I washed, scrubbed, buffed, shaved, and cleaned every orifice of my body. Not that I have any plans for Crew to see any part of my body, but . . . a girl has to be ready for anything.

Not only that, but I needed to do something to take up my time because otherwise, I'll sit here coming up with a million scenarios about why he had to come see me.

Today.

Urgently.

And with a problem.

I look at my phone, anxious because he should be pulling in at any minute. Instead of meeting at the diner, it's so much easier to just come here. So, Grady is driving him to the house.

So freaking awkward.

Headlights shine down the drive to where my cottage is, and I look in the mirror for the five hundredth time.

"You are a confident, smart, and amazing woman. Don't be a bumbling fool."

My reflection doesn't exactly show that same level of confidence, but the knock on the door says it's time to fake it.

I walk out to the living room and open the door. Crew is there, in a three-piece suit, looking so damn hot I might be burned just from being close to him.

His dark brown hair is pushed back and to the side. The dimple on his left cheek looks deeper than yesterday, but there's a worry in his crystal blue eyes that has me concerned.

"Hey," I say softly.

"Hey. Sorry to drop in like this."

I shake my head. "No worries. Come in."

He turns back to my brother. "Thanks for the ride. I'll have Cliff meet me out here to drive back. I know you have the kids and it might be late."

Grady looks like he's ready to crawl out of his skin. Crew is both his boss and he delivered him to his little sister. I grin, loving this moment. "Bye, Grady!"

I pull Crew in and close the door. I laugh a little and Crew stares at me with a smile. "Enjoying yourself?"

"That moment was priceless. He wanted to rip your head off, but couldn't. Oh, if only I had recorded it."

Crew chuckles. "As an older brother, I can imagine exactly how that must've felt."

I shrug. "Serves him right."

Crew looks around my cottage, shaking his head. "You know, this place is a hundred percent you."

"How so?" I ask, not sure if that's a compliment or not.

"It's just warm, comforting, filled with everything you'd want a home to be. The couch looks inviting and well loved. Everything is in great condition and it's a place you want to be in."

Definitely a compliment. "I'm sure yours is a dream."

"Mine is a museum. I hate the couch, it's fucking hard as a rock, but the designer was adamant it was the best piece for the space. Everything is spotless. You'd never know a human lives there."

"Still, I'm sure it's stunning."

Crew walks over to my sofa and sits, melting into the broken-in furniture. "No, this is stunning and a dream, Brynn. This is a home."

I move over, taking the seat next to him. "Why did you fly out here?" I ask, not really able to hold back.

His beautiful Nordic eyes meet mine. "Marry me."

eight

CARSON

I've found in business it's best to stun the person and then explain.

Brynn is definitely stunned.

"I . . . you want me to . . . *what*?"

"Marry me, Brynn. Not for all the reasons that might be going through your head, but because you're the only one who can help me save my daughter."

She blinks a few times. "I'm not following."

"I got a call last night from a friend after we dropped you off. There are photos of us together in the car and at dinner. Photos where I had my hand on your back or when you almost fell and I caught you. My security team intercepted the guy too late, and those photos had already been sent to my ex-wife. She's building a case that I'm always seeing another girl, I'm unreliable, I travel too much and therefore can't take care of Layla." I swipe my hand through my hair. "Layla is being neglected and living in a home with an unstable mother. I need to get her out of there, but Jacqueline only cares about the money, and even with the settlement I offered her, she wants more and knows Layla is the way to get it."

Brynn lifts her hand. "I understand all of that, but how does me marrying you come into play?"

"My lawyer is adamant I need to settle down, give the appearance of a stable home with a family. That photo of us is going to be leaked to the press. There is going to be a story and I can't stop it. Jacqueline paid some tabloid to expose me to help solidify her claims. My lawyer, after she lost her shit, urged me to come to you and get married. Especially now that you've met Layla because there's a photo of us leaving Jacqueline's house holding hands. Which, you can imagine, my ex-wife went ballistic over."

This sounds ridiculous even to me, but I know it'll solve both our problems because I can help her financially. The thing is, if Brynn is anything like the girl I fell for years ago, money is not going to be a motivator. She is selfless, kind, and will help others. Which is really why I need her anyway.

I need her help and in turn, I can help her.

"I understand your lawyer's concern over giving the right impression to the judge, but marry you? I can't."

"I know this is a big ask. Jesus, I know it's impossible, but we'd be able to help each other. You can help me make sure Layla isn't harmed and I'll be there to take care of you and the cost of your surgery. We'll make an arrangement that works for both of us. You'll be able to recover in my home, with people there to help, and have my insurance to cover the costs. Your business is starting up? I have contacts for days. You can help me just as much as I can help you. No, not me." I shake my head. "Help Layla, then I'll do anything you need, Brynlee. If it's money or business or my fucking world, you can have it."

She stands, moving around her living room. "I want to help you. I want to help Layla, but marriage, Crew? Us? You hadn't seen me in ten years before a few weeks ago!"

"There is nothing I won't do for Layla and there's no one else I'd rather do this with than you. I know you, Brynn." I get to my feet, going to her. "You know me better than anyone else in the world. No one in my life would question this."

"Everyone in my life would!" She raises her hands and drops

them. "I'm the steady one. I don't do things like this. I understand you want to help Layla, I get it more than anyone. I was her. I wanted someone to get me out of my hell with my father—"

I grab her hands. "Then you know why I want this for her. Why I'll do anything to make it happen. If we get married, we'll ride the storm of the photos together. We'll be able to over-shadow the rumors with the news of our engagement, and my family and friends won't even question it."

Her beautiful brown eyes find mine. "Why?"

Time to give her the truth. "Because since the day I walked away from you, I've never let it go. I begged my grandfather to let me go to you, to beg for a second chance, but he demanded I marry Jacqueline."

I want to say more. To tell her the final part, but I can't because she'll never agree to marry me if I do.

I never stopped thinking about what we had. I wanted that—you —and I couldn't have it.

She shakes her head, stepping away and moving to the small fireplace. "That makes no sense."

To her, it wouldn't.

To me, it was decided without my consent.

Jacqueline's family wasn't as powerful as my own, but they had connections that my grandfather coveted. We met when we were kids and were basically told this was our future. It wasn't until my grandfather got sick that he saw the misery I was living in and he removed his ridiculous rules regarding our lives.

I wait for her to turn and face me because reading her face is the only way I'll be able to try to get her to agree to this.

"It may not make sense to you, but it's the truth."

She lets out a heavy sigh. "I have to think about this, because while your family might not question it, mine will. My brothers will have a lot of opinions and . . . I hate lying to them. I don't do it. I learned the hard way about how that turns out."

"If this was just about me, I would never ask it. I'm asking you to help me help my daughter, and for her, there's nothing in the world that I won't do. I can also give you what you need. I will help your business, pay for the surgery, and take care of you after."

Brynn shakes her head. "I'm not taking any money. Not a dime. I'm waiting for the charity to come through and I'm not taking your money. I'll find a way, this would only be to help Layla and . . ."

"Okay. But if you change your mind, it's yours," I offer. "All I'm asking is to help me stop a little girl from being hurt."

She closes her eyes for a moment, then opens them. "You're not fighting fair."

"I never said I would."

There is no fair in this, there is only my daughter's future.

Brynn paces around the room. "This is crazy, you know that, right?"

"I know it's extreme," I admit. "I know that when these photos leak tomorrow, if we're not announcing an engagement, the picture that Jacqueline is going to paint will only make things worse. I know that Layla is being hurt and I can't fucking stop it. You saw the tears, Brynn. You were there."

Her hand rests on the base of her throat, gripping the necklace pendant. "There's no guarantee that this will work."

She's right. It could all end up where I lose anyway. But I need to keep this about Layla with Brynn. It's Layla that she's going to want to do this for. I hate using it. I hate using her, but there are choices about who to protect and my daughter will always come first. "It's her best chance."

"I need to think," she says.

I shake my head. "I need an answer now. If we're going to beat the story, it has to be tonight."

"Tonight?" Her voice rises. "You're asking something impossible!"

"Am I? I'm asking you to marry me. To be my wife and help me take a little girl who is innocent away from her horrible mother. I'm asking you to let me take care of you, give you whatever you want."

Brynn moves her hand back and forth. "What I want? I want

love. I want a husband, not a business arrangement. You talked about how horrible it was being married to her when there was nothing between you. Now you're asking me to enter into the same thing?"

Maybe I'm tainted. Maybe because of the fucked-up relationships I've had my whole life, marriage never meant a damn thing to me. Most are a business arrangement in my circles, but Brynn isn't from that world.

"You want the fairytale."

Her brown eyes move to mine. "I'm not a little girl. I've met the Big Bad Wolf, and I thought I found a real boy once." The sting hurts. I know I broke a part of her and I've never forgiven myself for that. "I also know true love, Crew. I've seen it on my brothers' faces and I want it."

"I won't stop you from having it. We'll get married and you give me a year to get Layla settled and get you back on your feet. And then I won't stand in your way."

"A year?" she asks.

"I figure it will be enough time that you'll be recovered and I'll have Layla fully established at home. A year will hopefully be enough to keep Jacqueline from trying to fight me again. I'm not tied to the timeline as much as the circumstances." I could lie, put a contract in place where there is a firm timeline, but that seems unfair. If Brynn is willing to help, I won't push it.

"So if it goes over a year, then what?"

I shrug. "Name your price."

She lets out a soft laugh. "I wouldn't be doing this for money, I've made that clear. It would be for Layla."

"I understand that, but my money is yours, Brynlee. I won't ask for a prenup. You can have it all if I have Layla."

Her eyes widen. "*Are you nuts?* Of course we'll have a prenup! I don't want your money."

The fact that she just said those words tells me she's going to do it. I step toward her. "You'll do it?"

Brynlee looks torn. "This may not work."

"I know."

"If you don't get custody of Layla, then what?"

"I try again. I just ask that you stay with me until we have her."

I wait, letting her think through whatever it is she needs to. I know Brynlee, maybe not as much now, but at the heart of her, she is selfless. She has a deep desire to help others, always sacrificing to make things better for another. Look at what she's willing to do for a man who hurt her as a child, who hurt her mother and family. Even after all her father did, she's willing to literally give him a part of herself. To put her own wants, hopes, and dreams to the side for someone who wouldn't do the same for her.

Brynlee saves the people and things around her. It's who she is, and it was a gamble to think she'd do this, but deep down, I knew she couldn't let Layla hurt.

She sighs heavily, rubbing her temples. "I don't want my brothers to know why."

"I don't want anyone to know why. If anyone knew that this was fake and not because after ten long years we found each other again, then the chances they'd sell the story to the press are too high."

"My family would never," she argues.

I lift my hands. "I didn't say they would. I don't think they'd ever risk hurting you, but a secret is only a secret when it's between two people."

"I swear, I'm the biggest idiot to ever live. To consider this is lunacy."

"No, it's kindness. It's everything to me. Everything, Brynn."

Her gaze meets mine and she smiles softly. "I don't want my brothers to know about the surgery. Not until I'm ready."

"Understood."

I'll keep every secret she wants.

"Do you have a plan on how this all works?" Brynn asks as she sits back down on the couch.

I walk over, sit beside her, and take her hand in mine. "We announce our engagement in tomorrow's paper. It should over-shadow any gossip that Jacqueline could possibly have, and negate whatever she says. Then, we get married by the end of the week. We'll fly to an island, have a small ceremony on the beach, surrounded by our closest friends and family. It will get you on my insurance policy immediately, which hopefully will cover the surgery and if not, I'll pay for it."

"No!" Brynn jumps in.

"No?"

"No, you're not paying for it. I'm not taking money from you. At all."

I sigh. "Okay then, you'll have the answer from the charity by then, right?"

"I think so. They know this is an urgent request. Guardian Angels made it seem like it was a rather quick process."

I file the name away, knowing I'll be making an incredibly large donation tonight. No matter what, her surgery is taken care of. I will not have her worrying over money, not when she's giving up everything for me.

I rub the back of her hand and she trembles. "What's wrong?"

"I *hate* lying." Brynn's voice aches and I truly hate myself for asking her to do this.

"Is it all a lie?"

Her lashes flutter and she stares at me. "That we're madly in love and can't live our lives another day without each other? Yeah, I'd say it's a lie."

I shake my head. "It's a stretch, sure, but it's not a lie. We were madly in love with each other. We did dream about spending our lives together. Fuck, we sat on the beach with my arms around you and we talked about what it would look like. We wanted a house on Long Island where we could have land and a farm. I was going to commute into the city and we'd ride home together."

That conversation is burned in my mind. I remember it all. I longed for it to be true for so many years.

Brynn's lips part. "I was going to run a charity."

"And we were going to be so fucking happy," I finish.

She smiles and laughs quietly. "None of that is going to be this

79

story, Crew. We're going to live in Manhattan, in a high rise, while we're fighting for custody of your daughter. We haven't been in love for the last ten years. Hell, we haven't even kissed each other since the night you left me."

"Do you want to kiss me?" The surprise in her eyes causes me to smile. "All you have to do is ask."

Her cheeks redden and it's the most adorable thing.

"I have to ask?"

"Is it what you want?"

I can see in her eyes it's exactly what she wants now. If we're going to sell this marriage, we're definitely going to have to kiss. We're going to need to be incredibly affectionate, but not ridiculous.

"I'm not sure," Brynn admits.

I lift both hands up to her face, moving my thumbs along her cheekbones. "It's what I want. It's what I've wanted since I saw you again. It takes every ounce of restraint I have when I see you not to pull you in my arms and make you remember how good we were."

"I don't have any issues remembering, if anything, I wish I could forget."

Her words slay me, and I lean in, brushing my nose against hers. "Marry me, Brynlee, and we'll seal our promise with a kiss."

She brings her hands up to my wrists, holding me as I hold her. I wait, desperate for her answer. "Yes."

And then, slowly, cataloging every breath we share, I bring my lips to hers, and kiss her like I've wanted to for so long.

nine

BRYNLEE

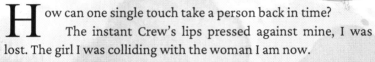

How can one single touch take a person back in time?

The instant Crew's lips pressed against mine, I was lost. The girl I was colliding with the woman I am now.

I've replayed the kisses we've shared over and over so many times that by now, it shouldn't feel this way. I should be immune because we've kissed a million times in my dreams.

But this isn't a dream.

This is real and I'm so freaking screwed.

He tilts my head to the side, coaxing me to open to him, and I couldn't resist if I tried. I'm needy for him—for us. Crew takes control, as he always did, and I find myself on my back, him above me. He kisses me deeply, languidly—it's everything.

My fingers tangle in his dark hair, feeling the silky strands glide across my skin, while he keeps his mouth to mine.

I didn't realize how starved I've been. How much I've missed him. How good this man kisses.

Much too soon, he pulls back, both of us fighting for breath, and he looks down at me. His blue eyes are swimming with desire. "I'm sorry I got . . ."

"Carried away?" I finish for him.

"You always made me lose my sanity."

He brushes my hair from my face, smiling down at me. "You always made it easy."

Crew kisses me again, this time much more innocently, and then shifts, pulling us both back to sitting. "I don't think we'll have to fake the chemistry."

I clear my throat. "No, definitely not, but . . . if I'm going to do this. If we're going to be married, but only in name, I don't think it's smart if we let our hearts get involved."

I have to lay ground rules because without them, I'll fall so deeply in love with him that I'll never be able to see a way out. While that sounds all well and good, that isn't why he came back. It was never for me, it was for his daughter.

"Agreed. However, we're going to need to be affectionate," Crew reminds me.

"And we can do that in front of people, but in private, we have to maintain some distance. I'm going to be working a lot and I'm going to assume you will be too?"

He nods. "I travel frequently for business. When you have your surgery, I will be home, though. I'll stop all travel and be there to help you."

I bite my lip, looking away. "I'm sure we can find a nurse."

"I'll be there, Brynlee."

I turn to him, seeing the promise and determination there. "Okay."

"In sickness and in health, right?" he says, more as a joke than anything, but I go along with it.

"Till custody do us part."

He laughs. "Something like that." Then he stands, reaches into his pocket, and pulls out a ring box.

Even though this is all for show and I know it, my heart races. I've dreamed of being proposed to. Where the man I love would get down on one knee, pull out the box, and tell me all the reasons he wants to spend his life with me.

This isn't the dream, though.

This is business. I tamp down my emotions as he gets to his knee and I shake my head. "Please don't."

His head tilts as he watches me. "Don't?"

"Don't ask me to marry you. Don't take this . . . please just don't."

It seems to dawn on him why I'm asking, and he nods, sitting beside me and opening the box. There rests the most beautiful ring I've ever seen. It's nothing like I would've expected from him. It's delicate, with scrollwork on the sides and up to a very large emerald-cut diamond surrounded by others in a beautiful halo that looks almost like a picture frame. It's antique, stunning, and exactly what I would've wanted.

I hate him for knowing what I would want, because I don't hate him at all.

"I bought this ring today. When I went to the store, I had the intentions of buying a disgustingly big rock, one that would possibly break your finger from the weight of it, but that didn't feel like us. We weren't about the money, we were about more. As I looked around for something I thought was us, I saw this in a case, alone, and I couldn't walk away. It's beautiful, like you, soft and yet strong, like you, and more than that, it has a past, like we do. Somewhere in time, I believe a man loved a girl so much he had to make something to show it," Crew says, clearing his throat. "I think he knew he wasn't good enough for her, and had to give her something to remember him by."

"Crew." I try to cut him off, but he continues.

"He wasn't good enough for her then, and he isn't now, and when she's ready to leave, he'll let her go because she is too beautiful to be in a cage. I know you want more than a marriage of convenience, and I fucking hate myself for taking this from you, but this ring represents how I've always seen you, Brynlee— perfect. I won't ask the question. I won't take that from the man who deserves to give you a proposal with his heart on his sleeve. When you're ready, put the ring on, and I'll know it means you'll do this."

My God. Doesn't he get it? Doesn't he see that he's ruined any fucking proposal that could ever come? I will never recover from that. He . . . ruined me. He will obliterate me by the end of this.

This is a mistake. I need to protect myself and say no, not put that perfect ring from my perfect idea of a man on my stupid finger.

But then I think of someone else who needs protection.

The little girl with Crew's eyes. The ones that were in so much pain, pleading for her father to save her.

I close my eyes and see those eyes, staring up at me, asking me to give her a chance.

I can't say no.

I will destroy myself if it means saving her. Just like I always do.

I grab the ring and place it on my left hand, where it fits perfectly. Like a moth to a flame, I will burn and turn to ash.

Things move incredibly quickly when you decide to marry in a week. After we agreed to the engagement, Carson stood and called his assistant, who contacted a wedding planner, who told me that anything I wanted was at my disposal. So many congratulatory wishes were cast upon us in the matter of an hour. His asshole friend from college, Ford, got on the phone, welcoming me into the fold.

I hated that guy then and I have a feeling he's not going to grow on me now.

Crew hangs up his last call and finds me in the kitchen, where I'm standing like an idiot, trying to make sense of my new life.

"Hey."

"Hi."

He smiles. "We have to go to the city. I need you to go to the penthouse, find a way to redecorate, whatever you want, so that it looks like we're building a home for Layla."

All of this is way, way too much. He needs to slow down. "We have to do other things first," I remind him.

"Like what?"

"Oh, like tell my brothers for one. I'm not going to run off with you tonight. We have to tell them. You thought facing your ex in court was scary? My brother is armed."

He exhales heavily. "Of course. I'm an ass. We need to tell your family. Whatever you decide for the destination of the wedding, I'll cover costs for everyone we include."

When is he going to get it through his thick head that money isn't what I care about? I sigh heavily. "I don't want a destination wedding, Carson."

His eyes jerk to mine. "Don't call me Carson. I'm Crew. Always to you. Always."

"Okay, Crew. I'm saying that you kind of told me the plan, which is great because you're clearly a great businessman, but my brothers know I would never want that. If we want to sell them, and anyone who knows me, on a wedding, they know I'd want to do it on this farm."

I watch as he processes this, his jaw tics a little and he studies me. "On this farm?"

I nod. "Right here."

"You want us to get married here and not on an island with everything you can dream of?"

That's just it, I don't dream of those things. I'm sure at some point or another I did, but that's not who I am. I step closer to him, placing my hand on his chest. "If this was really a magical reunion and we are so desperate to never spend another moment away from one another, I would want to do it here, where I spent all my days and nights dreaming of you. Either here, or on the beach in North Carolina, where we fell in love. I'm sentimental." I shrug because it's just who I am.

He smiles down at me. "Okay."

"You're agreeing to what?"

"To letting you plan the wedding and do whatever you want. If it's here, we'll do it here. If it's in North Carolina, I feel like that would be perfect too."

That was easy. "Then that's what we'll do. Here would be easy, but I think there'd be a really beautiful sentiment doing it at

OBX. We met there, fell in love there, only seems fitting to marry there."

"And it's still a destination wedding," he reminds me with a grin.

"Whatever. That was the easy part, now we move on to actually going to see my brothers. I need to handle Asher first because he's going to be the worst, and they all tend to follow his lead. If I get him alone and on board, the other two will be putty in my hands."

For the first time, I see a bit of hesitation in Crew. Good, he should have to suffer this. "We'll need to tell my siblings as well. We'll do a lunch or something tomorrow, even if the news will break tomorrow morning."

"Okay."

The two of us stand here, my hand over his heart, the diamond glittering in the light, and he lifts his hand to cup my cheek. "You'll never know how much this means to me, Brynn."

"I can guess."

"No, Bee, you really can't."

He leans down and places a soft kiss on my lips that I feel down to my toes.

I feel the loss of his heat when he lifts back up. "Tomorrow the world will know, so let's go tell our families and do what we can to sell this." Then, he raises my hand to his lips and kisses my ring.

I have a feeling it's going to be a lot easier to act like I'm in love with him than I hoped.

Curse me for having an open heart.

ten

CARSON

"You're getting married?" Asher asks with disbelief. "To each other?" He stares up at us from his couch after inviting us inside after he just got off his evening shift.

Brynn nods. "Yes. This week or next, I'm still planning."

That's when he gets to his feet. "What? What are you doing? Who the hell are you, Brynlee? You're marrying someone no one has ever met before!"

I tamp down my desire to punch her brother in the face for being a dick, but if this were Kimberly, I can't say I wouldn't be acting the same. My sister is the only thing my brothers and I are willing to stand up to our parents over. We protect her at all costs and Brynlee is much the same from what she's said.

She remains completely calm. "He's not some guy, Asher. I love him, I always have, and now he's back in my life and I don't want to waste another day without him." Brynlee takes my hand in hers. "We already know what it feels like."

He scoffs. "Give me a fucking break."

Phoebe, his fiancée, grabs his arm. "Sit down, Asher. You're being a prick." He stares at her, and then does as she asks. "Brynn, we're really happy for you if this is what you want."

She smiles at her soon-to-be sister-in-law. "It is, and we don't want to take anything away from your wedding, which is why we want to do it quickly and without fuss. We don't care about a wedding. I just want him to be my husband." Brynn then turns her glare to her brother. "I thought maybe you could understand that, being as in love with Phoebe as you are."

"Of course I get it, but we don't know him!"

"I didn't realize my brother needed to know *my* husband. You know, since *I'm* the one marrying him."

There's going to be about five more minutes of this where I can stay quiet. There's no way I'm going to allow anyone to yell at Brynlee. I don't care if he's her brother or not.

"This isn't you. You aren't an idiot like Rowan!"

That's it. I stand, pushing the chair out behind me. "As a father, I can imagine the love you have for Brynlee comes close to that. You want to protect her, make sure no one will harm her, and that's admirable. As the man who loves her, I want the same. She's not an idiot. She's the kindest, most selfless person I know. If you want to calm down, we can continue to talk about this, but if you want to yell at her, we're leaving."

Asher crosses his arms over his chest, looks at me, then his sister, and then his wife-to-be, who is grinning. "You have to admit it's sudden."

"It is. I'm sure my siblings are going to have the same reaction, but you can also understand that I've spent ten years without Brynlee, and I have no desire to spend another ten days without her."

He sits down, letting out a heavy sigh. "I have no right to say anything, she's an adult."

"Yes, I am, but I love you, Ash, and I'd like not only your blessing, but for you to give me away." Brynn's soft voice is gentle as she looks at her brother.

"I can never give you away, Brynn, but I'm happy to walk you to the man who loves you enough to stand up to me."

Phoebe claps her hand on the table. "Well, we're all shocked, but so happy for you. Olivia is going to lose her shit. You better go see her."

Brynn inhales sharply. "I need to do that very delicately. Ash, can you ask her mother to bring Olivia here?"

He nods and gets up, and Brynlee turns to me. "My niece and I are really close, and I need her to find out from me and meet you —officially. She's deaf and non-verbal so I'll sign and then translate."

"I hope she's happy for us."

She laughs. "Me too."

Asher returns, sitting back in the chair across from me. "So, where will you live?"

I answer. "I have space in New York City. With Brynlee's new company based there, and since my daughter lives there as well, we'll spend our time there."

"Of course we'll visit," Brynn assures him quickly.

Asher's mask slips for just a moment and I see sadness fill his eyes. "You're going to leave the farm?"

I reach out and take Brynn's hand, lending her any support I can. "We'll visit—so much that you'll be sick of me."

"Right. Sick of you." Asher looks away and Phoebe rubs his arm. "I'm going to check on the baby and call Grady and Rowan. They'll want to hear this joyful news as well. I'm surprised you didn't ask them to be here so we could all get it over with at once."

Brynlee laughs softly. "I figured you were going to be the worst so I might as well let you have your own session. If you're supportive, hopefully they'll fall in line."

Phoebe speaks quickly. "Not that it matters, since it's your choice. Asher knows how that is, don't you, honey? When other people's opinions can keep you away from the person you love." Her delicate brow raises as she tilts her head.

He rolls his eyes. "Yes, sweetheart, it's a shame."

She looks triumphant as she turns to Brynn and whispers, "I got this. You just be happy."

We continue to talk about logistics and then about the wedding itself. About fifteen minutes later, her other brothers and their significant others are in the room. Our news is met with a lot of surprise, especially from Rowan and Charlotte.

"Oh. Wow. I . . . didn't know . . . wow." Charlotte repeats herself and blinks repeatedly. "So, I guess we're all keeping the business in the family after all."

I nod with a smile. "It seems that way. Really, I need to thank you both, if you hadn't invited me to your wedding, I never would've found her again."

Rowan clears his throat. "Yeah, about that, you slept with my sister and disappeared? You're so fucking lucky I didn't beat the shit out of you at my wedding when I found out. I watched my sister sob on the bathroom floor because you hurt her, and now you're getting married?"

Seems Brynn filled her family in on our past. I'd like to tell Rowan to go fuck himself, that it's between Brynlee and myself, but we're not coming at this on equal footing. I hurt his sister and if this were my sister, I'd be the same.

"Rowan!" Brynlee steps in.

I squeeze her hand. "He's right. I hurt you, and then when I saw you again for the first time, I hurt you more." I look to her brothers. "I was wrong to ever walk away from her. I loved your sister more than I can say, and I truly believed I was protecting her when I disappeared ten years ago. I was young and stupid, and not able to give her the life I can now. But you know we're not talking about the money, because Brynlee couldn't give a fuck about my fortune. If you want to punch me, now is the time. After tonight, our past is behind us."

Rowan smirks, and Charlotte slaps his chest and shakes her head. Grady looks at us and smiles. "I have nothing to say other than that if this is what she wants, none of us have a right to say a word."

"That's right. None of you do." Brynlee points her finger at Rowan. "Especially those of you living in glass houses."

Grady is the first to approach me, his hand extended. "Welcome to the family, Carson."

I return the gesture. "Thank you, and please, call me Crew."

He nods, then I repeat the same sentiment with her other brothers. I pull her to me, wrapping my arm around her and kissing her head. "That wasn't so bad."

She smiles up at me. "That isn't even the half of it. Wait until Olivia gets here."

Her niece arrives twenty minutes later at Asher's house, and Brynlee takes us up to her room for privacy. Olivia has the entire upstairs, which is more of a loft. There's a bedroom on one side and a playroom on the other.

We're sitting on the couch and Brynn's leg is bouncing. She releases a heavy sigh and lifts her hands to sign, speaking aloud as she does so. *"Olivia, this is Carson, but we call him Crew."*

I wave and she does the same.

"Crew and I liked each other a lot when I was in college."

Olivia's eyes widen and she signs. Brynn smiles and nods.

"What did she say?" I ask.

"She asked if we hooked up."

I laugh.

Brynn ignores me and returns her attention to Olivia. *"He came to Uncle Rowan's wedding, and we started talking again."*

Olivia signs and Brynn speaks. "She said she remembers you being there and wants to know why she had to come here."

Brynn replies to her niece. *"I asked you to come because I wanted to tell you myself. Crew and I have been spending some time together and I mentioned I liked him a lot, but I loved him too. He asked me to marry him and I said yes."*

Her voice trembles as she speaks, and I wish I could take her fear away. Olivia looks to me and then to her aunt. Brynlee and Olivia speak back and forth, though she's stopped interpreting, and I remain patient. It's clear whatever conversation they're having, it's more important for her to talk to Olivia than to me.

After another minute, Olivia launches herself into Brynn's arms and they hug. She turns to me.

"Olivia was worried, but she's so happy for us. She also thinks you're cute."

I grin. "And you were worried she wouldn't take it well. I'm a catch, you know, all the girls love me."

She rolls her eyes and then Olivia leans back. "Olivia wants me to tell you that she would love to meet Layla."

I look to Brynn. "How do I sign that she'll love meeting her?"

Brynn shows me and I do my best, but I'm sure I butcher it. The two of them smile and Brynn corrects whatever I got wrong.

Olivia replies and Brynlee laughs. "She said you did it wrong, but she appreciates the effort."

It seems like Olivia has more questions for Brynn and is probably uncomfortable with me there.

"How about I give you guys some time to talk? I'm sure she has questions," I offer. It's clear the two of them have a very special bond.

"You're sure? I know my brothers are down there . . ."

I lean in and kiss her temple. "I'll be fine. Two of them work for me. They can't be too bad, and the other I can handle."

Olivia giggles and Brynn tries to hide her smile. "She can read lips really well."

I give her a wink. "Any tips?"

Olivia raises her hands and talks to Brynn. "She said the key to her dad's heart is her and her sister. She said Rowan likes mischief and Grady is boring and just likes planes."

"Thank you. I'll do my best to stick to those topics."

She nods once.

I head downstairs, giving them some privacy. When I get to the bottom of the stairs, Asher is there.

"Did it go well?" he asks, his voice terse, but not filled with venom like earlier.

"I think so. Olivia is really sweet."

"She loves her aunt very much." He runs his hands through his hair and sighs. "Want a beer?"

I fucking hate beer, but it seems I'm going to drink one tonight. "I'd love one."

"Come on."

I follow Asher out to the back deck, where he opens a fridge and hands me a beer. We both open them and he points to the chairs that are by the firepit. "Sorry I was a prick, as Phoebe said before. Brynlee is like a daughter to me in some ways, more than a sister."

"I get it. I'm a father and I can't imagine that I'd handle it well if Layla came home with a guy I'd only met once in passing."

He takes a long pull from the bottle and then looks up at the sky. "She has a piece of shit for a father. Howie was my mother's last marriage after our dad ran off. When my mom finally left Howie, and moved here, it was rough on her. Then Mom died and I did what I could to protect her, but I failed in a lot of ways. One of them I'll never forgive myself for. It's why when it comes to men in her life, I'm a little over the top."

I know he's talking about her ex. She told me bits and pieces of the guy before me who lied to her and how he was her brother's best friend. "I don't ever want to hurt Brynlee."

"But you did," Asher reminds me.

"I did. I regret it," I assure him. "I plan to spend our time together making it right. Brynlee will want for nothing, and I'll do what I can to keep her safe and healthy."

That's the best promise I can make at this time. He doesn't know about her surgery and all the reasons we have to make this work. But I do care for Brynn. I always have and always will. If she needs something, I'll do whatever I can to make her happy.

"Then don't take her from here and think she'll fit into your life there. Brynlee has always needed to save the world. Any time there was a person or animal that was hurt, she took responsibility for it, wanted to fix it, give it a second chance. I've watched her break more times than I care to admit when it doesn't work." He pinches the bridge of his nose. "I don't know why you guys feel the need to rush and get married this week, and while I may not be a genius, I'm not a fool, and I'm pretty sure there's some other reason behind it."

"Brynlee told you her reasons."

"Yeah, and I'm not buying it, but I won't say anything more on it. I hope you understand the gift that my sister is. I hope you don't break her heart, because I'm not sure how many more times it can happen before it can't be fixed."

I open my mouth to promise I won't do that to her, but the back door opens, causing us both to turn. Olivia and Brynlee are there, Olivia has a big smile on her face and Asher and I both stand.

"Here you both are," Brynn says and the two of them step out.

Asher signs to his daughter and she signs back.

Brynlee stands beside me, whispering what they're saying. "She told her dad she's going to be in the wedding, her mother said it was okay already, and that you tried to sign to her and it was terrible and also very sweet."

I laugh once.

"Asher is happy for her and thinks you're an idiot," Brynn says with a laugh. Olivia turns to me and signs with Brynn speaking it. *"I am very happy for you. Aunt Brynn is the best and I hope I can come to New York and visit you."*

"Can you help me sign this back to her?" I ask Brynn. "I want to try again, even if I'm bad at it."

Her smile makes my chest ache, but she helps me, moving my hands as I say the words, knowing she can read my lips if I screw up too bad. *"You are welcome any time, and I agree, she is the best."*

Olivia signs back. *"Thank you and you did much better."*

I grin and speak so she can read my lips. "Hopefully your aunt will teach me more."

Brynlee's eyes find mine. "You want to learn?"

I look at Olivia and then to Brynn. "Of course I do, it's important I can communicate with your family."

Her eyes fill with unshed tears and she looks away, but Asher is staring at me he tips his bottle at me and smiles. "I get it now."

I'm not sure what he gets, but before I can ask, Phoebe comes outside, ordering us all inside to help settle a fight between Rowan and Grady.

eleven

CARSON

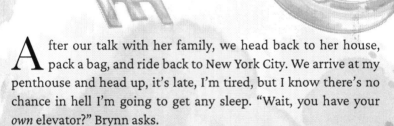

After our talk with her family, we head back to her house, pack a bag, and ride back to New York City. We arrive at my penthouse and head up, it's late, I'm tired, but I know there's no chance in hell I'm going to get any sleep. "Wait, you have your *own* elevator?" Brynn asks.

"*We* do."

This will all be hers in eight days.

"Right, I'm going to live here." The way she says it is almost like she can't believe it. "Because I'm marrying a billionaire and he has his own elevator."

I laugh a little. "I'd probably have this same thing if I were just a millionaire."

"Oh, of course, us common folk just use the stairs."

My gaze moves to the area where the stairs are. "You're welcome to do that, but it's one hundred and thirty floors."

Her eyes widen. "*What?*"

"It's a long walk."

She nods. "I'd say."

"Come on." I laugh as I guide her over, scan my fob, and the elevator door opens. "It takes us directly into the penthouse."

"Of course it does," she laughs to herself as she gets in. "How big is it? The penthouse, not the elevator."

It takes a few minutes to get up to the entrance, since we have to go up over a hundred floors.

"It's a good size. There are seven bedrooms and eight bathrooms and it's three full floors."

Brynn's mouth drops. "It has more bathrooms than bedrooms?"

"I told you it's ridiculous."

"And you live here alone?"

I shake my head. "No, Cliff and Celeste live here too."

She laughs at that. "Let me guess, Celeste is your . . ."

"Housekeeper. She cooks and keeps things clean, not that I'm much of a mess maker, but she's a godsend and I can't imagine life without her. If you need anything, just ask."

"I'm not sure I'm going to do well with this."

All of this is going to be extremely strange for Brynn, but it's going to be her new life for the time being. "It gets easier. Cliff will be your driver. Ford already hired someone new for me. I want you to be with someone I trust. If the media starts to harass you, I'll have my security team assigned to you as well."

She lifts her hand, covering my mouth. "No more. Let's . . . take this slow and let me ease into this, okay?"

I smile, pulling her hand down. "We're getting married in a few days, we don't have slow."

"That may be, but I'm going to end up having a panic attack in your very nice, private elevator. Cooks and drivers and security teams are all a little much on the night of our engagement. Between the fact that we are engaged, told my family, and we're already mid planning a wedding, and then there's telling your family, who I've never met, in like, twelve hours . . . it has me on edge."

She's so fucking cute when she's flustered. "So you don't want to know about the private ballroom?"

Her hand is back on my mouth. "Zip it."

To keep her from freaking out, I push the button to go to the second floor of our penthouse. It's the level with the primary bedroom and Layla's room. It'll . . . ease her in, maybe.

"Why did you do that?" Brynn asks, removing her hand.

"I figured it may work better if we go to the bedrooms first."

Her eyes widen. "Bedroom?"

Shit. I didn't think that through. "I just meant to show you our rooms, Layla's room, that's all."

"We're not sharing a room," she informs me as we stop on the second floor of the penthouse.

"Of course we are. We're going to be married."

"Yes, but . . . that wasn't part of the plan."

"Technically, we didn't really have a plan about that," I remind her.

We step off the elevator and Brynn gasps. We enter the hall-way, where the floors are marble, gleaming because Celeste washes them daily. There is a huge spiral staircase to the left that opens to the main and upper levels. I guide her the other way, where the guest rooms are. Maybe that'll keep her calm.

"You live here?" she asks again.

"*We* live here, Brynlee."

She laughs once and sighs. "You understand my entire house fits in just that space where the staircase is?"

"It's a lot, I know."

"Crew, it's . . . more than a lot."

I shrug because it is what it is. "I entertain here at times and there's something to be said for intimidation when you're brokering a deal. Bringing my adversaries here has helped me remind people of who I am and exactly what I own."

Brynlee seems to consider that and rests her hand on my arm. "I'm sorry. This has been a very . . . unexpected day."

"Don't apologize. Here, let me show you Layla's room."

We walk down the hall and I open the door. It's like cotton candy threw up in here. The room is overdone, but Layla loves pink, so when I told the designer that, she ran with it. There is a large canopy bed, a gold dresser, and more toys than the kid could ever want. This room is soft, girly, and all I want is for her to be happy when she's here.

Brynn smiles up at me. "It's very pretty."

"She loves it."

"I'm sure she does. Do you show your business adversaries here first?"

I grin. "No, should I?"

"Might scare more of them off."

I laugh and take her hand. "Come on, let me show you the rest."

We open the other guest rooms on this floor, the gaming lounge, in case she decides she wants to throw darts or whatever. I never go in there. Then I bring her to the primary wing. It's masculine, because I live here alone, and it's massive.

Brynlee doesn't say anything as she walks around the space. There are two bathrooms, two dressing rooms, a sitting area, and floor-to-ceiling windows that look out at Central Park in the bedroom area.

"I get my own bathroom?" she asks.

"I use the smaller one."

Her brow lifts. "Why?"

"Because I don't need anything more than that."

"Crew, you don't need any of this!"

She's not wrong, I don't need it, but I wanted it. I needed to own something that Digger could never touch. This place is the opposite of the brownstone. It's big, over the top, and is so damn ostentatious it's basically the definition of the word. It drips of someone with too much money on their hands, and the day I bought it, I felt fucking free.

Everything she ever wanted was in this place and it wasn't hers.

I walk over to Brynn, incredibly happy that she will be the person who lives in this place with me. She'll be the woman who can say this was hers, even if only for a while.

"I needed control in a time when I had none. When everything I wanted was out of my reach. I was so fucking angry at her for keeping Layla from me, I needed to punish her. To get something she begged for and to know she couldn't touch it. I don't need this space, this many bedrooms, this many bathrooms, but I needed to feel like I had something."

Her hand reaches up, pushing my hair back. "Did it make you feel better?"

The question isn't sarcastic, it's soft and curious.

To be honest with her, to tell her that I felt nothing after it became mine, is an admission I don't want to make. But this is Brynlee. She's the girl who knew my most inner demons and never shied away from them.

"I felt alone, with a lot less money."

Her thumb moves across my stubble. We're silent, just standing here, her touch is a caress, and I don't want it to stop.

Brynn's eyes meet mine. "I'd forgotten about this scar." She grazes the place where I had stitches after my first collegiate crew race. After we won, one of the oars came loose and hit me in the lip. "I thought I'd memorized you so well that I wouldn't have forgotten about that detail."

"There's nothing about you that I don't remember."

She steps back, her hand dropping, and I try to figure out what I said that has her pulling back.

"I don't think us staying in the same bedroom is smart."

I run my hand through my hair. "Maybe not, but we can't sleep apart. While Celeste and Cliff would cut their arms off before ever breathing a word to the press, there are many others who I don't trust that implicitly. Layla is little and if she notices, and mentions it to anyone, then our entire arrangement would be screwed. We can't give anyone any possible idea this isn't real. Too many things can go wrong if we start putting up barriers."

"Fine, but I have rules."

I laugh. "I can't wait to hear them."

twelve

BRYNLEE

R ules are the cornerstone of my life.

Therefore, the only way this marriage will work is with very set ones.

I just need to come up with them.

Crew stands there, arms crossed over his broad chest, looking like the delicious man I want nothing more than to climb into that monster of a bed with and forget life exists.

However, that would be stupid.

Stupid is for young girls and I'm not that anymore.

"Do you have rules or are you just going to come up with them on the fly?" he asks.

"I'm not sure yet."

He grins and God, he looks so hot when he does. This! This is going to be my first rule. No thinking that Crew is hot.

But then his stunning blue eyes are staring at me and I can feel my insides start to go mushy.

I clear my throat. "Rule number one, no sex."

"You want us to have a marriage with no sex?"

No.

"Yes."

"Okay, if that's what you want. I will not initiate sex with you," he promises.

I purse my lips. "You think I'm going to initiate with you?"

Crew walks over to his—our—bed and sits, tossing his shoes off. "If I remember, it was you who threw herself at me that night. I think I was trying to hold off on us having sex."

I gasp. "Umm, absolutely not. We made out, you went down on me, and then somehow, I was on my back, and you kept asking if it was okay."

Crew shakes his head. "I don't think that's how it went."

"I promise, it is."

I remember everything about that night. I also remember me begging at some point, but we're not going to bring that up.

He pulls his tie loose, letting it hang around his neck. "You asked me to come to your room, you kicked your roommate out, and we were lying there. Then you said, 'Crew, please make love to me.'"

Oh, he's so full of shit. "I never, *ever* said that."

"Pretty sure that's how it went."

"Then you've lost your memories somewhere in your old age. I assure you, I did not ask you to make love to me."

I probably thought it, but he doesn't read minds so . . . I win.

"I don't know about that," he says and then smacks his lips. "If your mouth didn't say it, I know your eyes did."

I stare at him, glaring more than anything. "What are my eyes saying now?"

"That you are trying to undress me."

I huff. "Not even a little. Time to get an eye exam."

Crew gets back to his feet, moving toward me. "It's fine. Like I said, I will not seduce you and if you try to seduce me, which is probably going to happen, I will do my best to resist you . . . or not."

Self-absorbed man.

"I'm so glad you've enlightened me on your plan. Rule number two, I need for us to abide by the fact that this isn't real."

"Meaning?"

I sigh, hating that I have to say it, but I need to put it out there. "We had a whirlwind romance. We were those people that fell in love in a week, fell hard, and when you left, it broke me."

"Brynn—" I raise my hand.

"It broke my heart, Crew. I haven't dated or been with anyone since you. I'm not saying this to be dramatic or hurt you in any way, I just need you to understand that I've been with two men in my life, and both relationships ended horribly."

He winces and I know that he and Jonathan aren't the same, but the damage to my heart didn't differentiate. I loved him, trusted him, and he left me. I've forgiven and moved on, in a way, but that scar will forever remain on my heart.

I need to have an exit plan for this because getting married like this, building everything on lies and deceit, isn't going to end well.

I know it and I'm pretty sure he does.

"I never meant to hurt you."

"And you've said that, but it doesn't change the fact that it did. It hurt and it still hurts, and I've tried so hard to move past it, and I have, but . . . I don't know, maybe I haven't."

The admission causes a pain in my chest, but I need him to understand why I need these rules.

"So let's have it out," he says, moving closer.

"Have what out?"

Crew starts to pace. "The past. The anger. The whole damn thing. I'll go first. I hated you for making me question everything in my life."

My eyes widen. "What? How the hell are you mad at me?"

"Because I was perfectly fine letting my life be what it was going to be. I fucked around, had fun, never felt a damn thing for any girl I spent time with, then I met you. You were so much more than I ever imagined."

Well, that's rich. He's pissed at me for having a football thrown at my head. "Yes, I'm so sorry I was in your orbit when you and your idiot friend wanted to throw things at the pretty sorority girls."

"That's another thing!" he bellows. "You had to be nice about it."

I glare at him. "Oh, don't you even make this my fault! You couldn't catch a football! You were the one who came to me, asking me my name and all that."

"And I knew the first moment I met you that I needed you in my life. I couldn't walk away. I couldn't even think about leaving you at that moment."

"You left me forever! You could've been honest and told me what our reality was! Instead, you let me love you. You pretended we could have more than just that week, let me live in that euphoric heaven and then dropped me in hell. So don't you dare come at me like I did anything wrong. You broke me, Crew. You left me alone in that damn house, waking up after giving everything I had to you. You chose to leave me without even a damn note. I woke up, alone, naked, and searching for you, hoping that maybe you just went to get gas or breakfast. I thought you'd come back, and you never did. So, yeah, I need rules. I need to protect my heart because it wouldn't take much for me to just let you back in and let you break me apart again."

My chest is heaving as I let that all out. He moves closer, stopping a few feet away.

"I know you won't understand it, but I couldn't look you in the eyes and say the truth. I couldn't see me hurt you that way. For the first time in my life, I hated my name, my family, my fucking mapped-out life. I thought, maybe if I don't say it, I can fix it. I thought I could go to my grandfather, explain how I met someone, and I loved her, and he wouldn't push the issue. I had a plan to come back to you, Bee. I'm sorry that plan was flawed from the start."

I look down at the floor before I can return to his face. "We were young and stupid to think it could last."

"But you're still angry."

I shake my head. "No, I'm just still trying to recover from another man making me think I could have something and then taking it from me."

And that's really what it comes down to. I believed in him—in us. I thought that he was going to be different, and I let my very trusting heart have free rein. That can't happen now.

"So what are you asking me for?" Crew's voice is low.

"I guess I just need us to be careful and not get caught up in the past. We had something special then, but we're not those kids anymore. You and I don't really know each other now. This . . . relationship . . . is flawed to start with, and to pretend otherwise is stupid."

He nods. "I understand and see your logic."

Well, that's good—I think.

"All right. Do you have any rules?"

Crew runs his hands through his thick hair. "Two rules. One of them is that we don't lie to each other. We have to be able to trust one another, even if we're in this for unconventional reasons. I don't want you to tell me you want something you don't or the other way. You'll never have to wonder if I mean what I say because I won't lie to you."

"Okay, I can do that." Honestly, it'll be nice to not have to question everything, and I hate lying, so this is great. "What's the second rule?"

"No matter what, Layla comes first," Crew says with a firm voice I imagine he uses in business.

"I would never ask otherwise."

He shakes his head. "I didn't think you would. I just mean that her happiness, her needs, they'll always be my first priority. I need you to understand that. Whatever we need to do to protect her, keep her safe, and help her recover from whatever hell her mother is putting her through, that's what we do."

The way he says 'we' makes my chest tighten. I may have only met Layla once, but already she matters to me, it's why I'm here with a big ole rock on my hand. I move to him, taking his hand in mine. "Of course."

He smiles hesitantly. "I have one more offer."

"What's that?"

"If you change your mind, you're welcome to use my body in any way you want."

We both laugh and I drop his hand, rolling my eyes as I do. "Such a man. Now that we have that settled, I need to change into something comfy and try to familiarize myself with my new home. When do you have Layla again?" I ask.

"This weekend. There's not a chance in hell that Jacqueline will let us have her for the wedding. She's going to lose her ever-loving mind tomorrow when this all breaks. Are you ready for it?"

"As much as I'll ever be."

He lifts my chin up so our eyes meet. "I will never let her hurt you."

It's him that I'm worried will hurt me, but I just smile and let him kiss me softly before he walks out.

"Oh, this is the best news ever!" Celeste, the housekeeper, says as she rushes around the kitchen island to hug me. I unpacked my small bag and then came down to find the kitchen for a cup of tea. "I'm so happy to hear about this! I've hoped and prayed that Mr. Knight would find someone. To think, ten years you two were apart and to find each other after all this time." She dabs at her eyes and then smiles. "Anything you need! Anything! You just ask."

"Thank you." I can tell I'm going to absolutely love her. "I can't tell you how much that means to me."

"Are you telling her how much you love me?" Crew walks in, wearing a pair of basketball shorts slung low on his hips, and his shirt leaves little to the imagination. Dear God. I am pretty sure I'm drooling.

His body is absolutely stunning. I know men aren't supposed to be beautiful and all that, but he is.

He's beautiful and hot and . . . we are *not* going to have sex.

I'm starting to think I'm a damn idiot for that rule.

"Yes, I can't seem to stop myself," I say with a sugary sweet lilt.

He chuckles and then slaps me on the ass with his towel that's draped around his shoulder as he walks past me. "I'm going in the gym, then maybe we can watch a movie on the big screen before bed?"

"A movie? Do you have a theater in here too?"

Celeste giggles. "He does."

Of course he does.

"Sure, that sounds great. Wait, you're going to work out?" I ask, looking at the clock. It's almost eleven at night.

"I didn't this morning and I need to run and clear my head."

"Right. A run. Totally makes sense."

Crew winks. "Walk around and check out the house, I promise you'll love the library."

What the hell have I gotten myself into?

When Crew leaves, I turn to see Celeste watching me closely. "I'd be happy to show you around more."

I think I need a little alone time to sort my thoughts out. "I'm kind of overwhelmed, do you mind if we do that tomorrow?"

"I don't mind a bit. You go look around and I'll be preparing for tomorrow with his family."

Yes, brunch tomorrow. Crew called his brothers and sister, asking them to come to his place to discuss our big news. Not that they won't see it in the papers tomorrow. He said it will be completely uneventful. Apparently, his family doesn't do emotions or outrage. I was assured it will all be very civilized.

I wave and head out of the kitchen. I look around the second floor, where Celeste and Cliff reside, checking out the areas Crew didn't show me, which is everything other than the staff quarters and the main kitchen. As I meander around, I find a dining room, family room, another guest room, and the movie room he talked about, which is literally like a damn movie theater. Then there's another room that is nothing but windows, which is attached to the library, and I realize we must be directly below the master bedroom.

I head down the stairs and I seriously can't comprehend it. The first door I open is a massive room with tables in the corner and I can't tell what the room is, but it's clearly for entertaining.

I head back out and see the terrace. Although, I don't even know if you can call it that, because it's freaking huge. Like the size of the dining room and kitchen combined.

It's a little chilly, so I don't plan to stay out here long, but the views are . . . well, billionaire views.

The terrace has two large couches, lounge chairs, and three separate firepits. The wind whips my hair in my face, but I can't seem to go back inside. I pull it around to my side, holding it as I stare out above the trees, above so many other buildings, just looking out at Central Park and the city that never sleeps.

"It's beautiful, isn't it?"

I gasp and turn to see Crew leaning against the door, his towel draped around his neck with a grin on his perfect face.

"It is."

"The view isn't bad either," he says, walking toward me.

Heat rushes to my cheeks and I face away, working to control myself.

Why does my traitorous heart not remember the pain of him leaving? Why do I look at him and go back to the smiles, kisses, the way he made me feel like nothing in this world could ever hurt me again?

But he did.

Crew left me, reminding me that not all love stories have a happily ever after. Sometimes, it's a damn tragedy.

He stands beside me, his arm brushing mine. "As much as I love the city and the views of the park, it's nothing like the tranquility of Sugarloaf."

I look at him as he turns, putting his back to the view. "I sometimes think Central Park is a mirage. A way for New Yorkers to feel like there's a bit of beauty and peace among the greed, shopping, and filth."

"Everyone needs a place for peace."

"True. My brothers and I used to play football at the park

every Friday when we were kids. We grew up on the Upper West Side in the house my grandparents owned that has been in my family for generations. We would sneak out after my parents left for whatever business dinner or gala they were attending and play football for hours."

"They didn't let you play?"

He scoffs. "A Knight? Play a sport as undignified as football? Absolutely not. We could row, fence, or play soccer. That was it."

"And you picked rowing."

He smiles at me and pushes off the railing. "I hated running, so soccer was out, and there was no way I was going to fence, so . . . that left me with one option. I would've kicked ass in football, though."

I smile at the image I have of a twelve-year-old Crew, sneaking out the back door to play football.

"I'm sure you would've. There's not much you don't excel at when you want something."

"I'd say the ring on your finger is proof of that."

I look down at the incredible diamond, nestled snugly around the others. "We both have our reasons to agree to it."

He nods once. "Tomorrow is going to be . . . interesting."

"Your family?"

"Kimberly will be overjoyed, truly. She may be a giant pain in the ass, but she's a hopeless romantic. My brothers are assholes."

"More than my brothers were?" I ask with a raised brow.

The wind whips up again and I shiver. He notices and extends his hand. "Come on, let's go inside."

I take his hand and he doesn't bring me back in the door we entered, he walks us down to the end where there's another door.

"This is the gym here and there's another room back there, but I don't use it."

"Do you use half the rooms here?" I ask with a laugh.

"Nope, but once we're married, we'll need to throw a party to celebrate our marriage. I can finally use the ballroom and Celeste will be excited she can order a catering company around."

Great. A party. "I'm going to be preparing for my surgery. I don't know that I can plan a party."

"You won't have to worry about anything, Brynn. We have plenty of people who will handle it all. I know your priority is your father. I wouldn't do anything that would hinder that."

I nod, relief flooding me. "Thank you."

"Did you hear back from the charity yet?"

The relief is gone. "No, but I'm hoping by the end of the week."

His smile doesn't quite reach his eyes. "I hope so too. At least that would be one less thing for you to worry about."

Yeah, it would, but I can't do anything about it. "Well, for now, the thing I'm most worried about is meeting your family tomorrow when we tell them we're engaged."

Because that's going to go over like a lead balloon.

He shakes his head. "They'll love you and if they don't, they'll pretend because that's what we do. Don't spend another minute thinking of them, I promise, none of them will upset you."

thirteen

CARSON

I wake up to Brynn curled against my chest, leg thrown over mine, hair in my mouth, and I can't think of any other way I want to wake up.

Which is fucking stupid to think.

I mentally slap myself and remember to keep my head in the game. We're playing house, nothing more.

Brynn rubs her cheek on my chest, mumbling in her sleep, just like she did when we were young.

"You are the best pillow in all the world."

I pushed her long red hair back, not sure where her face was under that mess. "I swear you're in here. At least you were when we went to sleep."

Brynlee grumbled something about sleep and hating being awake. "Five more minutes."

"I wish we could, baby, but we have plans."

I only had twenty-four more hours with her, and I wasn't going to waste any of it sleeping.

"Plans?"

"Yup."

"That include being awake?" Brynlee asked, tightening her grip around my chest.

"Most plans do." I chuckled. "Come on, Bee, get up."

She lifted her head, brown eyes with flecks of yellow around the iris staring at me. "This better be worth it, Crew."

And there was the stinger. She may have been sweet, always giving parts of herself in service of others, but she had her defenses, and she could definitely pack a punch when her back was to the wall. It's why I called her my little honeybee, which she found adorable.

"It will be," I promised.

At least I hoped it would.

For the last six days I'd questioned everything I'd ever thought about love. Not that my parents or grandparents showed any of us what love looked like, but I believed it just evaded the Knight family.

We'd been punished, thanks to the generations of shithead men who married for duty.

Which is what I'd been told I'd be doing.

But what if I could have this? What if I could have her?

She whined and dropped her head back on my chest. "I want to just stay here. Forever."

As though she read my mind. "And what would we do?"

I could feel her smile on my skin. "Stay like this. Stay in bed, wrapped around each other while the world moves on, and we have each other. Although, I'm not sure any company we work for would allow that," Brynn joked.

Little did she know I owned my own company at that point and I could've probably found a way to work that into the bylaws.

"Probably not, but I want us to do something fun today, and then tonight, we're going to dinner, just the two of us."

She looked up at me with her long lashes fluttering. "A date."

"A date."

Our last one.

Brynlee pushed herself up higher on my chest and kissed my nose. "How have we spent this entire week together, each night sleeping together, and not gone on a date?"

I chuckled, pushing her hair back. "I'd say we've been on the longest first date in history."

"I don't want it to end," she admitted.

Neither did I, but I knew there wouldn't be a way to continue, not with my family. Not with my future mapped out, but I could give her one date. One that she'd remember forever, and that's exactly what I planned to do.

My phone rings, and I glance at the clock, seeing it's five in the morning. Great. It begins.

Sure enough, my father's face is on the screen, and I shift, trying not to wake Brynn. She rolls over, clutching a pillow, and I grin.

She's the same in so many ways.

Once out of the bedroom, I swipe the phone. "Hello, Father."

"You're engaged?" he yells, and I pull the phone away from my ear. "Are you fucking kidding me?"

"No, I'm not kidding, it's why we're all having brunch today, so you can meet Brynlee."

He's silent and I remain the same. The name is not foreign to him. Which is why this will work in my favor. My family will have no problem understanding exactly why I'm marrying her.

"Brynlee?"

"Yes."

"You found her?"

If I hadn't been such a fucking asshole, I would've looked for her sooner. "I did, by chance."

"So, you're going to marry her?"

"Yes, and I *appreciate*"—I emphasize the word strongly— "your support and welcoming of her into the Knight family."

"Crew." He huffs my name.

Sometimes I think my parents think we're all still kids. That we are awaiting our inheritance and will play by their ridiculous rules. My grandfather signed over my inheritance when I married Jacqueline. I built my own fortune, making sure I never needed to be a part of this game anymore.

"I'm not fucking around. I don't need your money. I don't need your support. I don't need this company, I have my own. I'm not a child. I know what I'm doing, and I love her. So, you'll support me, or you can fuck off."

"Jesus, calm down," my father says with a half laugh.

It's not often any of us go against him. We've been trained to be obedient. The Knight name is more valuable than any amount of money we have in our accounts.

I stay quiet, letting him sweat for a moment.

He speaks again. "It just feels sudden, Crew."

"It's not. It's ten years too late. If I wasn't forced into the bull-shit marriage with Jacqueline, then I wouldn't be suddenly doing anything."

His deep sigh fills the silence again. He regrets everything about pushing me to marry Jacqueline. He disliked her but would never go against his father's wishes. Jacqueline was like chimera. We hoped she'd be this perfect idea of a wife. She came from a good family, wasn't as rich as us, but wasn't poor, and she knew what her job was. However, she ended up being none of those things. Her family reputation detonated a month after our wedding when her father was arrested for embezzlement and her brother was accused of assault.

"Well, congratulations then. When is the wedding?" my father asks.

"In seven days, in North Carolina. If you come today, we'll have more details."

In the heaviness of the moment, I know he wants to say more. However, for maybe the first time in his life, he doesn't. "I look forward to meeting her."

"I'll see you in a few hours."

I hang up and look at my phone; there are text messages and emails piling in.

"Everything okay?" Brynn's sleepy voice calls.

When I look up, she's standing at the door, head resting on the jamb, long, lean legs crossed at her ankles, and I want to lift her, toss her on the bed, and fuck her until neither of us can walk, but I force myself to stay put.

"My father found out through the article this morning."

"I take it he wasn't happy for us?"

I grin. "He's fine now."

"Maybe there's another way, Crew. Maybe we don't have to do this to win Layla."

"I wish there was. I analyzed it all day before coming to you. The issue was the photos of us, I couldn't find a way around them. Even if I explained that we were old friends, the way they were going to spin it would have just solidified her case. I need to give the courts every reason to believe that I'm a family man. Being photographed with women and letting the papers spew whatever bullshit they want isn't going to help."

Brynn walks toward me. "I never saw you in the papers. In all these years."

"I work very hard to stay out of them. My company takes the credit, I'm just the man behind the curtain. Jacqueline is using my name now to build her case. Suddenly, what I do and who I'm with matters."

She stands before me, looking so damn perfect it actually hurts. "Then we'll give them a wedding and photos of us in marital bliss."

I smile down at her. "I don't know that you'll have much bliss, but . . ."

"Well, you are pushy."

"And you still hog the covers."

Her eyes widen. "I do not."

"I woke up to you climbing me like a tree."

"I'm so sure," she huffs. "Anyway, what are our plans after brunch?"

"I have to go to the office. I'd like you to come with me and meet some of the people there. My lawyer will be meeting us there as well, she wants to talk to you about the case and make sure you and I are on the same page. Then we pick up Layla for dinner."

That's if her piece of shit mother doesn't pull some bullshit after she wakes up to see the news.

"Do you have a plan to tell her?"

"I think we just tell her that we're getting married. She's four, so I don't think we'll have issues. She's a really sweet kid."

Brynn smiles. "I know, I just wasn't sure what the plan was."

I wish I had one. I wish I knew what to do in this situation, but it's all uncharted water.

My phone rings again, and I toss it over on the chair. I'm not in the mood for any of this. "Are you hungry?"

"For breakfast?"

"You know, that meal after you wake up," I tease her.

"I know what breakfast is, ass."

"Come on, I need to eat and I'm craving eggs and bacon."

Brynn eyes me warily. "Do billionaires even know how to cook?"

I grin. "Some of us do."

"Wow, who would've thunk it."

"Luckily for you, you got the upgraded version."

She laughs and playfully taps my chest. "Yes, lucky me. Let's see you in action and I'll let you know if your upgrades are complete or if you need a new version."

"And how was brunch with your family to announce your engagement?" Ms. Banks asks as we're sitting in my office a few hours later.

Brunch was exactly what I thought it would be. My sister was incredibly supportive, hugged Brynn and welcomed her to the family.

My brothers were reserved but wished us well, and I got text messages from both of them letting me know I wasn't behaving like myself and they hoped I wasn't being blackmailed.

Dad was . . . quiet. Mom was in her own world, but both said they hoped this marriage was better than the last.

Which is comedic since they're the ones who basically forced me to marry Digger.

"It went well," I say, because that's about all I can say.

"I've gotten four calls from your ex-wife's legal team. All stating that this is a sham of an engagement, and she is going to be working to ensure you're not allowed near Layla until after the custody hearings due to your upcoming nuptials."

My vision has a red haze over it, but I keep my composure. Brynn's fingers lace through mine and she squeezes lightly.

"On what grounds?" she asks Ms. Banks.

"Stating that you are going to be too upsetting to Layla."

Brynn clears her throat. "I'm sure you informed the former Mrs. Knight that she cannot control who Layla interacts with during Carson's allotted visits? If that was the case, Carson would be well within his rights to demand the same thing, and since it's been . . . alluded to, that she's dating someone, he'd be able to restrict her life as well."

Ms. Banks grins. "I did, in fact. However, as happy as I am for you both to have found love again, it's going to enrage her, and I don't doubt the games she plays will be something we will have to combat."

"I'm not sure Carson has told you, but I'm also a lawyer who worked in family law for a short while. I'm very aware of what we need to do to make this easier for everyone. Layla is our main concern. Her safety and well-being are the only things the two of us want more than anything. Last time we saw her, she was terrified because her mother is drinking constantly and screamed at her, and the nanny has even written a report. We need to get Layla out of her unstable environment."

My fucking God. The way her voice never wavers, how she
holds herself, makes me want to lay at her fucking feet and
worship her. I squeeze her hand, lifting it and kissing her
knuckles.

Her eyes find mine and she smiles a little. "I just want her
safe."

I can't speak because I'll say all the things I promised I
wouldn't. Brynlee's speech from last night, the way she explained
the pain I caused has me staying silent.

I won't make this harder for her. No matter how I feel. She is
giving me everything and I can give her the one thing she
asked for.

Ms. Banks clasps her hands, placing them in her lap. "We all
want the same thing, and the news of your engagement is being
received well in the press. It's a love story that people will talk
about, and that's what we need. Good press. It doesn't hurt that
you're a lawyer who is practically a saint."

"I wouldn't . . ."

She cuts Brynn off. "I would. You run an animal sanctuary in a
small town, took care of your niece, put yourself through law
school, and just started your own company. Now, I'm not a
complete fool, it's clear that this moved incredibly fast and I'm
going to assume the story is not entirely true."

"Parts of it are embellished," I admit.

"This will quell the rumors and the case that your ex-wife has
created. There will be no playboy image with *Little House on the
Prairie* beside you. Whatever the terms of your agreement are,
don't tell a soul. Not me. Not friends. Not family. No one can
know, and if it is this grand love story, then . . . congrats."

She stands, and Brynn and I do as well, and she leaves
without a backward glance. Brynn turns to me.

"Anyone else I'm going to meet where I might need a change
of clothes?"

I stare at her in confusion. "Change of clothes?"

She flops back on the couch and sighs. "From sweating. So far, everyone I've met has been terrifying. I'm just wondering if we can get it all out of the way in one day."

"Well, we have to pick up Layla in an hour, so I'm going to say we have more to go."

Brynlee groans. "Great. I just love crazy ex-wives."

I laugh, squatting down in front of her. "Then you're in luck. I have one of those."

fourteen

BRYNLEE

The first time I met Layla, I knew she was amazing, even though it was just a few minutes.

We're now at the table, coloring, and she's telling me all about her school, and I'm head over heels for this little girl.

"Can you color this page?" she asks, batting her long eyelashes.

"I can."

Crew is sitting at the table with us, going over emails on his phone that were the result of our entire day being taken up by our engagement.

It was one phone call after another. He had business associates, friends, family he hasn't spoken to, his lawyer assuring us that Layla would absolutely be ready when it was time for us to get her, and people I don't think any of us knew.

I was so not prepared for my newfound fame, either. All these years I've never heard Crew's name or seen photos. Not that I really cared about gossip, since I grew up around Jacob Arrowood, the famous actor who was a heartthrob—well, still is. Everyone in our town knew we couldn't believe anything we saw on television or online about him and I never cared enough to look.

"Daddy, can you color too?" Layla extends a crayon to him.

"I would, but I might ruin your pretty picture."

She smiles. "You won't."

"Okay, then." He puts his phone in his pocket and starts to color.

The three of us work on the book, Layla instructing the two of us where to color and which color she prefers. I catch Crew glancing at me with a smile several times, which I ignore because it fills my stomach with butterflies each time.

"Can Brynn"—which is more like Rin—"play with me in my room?" she asks, as she's clearly done with coloring now.

He glances at his watch and sighs. "It's almost time for you to go back home, Ladybug."

I grin at his nickname for her. Apparently, he has a thing for bugs. I'm his honeybee and she's his ladybug. It's kinda cute.

We spent the last few hours coloring, playing dolls, eating dinner, and then Layla painted my nails and Crew's. She's so damn adorable and easy to love. The fact that anyone could hurt her is unimaginable to me.

Although, the idea of anyone hurting any child feels the same.

Whenever I've come in contact with a child who has been abused, it's different for me. The feelings, emotions, and trauma that I experienced are triggered. I remember it all—the fear, the pain, the wondering what was wrong with me and why Howie didn't love me. I remember questioning what I did wrong, and how I could never make it make sense.

Because it doesn't.

There's an unspoken understanding, I believe, between victims. A silent language, a sign, a look that tells the other it's okay and that this person understands as well.

I feel as though we had that moment.

Layla crosses her arms over her chest. "I don't want to."

"I know, but I'll see you very soon. Just a few sleeps," Crew reassures her.

I smile and Layla turns to me. "I see you too?"

My eyes find Crew's and I wait for him to say something and tell her we're getting married. He reaches out, pulling Layla onto his lap. She nestles into him, and he hugs her tight. "You're going to see Brynn a lot more."

Her eyes brighten and she looks to me. I nod.

"I like her."

"Me too," Crew agrees.

"Rin is pretty."

"I think you're pretty," I tell her.

She ducks her chin.

"Layla, you'll see Brynn at my house when you come. She's going to be here all the time."

"Yay!" She claps and giggles.

I can see him struggling with this, to tell her the whole of it. She may like the idea of me being here sometimes, but who knows if she really understands what that means. He clears his throat. "Do you know why she'll be here?" he asks.

She shakes her head.

"It's because Daddy and Brynn are getting married."

Her mouth falls open. "Today?"

We both laugh. "No, not today, but very soon. Brynn is going to live here with me and be my wife."

"Forever?"

My heart breaks because it's not said in sadness, more like hope. How do we tell her that we actually have an end date?

We can't, and the idea of hurting her hurts me more than I can say.

I reach out, pushing her blond hair out of her eyes. "I'll be here a lot. We can play and I would really like to be your friend, is that okay?"

She nods. "I like friends."

"Me too."

Layla giggles and hugs her dad. "I want to stay with you forever, Daddy."

His eyes close and he pulls her tight to his chest. "I hope soon, Ladybug, I hope soon."

I hope so too.

I'm standing in the beach house where I met Crew ten years ago. So much has changed since I was here last. In just a few hours, we'll be married.

Everything in the last week has been a whirlwind and I swear the days bled together.

The day after we had Layla, our lawyer informed us that Jacqueline requested the court date be pushed back due to a medical condition she developed, which sent Crew over the edge. I'm hoping the judge will see through the game and not allow it, but . . . who knows?

Then, at my request, a prenup was drawn up, which the two of us signed. I wanted it to be crystal clear that we weren't marrying for money. Not just for my own peace of mind, but also for any argument in the custody battle.

Now, I'm here, at my wedding, with a custom-made dress that was sewn in just six days, that I'm sure cost a fortune, but I wasn't allowed to see any prices of anything. And I'm on the verge of a panic attack.

What the hell am I doing?

There's a knock on the door and Phoebe peeks her head in. "Hey."

"Hey," I say with a smile.

My family got in late last night. Crew paid for Grady to fly everyone on a much bigger and fancier jet than he usually uses.

"Are you ready?" she asks.

What a loaded question. "Can I say yes and no?"

Phoebe laughs. "I would expect you'd be a little freaked out."

"A little? I'm ready to pass out."

She comes to me, taking my hands and pulling me to the sofa. "Do you want to tell me the whole story?"

I want to, but I can't and won't. Like Crew and I agreed, no one can know the truth behind it all.

"What story?"

"Brynn," she says my name on a sigh. "I was with you when you texted him. How did it go from he didn't have your number to marriage in a few hours?"

In all the excitement following, I didn't even think about the fact that Phoebe had been with me. Shit.

"It really was like that, though," I explain. "I told you how I felt after our dinner, how sweet he was."

"Yes," she draws the word out. "I don't know that means marriage in a week, though."

I need to remind her how fast she and Asher fell. And they didn't have the history that Crew and I do. "When you realized how much you loved Asher, didn't you want to be with him? If you'd broken up, and went years without him, wouldn't that have been enough wasted time?"

Please let this lie stop feeling like the truth.

"I get all that, I just . . . I worry. You're moving to New York, starting your company, and . . . you know . . . your upcoming surgery . . ."

I nod. "Yes, I know."

"It's just a lot of things all at once, Brynn. I just want you to be happy and also not make decisions you'll regret later."

Before I can say anything else, there's another knock on the door. Thank the Lord.

"Come in!" I say quickly.

Kimberly peeks her head in. "Sorry to interrupt, I just have something for you."

"For me?" I ask.

"From my brother."

She walks in and hands me a narrow box. I take it but hesitate to open it. I don't know what the hell Crew gave me, and I didn't even think to get him anything.

Now I feel like an ass.

"Open it!" the ever-impatient Phoebe demands.

I lift the lid and burst out laughing. There is a football nestled in white silk.

Kimberly looks at the gift and huffs. "What the hell is he thinking?"

"It's how we met," I explain with my cheeks burning. "We were on the beach, he was throwing a football with Ford and I caught it."

I lift it and there's a note at the bottom.

With shaking hands I unfold it to see his handwriting.

Dear Brynlee,

Ten years ago you caught this ball. I've had it, held it, and kept it with me. I never forgot a moment we shared, and just like this ball, I'll hold onto today's memories the same. Thank you for all you've given me.

Yours,
Crew

Oh my freaking God. He saved the ball. It can't be. How can this man keep doing this to me? I'm not emotionally prepared for this. I thought it was a toaster or some other random gift. Not this. Not him giving me the ball from the day we met.

Why is he so intent on making me fall for him?

Tears roll down my cheeks and both girls are reaching for my face with tissues. "No, no tears!" Phoebe fusses. "You'll ruin your makeup."

I laugh once, lifting my face to them as they fan and dab.

Kimberly places the note and the football back in the box. "Do you need help getting dressed?"

I nod. "That would be great."

Phoebe smiles and walks over, unzipping the bag the gown is in.

It's simple, elegant, and exactly what I wanted. It's a long silk backless gown with a sweetheart neckline. The fabric pools right at the small of my back, creating beautiful layers. The train is short, but it seemed perfect for a beach wedding.

When I turn to see myself in the mirror, I gasp. My red hair is pinned to one side, curled in a wave that's classic and timeless. My makeup is subtle and soft. I almost wouldn't recognize this woman in the mirror.

"Oh, Brynlee, you're absolutely stunning," Phoebe says from beside me.

Kimberly, who will be my sister shortly, nods. "Seriously, Crew is going to lose it. You really are a vision."

I smile and inhale deeply. "Thank you both."

There's another knock on the door and Phoebe opens it and tells whoever we'll be just a minute.

"It was Ash. They're ready for you."

Ready. Right. Ready to get married.

Ready to walk to Crew and become his wife.

Dear God.

Kimberly pulls me in for a brief hug. "I know we just met, and you don't know me, but I know my brother. He talked about you to me a few years ago. Talked about the trip here and how he met the only person he ever imagined sharing a life with. I told him he should find you, tell you the truth and explain what an idiot he is. I'm glad he listened. I'm truly happy you both were able to find each other."

My hands start to shake and I fight back tears. How wrong she is in some ways. We did fall in love here. We shared our hopes and dreams, and all I hoped for was this exact moment. Only in the fantasy, we were getting married for other reasons.

Still, part of me, that part that caught a football and fell in love with a boy, is banging on the walls of my heart, desperate to feel more.

I won't let her out, though. I won't let myself believe the lie. I can't end up wrecked worse than I was before.

I meant what I said to him about being broken.

I need to be stronger this time. I've taught myself how, and the wall around my heart was erected for a reason.

"Thank you," I say, holding back the emotions with all my strength. I look to them both. "Can I just have a few moments?"

They each squeeze my hand and then leave.

I turn back to the mirror. I fix my necklace, the one my mother gave me before she died. It's a heart-shaped diamond pendant that her mother gave her. "Oh, Brynlee, I hope your heart is as hard as this stone. Otherwise, it'll become dust if you let him in even a bit."

Then I grab my bouquet and walk to my brother, ready to marry a man who has the power to obliterate me.

fifteen

CARSON

"To the bride and groom! May they find many years of happiness!" Ford says after giving the worst best man speech in history.

Everyone toasts and Brynn shakes her head as she sips her sparkling cider that we had to hide since no one knows about her surgery. "Sorry about that," I say to her as I place my glass down.

"Who doesn't love telling both sides of the family how we slept together on spring break?"

I sigh. "I'll dock his pay for a few weeks."

She grins. "It's no less than he deserves."

"Well, you deserve more," I tell her and rise to my feet. "Dance with me?"

Brynn places her hand in mine, and I escort her to the dance floor. Her hand rests on my chest and I graze the bare skin at the small of her back. "I know I said it before, but honest to God, Brynlee, you look gorgeous."

"Thank you. You look very handsome." She pulls her lower lip between her teeth, and I focus my gaze on the dance floor and think of anything else to keep from growing hard.

"I'm glad you approve."

She laughs once. "You know I've always thought you were hot."

"And I've always thought you were the most beautiful woman in the world."

"We've got that going for us at least."

I turn her, moving to the music as our families watch. "We've got more than that."

"I hope so."

What does she hope for? I wondered this as we said our vows, promising to honor each other until death do us part. Does she want a friend, a lover, a husband who will give her a family she deserves?

All of those things I wish I could open myself up to, but I can't even consider more until we have Layla safe.

"Your family flies back tonight?"

Brynn glances over at them and smiles. "They do. I promised we'd visit. I'd like if we can maybe bring Layla there the next weekend we have her? I think she'd like the farm and my nieces and nephew."

"I'd love to do that."

I know how hard leaving her family is and it would be good for Layla to get away from the city, see cows and all that.

"Really?" Brynn asks, her eyes lighting up.

"Why are you so surprised?"

"I don't know, I just figured it's easier to stay there. I just . . . I miss Sugarloaf. I'd love to show you around, and I miss my animals."

I brush my thumb on her back as we sway. "Then we'll go every weekend, whether we have Layla or not."

"You don't have to do that."

"I know I don't, but I want to."

Maybe some small-town life is exactly what I need. Plus, I can visit some of the farms we've contracted with for Knight Food Distribution, including her brother's. It's a win-win.

"Thank you." Her voice is soft as she looks at me.

"I told you, Brynlee, there's nothing I won't give you. I know that you gave up a lot to do this, and I'm willing to do the same. Not that I think going to your hometown and spending the weekends there is a sacrifice."

Her brown eyes fill with unshed tears. "You have no idea how much that means to me. My farm, those animals matter a lot. I've worked so hard to save them, give them a place to thrive, and while I love Rowan, and he's great at some things, he hates that damn farm and I worry he's not going to keep up."

"Then we'll have to check on it often." Brynn pulls her lower lip between her teeth and nods. "What's the saying anyway? Happy wife, happy life."

"I'm pretty sure a woman came up with that one."

"And a man would be stupid not to follow it. That's why we have donuts as our wedding cake."

She laughs softly. "Donuts are the superior dessert. You can do so much with them."

"I'm sure."

"Either way, I got the donuts and you got a wife."

"Is she happy?"

Brynn tries to hide her smile. "I'm happy-ish."

"Then I need to up my game. Since I'm a smart man who is all about making his wife happy."

"And you think you can accomplish that?" she asks.

I lean in, my lips just grazing her ear. "I think you already know the answer to that." The sound of forks tapping glasses fills the small tent and I pull back to look at her. "I think the people want us to kiss."

She blushes. "Make it a good one, Mr. Knight."

My face moves to hers slowly. "Anything you want, Mrs. Knight."

Then I kiss her, and the sounds of hoots and cheers fade away as I hold the wife I've wanted for so many years in my arms.

The wedding is over, our families have left, and it's just us in the house in Kitty Hawk. Brynn has changed out of her wedding dress into a pair of white silk pajamas. We're sitting on the couch as I go over emails and send instructions to various employees, and there are bottles of cider and champagne next to her as she sits, flipping through her phone.

I really hope she's drinking the cider.

I send the last email and look up to see Brynn watching me. "Everything okay?" I ask.

She nods. "Just . . . wrapping my head around the fact that we're married."

"I have the paperwork to prove it," I joke.

"I have the ring to show for it too, which I love. I'm glad that you picked a solid band. It's really what I hoped for."

I hated the idea of not giving her more, but Kimberly was emphatic that a plain band would work best with the engagement ring.

"Good. I'm glad you like it."

"I do." She smiles and then takes a sip. "I poured you a glass too. I didn't want to drink alone."

I grab the other glass sitting on the coffee table. "Yes, no one should be drinking sparkling cider alone."

"Shut up," she says with a laugh. "I got you the good stuff. Someone should at least get to enjoy themselves. Should we toast?"

"We had so many freaking toasts today, I'm all toasted out." I laugh and raise my glass anyway. "This is for us."

"All right." Brynn sits up, tucking her legs underneath her. "Let's hear it."

"To the girl who saved me twice."

She rolls her eyes. "I never saved you."

"No?"

"Nope."

I raise one brow. "Are you sure?"

"Absolutely positive."

Oh how wrong she is. "The first time you saved me was just outside that door." I point to the beach area.

"How did I save you?"

"You said hello," I tell her honestly.

Brynn giggles and covers her mouth with her hand. "You don't have to woo me, Crew. You already put a ring on it."

"I'm not wooing you."

"Fine," she says, putting the flute down. "Seducing then. I'm not seducible."

I throw back the champagne and place my glass beside hers. "No?"

"Nope."

"Is that a challenge?"

Brynn smirks. "If I remember, our agreement was that you would not try to seduce me."

I lean back, nodding slowly. "That's correct. I said I would allow you to seduce me. So, I invite you to try."

"Oh, please. You'd like that."

"I would, actually." I'd like that a whole hell of a lot. All day I've kissed her, touched her, held her in my fucking arms knowing that I couldn't do more than that.

We put on the show of a lifetime, my whole family bought it, telling me how happy they were because watching me with Brynn explained it all. Like that wasn't a kick in the fucking nuts.

"Anyway," Brynn dismisses the talk of seduction, which is probably for the best. "We got some good gifts."

I chuckle. "Yes, nothing says congratulations like the turkey platter my mother gave us."

She swats at my chest. "Stop it. It was really nice."

"Your brothers gave us the best gift," I remind her.

"Oh, God. The three of them are so happy that I'm your problem now."

I pull open the bill of sale that states no returns or exchanges with our names on the contract. "Seems there's some fine print about returns."

She grabs the note and tosses it behind her. "I hate them."

"You don't."

"I know, I wish I did."

"They seemed really happy for us today." I drink some of the champagne and refill her glass with the cider.

"They were. It helps that two of my brothers work for you so they'll always be nice."

I chuckle. "You think that's why?"

"No. They actually like you, heaven knows why."

I pull her glass from her. "No more cider if you're going to be snarky."

She takes it back. "Please, I'm not even a little tipsy. Carbonation makes me tingle."

"How many have you had?"

Brynn rolls her eyes and sighs. "I wish I could've had a drink. It would've made the glares from your friend a little easier. I couldn't even hide behind a buzz."

"I'll handle him."

She sits up quickly. "Absolutely not. I can handle it, Crew. I was more worried about your brothers, but they were funny and really sweet."

That's not the way most people describe my brothers. "Ryan was really happy for us. He wants us to come to dinner in a few weeks."

"We'll have to do it before the surgery. All of it's coming so fast, you know?" It really is. Brynn's surgery is in four weeks and then three weeks after that is Layla's custody hearing. I have seven weeks until we find out if I'll have her for good.

"Well, *husband*, I'm exhausted, emotional, and married. I feel like I could sleep for days. It's been a whirlwind and I swear I don't know what end is up since you came back into my life." To punctuate that, Brynlee lets out a long yawn.

"I have that effect on women."

She grins and then sighs, looking around the living room. "This place is filled with so many memories."

"It is."

Any time I come here, it's like the past haunts me. Not in a good way either.

She rests her head on the back of the couch, turning to face me. "It was amazing we were able to get it for this weekend. I figured the owners would've had it rented since it's almost high season."

"I knew it wouldn't be a problem. I own it."

Her head lifts, eyes wide. "What?"

"I own this house. No one stays here but me."

It seems like a storm rolls through her, confusion, disbelief, and something else settles as she blinks a few times. "You bought *this* house?"

"Yes."

"When?"

I wait, not sure if I should tell her, but knowing I won't lie. I don't know if she's angry or happy. "I bought it nine years ago."

"Nine . . . you own this house? The house we . . . the place where we . . . Why?"

Why does she think? I bought it because it was the house I met her in, loved her in, and where I left her. I bought it because it was the only link I had to her. The only one I would allow.

I promised not to seduce her. I promised to let her keep her walls because I hurt her enough and I don't want to do it again, so I keep silent.

Brynn runs her hand down her face before resting it on her neck. "Why, Crew?"

"Because it meant something to me."

Her eyes fill with tears. "You kept the football, bought this house . . . I don't understand."

I think she does. I think she knows exactly why I did all of it. I walked away from her because I thought I had no choice. I gave her up to save her from a life she wouldn't have wanted. All of that didn't matter when it came to how I felt, though.

How I fucking missed her smile, the sound of her laugh, the way she'd plaster herself to me as though she could fill every gap in my heart the closer she was.

So, yeah, I kept, bought, and saved everything I could of her.

She shifts her weight, coming to her knees in front of me. Her hands cup my face, keeping me from looking anywhere but at her. "Brynn . . ." I caution her.

"Don't talk," she says, as she sinks back down, bringing her face closer. "Just . . . don't say anything."

Her lips touch mine, soft and sweet. I let her kiss me, seducing me even though she doesn't have to try. I've been under her spell since the day I met her.

Brynn's hands move from my face down to my shoulders and then rest on my chest. Her lips part and our tongues meet, moving like a dance as I stay still. Her fingers slide down to my wrists and she moves them until my arms are around her. I hold her, letting her have the control, even though every part of me wants to take over.

To lay her down, strip her bare, make her scream my name. Maybe it would erase the memory of the past, and give her a wedding night filled with passion where she wakes up with me still there.

Her body moves closer, my hands holding her hips as our kisses become deeper. Brynn's fingers grip the back of my neck, pulling me tight. The feel of her breasts against my chest has me releasing a long moan.

"Brynn, you don't . . ."

"Just this once. It's our wedding night."

One time is never going to be enough, and as much as I want her, more than my next breath, not tonight, not like this.

Not when she's just feeling the effects of the day and will blame me later for it.

"Brynn, we can't."

She pulls back. "What? Why?"

I push her hair back, running my thumb against her shoulder. "Because you set the rules and the only reason you're breaking them is because you're emotional and exhausted."

"That's not—"

"It doesn't matter. I'm not ever going to be the man who takes advantage of you. If or when this happens between us, it won't be because you found out I bought this house or kept the football. It won't be because you've been run ragged trying to deal with the wedding, an engagement you didn't plan on, and the stress of becoming my wife. I won't be another guy to use you that way."

I know about her past, about the man who used her and then discarded her. I also, in some ways, fall into that category. In my mind, it wasn't that way. I did what I did to protect her from my reality, but my sister showed me how it would look from Brynn's angle.

Another man who slept with her and then walked away.

"No matter if I want this?" she presses.

I move my hand back up to her cheek. "Will you want this tomorrow? Will you hate me when you realize you didn't want this in a few days? Can you actually answer any of that right now and know you'll mean it? No matter how much I want this—you —I won't take anything from you."

Even if it fucking kills me.

sixteen

BRYNLEE

I stare into his crystal blue eyes—my husband, the man I have wanted for so long—and hear his questions bouncing around in my head like a pinball machine.

Tomorrow, if I woke up naked beside him, would I regret it? I don't think I would, but . . . ugh. The one thing I do know is that sleeping with him will only make those pesky feelings I'm trying to avoid resurface.

Instead of answering all the questions, I give him one response, and there is no question that it's the truth. "I wouldn't hate you, Crew. Even if tomorrow we woke up and I thought it was a mistake, I wouldn't ever hate you. I've tried so hard to hate you."

His grin is soft and his thumb moves against my cheek again. "I'm pretty sure you hated me before."

"No, I didn't. I loved you far too much to hate you."

That was stupid to say. Maybe I am over-emotional since it's my wedding night.

"If we went back to the day I left, I bet you'd say different."

I sigh. "Probably, but I don't want to go back in time. I don't want to remember how much it hurt. We can't change the things that hurt us then, so I refuse to dwell on it. Yes, you hurt me. Yes, I was angry, and more than anything, confused. Time healed some of those wounds and—" I glance around. "Being back here is both happy and sad."

"Tell me about the happy," he urges, adjusting me so I'm beside him.

Like it's the most natural thing, I shift, pushing him to lie down, and I curl up against him, my head on his chest. "You kissed me for the first time out that door."

"You asked me if it was possible to love someone so fast in that kitchen." He brings up what I said two nights before he left.

I smile, remembering him wrapping his arms around my middle as I tried to cook. The way his scruff felt against my neck when he kissed me. "You told me it was not only possible, it was happening to us."

His fingers make patterns on my back as we lie here. As if this marriage was real and we weren't just playing house.

"I didn't understand how someone could literally be everything I wanted in life. You were smart, unbelievably beautiful, funny, quick, and sarcastic. I didn't even have to explain things, you just understood. I remember the one day I purposely said stupid shit to see if you were going to just be meek, but you weren't."

I lift my head. "You did that on purpose?"

He pissed me off so much that day.

"Don't be mad, I was convinced you were a fantasy and that when I woke up, it was going to be painful."

"It was the first day I thought that maybe you were an asshole who I should've kicked out."

Crew smiles at me. "You stood your ground."

I roll my eyes. "Of course I did. You were being an idiot."

"I was, and the fact that you told me in about twenty different ways made me love you more. I wasn't used to girls standing up to me. The girls that were around me knew who I was, so they wanted something. You just wanted me."

I huff, laying back down. "Clearly there's something wrong

with me." He tickles my side and I burst out laughing, squirming, and begging him to stop. "Oh my God! Crew!"

He stops and I work to catch my breath. "There's nothing wrong with you."

I grin, staring into his beautiful eyes. "You're right, it's you who is a mess."

"You're not wrong, but you married me."

"I wonder what that says about me?"

"That you are a kind soul who took pity on a poor man," he says back.

"Poor?" I toss at him. "There's nothing poor about you, babe."

"Ahh, but am I rich in life?" Crew asks and I shake my head.

"Considering you have me as a wife now, I'd say so."

Crew brushes his thumb against my lips. "You're the best decision I've ever made, even if it won't last."

My heart pounds as the idea of not having him again hits me hard. This arrangement just started and already I'm sad thinking about the end.

"Are you trying to seduce me again?" I ask playfully, not wanting to think of sad things.

"Is it working?"

I grin and then lay my head back down. "Nope."

"I guess I need to up my game then."

I wrap my arm around him a little tighter and listen to the sound of his heartbeat replaying the good parts of today.

Like his face when he saw me as I walked toward him or the way he held me as we danced. I think of how his voice wavered when he made false promises to me and I repeated them to him.

All of it plays like a movie behind my eyelids and the one I watch the most is the kiss we shared on the dance floor . . .

Crew shifts under me, and I open my eyes to the sun blaring through the windows.

Crap. We fell asleep on the couch and slept with me practically on top of him.

"Are you awake?" he asks with his deep sleepy voice.

"Barely."

He chuckles. "I need to get up."

I nod and try to adjust, but there's literally no room, and when I move my leg, he grabs it quickly. "What?"

"Your knee was close to a certain part of my anatomy."

"Sorry," I mutter and let him move us both.

He heads to the bathroom, and I force myself to sit up. My neck is freaking killing me. Being stuck in that spot all night when there are six bedrooms with beds was probably not our brightest idea.

I see my phone light up and I mentally groan imagining the number of messages. There are eighteen text messages from people in Sugarloaf who saw photos of the wedding, sending their well wishes and asking where their invites were.

One is from Phoebe with a link to the article online about us and our story, and one from my father, saying how happy he is for me and wishes he could've seen it.

I sit back, feeling a horrific amount of guilt for not inviting him. It just was too fast to ease my brothers into seeing him, and while Howie and I have come to a place of understanding, it will never happen for them. Not after they saw the damage he did to me and my mother.

Howie said he understood and would never want to ruin my day and asked if Crew and I would have dinner with him when we're settled a bit.

Then an email pops up from the charity about the surgery.

I open it quickly, scanning it for the words I'm desperate to see.

Dear Ms. Whitlock, we received your application . . . *blah, blah, blah*. We would like to set up an interview for next Monday at noon, where we'll be able to render a decision.

Monday. Like this Monday. Okay, this is good, if I get the money from them, then the surgery is completely covered. If not, I'll hopefully be on Crew's insurance, so they will cover a good amount. Whatever they don't cover, I'll just pay over time. It'll be fine. This will work and it's one less thing on my never-ending list of crap.

I send messages back to everyone then reply to the email stating that Monday at noon is wonderful and I'll be there. Crew comes back into the living room with a bottle of water, Tylenol, and a donut. "Here, in case you weren't feeling great."

I laugh. "You can't get a hangover from sparkling juice."

"Still."

A very mild headache is lingering, but I don't know if it's from the neck pain or just the entire day. I take and swallow the pills, grateful that he even thought of it.

"Thank you."

Crew nods once. "Flying with a headache is the absolute worst."

I take a bite of the donut and swallow. "We have to fly back tonight, right?"

"Yes, I wish we could do a honeymoon, but we have to get Layla in two days."

"I understand. I don't need a honeymoon."

I really don't. Would it be amazing to go somewhere? Yes. I've never been out of the country and to go with Crew just seems like a dream. Then I remind myself that this marriage isn't real, and there is no reason to honeymoon since we're already planning a divorce.

"You deserve a honeymoon, Brynn. If I could, we'd go to Paris or Italy or Greece or whatever the hell you wanted. It's just that we have to . . ."

I lift my hand. "I know, I'm saying it's fine. Layla is our priority and I have to be in New York anyway. Paris, Italy, and Greece will be there for me someday. I have my passport and one day I'll get a stamp in it. I promise, it doesn't have to be now."

"Okay. I'd like to get some work done and then pack up to head to your house for the weekend with Layla."

He was serious about that. "You want to go to Sugarloaf this weekend?"

"You need to check on the farm, don't you?"

"Yes, but . . ." I don't know why I'm hesitating. I miss my home and Layla can stay in Olivia's room, where I think she'll be happy, but having him there is another thing. More people he'll meet. More lies we'll have to tell.

"But what?" Crew asks.

I can't un-ring this bell so there's no point in making this into his problem.

"We need to be back by Monday. I heard back from the charity, and they want to do an interview at noon."

Crew sits beside me. "That's great."

"It is. I know we got married so that we'd have the insurance, but when your assistant explained what they covered, it wasn't everything. Hopefully the charity will cover the remainder of it. If not, it'll be fine." I take another bite and fight back a moan inspired by the best donut I've ever had.

I don't know who the wedding planner used, but these are amazing.

"You're not paying a dime," he says without room for argument.

Gone is the girl loving her donut. My inner lawyer is riled because I can always find an opening to argue. "Neither are you. I didn't marry you for money. I married you so that we can help the people we love."

"And you're my wife now, which means there's not a snowball's chance in hell that I'm not going to take care of you." He shrugs.

After putting my sugar delight on the table, I pull my legs up under me. "Taking care of me doesn't mean paying my bills. It's things like this, Crew. It's bringing me medicine because you know I had a rough day, making sure I don't go into that surgery alone, being the someone who cares about me who's there. That's what I want, not your money."

He releases a deep sigh. "I'm not going to fight with you about this."

"Good, neither am I."

His blue eyes find mine. "I think we have different ideas about what the ending of the argument is."

I smile. "I'm sure we do. Now, are you ready for Sugarloaf? It's your quintessential small town, full of nosey neighbors and people all up in your business."

He laughs, but there's a hardness in his jaw. "So it's different from the nosey snobs who are in my business now or the camera crew that's been following us around all week? I think small-town people are exactly what we need."

Yeah, I think he has a very different view of what that looks like, but I miss my animals so I'm not going to argue the point.

"If you say so."

"I do, besides, it'll give us some alone time, which we haven't had since we got engaged. Layla will love the farm and we will have time to reset a little."

"Oh, yes, nothing like doing a reset on a farm that needs work."

"You keep saying that, but isn't that the point of the farm?"

I let out a breath through my nose. "Yes, but Second Chances is different. There are more chores than hands and every animal there has a special need to some extent. Don't get me wrong, I love it. I love helping them, loving them, giving them a second chance, but I can only imagine the state it's in with me being gone. Rowan is great and all, but he's not exactly the 'sit on the floor with the goats and tell them they're pretty' kind of caretaker."

"I'm not sure any guy is going to do that."

I shrug. "Well, Desiree needs to have her leg rubbed with the oils or it gets tight."

"Desiree?" he asks.

"The sheep who has arthritis," I explain and move on. "Toby can only eat grain once a week or he gets gas." Crew's brows pinch and I smile. "He's my donkey. The alpacas don't like rain and I have coats for them, but Rowan will never put them on, so I'm sure they're a mess, and the chicken coop is at its max capacity and is being held together by duct tape at this point. Asher and I were going to work on fixing it in the next few weeks."

"I'll help," Crew says, and I laugh.

"Help what?"

"We'll get them all set up this weekend."

I stare at him, wondering what planet he just came from. "Have you ever worked on a farm?"

"No."

"Have you ever taken care of animals before?"

He smiles. "Nope."

"Well, this should be a fun and enlightening weekend," I say, leaning back.

Crew tilts my chin up so our eyes meet. "Think of it like a long weekend date. We'll teach each other new things."

"Aren't you doing this whole relationship thing a bit backward?" I ask, since we're married and all.

"I think you and I are rather unconventional no matter what. Besides, just because we're married doesn't mean I don't want to date you. You know, so that after we're divorced, I have a chance to see if you might want me back."

I'm totally pretending that doesn't make my heart flutter at all.

"So you want to divorce me to date me after?"

Crew smirks. "It makes sense in my head."

I roll my eyes. "I'm glad it does somewhere because that's the dumbest thing I've ever heard."

He steps closer and I gasp as he pulls me against him. My head doesn't even reach his shoulders. So damn embarrassing. "I thought about you, us . . . marriage, for so long and I hate that this is how it happened. If I could go back, I would've found you years ago, begged for your forgiveness, worked every fucking day to prove that I was worthy of you, not stolen you like this."

"You didn't steal me," I say, my heart beating frantically.

"No?" he asks, pulling my left hand up between us. "I didn't win you, Bee. I didn't do or say all the things I should've. I married you so that my custody case wasn't blown. I married you so that you'd have insurance and the means to save your father. We married for other people and while all of it makes sense, I'm having a really hard time remembering it. Because when I look at you, in this house, on that couch where we slept, all I can think about is what a fucking asshole I am to have taken something else from you. So, yeah, I stole you, and now, I plan to try to earn you."

He kisses my lips softly, releases me, and walks away, leaving me feeling like I've just been kicked in the stomach.

Dear God, I'm so screwed.

I'm sitting in the conservatory, responding to some emails and potential clients when there's a knock on the door.

Celeste is there with her warm smile. "Sorry to bother you, darling, you have a visitor."

Who the heck could be here? "I do?"

"Well, visitor is a loose term," Grady says as he walks into the room.

I get up, breath filling my lungs, and I could cry. I wrap my arms around my brother. "More like pain in the ass," I joke.

He pulls back to look at me. "Just seeing if you've changed, now that you're a billionaire's wife."

I roll my eyes. "Har, har. I'm still me."

Grady takes a second to look around the room. "Jesus. What the hell is this room?"

"You have no idea," I tell him with a laugh. "This, my brother, is the conservatory." I'll never be used to the size and opulence of this place.

He turns to Celeste. "Tell me your name isn't Scarlett and you don't have a rope?"

She looks puzzled and I roll my eyes.

"He's making a reference to Clue. A bad one clearly, but we played that board game all the time as kids."

Grady grins. "And I kicked your ass each time."

"Yes, beating a child was so difficult," I quip back. I didn't realize how much I missed him until now.

Seeing my brother here, though, makes it feel a little less

ridiculous. I guide him over to the curved sofa that overlooks the city.

Celeste smiles. "I assure you, Mr. Whitlock, I do not have a rope, gun, or candlestick handy."

He lays his hand over his heart. "I feel much safer now."

"Do you need anything? Food? Drinks? I can whip up something, no problem."

Grady smiles. "I wish I could, but I don't have long. Thank you."

"I'll leave you both. Just ring me if you need something."

"Thank you, Celeste."

She leaves and I hug Grady again. "It's so good to see you."

His eyes narrow. "It's only been a few days."

"Yes, well, I guess I'm dumb and miss my brothers, even though you all drive me nuts. You're sure you don't want anything?"

"No, I'm good. I just met with Carson about his schedule over the next few weeks. He's taking some time off, so I won't need to fly into the city much."

I keep my face stoic. "Yeah, we have some plans," I try to explain.

"Are you guys going away?"

This is my opening. This is my chance to tell one of my brothers. Really, the most rational and even-keeled one too.

"Not really. We are just going to spend time together."

He nods. "That's good. You guys probably need to do that. I'm surprised, since Carson doesn't seem like a guy who takes much time off."

I smile. "No, he's not."

He's doing it for me. He's doing it because I won't be able to do anything after the surgery and he refuses to let me struggle.

Tell him, Brynn. Tell Grady why he's taking off work. Tell him about the surgery.

"Addison said you're coming home this weekend with Carson's daughter?" he asks.

I nod, trying to get my mouth and my mind to work together.

"Good. Elodie and Jett asked if we could come by to see the animals. I figured you wouldn't mind, plus the kids are around the same age, right?"

"Yes, Layla is four."

He tosses his arm across the back of the chair. "I'm sure Elodie will love having a friend who doesn't want to play war with her Barbies."

"Yes, I grew up having that particular joy in life."

Grady rolls his eyes. "Please, you were picked on far less than Rowan. Asher and I were relentless with him."

Yeah, yeah, I've heard all about the torture they inflicted on him. Rowan was the youngest sibling for a long time. I'm eight years younger than him and my brothers wouldn't dare upset me. I was really, really good at crying, which is why Rowan was the easy target.

"Doesn't mean you didn't gang up on me when I wanted to play dolls," I remind him.

"Anyway, I'll bring her by if you text me."

"Sounds good."

"Brynn?" Grady says my name with a touch of apprehension.

"Yeah?"

"Are you okay?"

I turn to face him. "Why do you ask?"

"I may not have been around as much when you were growing up. I know Asher and Rowan are your closer brothers, but I'd like to think I have a pretty good read on you. You're a lot like Mom. She was good at hiding things, but it was always there, simmering underneath. You have the same mannerisms, and I'm concerned."

Oh God, he knows something.

Of all my brothers I thought might pick up on something, it wasn't Grady.

I don't want to lie to him. I've done enough of that, but I also don't want to tell him about the surgery. There's no way he'll keep it from Asher and Rowan, who I don't plan to tell until the day before.

"Can we talk in a week or two?" I ask hesitantly. "I'm fine, everything is fine, I promise, but I'm just not ready to talk about it yet."

"Is it about your marriage?"

God, if he only knew how all of it ties together.

"No, it's not Crew or anything like that, and no, I'm not pregnant. So, you can calm down there too. It's just something that I need a little more time with before I can share with you guys."

He reaches out, taking my hand. "Brynn, you can tell us anything. There's literally nothing the three of us wouldn't do for you."

"I know that, Grady." My brothers are the best and they'd lay down their lives to protect those they love, me included.

It's why I'm just not ready to tell them about this. Asher will never understand that I'd be willing to give a part of myself to Howie. Rowan literally hates my father and I wonder if he wouldn't kill him before the surgery. Grady may not harbor the level of animosity that they do, but he would struggle.

I don't need to be the reason they suffer.

"All right, if you're okay, then I'll be here when you're ready."

I lean in and kiss his cheek. "You're the best big brother a girl could have."

He chuckles at that. "I don't think you were saying that when Jett and I were living with you."

"That's because you're annoying as fuck."

"Yeah, and you're a dream."

I shrug. "We're not talking about me."

"Maybe we should. When does your husband get home?"

Glancing at my phone, I see it should be relatively soon. Crew said he had to go into the office, do some work, and then set up the next week of meetings. He promised he'd be home for dinner, but I told him not to rush. The whole point of this marriage is for convenience. The last thing either of us wants is for the other to be needy.

"Soon. What time are you heading back to Sugarloaf? Did you fly in?"

"Yeah, I flew in to pick up a package from his office and I'm flying out to Pittsburgh in the morning from Sugarloaf. He had a driver bring me here so I could say hi before heading back home."

I smile. "That was sweet."

He huffs. "Or he's the most strategic person alive and knew that he'd be late, so best send her brother to check on her and take up her time."

"Or that." I nudge him with my shoulder. "Any new pictures of the kids?"

And with that, my brother launches into a twenty-minute conversation about the new things that Jett and Elodie are doing at school and a part of me feels like I'm home.

seventeen

CARSON

"We are not doing this, Jacqueline. Go get Layla." I remain calm as Jacqueline rages at me. The agreement is that she will not be present when I pick Layla up, but today she felt she didn't need to adhere to that.

"You're not going to bring our daughter to your whore! I refuse! You'll have to kill me before I let her around that slut!"

I count to ten before I open my eyes to look at her. Ironic that the woman who cheated on me more times than I can count is calling Brynn a whore. She wants to bait me, and I remember what Brynn said as we approached and saw that Jacqueline's car was out front. *No matter what, don't let her get your anger up. Let her rage and let it go. Don't give her any ammunition against you. Just get Layla and we'll have a great weekend together.*

If she only knew how hard that would be. Listening to my ex-wife talk about Brynn has my anger so high, I can barely see straight.

"I'm happy to contact the police, show them the court documents if you need me to," I say, forcing myself to remain calm.

"I don't care what you have, you won't have Layla this weekend."

I keep my voice even, using my negotiating skills even though

I want to rip her throat out. "Jacqueline, I don't think you want this kind of press, do you? Not after your brother's last arrest. It would be a shame for your parents to have to deal with yet another child of theirs out of control."

Her jaw trembles and I wait. If there's anything she hates, it's having her family's name brought up in the papers in a bad light.

"You can't do this to me."

"I'm not doing anything to you."

Tears fill her eyes. "You married her! You never loved me, I knew that, but then to marry her. You're not going to take Layla from me, Crew. I won't let you."

"That'll be determined in court, but you and I both know if I call the cops now, I'll leave here with Layla and you won't be able to stop it."

She clenches her fists and starts to move around the room. "I'm going to do everything I can to make sure you don't win."

"I don't doubt that. Get my daughter and let's avoid any more trauma for her sake."

Jacqueline glares at me and then walks out of the room. I stand here, hoping she does the right thing for once. A minute later, Layla comes running into the foyer. "Daddy!"

It's like I can breathe for the first time since entering this house. "Ladybug."

I scoop her up in my arms and the nanny comes toward me, a bag in her hand. "I'm sorry, Mr. Knight. There is very little . . . in the bag. I did my best."

I nod to her. "It's fine. I'll get her whatever she needs."

I have her, I don't care about anything else.

We exit the house and Layla squeezes my neck. "Did you get married, Daddy?"

"I did."

She claps my face between her hands. "Can we go to your house now?"

Oh the mind of a four-year-old, always changing gears. "I have a surprise," I say, as I walk toward the door with her very empty bag.

"You do?"

"We're going somewhere super fun this weekend. You, me, and Brynn."

Layla smiles and gasps. "Where?"

"A farm, with lots of animals."

"I love animals!"

"I know. Brynn has her own farm with lots of animals. We're going to stay there so you can help her, does that sound fun?"

She nods and Cliff opens her door. Layla gives him a big hug and then I get her in the car. "Rin! We are going to your farm!"

"I'm so excited to show you all the animals. Do you like chickens?" Brynn asks.

"I don't have any chickens."

Brynn giggles. "I have lots. Maybe you can help me feed them?"

Layla nods enthusiastically.

We spend the next two hours with Layla chattering nonstop to Brynn about her animals, what they have there, where she's going to sleep, and any other question she can ask. Brynn tells Layla about her nieces and nephew, and how maybe tomorrow Elodie and Jett, Grady's kids, will come over and play.

I'm barely in the conversation, and that's just fine by me. I've never seen Layla take to anyone the way she does Brynn. They're like two old souls finding each other.

As we enter the town, Brynn points out some landmarks and smiles at me when she catches me staring. We travel down the winding roads and pull up to her small cottage.

"Daddy, can we see the animals *now*?" Layla asks with wide eyes.

"Let's get settled first and then we can go."

She pouts but Brynn is quick to jump in. "Do you want to see where you'll sleep? It's very pretty."

Layla grabs Brynlee's hand and they walk into the house. It's a little nuts to think the last time we were here was when I proposed. Now, we're married and bringing my daughter to spend the weekend.

I look around, taking in the small room in a different light. This is where she lives, where she has spent her days and nights. There are photos on the mantel of her brothers and their kids. A picture of her and Olivia with their tongues out and fingers making the 'I love you' sign. Brynlee as a little girl with a woman I assume is her mother.

"That's my mother," Brynn says, and I turn to see her staring at me.

"You look like her."

She smiles. "I think I'm a good mix. I get my red hair from my father, but I've definitely taken more of my mother's features as I've aged."

"Well, you're stunning and so is she."

She turns her head to hide her face and then sighs. "Layla loves the bedroom. I want to change a few things so it's more age appropriate. Olivia doesn't really stay here anymore and I'm sure she'd be okay with it."

"You don't have to do that."

Brynn shakes her head. "I want Layla to feel like this is a home for her. I went to put her things away, but the bag is empty."

I grit my teeth. "Her mother."

"I figured."

"I have Cliff going to the store now. He'll be back as soon as he finishes shopping."

Brynn moves closer, touching the photo beside the one of her and her mother. "I will never understand how a parent can use their child as a weapon. Layla deserves better, and you're giving her that. When she comes to live with you, she'll never have to worry about having caring parents."

Her hand rests on the mantel and I cover it with my own. "If it weren't for you, it wouldn't even be possible. I would've lost before I started."

"You'd have found a way."

"I don't even know if I'll get her now."

Brynn rests her head on my shoulder. "I have faith."

Layla comes running out. "Can we go *now*?"

"Yes, let's go see the chickens," Brynn says with obvious excitement. She turns to me. "You too, it's an all-hands-on-deck farm here."

I look down at my suit. "I'm not dressed for farming."

"Well, I helped pack your bag this morning, so go get changed and we'll wait for you."

"Yeah, Daddy! Get dressed."

My brother talked to me about when he met his wife. How there was this one moment where he saw his future with her, and it all clicked. I thought he was a fucking idiot because all I ever saw with Jacqueline was prison, but I'm standing here, looking at Brynlee holding Layla's hand, and my chest is tight.

I can see that future, where they wake up, work at Second Chances during the day, and bake cookies. I can see me working in the living room, with photos of us around and the two of them coming in to stop me to pay attention to them.

I watch years go by, Layla growing up, and Brynlee pregnant, hand on her belly as she calls after her.

All of that flashes before my eyes and then disappears, because none of that will be my reality. Not when I know Brynn has her exit strategy.

"Crew?" Brynn's voice is full of impatience. "The bedroom is that way."

I blink and force a smile. "Right."

I head into her room, opening the bag and grabbing the jeans and T-shirt. God, I can't remember the last time I wore jeans. I change and head out where the two girls are dancing around.

"Am I interrupting?" I ask, amused.

"Nope, we are just ready to see the chickens."

So am I.

"Let's go, then."

We head out to the barn a few yards from the house. There are fences around it where various animals are moving around.

Layla is between us, holding both our hands as we walk. "Do the chickens bite you?" Layla asks.

167

"They don't bite, they peck if you have food in your hand, but it doesn't hurt."

My daughter looks up at me, her eyes bright with excitement. "They eat out of your *hand*!"

"Are you going to feed them?" I ask.

She nods enthusiastically. "I love chickens!"

I don't know that this girl has ever seen a chicken outside of the store, but I'm not going to argue with her.

When we get around the side of the barn, Brynlee stops. Her eyes are wide, hand covering her mouth. "What is that?"

Praying there's not a heap of dead chickens, I look to see what has her looking horrified and move Layla behind me. "What's wrong?"

She points. "That coop isn't mine. I'm so confused."

Feeling a bit of relief, I pull Layla back around. "It's yours," I tell her.

Her eyes meet mine. "What?"

"You said your coop was falling down. I called Rowan, who confirmed it wasn't working and had this one delivered a few days ago."

Her jaw opens and closes. "Crew, this . . . no, this is too much."

In front of us is a very large coop, it has two extensions off each side where the chickens can be contained, which the man on the phone was very adamant were necessary. I also had a team of people come and build a garden around it, because they also said chickens like to forage and it was a good idea to have space for that.

Thankfully, Rowan was here to oversee the project and make sure it would be up to Brynn's standards.

"Do you like it?"

"Like it? I love it! It's just too much!" She moves toward it. "It's more than I've ever . . . you shouldn't have done this."

"You're my wife. You love the chickens, said you needed a new coop, and I agreed."

She turns to me, tears in her eyes, and one falls. "You had them build a chicken palace."

I shrug. "If you say so. I just thought you'd want something that wasn't falling apart."

Brynn wipes her tears and leans in to give me a sweet kiss. "Thank you."

Hell, if she'll kiss me each time I do something nice, I'm going to make it a daily occurrence. "You're welcome."

Layla taps Brynn's leg. "Are the chickens in there, Rin?"

Brynn gets down to Layla's level. "They sure are. How about we go bring them some treats?"

"I want some treats."

Her eyes lift to me. "I'm pretty sure we're all going to get a treat today."

Then she takes Layla's hand and heads off into the chicken coop.

"Are you ready for this?" Brynn asks as we're in the parking lot of the famous Sugarlips Diner. And when I say famous, I mean to the town of Sugarloaf only.

"Is this like facing a firing squad?"

"That's a good analogy."

Great. "It can't be any worse than the business meetings I deal with."

She cocks her head to the side. "Wanna bet?"

I grin and hoist Layla into my arms. "No one can be cruel with this face here."

Brynn smiles. "That is true."

"Come on, let's get it over with while we have our secret weapon."

We enter the diner and like a scene from a movie, the place quiets and everyone's head turns to see the three of us. Brynlee doesn't seem to care and waves. "Hey, everyone! This is my husband, Crew, and his daughter, Layla. We wanted to come say hi so I could introduce them to the warm and loving people that I described you as."

The room goes from complete silence to being so loud it's hard to think. There is clinking of silverware, scraping of chairs, and people moving around to come greet us.

The first to come is an older woman, maybe in her late sixties. "Hello, dear, I'm Mrs. Symonds. I was Brynlee's principal in school. She's a lovely girl, you're very lucky to know her. I make the best chili in the town, just ask around."

I'm not really sure why that last bit is a thing I need to know, but I just smile. "It's nice to meet you."

Another older woman shoves her out of the way. "Move aside, Alice." The two of them glare at each other before she turns to me. "I'm Mrs. Cooke, but you can call me Marie. I've been around this one since she was a little girl. Her gran and I were close friends."

"We were close too, you heifer," Mrs. Symonds cuts in.

"Yes, yes, everyone is friends with you since you're just a peach," Mrs. Cooke says, sighing heavily.

"My gran loved you both equally," Brynn says, resting her hand on both their arms. "We'll be around to talk more soon, but Layla is hungry, and we need to eat."

The one thing neither of us thought about was that Brynn hasn't been in the house in two weeks. There were very few food options in the house. We were going to order something in, but Brynn thought maybe getting this over with and being seen in the town would make it easier for us going forward.

"Of course, honey, don't you worry about us," Mrs. Symonds says, stepping to the side.

Brynn maneuvers past them and we're stopped at least ten more times before we're at a table. The patrons continue to watch us though, and she huffs loudly. "Go back to your dinners. We're not going anywhere."

They take direction well. I can at least give them that. We go from being openly stared at to being on the receiving end of more subtle glances.

Layla is plastered to my side and Brynn pulls something out of her bag. "I brought us a coloring book."

"You did?" Layla asks excitedly.

"Do you want to color with me?"

She nods enthusiastically.

Brynn places the book on the table and pulls out some crayons. After a minute, Layla pulls the book to her, taking over the activity.

"Sorry about that. I knew they'd be excited, but I wasn't prepared for that level of craziness."

"Don't worry about it. It's clear the town loves you," I say with a grin.

"They do. We're very protective of the people who live here. It's more of a family than just a town, if that makes sense."

I nod. "It does."

"Most of us have lived here our whole lives. The farms here are generational and each person has a very deep pride about being from Sugarloaf."

"While I didn't grow up in a small town, I do understand generational pride." It's why I couldn't be with Brynn when we were younger. "It's nice to see an example where it's not trying to ruin people's lives."

Brynn laughs softly. "I wouldn't say it doesn't happen, but they mean well."

"When I reached out to Rowan about your sanctuary, he put me in touch with some guy named Albert. I spent an hour on the phone with him as he told me all the things I needed. The thing is, only about ten minutes was the actual advice about the farm, the other fifty was about how amazing you are, as if I didn't know that."

Albert had gone on and on about Brynn and the treasure she is. He talked about how his horse had the beginnings of colic and she came over each day to help because he was sick and couldn't. Then there was the story about when she was a little girl and she'd leave out bowls of food for the animals who might be hungry. It was story after story about how special, kind, and loved she is.

While I may not have known all the stories, I didn't need to hear them to know that I don't deserve her.

I never did.

"Crew . . . I . . . I wanted to say—" Brynn starts but is cut off.

"Rin, look at my pretty butterfly!" Layla beams, lifting her picture up.

She smiles wide. "That's beautiful, Layla."

"It's for you!"

"For me?"

Layla nods.

"Thank you, sweetheart. I love it. We'll put it on the fridge at the house," Brynn tells her and Layla beams.

If I didn't already love this woman, seeing her with Layla would've done the job. Layla has always been a reserved child. She spends most of her time with the nanny or alone with me. She also is simply shy, but with Brynn, she can't help but be happy.

"I color another one!" Layla announces and goes back to it.

"She loves you," I say to Brynn. "She's not even like this with Kimberly."

Brynn looks down and then lifts her gaze to me. "She's an amazing child and I adore her."

"You have no idea how much I want to kiss you right now."

Her eyes widen. "Crew."

"What?"

"You can't say that!"

I grin. "Why not?"

"Because . . . well . . . because."

I chuckle, enjoying that I rattled her. I lean back in the booth. "Tell me more about the farm."

"You probably know more about it than I do at this point. I'm sure you had a research team learn everything you could before you decided to work with Rowan," she challenges.

She's not wrong. My team is very thorough, and when I

considered Rowan Whitlock's farm and the one next door to help increase our organic milk production at Knight Food Distribution, we actually were going to choose Charlotte's farm. But in the end, we liked that Rowan had more land and was able to scale up.

"I know a lot, but not the reason why your brother expanded a year ago."

She sighs heavily. "Rowan expanded to upset Charlotte."

I'm not sure I understand that. "Meaning?"

"Well, you know they were fighting for your contract. That wasn't all they fought about. Charlotte's sister dated—well, thought—she was dating Rowan. It ended badly and Charlotte literally hated him for hurting her sister. Rowan thought she was terrible too. It went on for years, this . . . animosity. Then, I don't know, they went against each other head-to-head for your business and they somehow ended up . . ." She looks at Layla and then me, wiggling her brows. ". . . which led to real feelings and now a marriage."

I didn't realize there was that much history. When I met them, it was clear they weren't exactly friends, but each spoke of the other's farm in high regard and with respect. I never would've guessed they hated each other.

"And Asher is marrying Phoebe, who was his daughter's nanny?"

Brynn gives a tight smile. "Yup."

"Who also knows your ex who I'd like to destroy?"

"Same one."

"Grady and Addison seem to be normal," I note.

Brynlee laughs. "Normal? Please, those two are another story. However, each of my brothers found the other half to his soul. No matter how they got there."

"And what about you?" I ask, not sure what the fuck I was thinking asking that.

"My story isn't over."

eighteen

BRYNLEE

My brain is a mess. A big freaking mess.

He bought me a new coop.

Not just a small one either, the damn thing is huge. It has an automatic door, watering system, and large feed containers so it'll keep mice out and I only need to refill it once a week.

Then, to top that off, he had the food storage adjusted so I won't have to carry bags all over the place. They'll stay dry and protected in an area inside the new chicken palace.

I wanted to cry. No one has ever done anything like that for me. I made one stupid mention and not only did he take care of it, he went above and beyond.

Then I think about his eyes as he stared at me when he made it seem like it was no big deal. But it was to me.

It was everything.

All of the things start to pile up around me. The ball, the house in OBX, the coop, the things he says and how he looks at me.

What if I gave in? What if I . . . could have one night with him? I can handle the hurt, can't I?

Crew knows my past. Hell, he's part of that past. In just a few weeks, I'm going to have a major surgery where I'll spend weeks recovering, and I don't know what happens after that. I may never meet anyone else who makes me feel this way.

I pace the bedroom, waiting for him to come in after he finishes his business call. We got Layla down with no issues. She's really the sweetest kid ever and she's come alive on the farm, just like I hoped she would.

"Hey." Crew's voice causes me to jump.

"Hey."

"Did I scare you?"

I shake my head.

"I have something for you," he says with his hands behind his back.

"You do?"

"I do."

I try to peek around him, but I can't see anything. "What is it?"

"Oh, you want this?"

"You said you had something for me, so of course I'm intrigued now."

Crew grins. "I think you promised me treats . . . didn't you?"

I laugh and cross my arms over my chest. "So this is a quid pro quo?"

"No, just asking."

Pursing my lips, I lean against the mantel. "And what kind of treat are we thinking here?"

"Just a kiss."

I move toward him, kiss him very briefly, and step back. "Now, what's behind your back?"

He pulls a brown paper bag from behind his back and lifts it to read the name on it. "Hmm, I recognize this name." I'm going to grab that bag in about two seconds. I move to lunge for it, but he lifts it above my head. "Maybe you aren't going to get it now."

"Crew," I say his name pleadingly. "Please let me see what is in the bag."

I really hate this part of me. I hate surprises and yet I love them at the same time. I hate the anticipation of not knowing what's coming, but then love getting presents. I'm the worst at Christmas. My brothers absolutely hated shopping for me. Not only because of the obvious reason that they hate shopping, but because I was infamous for snooping to find the gifts.

This is even worse, having the damn thing dangling in front of me.

He opens it and puts his hand in, then pulls his hand out without whatever is in the bag.

"You're being very rude," I tell him. "I thought you subscribed to the happy wife mantra."

At that he laughs and shakes his head. "Now I see why you were a lawyer, you have an angle for everything."

I shrug, but then the blessed man hands me the bag. I open it immediately and find a cinnamon sugar donut. I gasp. "Is this the same one from our wedding?"

He nods. "It is. Is it what you wanted?"

This man. This beautiful, sweet, caring man. I hate him for making another brick in my wall fall to the ground. I need that wall to keep myself from being hurt when this ends.

But what if that is the only brick I lose? I'm still safe here, behind my wall. I can let that one go, and let myself feel good for a bit. Instead of letting my brain go in circles any longer about whether he and I make sense or this is right, I walk straight to him. "No. I want this."

His eyes widen in surprise as I basically charge him, my hands move to his neck, pulling him down, and I crush my lips to his.

It doesn't take but a second before he catches on, and his strong arms wrap around me, pulling me against him.

Our lips part and he slides his tongue in my mouth as the kiss deepens. He spins me around, my back against the door as his warm, hard body leans against mine. Crew's fingers dig into my hips, holding me tight against him.

I moan into his mouth, loving the way he tastes, smells, and everything he makes me feel.

One night.

One.

I move my hands down to the hem of his shirt and slide my fingers across his bare skin. His mouth leaves mine, panting for breath as he stares at me. "What are you doing?"

"Seducing you," I say, although it should be obvious.

"Brynn . . ."

"I'm not emotional. I'm not feeling the effects of a wedding. I'm sane, sober, and not afraid."

He brushes my hair back. "I don't want you to regret this."

"This is sex, Crew. This is two adults, who happen to be married and share a bed together, having one night."

His lips quirk up. "One?"

"One."

"So tomorrow we go back to the rules?"

"Yes, this is . . . I don't know, but I won't blame you for any of it, I'll blame the donut."

Goosebumps rise on my arms as he brushes his thumb against my lips. "One night isn't going to be enough, and do you know why?"

I shake my head.

"Because I'm going to make it so fucking good you won't be able to stop."

I'm not going to lie, I'm slightly afraid of that, but I'll cross that bridge when I get there. "You're sure of that?"

His lips brush mine in an almost kiss. "I'm absolutely positive. However, you're seducing me, so shouldn't you make the assurances?"

I pull my lower lip between my teeth. "I'm not as confident as you are."

Crew grins and then lifts me up, my legs wrap around his hips, and he carries me to the bed. "We'll work on that."

Our lips meet again, and I glide my fingers through his hair and then to his neck. His weight settles over me, holding me down, and I want to feel more of him. Those crystal blue eyes lock with mine, the emotions play like a movie and I can't look away. He's so beautiful, so perfect, so mine. Before I can think too hard, the warmth from his lips is on mine, sending waves of pleasure through my veins. Crew kisses my lips, my nose, my eyes, my cheeks, then down my chin and neck. I move my head to the side, giving him full access to every part of me.

"Crew," I say his name softly.

I can feel his smile against my skin as his hands move down my body, pulling my shirt up.

"Higher?" Crew asks, his teeth grazing my neck.

"Yes," I moan loudly.

His finger brushes right under my breast. "More?"

"Yes."

Then I shift, pulling my shirt up and off, tossing it to the side.

He kisses me again. I don't know that I will ever tire of his lips on mine. The way he knows exactly how to move in tandem with me has my heart fluttering as if it could leave my chest.

"I want you so bad. I've dreamed of this," he says between kisses.

"I didn't want to want you," I admit.

He smiles softly. "I'm really glad you do."

My heart pounds so hard as he leans in a little, moving his finger from my throat down to my breasts. He traces a pattern from one side to the other, just faintly touching the area where the bra covers my nipple as goosebumps rise against my skin.

He moves back up to the straps, pulling them off my shoulders. "If you want me to stop at any point," Crew says, staring into my eyes.

"I don't."

"Just tell me."

That same offer he made ten years ago. All week we'd fooled around, kissed, he went down on me and vice versa. We touched and played, and he never pushed me for more than I could do.

One night I thought we were going to make love, but I panicked, and he just held me as I apologized.

He moves his hand to my back, unhooking my bra easily. He watches me, maybe waiting for me to stop him. I'm supposed to be seducing him, so I push up, pulling my bra free.

Still, he doesn't look. His blue eyes are trained on mine.

"You're sure?" he asks again.

"Touch me. Kiss me. Love me," I say before pressing my hand to his cheek. "I want you."

His hand moves to my breast, cupping it gently, then he pinches my nipple and I moan. My head falls back, and I focus on the fact that he's touching me. Ten years of being without this, without him, and now I have it.

Crew's head moves down my body, he takes my nipple in his mouth, sucking gently, and my body tenses. Both my hands move to the back of his head, holding him there. It's so damn good. So freaking good.

He moves to the other side, doing the same thing, but this time he bites down just a little.

"Crew," I moan his name softly.

"You have to be quiet, Bee. Can you do that for me?"

I nod, remembering that we're not alone.

"Good girl," he praises. "Now, I think I'd like to kiss somewhere else."

I close my eyes, heat rushing to my cheeks. Crew is the only man who has ever done this to me. The only person who made me fall apart in a way I didn't know was possible.

He kisses farther down my body, over my stomach to my jeans. "Look at me, Brynlee."

I take a second to find my courage before fluttering open my eyelids.

"I don't want you to hide or pretend this isn't happening. I don't want you to lock yourself up in your head. Watch me love you. Watch me make you feel good."

My breathing grows ragged as I am filled with fear and something else that I can't quite name.

I keep my eyes on him as he unbuttons my jeans. The soft sound of the zipper being pulled down fills the room. I'm surprised I can hear anything with the pounding of my pulse in my ears, but I stay in the moment.

Crew clears his throat. "Do you want them off?"

"Yes," I whisper.

"Good."

He slides the material down, shifting from side to side until they're off. He runs his hands up my legs and then hooks his fingers in my underwear.

I nod when he looks to me again. "I want this."

And I mean it. I want him and this and us and a chance to erase the memories from the last time.

He slides my underwear off and then grasps my leg. He kisses my foot, my ankle, and then the calf. Slowly, Crew moves up my leg, spreading my thighs apart. "So fucking beautiful."

The blood in my veins is like fire, burning me from the inside out. My chest is heaving as he moves closer.

"Watch me, Brynlee."

I can't. I shake my head.

He runs his tongue along my center and doesn't move. "Open your eyes. Watch me worship you."

Crew pushes me, my legs completely apart, holding me open to him. I do as he asks and meet his gaze.

"Good girl. Keep your eyes on me and I won't stop, but if you close them again or look away, I will. You get to decide how long I do this for. You're in control, Brynn."

My heart is pounding, and I nod because I didn't realize just how much I needed to know I can stop this or keep it going. That he's giving over the power to me so I can be comfortable.

He moves his head to my core and his flat tongue slides against my clit. I moan, but keep my eyes on him, watching as he does it over and over. Crew moans as he moves his tongue in different patterns. The desire to close my eyes and just get lost is enormous, but I don't want him to stop.

I move my hand into his hair, letting his silky dark locks slide through my fingers. He pushes my legs farther open and flicks his tongue faster.

"I can't . . . I can't . . ." I pant as I climb higher with pleasure. "Oh . . ."

He moves faster, sucking harder on my clit and changing the

pressure. My fingers move to the comforter, gripping the fabric. Still, his eyes don't leave mine.

"Crew," I say his name softly and I can't hold back much longer. "It's coming. Please. More. Don't stop."

I say that last part because I can't keep my eyes open anymore. The pleasure is coming so hot and fast, I have to keep myself from falling apart.

My orgasm rips through me as he continues, not letting up even though my legs are clamped around his head, fingers gripping the sheet so tight I swear it might tear, and holding my breath so I don't scream.

My body gives way to the intense pressure and he kisses his way back up over my belly, my breasts, and then my neck.

Slowly I open my eyes to see his face above mine. I run my fingers through his hair. "I'm in control still?"

He nods.

"Then I want more."

"Do you?"

I grin. "Yes. I want you. All of you."

"You have it."

I move to sit up and cup his beautiful face. "One night."

"Whatever you want, Brynn."

He may not think I can see what that costs him, but I do. Crew is used to being the one calling the shots, but tonight, he's not fighting me.

"Sit back."

Without pause, we move so we're both on our knees. I pull his shirt up, sliding my hands along his sides. I want him to be undressed as well. I need to feel his skin against mine. "Take your clothes off, Crew."

He reaches up with one arm, pulling the shirt over his head and throwing it to the side. I take him in, the way his body has only become more defined, more masculine. My eyes roam from his shoulders down to his chest, looking at the tattoos on his body that weren't there before. There's a Celtic moon over his chest with intricate knots and then something on his ribs.

"What's the moon for?" I ask.

"Layla means night."

I smile at that. "And what's over there?" I point to his ribs.

Crew hesitates for a moment and then turns, lifting his arm. My heart stops and I feel my chest tightening. I try hard not to let my mind make anything out of it because it could mean absolutely nothing.

When I meet his eyes, I see the emotion there. "A ladybug for Layla," I say, and then I stop, trying to get my breathing under control. "And a bee."

"For you."

My jaw trembles and I can do nothing but look at him. He has a bee on his ribs, next to a symbol for his daughter. I lift my finger, moving it along the black outline of a detailed bee with parts of a honeycomb around it. It's beautiful and angry at the same time, like a part of what we might have been.

The sound of my heartbeat echoes in my chest. I don't know what to say. How do I reconcile all of this? He has a tattoo . . . of a bee . . .

All of these truths slam into me, knocking the bricks down faster than I can put them up. The house, the coop, the tattoo, the way he looks at me, I can't breathe.

"Crew . . ."

He shakes his head. "Not now, Brynlee. Now I just want to kiss you, make love to you, hold you in my damn arms again and not leave in the middle of the night. We can talk about all the other shit tomorrow." His hand moves to my cheek. "Can we do that?"

The part of me that needs answers to everything rebels at the thought of letting this go. And yet, I don't want to talk anymore either.

I rest my hands on his chest. "No more talking," I promise.

"Unless you want to tell me the things you want me to do to you or how good it feels or you want to beg for more." He kisses me again, thwarting my ability to talk.

I work to remove his pants, wanting everything he promised and nothing between us.

Carefully, he lays me down and rests on his side. "You're so beautiful, Brynlee. Nothing compares to you. I've imagined this so many times in my head and this is a million times better than my wildest dreams."

I push back the hair that fell in his eyes. "And what did you dream?"

He grins. "I'd probably scare you off. The things I want . . . the ways I want to make you come apart . . ."

There are so many things in my life that have gone wrong. People I've trusted who hurt me or situations I found myself in where I made the wrong decisions.

My father, Jonathan, and even Crew.

I've struggled with trust more than anything because I've failed so many times.

But then I think about the coop. About how he promises me he'll be there. How he cares so much for his daughter.

And the bee on his side.

I look into his blue eyes, seeing the man who is willing to do whatever I ask. I know what I want.

I rest my hand on his cheek. "Show me what you've dreamed of."

nineteen

CARSON

To do this tonight is like a goddamn miracle, and the fact that she just said those words has my insides in knots.

I've loved her more than I've ever loved any woman.

I've wanted her more than I've ever coveted anything.

And she's here, in my arms, in her bed, asking me to make love to her. We reach for each other, bringing our lips together, and I kiss her deeply.

She tastes like happiness and heaven. My hands move down her back and over her perfect ass.

Her body arches into mine and the feel of our skin against each other is consuming every part of me.

She breaks away from my mouth, letting out a soft moan as I rock against her. My cock slides against the heat of her cunt.

"Crew," she pants. "Please."

"Please what?"

Her eyes find mine, her long red hair pulled over her shoulder. "Take me, please. I need you inside of me."

Like a rubber band that's been pulled too tight, I snap. I've wanted this, her, for so fucking long.

I lift up, pushing her so she's on her back, and I climb over her. "You're sure?"

"Yes."

I fucking love that word right now.

"Condom?" I ask so I can find it.

Her eyes widen. "Oh my God, I don't have any. I haven't . . . needed it."

"Fuck."

"Crew, I have an IUD and I've been tested. I trust you—if you want."

She's telling me I can make love to her without a barrier and thinks I won't want it. "I get tested every year for work. If you're sure . . ."

"I'm sure."

Dear God, I am never going to be the same after this.

Her legs move farther apart, cradling me to fit right where she wants me. It's been a long time for her, and I need her to be fully primed. I reach between us to find she's already drenched. My thumb finds her clit, rubbing it and alternating the pressure. "You're so wet for me," I murmur against her ear, and she moans softly. "That's it, baby, just let me make you feel good."

I keep doing that and then slip a finger into her pussy. Her walls tighten around me, and I have to keep myself from taking her now. I rub her clit and then finger her before adding another finger.

Brynn's nails dig into my shoulders. "Crew, please."

"Not yet. I want you closer."

"I'm so close," she whimpers and I grin.

"Closer." I finger her deeper and her legs open even more. I use my cock this time, rubbing her clit.

She arches her back, moving her hips as I slide my entire dick against her as though I was inside her, moving, and she pants.

When I move my hips back, I push inside her slowly. Her eyes open and her grip increases.

I pause, not wanting to hurt her.

"Tell me when to move," I say, holding myself statue still. She's so fucking tight, so hot, so perfect. Every part of me is screaming to go deeper, to thrust hard.

"Try now," she says, but I feel her body tense when I go another inch in.

"Put your hand between us, baby," I urge. "Feel where we meet."

She releases one hand and does so, and the pads of her fingers touch my dick and I let out a groan. "Now what?" she asks.

"Touch yourself. Make yourself feel good like I did before."

I would give my life to be able to watch her right now. Instead, I get to feel parts of it when her hand moves to my cock, sliding her wetness against the two of us joined.

When I hear her breathing increase, I push a little deeper. "Fuck, you're so tight."

"More," she pants.

"Keep touching yourself," I urge. "I want to feel you come when I'm inside of you. I want to feel your pussy tight around my cock."

"Oh God."

"Look at me, Brynn," I command, wanting her eyes while I sink deeper.

She does and I push more. "Stay with me. Stay here with me." I pull my hips back, sliding into her deeper still. There's no pain in her eyes, only pleasure and something else.

The connection is like nothing I've ever known two people could share.

Brynn's hand comes to my face, resting on my cheek. "Crew."

My hips continue to move, the two of us setting a slow, steady rhythm. There are no words spoken between us, but we say what we need to. I give her everything I can, wanting this to be good for her.

I'm close though. She feels too good and I have to use every trick not to go too fast. I want her to come again.

She bites down on her lower lip. "Oh, I can't hold on."

I watch her head tilt back as she orgasms. Her fingers dig into my back and then scrape down my sides.

I can't stop myself, I follow right after her, kissing her and moaning into her mouth.

The two of us work to catch our breath and her hands move up and down my back. Slowly, I lift my head, praying I don't see regret in her eyes.

She smiles. "I'd say your dreams have been really good."

I laugh and kiss her again. "That was just a daydream, I have no shortage of ideas."

I roll to the side, and she exits the bed, wrapping herself in my shirt and heading into the bathroom.

Once I've cleaned up, I get into bed and watch for her. She exits wearing my shirt and I realize how fucking sexy it is. She climbs in, her cheeks red, lips swollen, and hair in a ponytail.

"Come here," I say, opening my arms. Brynlee doesn't hesitate, she plasters herself to me and I pull her tight. "I'm going to hold you all night and you don't have to worry about me being gone in the morning, I'm not going anywhere."

Her eyes find mine. "Thank you for tonight—and today. The coop, the diner, and then . . . you know."

"The orgasms?" I ask with one brow raised.

"Yes, add that to the list."

I chuckle and kiss her forehead. "If I get nights like this, I'm going to build you a barn starting tomorrow."

She sighs heavily and then wraps her arms around me, and we fall asleep literally wrapped in each other's arms.

"We need to put the pig in the pen with the sheep and the cow," Brynn explains as she's herding animals around.

"Daddy, I got a chicken!" Layla calls, showing me the chicken scooped under her arm.

Brynn turns to her. "That's Bonita, she's been with me since she was a baby. She's very sweet."

"I love her."

"Can you bring her back in the chicken area so she's nice and safe when we leave?"

Layla nods and looks to me. "Will I see her again?"

"You will. We'll come back here next time you're with me. Would you like that?"

My daughter's eyes brighten. "Come on, Bonita, I'll put you somewhere safe." Layla pets Bonita and talks to her, telling her about her toys as she walks into the large chicken area.

I smile and glance at Brynn who looks ready to cry. She turns to me. "Come on, we have to work, or we won't get her home in time."

"Right. Pig in with the sheep and cow."

I'm able to locate the cow, since it's huge and all, but I'm not exactly sure how the fuck I'm supposed to move it. "Come on, cow, we have to go in the barn."

And when I say barn, it's more like half of a building. I'm sure at one point it was a very beautiful barn, it's not now. It's missing large parts of siding and has some plastic roofing sheeting around it. The stalls inside don't have doors, they're more like makeshift wood slats that are propped up.

I sigh as I try again with the cow, this time pulling a little on the harness. "Let's go inside."

The cow doesn't move.

"You're making me look like an idiot," I tell it and she swishes her tail. "I'll give you an apple or whatever cows like if you don't make me have to ask her how to do this."

The cow just stares at me.

"Any tips?" I ask Brynn as she lifts a sheep in her arms. Not like I can lift the cow and carry it.

"Bridget, barn," she commands, and the damn thing starts to follow her.

"Really?" I ask Bridget as she passes me.

An hour later, we have all the animals where they need to be, Layla is in the house with Cliff, getting all her new clothes and toys together, while Brynn and I are walking hand in hand.

"Thank you for helping." She rests her head on my upper arm. "I'm glad we came, and it seems Layla likes it here."

"She definitely does. I see why you love it here."

Her beautiful brown eyes find mine. "It has its weaknesses too."

"Bad Italian food."

She laughs. "That and while having a ton of land and nothing around for miles, you have very little privacy, thanks to the people."

"In New York, we have no privacy, and no one gives a shit about you. I'm not sure your end of the deal is all that bad."

As we get closer to the house, we see her brothers leaning against the fence rail, watching us with shit-eating grins.

"Well, look who became a country boy," Asher says as we walk toward them. "She broke him in in no time."

Brynn shakes her head. "He at least helps, unlike you morons."

"I'm pretty sure he has his reasons," Rowan jokes.

Asher slaps him in the back of the head. "Gross. She's still our sister."

"We came to actually do this stuff for you, but you guys were already knee deep in animal shit, so we decided there was no point messing up our boots," Grady tacks on and then looks to me. "Boss."

"Grady," I say, not really sure exactly what footing I'm on here. These are my brothers-in-law, but two of them work for me as well. Right now, we're family, on their land. "Thanks for coming, but we've got it handled." I look to Rowan. "We really appreciate all your help while we're in New York during the week. I know you have a lot of responsibility on your own farm, but the fact that you've come here daily matters to both Brynn and me."

He nods once. "Anything for Brynn."

She scoffs. "Please, I had to beg."

"I was able to find two people who will alternate starting tomorrow. They've already been paid, but they'll come, do whatever they need to for Second Chances, and then we'll be here most weekends," I explain.

Brynn's eyes dart to mine. "What?"

"I know you were worried about it."

The two of us look at each other for a minute, forgetting her brothers are there. I'm not sure why she's so surprised. This is something she was concerned about, especially once her surgery happens. I figured if we found someone now, then she'll be more at ease later.

"He must really love her if he's willing to care for the animals," Grady notes.

Asher pushes off the fence. "Well, our work is done." He makes his way to where we're standing and Brynn turns to him, breaking our moment. "Get back safe. Love you."

"Love you too." She seems kind of dazed. She hugs her other brothers and I shake their hands.

We start to walk toward the house, and she stops. "You hired people to run the farm?"

"I hired people to help your animals."

"Why?"

"Because you mentioned that things were hard for you. You had the animals, the coop that was falling apart that Rowan promised to fix, but hadn't. You said you have the surgery, the costs of it, the never-ending repairs, your company. All of those things and more." I push her hair behind her ear. "I know that my money makes you uncomfortable, and you're more than capable of doing all these things, but I don't want you to worry. I promised, hell, I vowed to take care of you, Brynn, and that's what I'm going to do."

And when we're back next week, she'll get another thing off her list. I plan to whittle them down until there is nothing left.

twenty

BRYNLEE

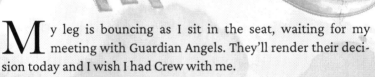

My leg is bouncing as I sit in the seat, waiting for my meeting with Guardian Angels. They'll render their decision today and I wish I had Crew with me.

He asked, but I was adamant he didn't need to cancel his meetings. He's done so much of that since our whirlwind marriage began.

The door opens and a short, stocky man enters. He smiles warmly and I stand to shake his hand. "I'm sorry to keep you waiting, Ms. Whitlock. Oh! I'm sorry, I mean Mrs. Knight. I saw you in the papers," he admits. "I'm Roger Bagwell and I'm your case manager."

"Please, just call me Brynlee. It's nice to meet you."

"You as well. We went over your paperwork and everything looked to be in order. I just had a few items I needed to clear up before we can either approve or deny you."

I nod. "Okay, I'm happy to help."

"First, I know your marital status has now changed. Do you happen to have the paperwork for that?"

I reach into my bag, extracting my marriage license, and hand it to him. "Here, I did send an email to update my application."

"Yes, I did receive that and thank you for sending. Based on the application that was submitted, we were able to qualify you for a grant. However, with the new updates, we need to double check."

My heart sinks a little. "Oh? Because I'm married?"

He shakes his head quickly. "No, no, not because of that. We work to help ensure that every living donor's expenses are as minimal as possible. It's the generosity of our donations that allows that. We want to make sure that the people we're issuing the grants for truly need them. They have to be uninsured and meet an income threshold, which you did . . ."

"But I don't now," I finish.

Because I'm married to a billionaire and why would I need money when Crew could probably buy the hospital?

I sit back in my chair, feeling defeated.

"It's not that your income has changed. We understand that you're newly married and without steady employment at this time. However, you indicated that you now have insurance?"

My jaw drops slightly. "Well, yes, but it's not active yet. I don't think I have coverage for this, as it was all set in motion prior to my marriage."

He writes notes down. "I see. Have you checked with them?"

"I haven't. I didn't even think about it. I don't know . . ."

"It's completely fine, Mrs. Knight. We know this is all new and there are a lot of changes. Do you mind if we call them and open a case to find out what, if any, benefits will be covered?"

"Of course not." I dig in my purse and grab my phone to call Crew. I don't have a card or even know anything about our insurance. "Can I have just a minute?" I ask.

"Please." He extends his hand toward the door. "The office to the right is empty."

"Thank you."

I head inside and he answers on the second ring. "Brynn, is everything okay? Did you get the grant?"

"Yes, everything's fine and no, not yet. I need the information on our insurance. One of the requirements is that my insurance won't cover any part of the surgery."

"I see. I'll have my assistant call as soon as we hang up, she'll get you all the information you need." He drops his voice. "I'm in the middle of a meeting or I'd do it for you."

"No worries, thank you and happy . . . meeting or whatever."

He chuckles. "Thank you, Bee."

Sure enough, three seconds later my phone is vibrating in my hand. His assistant, Ginny, gives me all the details as well as a direct contact she thinks I should call first. Apparently, being Carson Knight and owning the companies that pay the insurance is not without perks.

I write everything down, thanking her for her help, and then dial the number.

It feels like an hour later, I have all the right people to contact and knock on Mr. Bagwell's door. He calls for me to come in.

"Sorry about that, dealing with insurance is never easy," I say, and hand over the notes I made.

He smiles warmly. "Oh, I know that. Please sit. I just hung up with my manager and we're going to use your initial application to make our decision."

"What do you mean?"

Mr. Bagwell places both hands on the desk and laces his fingers together. "We had preliminarily already issued you the grant when you sent your updates in. Guardian Angels feels that you should be given the money without having to speak with your insurance first."

I'm so confused. "While I appreciate that, and I really do, I'm not sure I understand why the change."

"What we'd like is to give the requested amount with a contingency. We've done this several times before. If you will sign a document stating you'll allow us to pay the hospital directly after they've submitted to insurance, then we'll be given a refund back for whatever funds weren't used."

I sit forward. "Of course. I'll sign anything. I'll even go through and find out exactly what the insurance pays so that I don't take anyone's opportunity for the grant."

"That's very helpful."

I could cry. God, this is amazing. I have the money to cover the transplant and I don't have to do anything crazy to get the money. I wasn't counting out putting up a subscription site for foot porn if that's what I needed to do.

My chest is lighter, and I can't stop smiling. "Thank you. Thank you so much, Mr. Bagwell."

"Don't thank me, Brynn. What you're doing for another person is truly selfless. Here, just sign in these two places. The first page is accepting the grant and the second is allowing Guardian Angels to pay the hospital directly with any refunds being sent to us."

I read over the documents carefully, the lawyer in me never goes away. Everything looks to be exactly as he said. The addendum paperwork has everything laid out. For some reason, I glance at the name on the top.

Brynlee Knight.

It'll be the first time I sign my name as a married woman. As Crew Knight's wife.

I don't let myself think about it and sign quickly, only focusing on the fact that I can do this for my father. The tears I was trying to hold off stream down my face. They're tears of relief and utter happiness. We both stand. "I need to call my father and husband."

He extends his hand and I grasp it. "We will all be thinking of you and praying for a safe and successful surgery."

"Thank you."

I head out of there, sending Crew a text.

ME

I got the grant! There are some weird changes, but it's all good!

CREW

Congrats, Bee. I'm so happy for you. I'll be home around six. Let's do dinner to celebrate.

> **ME**
> Sounds good. See you soon.

Next, I call my dad, letting him in on the good news. He cries—a lot. Everything is coming together, and my cheeks hurt from smiling so much.

My phone pings with a text.

> **OLIVIA**
> Look, you're famous!

With that comes a photo of me and Crew laughing as we walked into the apartment last night. His arm is around my back and I'm looking into his eyes with a huge grin.

> **ME**
> Where did you see that?

> **OLIVIA**
> Online. There's a whole section about Carson and his new wife—meaning you.

> **ME**
> I knew who you meant. Why are you reading that crap?

> **OLIVIA**
> Because! It's gossip and now, Holly Carpenter wants to talk to me to ask about my uncle. She's never cared about me before.

> **ME**
> You don't need to be her friend if she didn't see how amazing you were before.

OLIVIA

I know, I know. Anyway, I have speech therapy
and Dad is staring at me with that look. Love you!

ME

I love you most.

I head back to the apartment and do some work. Thea and I got an email from Catherine about a possible publicist coming to work with us. Since we're a sub-branch from her California office, we had talked about expanding to celebrity clients once we were more established.

I'm kind of surprised she wants us to consider someone when we haven't even gotten the business and crisis management division launched yet.

Thea replied asking to do a video conference this week to discuss the plan for when I'm out.

Right now, I don't even know how I'm going to manage any clients when I'm going to be recovering from surgery in a few weeks.

That's another worry to add to the list.

I swear, for each one we remove, another goes on.

"Hey," a deep voice calls and I jump.

"Crew!"

He stands there smiling with a box in front of him. I don't even have to ask what it is. I smile taking in the light pink square that holds my favorite thing.

"I think we mentioned a celebration was in order."

I get to my feet and walk toward the box of happiness. "You're home early."

"I had something else on my mind and couldn't focus."

When I'm a few feet away, he puts the box down and pulls me into his arms. "What was on your mind?"

"You."

His nose brushes mine and I inhale his cologne. My eyes close as I memorize it all and how he makes me feel.

"And donuts?" I ask.

"Not even a little, other than I like the way your lips taste after you've eaten one." I glance up at him, and the warmth in his eyes causes heat to pump through my veins. All I want to do is bite into a donut and kiss him until neither of us can think.

Rules. I have them. I think I have them. What were they again?

Oh yeah, no seducing. He's totally doing that.

Instead of doing what I think he will, which is strip me down and make me scream, he kisses the tip of my nose and steps back. "As much as I want you to bite that donut, we have plans tonight."

That stuns me. "Plans?"

I was really hoping that donuts and sex was the plan.

"Yup. We're going on a date."

I should've known that Crew's version of a date wasn't normal. I figured since we're in New York, we'll go get dinner and walk around. I don't know, something like that.

What I didn't anticipate was having to pack a bag and my passport.

I have no idea where we're going.

I'm in my joggers and cut-neckline sweatshirt. Crew is wearing basketball shorts and looking delicious.

We pull up to the runway to his private jet and my eyes go wide when I see a familiar face standing at the red carpet to the plane.

"Really? My brother is flying us?" I ask Crew.

"He works for me."

That thought makes me curious. "Does that mean he also works for me?"

Crew smirks. "Technically, no, but I'm happy to play along if it'll make you happy."

"Oh, it does."

"Then by all means, have at it."

He exits the car and opens my door. I place my hand in his and when I turn to grab our bags, the driver is already doing that. Right, we don't do those things. Also, we don't pack ourselves. About ten minutes after Crew's announcement of our date, Ginny showed up with a large box that was for me but only to be opened when we reach our destination.

We walk over to where our plane staff is standing.

"Mr. Knight, Mrs. Knight," a pretty brunette woman, who is maybe early forties and stunning, says as we approach.

"Jessica, thank you for filling in. I know it was short notice and I truly appreciate it. Please meet my wife, Brynlee," he says with his hand on my lower back.

"It's nice to meet you."

"You too. I'm sorry if we took you from something."

"Please don't apologize. I'm happy to travel with you guys."

"How's Grayson?" Crew asks.

"He's great."

"And the Firefly Inn?"

Jessica smiles. "The Firefly is doing great. We hoped maybe you and your wife would've chosen it for the wedding. Willow Creek Valley is a beautiful place."

Crew chuckles. "I should've, but we wanted to be married on the beach where we met."

"I'm sure it was stunning. Are you ready to board?"

He nods and we get to where Grady is standing. I grin. "And you are?"

His gaze lifts. "Hello, Mrs. Knight, my name is Captain Whitlock."

"I see, that's a great name."

"It is."

I fight back a smile. "And how long have you been a pilot? You look awfully young and inexperienced."

Crew laughs. "This is like when I was in Sugarloaf when you all chastised me."

202

I look over at him and nod. "Isn't it fun being on this side? I mean, right now, Grady is *our* employee. He has to be professional and it's killing him."

"Not at all, ma'am," Grady says. "I'm so happy to be the one who is flying this plane today, carrying such precious cargo."

I burst out laughing. "You're such a bad liar." I lean over and kiss his cheek. "I feel safe knowing you're the pilot."

"Yeah, this is every brother's dream to fly his baby sister on a date."

"Well, it's better than thinking about me joining the mile high club while you're flying, isn't it?" I ask, tap his chest, and walk onto the plane with a wide grin.

twenty-one

CARSON

Jessica brings us each a tray with food and a donut for dessert. Brynn looks over at me with a grin.

Wait until she finds out I bought the donut shop, but that's a surprise for another day.

For the next two and a half days, I'm going to give her a time she'll never forget.

Ford about lost his shit when I told him to cancel my meetings until Thursday because I'd be out of the country.

It was sort of fun.

"Are you going to tell me where we're going now?" Brynn asks.

"Not a chance. You'll see when we land."

She rolls her eyes. "Can you give me a hint?"

"Maybe."

"Okay, will we be warm or cold?"

I tap my chin. It's March so the weather there isn't warm yet, but we won't be freezing either. "We'll be comfortable."

"Ugh!" she groans and lays her head back. "You could just tell me."

"I could, but then it wouldn't be a surprise." I know how she feels about surprises, which makes this a little more enjoyable than it should be.

Brynn changes tactics and leans in close. "What if I offer a bargain for the information?"

This could be even more enjoyable.

However, that's not what my plans for tonight are. We'll be flying through the night and when we land in Paris, we'll be hitting the ground running. I want to show her everything I can, take her to the best restaurants, and then we'll end the night at the Eiffel Tower.

"I'm listening," I play along.

"Well, I'll give you something you want for every piece of information you give me."

"And what do I want?"

She pulls her lower lip between her teeth. "You tell me."

I turn my body to face her, moving into her space, forcing her to retreat a touch. "What I want"—I drop my voice so only she can hear—"is for you"—I move my hand to her cheek—"to eat your dinner and then nap."

Brynn's eyes flash and she grunts. "You're the worst."

"I've been told that several times. Now, eat, because we both need to rest before we land."

"And where are we landing?" Brynn asks, all innocence.

"On the ground."

She pouts and I fight back a laugh. After we're in the air, she eats her food and I convince her to come lie in the bedroom with me.

We still have about five hours before we land. I pull her to my chest and she drapes her leg over me.

"I hate surprises."

"I know."

"And yet you're doing it anyway," Brynn grumbles as she nestles against me.

Clearly, she's not all that mad about it.

"I'm pretty sure I'll be forgiven," I say, pushing her hair back.

"We'll see."

And then Brynn sighs heavily and we fall asleep together.

There's a knock on the bedroom door. Brynn groans and pulls me closer to her. "Not now. I'm sleepy."

"Yes?" I call out to either Jessica or Brynn's brother.

"We're going to be landing in twenty. We need you both to come take your seats," Jessica instructs.

"Thank you, we'll be out in a minute. Please pull all the window screens down so my wife can't see where we are."

Brynn's head pops up. "We're landing and you're still hiding it from me?"

I stifle a laugh. "Come on, let's get in our seats."

Normally she's not this peppy when she wakes up, but this time she's moving a little faster.

We get to our seats, where Jessica has laid out a few pastries. The two of us snack a little and then we start our descent.

Grady lands the plane expertly and then he comes over the speakers. "Mr. and Mrs. Knight, welcome to Paris."

Brynlee turns to me, her face alight with joy. "Paris?"

"I thought we needed a honeymoon after all."

"But . . . we can't. We don't have time."

I take her face in my hands. "We wasted years, Brynn. I can take two days and give you Paris."

I'd give her the whole fucking world if I could, but for now, we'll at least have this.

Seeing Paris through Brynn's eyes is something I'll remember forever. She's damn near giddy as we stroll along the streets, grabbing pastries at different places along the way. Her smile never fades as she takes in the sights and shops.

"Crew, I do not need a purse that is over ten thousand dollars," she complains as we're in one of the high-end designer stores on the Champs.

"You're in Paris, you need a souvenir."

"No, I don't. This trip, the fact that you took me to freaking Paris when we agreed we wouldn't, is more than enough."

I take her hand, moving her to another section of the store. "Every woman I know would've jumped at the chance for that bag."

She shakes her head, looking up at me. "It's not about that for me."

I look at her, my throat getting tight because I've never met anyone like her. People always say they don't want the money or luxury, but they seldom mean it. Brynlee really doesn't. She just wants the people she loves to be happy.

And all I want is to make her smile. "I know that, which is why I want to give it to you all the more."

I turn to the clerk as Brynn is trying to pull me out of the store. "We'll take the green please, send it to the Four Seasons in my name."

"Of course, Mr. Knight."

"Crew!" Brynlee finally gets me outside.

I pull her into my arms and kiss her. "If this is our honeymoon, you will need to accept that I'm going to be ridiculous and buy you whatever I want. I can't seduce you, Brynn, but I can spoil you."

Brynn rests her hand on my chest. "We've only been married for a short time and already you've done too much. The wedding, the coop, this trip, all of it is so sweet, but I have never needed any of it. I could've gotten married in my backyard and taken a secondhand coop. If we got on a plane and went to . . . I don't know . . . Birmingham, I would've been happy."

"Birmingham?" I ask with a chuckle.

"I have no idea why that popped into my head, but it did." Her fingers play with the button on my shirt. "I'm just saying that I don't care about your money, I care about you."

Her words cut me open, leaving me open and exposed. "I never stopped wanting you, Brynlee." Our eyes are locked and I want her to feel how I feel. "Even when I should've. Even when I married another woman. Even when I told myself over and over that there was no way I could fall in love with someone in a week, I still loved you. So, while our marriage and all the things you've named may seem like enough, it'll never express how much I care about you."

"You're not allowed to say that," she says with tears in her eyes.

"Why not?"

"Because I can't let you love me."

"If I haven't figured out a way in ten years to stop, what makes you think I'll be able to now?"

twenty-two

BRYNLEE

I'm trying to stay grounded and remember all my damn rules, even though this has been the most incredible day of my life.

We finished eating dinner *on* the Eiffel Tower with views that took my breath away. In just sixteen hours, we've seen so much, thanks to Crew paying to cut the line at pretty much everything.

We went to the Louvre, the Père Lachaise Cemetery, which was the most incredibly beautiful place I've ever been, and don't even get me started on this freaking hotel. We walked the Seine holding hands and he kissed me on the bridge, like I've seen in the movies. I've probably walked more than I've ever walked before and yet, I'm not even tired.

Crew opens the door to the hotel room and the high of the day and all the things we've done sort of crash down on me.

I want to talk about the things that happened, put in place the rules we agreed on, remember the hurt that I've endured, but I can't.

The two of us look at each other in the foyer of this ridiculous suite.

Like magnets, we're pulled to each other. Each step takes us to the next before I'm reaching for him and he's reaching for me. I'm not sure who kisses who, but it's intense and I feel it everywhere.

He moves my head to the side, devouring my mouth. I push his suit jacket off and toss my shawl somewhere in the room. My hands go to the buttons on his shirt, and I fumble trying to undo them.

Crew pulls back, both of us panting, and I wrench the fabric apart, causing buttons to fly everywhere. His eyes flash with heat and then he lifts me, walking us to the bedroom.

"Brynn," he sighs my name as he puts me down. His hands move to the clip in my hair, freeing it. "I want you more than anything, but I'll stop if you want."

His fingers move down my neck and over my shoulders.

While he may want me, I need him.

"Don't stop." Our mouths are close thanks to the increased height I get from my heels. "Don't stop at all."

His lips are on mine in a second and then I'm pressed against the poster of the bed, his warm body against mine. We kiss and I'm lost to him, constantly warring with my emotions and losing.

How in the hell does he do this?

Why do I let him?

Oh, I know, because I'm still in love with the man.

I shove that thought down, refusing to think about it as his lips slide against the column of my neck. "Crew," I sigh his name as he nips at my skin.

"I'm going to peel this dress off and taste you."

Thank you, God.

He turns me, the cool metal of sliding the zipper down in contrast to the heat of his body. I shiver as his hands move from my back up over my shoulders, just brushing the skin at the top of my breasts. The sound of his breathing is heavy as my head falls against his chest and he cups me gently. His hand slips under my bra and he rubs my nipple between his thumb and forefinger. I turn my head to him and he kisses me, then pushes the dress completely off and my head spins.

"Turn around," he commands. I face him in just my black lace underwear and heels. "The last time we made love, I gave you control. Do you need that again, Brynn?"

212

My heart is pounding and I'm unsure what to say. I glance at the floor trying to decide whether that's what I need. Is it control or do I trust him? I already know the answer, I do trust him, more than maybe I should, but being with Crew is like being home. He's a feeling, a part of my soul that knows it's found its other half.

I hate it because I know that half is going to leave at some point.

But my trust is his. It's always been his.

He lifts my chin to look in my eyes. "Do you trust me to make you feel good?"

"Yes."

Crew's lips touch mine and we cling to each other as my emotions flood me and he drinks them in.

He pulls back. "Get on the bed, keep your heels on, and go all the way to the top."

I do as he says, and he stands at the edge, looking at me with a heat in his eyes that could burn the hotel down. "Like this?" I ask.

"Just like that." His hand moves to his belt and he removes it, tossing it to the floor. Then he unbuttons his pants and leaves them hanging on his hips. "I've had more fantasies of you like this. Waiting for me, wet and ready. Are you wet, baby?"

I nod, feeling flushed at the question.

"I bet you are. I bet right now your panties are drenched," Crew says as he unzips his pants. "Open your legs." Slowly I part my knees. "Pull your panties to the side, let me look at your wet cunt."

My heart pounds against my chest, but I do as he asks. His eyes stay locked with mine and I wonder if he's testing me, so I stay with him, in the moment, letting him know I'm completely fine with his bossiness.

The corner of his lip turns up. "Does this turn you on, Brynn? Do you like me being in charge?"

"Yes," I confess.

"Good. Come here and take my pants off, but crawl to me."

I get on my hands and knees on the bed and do as he says,

crawling toward him. When I reach him, I place my hand on his chest and he lets out a low grumble. "Can I touch you?" I ask.

"Anywhere you want, baby."

I run my hand down his hard chest, touching the moon there, then down his ribs. I kiss him softly while my fingers rest on the bee that's tattooed there.

I feel him smile against my lips. "You like that?"

"I like that I've been here with you all this time," I admit.

His hand threads into my hair, holding me against his mouth. Crew's kiss grows more urgent and intense. I grip him tight, holding on and never wanting to let go.

"Fuck," he groans as he pulls away. "You have always been with me, even when I couldn't have you."

"I'm here now," I say, my hand moving up and down his spine as I look into his blue eyes.

"You are."

And I want him. I want to touch him, kiss him, feel him inside of me where he's always been.

"So what are you going to do with me?"

"I'm going to make you scream."

Well, I like the sound of that. I move my hand down to his pants and push them and his boxer briefs over his hips. He kicks them off and then he's gloriously naked in front of me. Crew takes a step back and wraps his hand around his cock.

I watch as he pumps up and down slowly as he looks at me. "Take the rest of your clothes off. Stay on your knees, I want to see all of you."

I unhook my bra, pulling the straps and letting the bra fall to the bed. Then I remove my underwear and throw it on the floor. "Do you like what you see?" I ask, feeling self-conscious.

I don't know why I feel that way because the look in his eyes tells me I have nothing to worry about.

"No, Bee, I fucking love what I see. There isn't a more beautiful view in the world than you, naked and ready for me."

I am so damn ready.

He strokes his cock again and I'm mesmerized by him. "Crew, I want you."

"I'm right here, baby."

I move toward him, getting off the bed, and put my hand where his hand was. I move slowly, trying to learn what makes him feel good. "Like this?"

"Just like that."

"I want . . ." I start, but stop, feeling embarrassed to say it. I liked when he was talking to me so I didn't get in my head. "Tell me what you want."

"I want your lips around my cock while you play with your clit." I kiss my way down his chest and sink onto my knees. Crew looks down at me, his fingers slide through my hair, guiding me. "Touch yourself while I fuck your mouth."

I open my lips and take him in. He groans loudly as he fills my mouth and I move my hand to my clit. I moan around him, and he pulls his hips back and holds my head as he moves forward.

I rub myself as Crew sets a pace. "That's it, baby," he croons. "You feel so fucking good. Play with yourself, make yourself ready for me." I was ready before we even started this, but I do as he says. I can feel my orgasm starting to build and Crew's fingers tighten in my hair. "Don't come, Brynn. Hold it off. You're going to come against my tongue, not before."

Yeah, I'm not so sure that's possible, but I grunt in acknowledgment and slow down the circles against my clit.

I lift my gaze to his and he moves his hips again before pulling out. "I need you, lie down."

Crew helps me to my feet, moving me where he wants me. I'm on the bed and he's pulling my legs forward, so my ass is at the edge of the bed. He drops to his knees, tossing my legs over his shoulders. My heels go flying to the floor, and he doesn't waste a second as his flat tongue licks me.

"Oh God," I pant. "I'm close already."

He is like a man starved. He licks and flicks his tongue over and over. I moan and writhe against the bed, my toes curling as pleasure floods my senses.

All that exists is Crew.

He continues to devour me and I'm panting and struggling to breathe. It feels so good, so damn good and I need to release. "I can't," I breathe. "Please, I can't take any more."

He doubles his efforts, and he starts to finger me. It's too much. I fall apart, crying out his name and incoherent words as my orgasm rocks through me.

He climbs up my body, taking my arms and putting them over my head. His hand holds my wrists, and I feel him at my entrance.

Our eyes meet and I nod as he pushes inside of me. My mouth falls open as I'm filled with him. I swear, I could stay like this forever because when he's with me like this, I feel healed. I feel like this could be more.

He could be everything.

The circumstances of our marriage don't seem forced or convenient, it feels real.

The years of hurt disappear with each thrust.

He releases my hands and I hold onto him. "Fuck, Brynn. You feel . . . fuck . . . you are . . ."

I don't need him to say it because it's the same for me. "I know."

He kisses me hard, his hips moving, and then his hand is under my ass, adjusting the angle.

He's so deep I have to hold onto his shoulders so I don't come apart.

Crew pulls out suddenly and I gasp at the emptiness. "Ride me, Bee."

When he's on his back, I climb over him. I hesitate, looking down at him, unsure exactly what to do.

He moves my hips and I feel the tip. "Crew, I've never . . ."

"I'm right here with you, baby, you control how deep I go."

I want him all the way. I sink down, my head falling back at the sensation. It's different and amazing and so much.

"That's it," he coaxes. "Take all of me, Brynn."

A low moan falls from my lips when there's no more to go. "Oh, God. So full."

"Now rock."

I move my hips again, rubbing against him, and I swear, I'm going to die. It feels so good, so much pressure everywhere. My hands are on his chest as I rock, staring down at him as he looks at me.

My body starts to tremble as the friction grows. "I can't again," I say, feeling exhausted and overwhelmed.

"Yes, you can." He grabs my hips and starts to rock for me. "Come around my cock, Brynn. Let me feel you contract around me." I fall forward and his lips are at my ear. "You feel so fucking good. You're so hot, so wet. Listen to the sounds of us together, how your body wants me buried in your tight cunt. Let go, baby. Let it all go, I'll catch every piece of you as you fall apart and hold you together."

I can't take another second. I do as he says, letting go. Letting the sensations overtake me as I rock back and forth. It doesn't take long before I cry out again, letting another orgasm, an even more intense one, happen.

"Fuck. Fuck, you feel so good," he pants. Crew holds my hips as he fucks me from the bottom. "I'm going to come. Fuck, I'm going to come."

He slams into me and then grabs my hair, pulling my head back as he releases. After he's done and he releases my hair, his mouth finds mine. It's not a kiss as much as the two of us breathing each other in.

His fingers relax and I lie on top of him, still connected.

Crew pushes my hair back, kissing my nose. "Let's clean up and then lie here and enjoy the view."

I get up, heading into the most lavish bathroom I've ever seen, and that's saying something since Crew's penthouse is ridiculous. I clean up, pull the silk robe around me, and head back to the bed, where he's propped up on the pillow.

He opens his arms as I approach, and I head to my spot against his chest. Neither of us says anything, we just look out the double doors where the Eiffel Tower is lit up.

"Thank you for bringing me here. For giving me the most

incredible time in Paris, and for being you," I say as I cuddle deeper into him.

Crew's arms tighten and he sighs deeply. "It's me who should be thanking you."

"For what?"

"For everything." He kisses the top of my head and I yawn. "Go to sleep, Bee. I'll hold you for as long as you'll let me."

After the Paris trip, Crew and I fall into an easy routine. We get Layla on Wednesdays for dinner, where we stay in the apartment and let her run our world. He travels sometimes. Then, on the weekends we head to Sugarloaf whether we have her or not.

"What would you like for dinner tonight?" Celeste asks as I've taken over the dining room table with papers.

Thea signed three clients and my husband mentioned my company to some of his friends, so I've been swamped with drawing up proposals.

It's a good problem to have, and has kept me insanely busy as Crew has been trying to catch up on his work.

I glance up, my topknot falling in my face. "Huh?"

"Food, Brynn. You have to eat. Carson will not be happy if he comes home to find you starved and passed out on the table."

I huff, causing my hair to fly out of my eye. "He'll get over it."

She smiles. "Maybe a sandwich or some soup? Just something to keep your stamina up."

"Both would be great," I say, feeling appreciation at her kindness.

I've spent a lot of time with Cliff and Celeste the last week. Crew had an emergency at one of the food factories in Arizona.

Since we got married, he's been home or with me and I didn't realize how abnormal that is for him until Celeste explained his regular schedule.

No matter how busy he is, he calls me every night. We talk for about an hour, he tells me about his day and I relay mine. It's really sweet that he does it. Not that I'm overly surprised, since he tends to make me see how much he cares all the time.

For example, every morning I wake up to a donut on the bedside table.

On cue, my phone rings.

I slide the button and his beautiful face fills my screen.

"Hi," I say with a smile.

"Hi to you. Where are you?" Crew asks.

"At the dining room table, which is basically my conference room."

He laughs. "You know I have two other offices. Take one."

"I don't need an office."

"I think you do, since you've overtaken the dining room."

I shrug. "I'll think about it."

"Don't think, Bee, just pick one. I'll have the decorator call you so you can make it how you need."

When he says and does things like this, it makes my head go in a million directions. I have my surgery in a little over two weeks and the custody hearing is scheduled for five weeks out. When all of that settles, what is he going to do with my office?

Am I even going to see him? Do we get a divorce? What if I want this to be more, be everything real because nothing about this entire thing has felt like a sham or a mirage?

Our entire marriage has been exactly what I would've hoped for in my life and more.

"You don't have to do that."

"One day you're going to stop arguing about this with me."

"High-handed man," I grumble.

Crew smiles. "How was your day?"

And he loves to change topics so I won't complain. I sigh. "It was good. I got three more calls from your friends."

"They're not friends," he corrects.

"No? What are they?"

"Businessmen who see value in your company. You and Thea have great ideas and ways you want to help corporations. They know you're a lawyer, she's a marketing manager. The two of you are also under Catherine Cole, which helps, since Anchor Light is a well-known name as well."

I try to let that be the truth, but sometimes I wonder if he's not calling in favors. Thea, on the other hand, doesn't give a flying fuck why we're getting business because now we're actually going to be able to float instead of sink.

"I hope that's true."

Crew runs his hand through his thick hair. "Let's just say it wasn't true."

My eyes widen. "What?"

"Let's pretend for a second that none of these clients came to you for the reason I just stated. Does it matter?"

"Well, I'd like to think it does, since I want this company to be built on its own merit."

Crew leans forward. "Brynlee, you are a start-up, love. No one company has any merit when it's just starting. You're only as good as the relationships you've built. Thea isn't bringing in clients because they think Anchor Light's corporate division is brilliant. They've never heard of it. They're taking meetings with her and you because of your friendships or working relationships. The people I've told about you are reaching out because they know me. They know the businessman I am. They aren't stupid and know there's a power move in having my wife in their ear. Take advantage of it."

"It just feels . . . I don't know, wrong."

He's silent for a moment. "Would you say that I don't deserve my success because my father built Knight Food Distribution?"

"Of course not! You busted your ass to get everything. Not to mention the other four companies you own."

"How do you think I was able to do any of it?"

Oh, I see where this is going. "I think you should've been a lawyer."

He laughs. "I'm just saying I have what I have because of who I am and who I know. My grandfather, father, mother's side, all of them are the stepping stones I had to climb. I'm a boulder you get to climb and use to your advantage. And I'm more than willing to have you hang all over me."

I smile and roll my eyes. "You have to be home for that to happen."

"I know, baby. I'll be home tomorrow. Your brother is flying out tonight so we can leave early."

"Do you still have a meeting with your lawyer?"

He makes a face that I giggle at. "Unfortunately."

"Why don't we stay in the city this weekend? We don't have to go to Sugarloaf."

"Absolutely not," Crew says with authority. "It's a weekend with you, in those jeans, without Layla, and absolutely no one around for miles. We're going to Sugarloaf, and I'm going to see just how much noise we can make in the silence around us."

I blush and really look forward to that threat.

twenty-three

CARSON

"Is the barn finished?" I ask Ford as I'm at my desk, going over all the things I missed here while I was in Arizona.

"The barn?"

I huff. "The one I told you to get built by this weekend."

Ford sighs heavily, leaning back in the chair across from me. "You know, I've done some weird shit for you over the years, but this is by far one of the strangest things."

"It's so strange to get a barn put up on a farm? Really?"

"No, that's not, but that you wanted it done in a week."

It may not make sense to him, but I don't care. When we were in Sugarloaf last, I saw what my wife was dealing with. Everything was crumbling around her and when I spoke with the two caretakers, they expressed some worries as well.

Brynlee gives everything to those animals and I'm not going to have her dealing with rotting wood and a roof that looks like it's one windstorm away from being taken off.

"She will never be okay with it otherwise," I explain.

"Why the hell not?"

"Because Brynn doesn't want a penny of my money. She hates gifts, trips, or designer names. She's literally the last person in the

223

world that sees me as a paycheck. If she knew any of this was happening, she'd flip the fuck out."

"So you're doing it anyway?" Ford asks with a shake of his head.

I shrug. "Better to ask for forgiveness than permission."

He laughs. "Yeah, totally worked out that way for me with my first wife."

"I'm pretty sure your marriage failed because she ran off with your accountant, not because you were being good to her."

Ford lifts his hands. "Ehh, I'm not crying about it, but we're not talking about me. To answer your original question, yes, the barn should be done when you get there tomorrow. The freaking cost to have one built in a week was ridiculous, but I did as you asked."

"Good."

"You know, you were more ruthless in that meeting this morning than I've ever seen you," Ford notes.

To be fair, the guy was a fucking asshole who wanted to push me around on price. I offered him a more than generous contract that would benefit him and my tech company. "I'm not in the mood to play 'whose dick is bigger.' It's mine."

Ford huffs a laugh. "And so is your ego."

"Rich, coming from you."

He lifts both hands. "Hey, I'm not saying mine isn't. You're just usually much more at ease in the meetings. I like to describe you as a venomous snake. You're patient, quiet, and unwavering when you're ready to strike. Sort of like how you got your wife back."

Yeah, there was nothing patient about how that went down. "Other than the fact that I married her a week after I put a ring on it."

"Other than that."

Best hurried decision I've ever made. "Well, it worked out for me in the end."

"So things are good with Brynn?"

Things are more than I ever imagined they could be. While I

know she's still trying to keep herself from getting hurt, she's doing a pretty bad job of putting distance between us. She sends me texts during the day when something good happens. Each night we end up naked and then she sleeps plastered against me. Yesterday after we talked, she sent me a text that she was going to get Layla some things for the house in Sugarloaf so we didn't have to worry about Digger being spiteful and not packing her clothes.

Everything about her makes me happy. Every time I think of her, I smile.

Falling back in love with her is as easy and natural as opening your eyes in the morning. She's so damn easy to love.

"Things are really good."

"I have to say, I thought this whole marriage was just for the custody agreement. I didn't know you guys really reconnected that way, but it's good to see you so happy."

"I am happy. Even if we married for all the wrong reasons."

"What wrong reasons?"

I realize what I just said, and I laugh once. "Meaning I knew I had to lock her down before she realized I was a mistake."

He grins. "Please, marriage is the mistake, but I'm glad you're happy. You deserve it, my friend."

"I'll be really happy once I get my daughter full time."

Ford sighs heavily. "I wish I could help you there, brother, but I got nothing. I just hope that your lawyer and the fact that every day there's some new article about you and your incredibly happy marriage will do what you need."

I shake my head. "Every day?"

My best friend looks way too happy as he pulls his phone out. "Ginny loved this one."

I take the phone from him and look at the two of us when we got back from Paris. My arm is around her shoulder, our fingers laced together as we entered the door of the apartment. The article, if you can call it that, says how I whisked my new bride to Paris for forty-eight hours of shopping and romance before returning to run my empire. Some of the facts are disturbingly correct.

"Where do they find this shit out?"

He huffs. "Fuck if I know. You know you're ruining her for any other man if this doesn't work out?"

I don't have a single issue with that. "There won't be another man."

At least I fucking hope not.

I know it's only been a few weeks, but I can't picture a life without her again. She's maneuvered her way into every crevice of my life and I'm not complaining about it. Before Brynn, I didn't head home from the office until after midnight most days. Sometimes, I just slept here.

Now, I'm packing my shit up by six, if not earlier.

"I hope this is forever for you. The two of you have waited long enough to find each other again, no matter what brought you together."

I hope the same, but I need to convince her.

"Brynn?" I call her name repeatedly, but she's nowhere in the house. I checked her normal places, which are her makeshift office, the bedroom, bathroom, and the terrace. Where the hell is my wife?

"Oh, Mr. Knight, I'm so sorry, I didn't get the alert you arrived home," Celeste says as she reaches out for my jacket. "Here, let me hang that."

"Thank you, Celeste, do you happen to know where my wife is?"

She smiles warmly. "I do, but she asked me to let you be surprised when you find her."

I laugh softly. "Surprised?"

"She said, and I quote, 'He wanted this big ridiculous apartment, he can search all the bajillion . . .'" Celeste leans in. "I didn't want to correct her that there is no bajillion." I grin and nod. "'The bajillion square feet of this monster of a house.'"

"I see. Well, I have a feeling you know whatever the surprise is?"

"Yes, sir."

"And you're not going to tell me, are you?" I ask.

"Not a word of it." Celeste reaches her hand out, resting it on my forearm. "She's truly a wonderful woman and I couldn't be happier that you found each other."

"Thank you. All right, let me get to searching for her. Any hints?"

Celeste looks over to the side and shakes her head. "I think it'll be more fun this way. Cliff is going to drive me so I can run errands, and he will spend the night out in Westchester so I can visit my daughter."

"I see."

"I made breakfast though, so don't worry about that."

I nod. "I appreciate it."

"It's good to see you smile again, Crew."

I don't tell her how good it feels because sometimes I'm not sure I can explain it. The world believes the lie we've sold, but most days, it's just the truth. Each day I'm around Brynlee, I fall deeper, I want more of her. I want it all.

"Tell Marissa I said hello."

"I will. Have a good night."

Celeste walks off and I decide since my wife wants to play games, I'll do the same. I head upstairs to my—our—bedroom and change into a pair of sweatpants, leaving my shirt off, since I'm hoping we end up naked tonight anyway.

This week has been incredible. When I got home from Arizona, we settled into this domesticated world. I never had this before. When I was married to Digger, I didn't rush home to her. If anything, I took longer trips, worked insane hours, did anything I could to avoid coming home to the woman who wasn't Brynlee.

"Marco!" I call out, hoping she'll play along.

"Polo!"

I smile instantly. "Marco!"

I walk down the third level hallway, thinking maybe she's in the game room. Nope.

She's definitely downstairs, then.

I walk around the spiral staircase, thinking how absolutely ridiculous this penthouse is. "Brynn?" I call out again.

This time I'm met with silence. Okay, so she's definitely on this level. I first check the movie theater, then the library, the conservatory, and last the family room, but she's not here. What the hell?

I head to the back part of this level where the dining room is and then, I find her in the kitchen.

Her hair is piled up on top of her head, random pieces falling out around her face. She's wearing a pair of leggings and a crop top. She's so damn beautiful.

However, she's covered in flour or something.

"You're making quite a mess, wife."

She turns with a grin. "I made dinner."

I raise one brow. "You did?"

I look around, wondering what exactly we're eating since there are just various ingredients all over the island.

"I did."

I walk over to her, wrap my arm around her waist, and kiss the valley of her neck and shoulder. "I could think of something else I'd like to eat."

She giggles and hip checks me. "Later. I cooked us a dinner, and I was trying to make cookies, but . . . that's not going to happen."

Brynn wipes her hands and then turns to face me, her arms coming around my neck. "You look beautiful," I tell her.

"I look like I don't know how to bake."

"You're still beautiful."

She smiles. "Did you have a good day at work?"

"I did. I closed another deal, and we landed a very large security company account thanks to my wife and her connections with Catherine Cole."

Brynn shrugs, her lips in a sweet smile. "I'm amazing. You can thank me later."

"I definitely plan to."

Brynlee was on a call with Catherine Cole who is married to Jackson Cole. His security company is one of the largest in the world, handling huge defense contracts along with private security. My tech company is now going to be handling the integration of some software that will help their communications.

"First we're going to eat."

Again, I'd much rather toss her up on this counter and do exactly that, but there's a look in her eyes that tells me she knows where my thoughts are and that's not happening.

"Is there dinner somewhere in this kitchen?" I ask, looking around.

Brynn sighs and steps out of my embrace. "Yes, go in the dining room and I'll bring it out."

"You cooked it? Or did Celeste?"

She slaps my chest playfully. "Do you forget that I have lived on my own for years? I babysat my niece for Asher all the time. Jett and Grady lived with me, and we ate during all that time. Yes, I know how to cook."

"All right, all right. I'm sorry. The most I can do is a bowl of cereal."

Brynn shakes her head. "Go in there before I put laxatives in your dinner."

I do as she says and sit, wanting to avoid whatever her wrath might be. A few seconds later she comes out with two plates. "Seriously, your whole plate warmer is a dream."

"Good to know."

"This is my mama's roast beef. It's my absolute favorite meal in the world. Besides Italian."

It looks amazing. On the plate are also potatoes and carrots. "Bee, this is incredible."

She shrugs off the compliment. "This is what I . . ."

I wait, but she keeps her eyes down. "You what?"

After a few seconds, she finally meets my gaze, her brown eyes filled with so many emotions that I can't place them quick enough. "I imagined being married would be like. We'd both come home from work, we'd talk, eat dinner, and fall asleep together."

"We do that," I remind her.

"I know, but we have Celeste, who does all the housework."

I grin, putting my fork down. "I'm pretty sure most wives would love having a housekeeper."

"Yes," she agrees. "I'm definitely not complaining. You have no idea how much I'll miss this when this is . . . well, anyway. I just wanted to have tonight be just us in domestic bliss."

I like that word. I like the idea of this being something we could share. I love having this shell of a penthouse becoming a warm home.

"Are you happy, Bee?"

She nods quickly. "Yes. I know we both have an end game here, but this has been amazing. To be with you, even if it's only for a short while, I've been happy. You've made me happy."

If she only knew I plan to make her fall so deeply in love with me that there won't be an end to this story.

"I want you to be happy." *I want you to be mine.*

"And I want the same for you."

Knowing that she'll start to become uncomfortable, and not wanting to ruin our date night, I dive back into the food. The two of us eat, our eyes finding each other a few times and after the last not-so-subtle connection, I speak again.

"So, what do I have to do to make this a regular thing?"

"What?"

"You cook for me, be my wife, and all that. I mean, we already have the fantastic sex down, maybe we try some more of this . . . domesticated bliss you speak of."

Brynn grins. "You think you deserve my wifely duties, do you?"

"I did take you to Paris, get you a driver, drop your name a few times to some friends who have now hired your PR company," I remind her playfully.

"Let's not forget the ridiculous bag that was a down payment on a normal person's house!"

"Sure, keep adding more on my list. Honestly, Bee, I'm starting to think that maybe you got the better end of the stick."

She laughs softly, leaning back with her arms crossed. "You do, huh?"

"If we're strictly going off the list."

"Well," she says, putting her fork down. Brynlee rises and moves to me. "I wouldn't want you to get the short end of any stick."

I push back a little from the table. "Love, I didn't mean it."

Brynlee's eyes twinkle. "I think you did."

"Come here." I lean back in my chair and she straddles me.

"Like this?"

"Exactly like this." I brush her red hair back and hold onto her jaw. "I didn't mean any of it. You and me, here or in Sugarloaf, is everything to me. I never had a reason to come home before. So, I don't need dinner or gifts or anything like that. I need you."

She pulls her lower lip between her teeth and then leans close. "Then have me you shall."

Then we clean the table a different way, one I'm all too happy to do nightly.

"Oh, shit," Brynn says with a deep sigh as we enter the main street of town.

"What's wrong?"

"It's Sugarloaf Day."

"Sugarloaf Day?" I ask in confusion.

Brynn turns in the seat to face me. "It's when the town celebrates the fact that we're the best town ever. This whole weekend will turn into sort of a . . . celebration, and it's a lot and now I'm worried because we're here."

"Why is that a bad thing?"

She smiles widely. "Well, with the trip to Paris, the stuff with Layla, and the surgery, I kind of forgot it was this weekend."

"Well, it's a good thing we're here then."

Her lips purse. "I don't know that you'll think it's good, but it is for me, because this year I'm the queen. Which means I have to ride on the float."

I burst out laughing. "I can't wait to see this."

If she could glare, I think this is what it would look like. "You will not laugh at me."

"I promise I won't, at least not when you can see it. Tell me, what does being the Sugarloaf Queen look like?"

"It's purely ornamental. If I'm being honest, my brothers have it worse than I do. Asher has to work and basically babysit the teenage boys who always try something stupid. Rowan has to run the petting cow area, which he absolutely hates. Then, Grady judges the chili cookoff and last time, he ended up needing an EpiPen because the Arrowoods put peanut butter or something in their entry. He swore he wasn't doing it again, but Addison demanded they have another go. Anyway, my part is just riding on the float holding sugar and a bread loaf."

I really want to hear more about Grady and the chili, but I can't stop picturing Brynn and what she's supposed to hold in her hands. "I'm sorry, holding what?"

"Think of it like royalty having an orb, which is the sugar and then scepter, which is the loaf."

"Brynn . . ." I can't even speak because this is beyond my imagination.

"I know, it's silly, but it's tomorrow and I think you should ride next to me."

My eyes widen. "No."

"Crew!" She leans in, her hands on my arm. "Please! It'll make the town love you. It's so special to them and just think of how much fun it'll be."

Fun is not exactly the word I was thinking of. "Bee, there's no way I can run the risk of that being a photo."

"What? You riding on a float with your wife in a small

232

town? How would that make you look bad? If anything, it would make you look like a doting husband who is completely smitten. Honestly, it can only help show what a great man you are."

I really doubt that. It's going to make me look like a fool, but at the same time, I don't know that I'm going to be able to say no to this woman. "I'm sure the judge will really see it that way."

Brynn smiles and leans close. "Please."

"I'm going to need more convincing."

Her lips are right up against my ear now and she whispers. "I'll work on that tonight."

"Yes, you sure will."

She giggles and then sits back as we head down the road to her family farm. We pass the sign proclaiming Sugarloaf Day and then take the fork over to Brynn's house. I have to lock my muscles so I don't give away my nerves about the barn.

I replay my conversation with Ford about her being upset, and I really hope she won't be. I know she doesn't want me to spend money on her, but it's not about that for me, it's about her being taken care of.

I want things to be easier for her and I have more than enough money to last me six lifetimes.

Her gasp is loud, and her hand grips my arm. "Crew, please tell me you didn't do this. No, don't tell me. I know you did. No one else would've done this in a week!"

"Before you get pissed at me, let's remember you want me to ride on the float with you tomorrow."

"I'm not sure if I want to kiss you or smack you."

"How about we go see it before you decide?"

Buying some time isn't a bad idea. She opens her door before Cliff can get there and I follow. Brynn is standing at the start of the path to her new barn, not moving. "If you can bring the bags in, then you're free to head to the hotel," I tell Cliff.

"Of course. Good luck with her," he says with a laugh.

Yeah, I'm going to need it.

I walk over to where she's standing, staying quiet. Her hand touches mine and she grabs it. When I look to her face, there are tears silently streaming.

Immediately I move, taking her face in my hands. "No tears, Bee."

She looks up at me, her lip trembling. "No one has ever done things like this."

"I'm not sure many people get a barn in a week."

Her laugh is short and she wraps her fingers around my wrist. "I mean everything, Crew. This is just one more in a long line of things you've done for me in a very short amount of time. You really don't have to do any of this. I'll never be able to give you any of this back."

"What makes you think I'm at all unhappy with what you give me?" I ask, brushing away a tear. "What makes you think you haven't done more for me than I can ever do? What makes you think I do anything because I have to? I want to, Brynn. I want to see your face light up. I want your worries to melt away and for me to be the man who does that for you."

I see her fighting my words, like she always does, thinking she's undeserving. I will never forgive myself for being one more man in her life who did that. The lack of self-confidence, the belief that she's not worth fighting for—I partially put that there. I need to erase it and make her see that she's worth everything.

"You're making it very hard to keep my heart guarded."

I lean in, just a breath from her mouth. "Good. I don't want you guarded, not with me."

Then I kiss her, hoping she feels just how much she owns me.

twenty-four
BRYNLEE

"You both were just so lovely on the float," Mrs. Symonds says as she stops us as we make our way through the festival.

"Thank you." I wrap my hands around Crew's arm and smile. "Carson was so happy to be a part of it."

Which is a big fat lie. It took sex last night and this morning before he was convinced. Although, I'm starting to wonder if that was the case, or if he'd already resigned himself to doing it when I asked in the car.

Either way—I win.

"And how is Layla?" she asks.

"She's good, very excited to come back to Sugarloaf next weekend."

Mrs. Symonds's smile grows. "Oh, I bet. The animals, fresh air, stars in the sky are a big change from that crowded city you've taken our Brynlee to."

"They sure are," he agrees. "I'm just glad we get to come here every weekend."

"Us too." She pats his arm. "It's not every day we get a celebrity in Sugarloaf." Seeming to realize what she's said, she lets out a laugh. "What am I saying, this tiny town has one. Although it's been a few months since Jacob has been around."

"We also have Sean and Austin," I remind her. The Arrowood family aren't treated like celebrities, but they are.

"Oh, that Austin is just out of control." She huffs. "He's going to need to hire you soon enough. The drinking, partying, and Lord only knows what else he's into."

This is going to be a very long conversation if I don't cut it off. I'm already aware of what's going on with Austin and I hate it. We were friends as kids, and we even went to prom together.

I hate seeing him struggling so much and måybe it would be a good idea to reach out and see if I can help.

"Thank you for stopping us, but we need to help Charlotte at Rosemary and Vine."

"Of course. We'll see you next week."

Crew and I head down the street, and I point out vendors along the white tent tops where all the local merchants are. We're stopped at least four more times so people can tell us how great the parade was, how much they love the new barn, and how happy they are that we're spending time in Sugarloaf.

I'm pretty sure Crew's ready to pack a bag and head home, but he smiles through it and is the consummate gentleman.

"Brynn!" I turn to see Melinda Temple waving frantically.

Ugh. I like her just fine, but she is one of those people who is only friends with those who can elevate her. I think I can count on one hand how many times we've spoken since high school.

"Melinda, hey. Long time no talk."

She smiles and nods. "It has been. So long. It's why I was telling Phoebe the other day when I came by for lunch that I was hoping you were around." Her eyes move to Crew. "Hi, I'm Melinda, a really good friend of Brynn's."

I look up at him and try hard not to laugh. He sees my face and winks at me.

She goes on. "Nice to meet you, Carson. I've heard such great things about you, and I just had to meet you."

238

Crew wraps his arm around me, pulling me to him. "Glad we were able to meet as well."

Melinda sighs. "Well, now that we're friends, we'll have to have dinner."

I fight back the urge to gag. "I'm not sure we'll have time. Every weekend we're really just trying to spend quality time together."

She looks at Crew and then me. "I'm sure you have one night to spare for an old friend."

I'm not sure who she's thinking of, because it's not us. We were never friends, since I'm two years older than her and we didn't run in the same circles. Once I graduated, I went to college and then law school.

Crew steps in. "I wish we could, but I'm selfish when it comes to time with my wife."

"Oh, of course. Brynn is great."

"She's the best," he corrects her.

I look up at him, my eyes swimming with affection. He has no idea how much I don't want to have dinner with her.

"We'll see if he feels that way in a few months," I try to joke. "It was great running into you. Take care, Melinda."

Crew expertly guides me away. "I take it we don't like Melinda?"

I shudder. "She's a strange one. Married some guy who was rich, took what she could and left. Since then, she's looking for a new meal ticket."

"Well, you don't have any reason to be jealous."

I scoff. "Jealous?"

"I'm just assuring you that my ticket has been punched."

"I'm going to punch you," I warn with a laugh.

Crew leans close to my ear. "You're the only thing I want to eat for dinner."

My eyes widen and heat floods my face. "Crew!"

"What?" he asks, all innocence.

"You can't say that as we're walking the streets." Seriously, I have known these people my whole life. If they heard that, I'd never be able to show my face again.

On the other hand—it was hot.

"Speaking of eating, do you want something here?"

"The pork belly street tacos are the best. We have to have them."

"Done," he says, making his way over.

Crew grabs us four tacos and we head over to the park where my nieces and nephew are.

Olivia spots us, waves, and rushes to me, wrapping her arms around my waist before stepping back. *"I missed you."* She signs.

"I missed you more. Did you see the parade?"

Olivia raises her brows. *"Yes. I will never do that, but you looked pretty. Even if it was lame."* She looks to Crew and waves.

He raises his hand, and I gasp when he starts to sign. *"Hi, Olivia."*

Olivia looks to me and then back to Crew. *"Did you have fun on the float with Aunt Brynn?"*

Crew clears his throat. "I think she asked me if I did something fun?"

I smile. "She asked if you had fun on the float with me."

He turns to Olivia and says what he is signing—kind of. *"No, but don't tell Brynn. Are you having fun today?"*

I feel like my heart might explode from my chest. He's learning sign language. Well, some of it. He didn't exactly sign what he said aloud, but it was close, and my niece looks as though she just fell in love with him a little.

"Yes, I am watching Jett and Elodie while Uncle Grady is trying to stop his tongue from being on fire."

I translate because there's no way he's going to get half of that. "Thank you. I lost her after watching," Crew admits.

I look over Olivia's shoulder and Jett is hanging upside down on the monkey bars. Oh boy. I look to Liv. *"You may want to get back to your babysitting."*

She turns quickly and runs toward Jett, her hands up trying to stop him before he does something very much like his father would and hurts himself.

Crew rests his hand on my lower back and I look up at him. "You're learning sign language?"

"I'm trying. I have someone come once a day for about an hour. I'm clearly not all that good, but I'll get there."

I face him, wrapping my arms around his waist. "Why?"

"Why do you think?"

I think I know. I mean, I feel like I know. He's shown me why. "Because Olivia is special to me?"

"Yes, and because what matters to you matters to me. It's why I did the barn, the float, the trip to Paris, Brynn. All of it is for you."

God, he's going to make me cry. My heart is pounding as my chest tightens. "I think tonight, I'm going to have to thank you for a very long time because my appreciation is going to take a while to show."

He grins. "I'm pretty sure I could do something else if you need more reasons."

I laugh. "I bet you could."

"Yes, fuck!" He screams as I take him deeper in my throat. His fingers are laced through my hair as he pumps his hips. "Don't touch yourself, Brynn. Keep your hands on my thighs."

I do as he says, loving when he's in control. I don't have to think or worry. It's a relief to let myself go. He's always so attentive to me that I trust no matter what we do is going to be good for both of us.

My palms are where he wants them, and he groans as he moves faster. After a minute he slows and glances down at me. "God, seeing you like this, on your knees for me, makes me feel like a king." He pulls out of my mouth and I gasp. "Lie on the bed, baby, I want to worship you now."

CORINNE MICHAELS

I lie on my back and Crew hovers above me. He stays like that, staring down at me, and I push my hand through his hair. "What's wrong?"

He shakes his head. "Nothing. I want to make love to you, Brynlee. Will you let me?"

There is a shift between us. Something that I can't explain, but can feel. His question hangs between us like fruit on a vine, ready to be picked. I think about what it means, what I'm agreeing to, and as much as I want to say no, to put distance between us, it's a lie.

My eyes meet his and I nod. "Yes, I want that."

His lids lower and he rests his forehead to mine. I feel him push into me slowly. When he's fully seated, his lips move to mine and we breathe each other in.

Neither of us speaks, we allow our bodies to talk for us. Every emotion is expressed through touch from love to fear as we move together. It was so easy to fall back here with him.

So easy to believe that I could keep my heart, which has never been able to listen to my head, in line this time. Crew stole my heart years ago, and I never was the same after. A piece of it always belonged to him, and instead of just letting him keep that piece, he put it back and stole the whole damn thing again.

We make love, because really there is nothing else to call it. His eyes find mine and stay there as tears trickle down my cheeks.

It's so good.

So much.

So damn hard to think and breathe because I won't survive this man if he leaves again.

I know he won't leave in the middle of the night, but after the surgery and the custody hearing, then what?

Where do we go? How do I go on with life knowing that I have felt this way?

He kisses my tears and shifts his hips, driving deeper.

"Crew," I breathe his name.

"I'm right here. Right here with you."

My fingertips dig into his back as my orgasm comes on so fast

242

I couldn't stop it if I tried. I cry out and he thrusts harder and faster. A few moments later, he yells out my name and collapses, panting against my shoulder.

I wait for him to move, but he doesn't, and I realize he's fallen asleep, inside of me in more ways than one.

"You're not alone, Bee. I'm right here," Crew reassures me as we're standing outside of Grady's house.

All my brothers and their families are here. They think this is just a run-of-the-mill barbecue, but it's so that I can tell them about my surgery in two weeks.

This is going to be the worst day of my life.

Well, that's a lie, but it'll be up there.

I nod, take his hand, and walk around the back.

"Brynn! Crew!" Phoebe calls out first and comes to give us each a hug. "You looked so regal on that float. I told Asher that next year, he'll have to dress in formal wear."

Asher scoffs. "Not happening, sweetheart!" He raises his tongs from the grill and we both wave back. "Don't listen to a word she says."

"My money is on your soon-to-be wife. You have what? Five days left?"

Asher looks to Phoebe and there's a hesitation there. "About that . . ."

Phoebe sighs heavily. "I guess we should tell them?"

My brother nods and turns to me. "The wedding is off."

"What?" I screech and move to them. "Why? What did you do?"

He chuckles and turns to her. "Told you it would be my fault."

Phoebe grins. "We got married a week ago."

Shock causes my body to lock and it takes me a second to recover. "You what?"

"We got married. We hopped on a plane last weekend, went

to Vegas, got married and came home the next day. We didn't want to tell you because you've been so busy and I didn't think that was a phone call kind of news. We told Rowan and Grady when we got back."

My gaze moves to Phoebe. "But you guys wanted a wedding."

She shakes her head. "I never did. Honestly, after your wedding, Asher and I were like, this is so not us. We canceled everything the night we got back and then . . . ran off. It was truly perfect."

I look to my brother. "Wow."

He chuckles. "We'll have a party after Phoebe graduates and we'll do it right then. For now, she's my wife and that's all I cared about."

I move to him, giving him a hug. "Congratulations."

"Thanks. She's everything I've ever wanted and we're both happy."

Phoebe tilts her head to the side. "Aww, my marshmallow's all burned on the outside but gooey in the middle. I love you too. I couldn't imagine hitching my wagon to anyone else."

I love that they're so in love. Phoebe wanted to wait until she had the baby and was settled in school. She loves Penn State, so much more than she ever thought she would. It has allowed her to be close to home and also still work with the app company that is working on making an ASL interpretation program for the phone. It's been really interesting so far and would help the Deaf and Hard of Hearing community so much. To be able to open their phones and have the camera be able to communicate with those who can't sign would change lives.

I give her a big hug. "I'm glad to finally call you my sister."

She kisses my cheek. "Imagine all the fun we'll have driving him crazy."

My brother groans and goes back to burning the burgers.

I lean into Crew. "Eat the meat with caution."

"Excuse me?"

"I should've warned you, Grady and Asher are the worst at grilling, and each thinks they're better. For whatever reason,

Asher is in charge today and I'm going to assume it's because he lost a bet, which means we all lose. Stick to the salads."

He grins. "Thanks for the warning."

We say hi to everyone else and I head inside to help Addison with all the sides as Charlotte and Phoebe head outside to try to supervise the grill. "So, how's married life?" she asks bumping my hip.

"It's good. We're happy."

Addison is the sweetest and most adult-like of my brother's partners. She's a little older, has been through a lot, and I can't help but be comfortable around her.

"You really look it. I don't know that I've ever seen you smile so much."

I focus on arranging the tomatoes on the platter, knowing that soon, I won't be smiling, and neither will anyone else in this house. "Thanks."

"Brynn?" Her voice is soft and full of concern.

"Yeah?"

"What's wrong?"

"Nothing. I just . . . I have a lot going on and my head is kind of a mess."

"Are you upset about Asher and Phoebe?" she asks.

I shake my head. "No, not at all. I'm happy if they're happy."

"Is it marriage things?" Addison asks and then looks down at what she is doing.

"No, nothing to do with Crew. I mean, we're obviously stressed with the Layla stuff, but nothing between the two of us," I lie. Then I remember the circumstances of her and Grady's relationship. "Addison?"

"Yes?"

"When you and Grady had your . . . arrangement, how did you handle it when your feelings became real?"

She places the knife down and wipes her hand with the towel. "I didn't handle it well. I made myself believe that it was going to end, instead of seeing that Grady never treated me like that was the case. We convinced ourselves that it had to be the end because that's what we agreed upon. It was stupid, and while we didn't handle it exactly how we should've, I'm not sure anyone does."

"What do you mean?" I ask, grabbing a carrot.

"We're human. We're flawed and stupid and we listen to the voices in our heads that have told us we aren't good enough our whole lives. We let fear guide us because it's so much easier to believe the bad things than the possibilities of good. I believed I'd never love again because I'd lost the love of my life, only to learn you can have two. I was so afraid people would judge me for loving him and from the outside, it's so easy to be like, 'you should do this.' When you're in it, you can't. You know?"

I reach out and take her hand. "Thank you."

"For rambling?"

"For being a part of this family."

She squeezes my hand. "The pleasure is all mine. I was an only child and now I have a very large family and one that has so much love it's impossible to absorb it all. Now, are you going to tell me why you're pale and seem nervous?"

Here I thought I was doing a good job keeping it together. Clearly not.

"I have to tell everyone something today, before Crew and I head back to New York. It's not going to go over well."

Her eyes widen. "Considering you just asked about me and Grady, I'm going to pray to God it's not about Crew."

I shake my head. No, that lie we'll be holding onto. "It's about me. I've been keeping something personal."

"Brynn, I'm not going to pry, but if you need me . . ."

"It's about my father."

A deep sigh of relief falls from her lips. "Oh, that we can handle."

I raise one brow. "Are you sure about that? The boys hate him."

"With good reason," she reminds me. "However, they also love you."

"This might tip the scales."

She laughs once. "Brynlee, you walk on water with those boys. There's nothing in the world you could tell them that will change that."

"I hope that's true. Do you think we could go out now? Before I lose my courage like I have the last year."

"Year?" Addison asks, her voice cracking.

"Come on, let's go tell them so we can watch the explosion together."

We head outside, her words circling around my head when I see Crew playing with Jett and Elodie. They're running around the playhouse Grady built for them as Crew tries to catch them.

Jett leaps in front of Elodie and roars, and Crew reacts by falling on the floor, clutching his chest.

I smile and wait for him to rise, but both kids pounce on him. Addison elbows me. "Kids are a real test of character. They're so pure and innocent that when they like an adult, I always keep that in the back of my mind. Seems like they love their new uncle."

"He's easy to love," I say almost absently because it's true. Every day I fall harder. Every day I try to put a brick up only to have him knock it down plus five more. There's really no chance of stopping it. If this ends, then hopefully my brothers, if they're still talking to me, will come sweep up the pieces left of me and glue me back together.

Addison calls the kids over and Crew stands, brushing the grass off his jeans and then running his fingers through his hair. His eyes find mine and I nod, hoping he understands it means I'm going to tell my brothers now.

He walks to me, taking my hand in his when he's at my side. "No fear, Bee."

Right.

"Ash, Grady, Rowan, I need to tell you something," I say, keeping my voice steady.

"She's pregnant already?" Rowan asks, glancing at Crew.

"I'm not pregnant."

"I knew that's why she wanted to get married in a week," he says to Grady. "You owe me fifty bucks."

I roll my eyes. "I'm not pregnant! Idiots." Asher is who I turn to, knowing it's going to be him I need on my side. "We talked about this a long time ago. Before you and Phoebe."

He scratches the side of his head. "We did? You hadn't even seen him yet. How the hell were you pregnant?"

If I kill them, I'm pretty sure a judge would let me off. "For the love of God, I am not pregnant!"

"Okay, if you say so."

Crew fights back a laugh and I glare at him. "Not helping."

"She's not pregnant," Crew tells them all.

I let out a heavy sigh and return my gaze to my brothers, who are now focused on me.

Okay, here it goes. I have to say the words and pray that they understand.

"About two years ago, Howie came to me as part of his twelve steps. He asked for forgiveness and offered some explanations, which I'm sure none of you are interested in. I'm well aware that my father is not your favorite person."

"That's a fucking understatement," Rowan says with a huff. "The only thing that man ever did for this family was sign his rights over to Asher when Mom died."

Rowan, my protective and always-ready-to-fight-anyone for me brother. "It's the one thing I'm grateful for. I've been lucky enough to have been a Whitlock in every sense of the word." I look to Asher. "You took me in and gave me your last name when Mom died. There's nothing in this world I wouldn't do for you. I love you all more than anything. Which is why I am literally sick to have to tell you this."

Rowan's body is tense, and he's going to take this the worst. I hate it. I hate that I'm going to hurt my brother. He's the one who saved me. Who came in, took Mom and me out, and hit Howie after we were both injured.

So much about that night scarred him.

"Brynn?" Asher asks, drawing my attention back to him.

My jaw trembles and fear takes hold, but Crew squeezes my hand tightly and I soldier on. "Howie came to me in the middle stages of liver failure."

"No." Asher crosses his arms over his chest. "I know where this is going and absolutely not, Brynlee."

I meet his gaze, knowing that this will hurt him, but also knowing I won't walk away from Howie when he needs me. "In two weeks, I'm going to donate part of my liver to him. We've gone through all the tests, and I'm a match."

Rowan curses, throwing his hands up. "Of course he wants to take more from you!"

"He didn't ask for this, Rowan. He doesn't even want me to do it, but I have to."

"You don't have to! You don't have to put yourself at risk for him. The man who broke your heart and never even checked in on you. Fuck him."

Asher turns to Rowan, putting his hand on his chest. "Stop."

A tear falls down my cheek as the weight of this secret is lifted. Crew moves himself forward a little, hand still in mine. "I know you're upset, but you will not yell at my wife and make her cry."

I step closer so I'm not behind him at all. "It's fine, Crew. He won't do anything more than this."

His blue eyes meet mine. "That's all he gets."

I return my gaze to them as Charlotte moves to be beside her husband, wrapping her hands around his arm as he fights to control his breathing. "So you're doing it no matter what?"

I nod. "He needs this, Rowan. I need to do this."

Asher walks to me. "You've been keeping this from us, why?"

"Because I knew this would hurt you guys, and the last thing I want is that."

"It's you that we're worried about," Asher tries to assure me.

The emotions I've kept buried since all this started come forward. I have been so afraid of telling them. So worried that my brothers wouldn't be able to see past the hatred they have, and I've hated myself for that.

They're not cruel. They're wonderful and loving and supportive.

All they've ever wanted is for me to be happy. They've given so much, and I knew, down in the depths of my soul, this would ultimately cause them pain.

I release Crew's hand and move to Asher. "I didn't want to disappoint you."

He shakes his head. "Brynlee, you've never disappointed us. While I hold very . . . unkind thoughts toward Howie, I wouldn't expect you to do anything other than give him whatever he needs. You're not like us, a bunch of hardened assholes."

"You think you're assholes, but you're not."

Charlotte snorts. "I think I can attest to different here."

Rowan scoffs, his eyes finally meeting mine.

"I know I'm asking a lot, but I would really love it if my brothers were at the hospital during the surgery with Crew. I'd like to see the people I love most when I wake up."

I look to Asher first who nods once. "I'll be there, holding your hand, like I always have."

My lips tremble and I look over at the other two. Grady, who is a lot like me in many ways, winks. "Of course. I may not understand your desire to be a good human *all* the damn time, but I wouldn't let you think I don't love you for it. I'll be there, just like you would be if it was any of us."

Rowan doesn't speak or move. Charlotte nudges him and he glances at her. The two of them share a silent conversation before she tilts her head. He looks back down at the ground and sighs. "I won't be there for him."

"Rowan," Asher says his name with a bite to it.

He looks up. "Don't pretend that you don't feel the same way I do. I get why Brynn is doing it. I get that she's literally a freaking saint. But don't ask me to go there and pretend I care about his outcome. Once again, Howie asks for something that will hurt someone else. What about Brynn, huh? What about her life?" Rowan asks, anger building with each question. "What about the fact that she just got married, is starting a fucking company, and is a new stepmom? What about her life? Why does she have to be the one to hurt too?" Then Rowan looks at Crew. "Tell me you're okay with this."

My husband shifts. "I'm not happy that her life will be on the line. I'd prefer to give him my liver than put her through any pain, but you let me know how you can control Charlotte and I'll try it on my wife."

Charlotte smiles at me and winks.

I stand before my brother. Under all the anger is fear, and it's so heavy in his eyes. "He didn't ask me, Rowan," I say steadily. "He didn't want me to even get tested."

My brother clenches his fists. "Finally he wasn't a selfish bastard."

"I know you hate him. I'm still angry for the things he's done. I'm not doing this just for him, a part of it is for me too."

"What the hell do you have to atone for?" he asks.

"It's not that," I assure him. "I just can't let someone die knowing I could help. I couldn't live with myself, Row. Please understand, I'd do it for anyone."

He laughs once. "Why are you such a damn good person?"

"Because I had the three best brothers, who allowed me to see the good in people."

At that he scoffs. "Nice try, Brynn. You knew that no matter what, the three of us would be there, that's not even a question. I'll be at the hospital, ensuring that no bright lights get anywhere near you, and if I do see one, don't get mad if I send it Howie's way."

I roll my eyes and smile. "I love you, you know that?"

"I wish you didn't wait until now to tell us."

"It would've given you more time to try to talk me out of it."

He nods. "Damn fucking straight." Then he looks to Crew. "You should've told us before today."

I feel Crew's hand snake up my back, resting on my shoulder. "It was her decision to tell you when she could."

"And you think this is a good idea?" Rowan asks him.

"No. Not even a little, but it's her decision."

I glance up at him, confused because he's never even expressed any feelings about it. He knew it was part of why I married him. I needed the insurance as a backup. Every time I've come home from an appointment, he's seemed supportive.

"Since when are you not on board?"

"Since the day you told me about it. I don't think he deserves it after the hell he put you through, but like everyone has said, you aren't us. You aren't petty and vengeful. It's why every person here loves you."

Does that include him?

He leans in and kisses me softly. "It's why every person here will be at the hospital as well."

I look around at my family and burst out sobbing. Crew pulls me to his chest, and I soak his shirt, feeling so loved and so damn lucky.

twenty-five
BRYNLEE

This last week has been a whirlwind. We had Layla for the weekend, took her out to Sugarloaf and she had the best time. Layla loved getting to play with Elodie and Jett, and I loved watching Grady chase them, as the three of them were menaces.

Yesterday, I had my final bloodwork drawn and a meeting with the surgical team to make sure everything is good to go.

Neither of us have talked much about the weekend in Sugarloaf where things shifted. I'm not really sure what to say. Why did we make love? Why did he call it that? Why does he keep doing things to show he loves me, but he hasn't said it since that slip in Paris? Was it a slip?

You know, real conversation starters—things every girl is dying to ask.

So I keep my mouth shut.

He's in Colorado now, but hopefully he'll be home sometime tomorrow afternoon. So I'm doing as much work as I can because he wants to spend the day tomorrow together before my surgery.

Thea and I hired Aarabelle Dempsey, a family friend of Catherine's, as a new publicist. She's going to work with Thea while I'm recovering. She was in California with Catherine the last year, working with celebrities, and wanted to move back to the East Coast where her parents live.

"So you've never really done corporate PR?" Thea asks.

"No, but Catherine did for years and when I went to her about being closer to home, she started to train me a bit on the other side of public relations."

Aarabelle and I are about the same age, she might be a year or two younger. She's smart, pretty, and eager to dive in.

Thea smiles. "All of it sounds great, Aarabelle. We definitely need the help right away, so the fact that you're willing to move to New York is imperative."

She nods. "Absolutely. I already have an apartment lease ready to sign. I just need the job first."

I glance at Thea and she nods. "Welcome aboard," I say to her.

"This is great. I also have a lot of contacts here thanks to my parents. I already asked for a few names that I can reach out to see if we can onboard as well," Aarabelle informs us.

"That's great," I say quickly.

"Absolutely," Thea agrees. "We'd love it if you have time this week to sit with both of us to go over some stuff. Next Tuesday is Brynn's surgery so we're trying to get everything done before then."

"Of course. Also, please call me Aara, everyone does."

We spend another hour with Aarabelle, signing paperwork, and then Thea calls Catherine to tell her the good news.

I'm working on a proposal I want to send today in the hopes they'll accept, and we can sign them on as well. The more people we get before Tuesday, the easier it'll be to have them meet Aarabelle prior.

My phone rings and it's Crew.

"Hey."

"Brynn, are you home?" he asks with a panic in his voice.

"I'm at the coffee shop right next door, what's wrong?"

"I just got a call from the police, they need me to come get Layla, she's . . . Jacqueline was drunk driving and hit a fucking cop car, so they're taking her to the hospital to be checked out, but I'm hours away. The nanny is visiting family. I can't . . . they said they'll have to put her in foster care until a family member can get there."

I'm already standing, gathering my stuff. "I'll go. Where is she?"

He tells me the hospital they're taking her to and I'm out the door. "I'll be there in a few minutes. Listen, call your lawyer right now. I need her to meet me there so we can get Layla released to me. I'll keep her safe until you get home."

I head outside and climb in the car with Cliff, instructing him to head to the hospital.

"That's not even . . . I know you will. I know you'd do anything for that kid. Fuck, Bee. I just . . . she was fucking drinking with my daughter in the car!"

"I know," I say, my heart breaking. "She's okay, though?"

"As far as I know. The cop said it was a precaution to have her taken to the hospital. He said there weren't any apparent injuries to either of them and Layla was in her car seat. I guess I can thank God for that small miracle."

"I'll be there in ten minutes. I'll stay with her, and I should be able to take her home to our place if she's released to me as a family member. I'll call the lawyer about getting custody signed over temporarily in light of the drunk driving charge. We'll do what we can. Just get home safe and don't do anything stupid. I'm here and I will protect Layla."

He lets out a half laugh. "I think I already did that when I married her."

"If you didn't, you wouldn't have Layla."

"Or you," he says softly. "Grady is working on getting the flight moved up so we can leave in the next hour. I'm going to push the meeting to finish now, even though it may be a mistake."

"Crew, take a breath, I won't let anything happen to Layla. I promise."

"Brynlee . . ."

"Go. Do what you have to and get back home."

"All right. Please call me when you get there," he begs.

"As soon as I'm with her, we'll call. I'm going to call your sister too, see if she can come to the house. While I love Layla and I know she likes me, it might be good for her to have her auntie around. I know it's what Olivia would want."

He sighs. "Thank you, baby."

"I'll keep you updated."

We hang up and my leg is bouncing as we make our way around the city to the hospital. I can't believe Jacqueline would do this so close to the court case. Stupid in every possible way, but if anything happened to that little girl, I would be devastated.

As soon as Cliff stops, I'm running out of the door to head into the hospital.

I give Layla's name, and thank God I now have her last name so they don't question me being there.

When I get to her floor, there is a police officer outside of her door, I take a deep breath and walk over to him.

"Hello, Officer. I'm Brynlee Knight and I'm here for Layla Knight. I'm family."

He nods and lets me pass.

When I open the door, my heart falls to the floor. Layla is lying in the bed, her eyes closed, and she's gripping the blankets. She looks like she fell asleep terrified. I make my way to the side of the bed, placing my stuff down in the chair, and I gently push her hair back.

Her eyes open, she nearly jumps out of the bed, but I quickly try to soothe her. "It's just me, sweetheart."

"Rin," she says my name with her chin wobbling. "I was so scared."

I sit on the bed, pulling her in my arms. "Oh, honey, I'm here. Don't be scared. I'm here."

"I want my daddy."

"I know, and he'll be here as soon as he can. He's getting on a plane and coming right here," I promise her.

She holds on to me tight and I rub her back, hoping she has a little solace knowing I'm here.

"My mommy was crying and I'm scared." She cries harder and

I just hold her. There's nothing else I can do, just be here and not let her be alone. Kimberly is a few hours away on a farm tour and won't be back until tonight.

I have never been more grateful that I was here, because the idea of her being alone breaks my heart.

I pull back after she starts to settle down a little. "How about we call your daddy now so he can see you're okay?"

"Okay."

I send him a text that I'm going to call him now and not to ask anything about the accident. We need her to give an account when we can record it.

Then I call and hand the phone to Layla.

Her eyes brighten as soon as Crew's face is on the screen. "Hi, Ladybug. Are you okay?"

"I'm at the hospital."

"I know. Does anything hurt?"

She shakes her head. "I want to go home."

"You will as soon as the doctors say you can."

Layla's lower lip juts out. "Daddy, I want you."

"I'm getting on the plane right now and I'll be home in a few hours, but Brynn is there, and she'll give you all the hugs you want."

She looks at me and I smile. "As many as you want."

"And you'll be here soon?"

Crew is already buckling up in the seat on the plane. "In three hours, baby. I'll be home just in time to tuck you in. Love you, Ladybug."

She leans her head against my shoulder. "I love you, Daddy."

He blows her a kiss and I smile at him. "We'll see you soon."

Layla and I lie in her bed, waiting for the doctor and watching television. I never thought I would be so grateful that Grady and Jett lived with me for so long, since I can talk to her about the characters on the show.

I'm pretty cool to her since I know all the songs too.

There's a knock on the door and we turn to see Crew's lawyer,

Ms. Banks, enter. She smiles warmly at the both of us. "Hello, Layla and Brynlee."

Layla grabs my arm. "I don't want to go."

"You're not going anywhere, Layla. This is Ms. Banks, she's a friend of your daddy's." Layla sniffles and I rest my hand on her cheek. "It's okay, I promise."

She relaxes and Ms. Banks waves. "I'm just here to make sure that you're okay and make sure that you can go home with Brynn or see if we have to wait for your daddy."

Layla scoots closer to me. "Can I see Mommy?"

"Not right now, sweetheart." She looks up at me and I give her a sad smile. I hate this for her. She must be so scared and confused about what's happening. I'm going to assume that Jacqueline is still being held, depending on how drunk she was. "Can you stay here while I go outside with Ms. Banks?"

"You're not leaving?" she asks.

"I'm just going right outside your room. I'll be back before you know it. Do you think maybe you can color a picture for me?" There's a stack of books and coloring books on the table at the foot of her bed.

Layla's eyes brighten and she looks animated for the first time since I arrived. I bring over a few options and the bin of crayons, kiss the top of her head, and we exit her room.

As soon as we're out of earshot, Ms. Banks starts. "I'm not able to get specifics but my contact at the NYPD said her blood alcohol level was at least two times over the limit. She's in the ER as well, being examined. She'll most likely spend the night in a holding cell, unless her lawyer can work his magic and get a bedside arraignment, which I'm going to assume he can't since she hit a police unit. Either way, I've already spoken to Child Protective Services and they've granted Layla to stay with Carson and you until Jacqueline's released. After that, you'll need to return Layla to her mother. I'm filing paperwork showing the child's life is in danger due to her mother's addiction."

All of that sounds pretty standard. "I think it might be smart if you approach Jacqueline while she's been dealt this blow. We know that Carson's case is solid and there was a good chance at him getting custody before she got drunk and drove with her child in the car."

"I've already considered that option as well. If this is a slow news day and it hits the papers, it could work in our favor. The other side is that if it doesn't become a news story, we can make it one and use that as leverage. My hope is that we can drop the custody hearing and get her to agree to signing her rights over to avoid a story. It's a pie in the sky dream, but I happen to be a great baker."

That would truly be the best-case scenario. Crew could skip a nasty, drawn-out custody hearing and have Layla full time. I pray that's the outcome, for everyone's sake.

As we're standing here discussing the possibilities, the doctor walks over. "Are you Layla's family member?"

"Yes, I am."

He extends his hand. "I'm Doctor Payne and I've been monitoring her since she arrived. Layla had no serious injuries that we could see. Her vitals all look good and thankfully, she was restrained during the accident. I'd like to go ahead and release her into your care."

"That's wonderful, yes, I'd love to take her home and get her settled."

"I'll get the paperwork drawn up and we'll have you out of here soon."

"Thank you."

The doctor leaves and Ms. Banks grabs her briefcase. "I'm going to head to the office and get everything in order. Tell your husband I'll send him an email with some options on how to proceed."

"I will."

She looks into Layla's room and sighs. "I hate that this had to happen this way, but it's truly a blessing for our case. Layla may just be living with you and your husband in a matter of a few days instead of weeks."

And with that, she leaves, and I head back to Layla, hoping Ms. Banks is right and we'll have Layla safe with us sooner rather than later.

twenty-six

CARSON

"**B**rynn? Layla?" I call out the moment the elevator door opens.

Not even a second later, Layla is running to me, arms wide, and I pull her to me. My heart is mended just a little as I hold her close. She's okay.

I knew she was, but having her like this is completely different.

She loosens her hold and I take a second to look at her. "Hi, Ladybug."

"Hi, Daddy."

I give her a kiss on her nose and lift her up, walking toward the kitchen, where Brynn is leaning against the door. "Hey."

"Hey."

I kiss her lips and then her forehead. "Thank you."

She smiles with a shake of her head. "We had fun. Layla and I watched television, did some coloring, then we had Cliff go get us some canvas and we did paintings."

"Paintings?" I say to Layla.

Her blue eyes are bright, and she giggles. "We made silly paintings, Daddy."

"Of what?"

"Rin made a cow, but it doesn't look like a cow." Layla ducks her head when Brynn gasps.

"Hey! It does too."

"No it doesn't!"

Brynlee purses her lips. "I think it does. Yours is the silliest."

"Nuh uh!" Layla protests. "Mine is a chicken!"

"A chicken with a smile? I've never seen one of those."

"I'll show you, Daddy!" Layla wiggles so I put her down and she rushes out of the room.

"She's okay?" I ask.

"She's doing great."

I go to Brynn, pulling her to me to savor the way she wraps her arms around me. "I don't know if I've felt that level of fear ever in my life. I couldn't get here any faster. I couldn't do anything."

"I'm sorry, babe," Brynn says, her brown eyes filled with emotion. "I'm sure it was impossible for you."

"Knowing you had her made me at least be able to stay calm."

"Good."

That was the only thing I kept holding onto in my head. Brynn would never let anything happen to Layla. She loves her and wants a better life for her, which is why she married me. Also, I know how Layla feels about her. The way she smiles when Brynn is around, always wants to sit by her, tells her stories . . . and Brynlee listens to each one.

I lean down, kissing her again, and then we just hold each other.

Layla's footsteps come barreling down the hall and I release my wife.

"Look! It's a chicken!"

I'm not sure I'd be able to see that if I wasn't being told it's a chicken, but I nod and go along with it. "It sure is. I love it."

"See, Rin, I made a chicken."

Brynn laughs. "You did and I love it too."

I look at my watch and see it's way past her bedtime. I'm glad she stayed up so I could see her, though. "I'm not going to work tomorrow, and I was thinking, maybe we can go in the movie room and all cuddle up on the couch. What do you say?"

"Can we watch the princess movies?" Layla asks with big eyes.

Brynn sinks down to her level. "Always the princess movies if I'm here."

She throws herself into Brynn's arms and they both laugh, and my world is back on its axis.

Jacqueline was released from police custody twenty-four hours after the accident. Her lawyer was unable to pull any strings thanks to my lawyer's connections. While I didn't love the idea of having the mother of my child spend a night in jail, I'm not unwilling to do what I have to for Layla.

The judge agreed to us having sole custody for the next three weeks leading up to the official custody hearing. Ms. Banks suggested that tomorrow we meet with Jacqueline and her lawyers to discuss an agreement to avoid the court hearing and keep Jacqueline's name out of the papers.

"I'm not doing this tomorrow," I say to Brynn as she's going through her overnight bag for the sixth time before we head to the hospital in the morning.

"The hell you're not! Call your lawyer, and get Layla officially."

I sigh, running my hand through my hair. "And leave you alone in the damn hospital? You are having major fucking surgery tomorrow. It can wait until after."

Brynn groans, tossing things back in the bag. "No, it can't! The whole reason any of this is our reality is for Layla. Damn it, Crew, don't let this even be a thing. I'll be fine. I'll be in the hospital, my brothers will be there, and you can take care of what you need to for her. She's what matters."

Now it's me who wants to shake some sense into her. "And you don't matter?"

"I didn't say that."

"No? It's pretty much what you did just say. I'm not leaving you during your liver transplant, Bee. I'm not going to have some meeting that can wait a day or two while my wife is undergoing surgery. It's not happening."

She throws the bag to the floor. "Then I'll cancel the surgery."

I roll my eyes. "Right."

"I'm serious." She fakes a cough. "I think I'm sick." Brynn coughs twice more. "Can't do it."

I'm not even sure why we're having this fight. Tomorrow, I could lose her. So many things could happen, and my life could be altered forever. Instead of making love or holding her in my arms, we're fighting about my ex-wife and her ridiculous request.

It's not happening. I'm not going to leave her at the damn hospital for anything less than a life-or-death emergency.

Kimberly will be here in the morning to hang out with Layla. She's going to take her shopping and who knows what other mischief she'll find so I can focus on my wife.

"You're not canceling and I'm not going to meet with my ex-wife when my wife is in surgery."

Brynn groans and steps toward me. "What were my rules?"

"What?"

"My rules when we got married. What were they?" she asks again.

"I don't fucking know, something about not loving you and not having sex with you, which, I'd like to point out lasted a whole week."

She glares at me. "Well, you're about to be on a six-week sabbatical coming up and maybe we'll start that today."

I smirk. "So you are having the surgery?"

I'm pretty sure if she could kill me, she would. "Anyway," she sneers the word. "I'm pretty sure you had a rule too. It was that Layla comes first. Always. Layla needs you to go meet with her mother and get custody. She needs to know that in three weeks, a judge won't be off his meds and decide that she's better situated with her mother. You need to get that done, Crew. So, tomorrow, you're going to meet with Jacqueline and get her to sign the fucking papers so I can recover without the stress of it!"

I step closer to her. "She does come first, Brynn, but so do you."

"You can't have two firsts. You have to prioritize her."

It doesn't work that way. I need them both. I will never forgive myself if I'm not at the hospital and something happens.

My hand lifts and I push her red hair back, holding my fingers against her neck. "There's no guarantee she'll sign it. For all I know, this is a game because she knows you have your surgery. She wants me to leave you and go to her. I can't do it, Brynlee. You're asking me to leave you and negotiate a deal that I doubt will even happen."

Her palm rests on my chest, right over my heart. "What if it could?"

"We could go back and forth about possibilities for hours. If Jacqueline wants to meet me, she could've done it today, or she waits until the day after. I'm not going to leave that fucking hospital until I see your brown eyes open and you tell me you're okay." A tear slips down her cheek and I brush it away. "Why are you crying?"

"I'm scared."

The confession breaks my fucking heart. "Of what, Bee?"

"What if I don't wake up? What if we don't get Layla and we have to send her back to her mother? What if my father rejects my liver and he doesn't survive? What if my business tanks because I'm spending weeks recovering? What if . . . what if . . . what if all of this was for nothing?"

I cup her cheeks, holding her face steady. "You will wake up because I need you to. We'll figure out a way to make sure Layla never leaves us. I wish I could give you some reassurance about your father, but we have to trust the powers that be. As for your business, it's already growing and thriving. If there's anything I'm good for, it's saving failing companies, so don't worry, I'll step in. As for this being for nothing, God, Bee, don't you see that it's already everything? I got to live with you as my wife. I've been able to have you, hold you, kiss you, love you in ways I only dreamed of. Even if we don't get Layla, you'll have been able to give your father this gift and it'll never have been for nothing."

She rises up on her toes, bringing her lips to mine. "When all of this settles, I want us to talk about us and where we go."

I don't need to wait for that, I already know. When I go to open my mouth, she covers it with her hand.

"After, Crew. Let's get through the surgery and the custody before we make any decisions. For tonight, I just want to lie in your arms and feel safe."

Neither of us slept. We made love, and cuddled, then made love again, and now I'm watching the inky blue sky turn bright, wishing I could slow time.

"I wish we had another week to prepare for this," Brynn says as she draws shapes on my chest with her fingertips.

"It wouldn't change the fact that you're nervous."

Brynn turns so she can rest her hand on my chest and then her chin. "It would just give us time. I wanted to take Layla horseback riding and get her more comfortable in her room. Now we're going to spend weeks away from Sugarloaf, and—"

I put my finger to her lips. "Stop. Layla loves the cottage, it's all she talks about. You're not going to die, so you can take her horseback riding when you're healed, and we can go to Sugarloaf as soon as you can manage the ride there."

Her brown eyes shimmer with unshed tears. "I just want this all to work, you know? I want you to get Layla and then my surgery to go well. I'm so worried that Jacqueline will fight you on this and we won't get her. That this whole marriage will have been for nothing."

"It's not for nothing."

I really thought that getting Layla was what was going to complete my life, and it will. I need my daughter to be with me so she's safe and loved, but I need Brynlee too. My world won't be the same if I lose one or the other. Therefore, I'm going to do whatever I have to in order to keep them both.

She shakes her head. "I didn't mean it like that. I'm sorry."

"I'm just saying, you'll get your surgery no matter what. Today, you'll go in there and give your father a second chance at life, just like you do for every living creature you meet. Your animals, your family, me, Layla, all of us are better because of you."

Her lips meet mine and I pull her closer.

Brynn sighs as our tongues meet, sliding together.

Her fingers lace into my hair, and she opens her legs wider. "Make love to me, Crew. Make my fears go away."

"You don't have to be scared, Bee. I'll fight all your demons."

She moans my name, and her hands move down my back. "Please. I need you again."

In a few hours, she's undergoing a serious and risky surgery. I'll have to feel as though my own life hangs in the balance until she's out and safe. I needed her last night, and I need her now.

I sink into her wet heat, letting it envelop me. She fits me perfectly in every way. I kiss her as I start to move, rocking us together, setting our pace. Her fingernails scrape down my back and then up my sides. Her hand rests on the bee that's been etched in my skin the way she's been in my soul.

"I . . . God, yes," she whispers against my ear. "You take it all away."

The two of us are panting and I can feel her tighten around my cock.

"I fucking need you, Brynlee. You." I thrust. "Own." Another thrust. "Me." Again. "Feel how much I need you."

She cries out, her fingers digging into my skin, head arched back as she lets go. I follow her over, unable to stop myself.

I push up on an elbow so I can see her face, and she's grinning with her lower lip between her teeth. "What?"

"I'm just happy, that's all."

271

I kiss her quickly. "Good. We better get ready so we're not late."

Brynn nods and we both head into the shower. Once done, she looks around the room, her arms over her stomach. Gone is the ease that we had before getting out of bed. I wrap my arms around her from behind.

"You're going to be fine."

"I know. I was just thinking about the first night I spent here. How I never imagined I could ever think of this palace as home." She glances up at me. "I guess I'm just laughing that leaving now, I just said how much I can't wait to come home, and I mean here."

"Just the same as Sugarloaf feels for me. I think that has more to do with you than the farm though."

Brynlee turns, her arms around my waist. "You mean you don't find the chickens and mucking the stalls to be fun?"

"As long as we get to shower together after, I might just be able to deal with all that."

It has nothing to do with animals or showering, it's her. It's always been her. She's my home. She's what I want the most in this world, and as soon as we're on the other side of this surgery, I plan to tell her all of that.

"Good to know." She rises up on her toes, kissing me softly.

I glance at the clock. "We have to go."

Brynn nods. "I want to say goodbye to Layla again."

She heads out of the room and I go grab her bag. I head to my daughter's room and lean against the door watching Brynlee, who has only known Layla a short time, be more of a mother than Jacqueline ever was.

Layla is asleep and Brynn is lightly brushing her hair. "I'll miss you and be back as soon as I can." She kisses her forehead. "Love you."

Her breath catches when she sees me there, but just shrugs, taking my hand when she reaches me, and I fall even more in love with her than I knew was possible.

twenty-seven
BRYNLEE

The doctor came in, explained the surgery again to my father and me, answered any remaining questions, which Crew had about a thousand of, and left us.

Asher, Grady, and Rowan came in the room before they brought Howie in. He was going through his own prep and then they wheeled him in here.

All three of my brothers showered me with love, the way they always have, and left me to have time with Crew. There's been something calming knowing that the four of them are here. As though the might of the Whitlock men and my husband can bend the whim of the world to their desires.

Now it seems my dad is going to have his moment. "I'll never be able to thank you enough for this, my Brynnalynn."

It's been so long since anyone has called me that. My brothers never would because Howie did. Still, the nickname takes me back to being a kid.

"You don't have to thank me, Dad."

He sighs and looks to Crew. "And thank you. You've given her a love that every father prays for his daughter. Someone who will be there for her, treat her the way she deserves, and care for her."

"As a father myself, I understand that, and you can rest

assured that there's nothing I won't do for Brynn." Crew looks down at me and my chest aches.

"I appreciate that."

Crew grabs the side of the bedrails, looking over at my father. "I hope that Brynlee going through this surgery shows you the kind of woman she is. How selfless and willing she is to risk her own life, her future, and her family without even a second's hesitation. All I ask is that you continue on whatever path you've been on this last year. I know I don't have that right to ask it, and that you're already doing everything to make amends, but she's important to me and I can't watch her be hurt."

Crew may support me doing this, but he's a lot like my brothers in the fact that he doesn't like my father. He only knows of the pain Howie caused in my life and now, he sees someone who is going to put me at risk again. I understand his views, to some degree, but if all we do is remember the bad things about every person, we would never love again.

My father meets his eyes. "The gift she's giving me is one I've tried so many times not to take. I don't want her in surgery. Hell, I prayed that she wouldn't be a match because I knew that Brynn would be the first to be in this hospital if she was. I struggle with this more than you can know. I have tried to convince her not to do this, not to risk her life for me, someone who has hurt her, but here we are." Tears fall from my father's eyes, and I wish I could get out of this bed to hug him.

Crew walks around to his side of the room and takes my father's hand, squeezing tight before releasing it as I fight back the intense emotions building. "She wouldn't be the woman she is if she wasn't willing to do impossible things for the people in her life. She loves you, Howie, and whatever feelings of unworthiness you struggle with, she doesn't see it. If she did"—Crew's eyes meet mine—"I wouldn't be in her life either."

There's a knock on the door, breaking the moment, and it's Asher. He looks at the three of us who are all in varying states of emotion. "I see I came at a good time."

I laugh because only Asher could ease the tension. He looks to

Crew. "There's a lawyer here that belongs to you. She keeps asking where you are and why you're not answering your phone."

"She can wait." He walks over to my bed, taking my hand.

"I figured you'd feel that way, but she's truly terrifying and I don't say that easily."

I look up at him. "You know she's here because of Layla. Go see what she wants."

"I'm not leaving you."

"I'm not saying to leave the grounds, but go out there before Rowan says something or . . . God only knows. Just go, ease my mind before surgery." I throw a little guilt on for good measure.

His blue eyes narrow and he sighs. "You're impossible."

"All I hear is you think I'm a delight."

Asher makes a choking noise. "I'll stay with Brynn, you go. I promise I won't let them take her until you're back."

Crew nods once. "Use bodily force if necessary." He kisses my forehead and leaves.

If I thought that Crew and my father were awkward, this is about a million times worse.

"Howie," Asher says, coming to my side.

"Asher, it's good to see you. Brynn tells me you're a sheriff and that you have the most adorable kids. Congratulations."

While Asher may despise Howie, and understandably so, he isn't the same man who wrecked my world all those years ago. He's thin, his hair is more gray than red, and it's very clear the alcohol and liver damage are wreaking havoc on his body. Gone is the vibrant man who was larger than life.

"Thank you. Brynn is very loved by everyone in the family."

My father dips his head. "All three of you were better men than I could ever be."

I clear my throat, not wanting this to go any further. Either my brother or father is bound to say something hurtful, and I want calm before we go into the operating room. "Did the lawyer say anything about why she was here?"

Asher shakes his head. "She just kept saying she needed him

to either answer his phone or come out and that it couldn't wait. Lawyers are pushy that way."

I grin at the jab. "We often know things and need to be."

"Still why I think you'd make a better lawyer than publicist."

"Leave the thinking to the smart people."

Asher huffs and plops into the seat next to me.

The nurse enters the room, heading to my father's bed. "It's time to head back and get you prepped, Mr. Fisher."

Howie's gaze meets mine and he forces a smile. "I'll see you on the other side, kid."

I laugh softly. "I'll see you when we wake up, Dad. Avoid going toward any lights, will you please?"

"You got it." He winks and then he's taken out of the room.

Asher takes my hand in his. "You know this world doesn't deserve you?"

I sigh heavily. "You're ridiculous."

"No, I'm not. There aren't many people in the world like you, Brynn. Fuck, if it were me, I wouldn't even consider doing this surgery, but I bet you didn't even think twice."

I didn't. As soon as I found out I was a match, I was full steam ahead. Even after Howie relapsed, I didn't hesitate. "You'd be right here if the roles were reversed. I don't care what you try to say."

My brother chuckles once. "Not a chance. If it were you, or Rowan and Grady? Sure. If it was my kid or my wife, absolutely. Anyone else, nope."

"Asher, you put your life on the line every day for people. You can try to pretend that you're this tough, grumpy asshole, but we all know better. I used to laugh that Phoebe called you a marshmallow, but she's right. No matter how charred on the outside you are, the inside is liquid. You love without restraint. You give to others without question. Everything you say that I am, this forgiving and kind person, I got from you. I learned to be the person I am because you were my role model."

I can't remember the last time I saw my brother tear up. Probably when Mom died, or when Olivia was born. It's not a normal thing, but here he is. My big, strong brother standing at my bedside with unshed tears.

He pulls me into his arms, hugging me tightly. "You make the world a better place."

I kiss his cheek. "So do you."

"I know."

We both laugh. Now that we've gotten all that emotion out of the way, I exhale and look over to where Howie was.

"He'll be fine, Brynn."

I look to my brother. "I know, it's just such a weird thing knowing we're both going under at the same time. He has no one to worry about him." Asher swallows hard and I rest my hand on his arm. "I'm not asking you to. I'm just telling you what I'm feeling."

"We'll let Crew worry about him, how is that?"

I grin. "I'll accept that, but I think you're going to have a hard time getting him to not worry about me."

"He can suffer having to deal with both."

I shake my head and smile. "You're a mess."

"Phoebe tells me that daily."

Crew enters the room, and I can feel my whole face light up. "Hey."

He walks toward me, forcing a smile. "Hey."

He and Asher share a look and my brother kisses my forehead. "I'll see you when you're out."

Nerves hit me, but I keep myself together. "Love you."

"Love you more."

Asher leaves and Crew comes around to where he was standing. "What's wrong?"

"Absolutely nothing."

Yeah, I don't buy that.

"Try again," I say with a brow raised.

"I swear, Bee, nothing is wrong. In fact, I'm just not even sure what to say or how to comprehend it all."

I shift, sitting up a little more. "Please just tell me. I'm assuming it's about Layla."

Crew nods. "It's over. She signed the papers, even without me being there to threaten or beg her to do the right thing. She wants to enter a voluntary rehab center and is considering moving to be near her family in Arizona. My lawyer offered to pay for the treatment and negotiated terms far better than I could've even wished for."

The heavy weight that's been on my chest lifts. "She's yours?"

He looks to me. "Yes. We have her full time. Jacqueline has agreed to supervised visits every other week once she's out of rehab. I'll pay her a small stipend for the next two years so she has a chance of getting her life back together. Layla is ours and I don't have to worry anymore. How is this even fucking real? How did I get everything at once?"

"Come here," I say softly. When he does, I take his face in my hands. "It's real and you don't have to worry anymore. Okay?"

He laughs softly. "I think I have one more big worry to deal with."

"I'll be fine."

"You better be, Brynlee Knight. I've lived in a world without your smile and I'm not going back to that. So, come back to me, okay?"

I smile and nod. "Okay."

Just then the nurse knocks and enters the room. "It's time to head back, Brynlee."

"All right." I barely get the words out and Crew crushes his lips to mine.

I pour my love into the kiss, wanting him to know just how much he means to me.

Crew leans back, then kisses me again. "I'll see you in a few hours."

I nod. "Yes, you will."

I close my eyes as the nurse wheels me away from the man I have fallen so hard for and I focus on the fact that for this one moment in time, the world feels right.

twenty-eight

CARSON

"You know pacing around here isn't going to make us get answers any sooner, right?" Asher asks and I sigh, forcing myself to sit.

It's been six hours. Six long, agonizing, exhausting hours. The doctor said it could take up to twelve hours.

"I'm losing my mind," I say, running my fingers through my hair.

Grady walks over, handing me a bottle of soda and some candy from the machine. "It's hard when you're waiting on answers and you're helpless to do anything if there's a problem."

"The last update was three hours ago, I thought we'd have heard something."

Asher grips my shoulder. "She'll be fine. I know my sister and she's far too stubborn to let this take her down. Just stay positive."

For as much shit as Asher gave me, he's been the most supportive out of everyone. He immediately rallied behind Brynn and I can see just how much she means to him. I may not have been his biggest fan, but I think all of his crap was because he just loves her and wants to protect her.

"How are you holding up?" I ask.

"I'm about as good as you are, I'm clearly just better at keeping it together."

I laugh once. "Well, there's that."

All of us lean back in the most uncomfortable chairs known to man and wait. Someone enters the room, the four of us pop out of our chairs. However, it's not the doctor, it's my sister.

"Hey," Kimberly says as she comes in the room, Layla right behind her. "Someone wanted to come give hugs."

Immediately a little part of my fear dissipates. Layla comes in the room and wraps her little arms around me. "Is Rin okay, Daddy?"

"She's doing just fine."

Her smile grows and then she hugs all of her new uncles. She's definitely taken to Rowan the most, but Grady's house is where her new best friends live, so she loves him as well. Asher is a little more reserved, but when she's tired, she loves to sit by him.

She's taking all their attention and my sister comes beside me. "It's kind of amazing seeing her with them. She's always been so shy, but since Brynn has come into your life, and you take her to the farm, it's like a part of her has come alive."

"They allow her to be a kid," I explain. "When we're in Sugarloaf, there is no competition or rules. She can chase chickens, pet a goat, fish and run around catching bugs. It's a different world than we grew up in."

Kimberly looks over at Layla who is trying to climb Rowan. "I'm glad her world is expanding, Crew. She's just so much happier and I wanted you to know that I see it, and now that she's yours full time, I think her life is only going to be fuller."

"I think so too. I know that Brynlee brings such a different feeling into the home."

She snorts. "I think you mean she made it a home. That penthouse was windows and walls, but now it's different. There's a warmth there."

"She's . . . well, she's amazing."

My sister nudges me. "I'm glad you found her again."

"Me too. She makes me so fucking happy." And I love her, but I won't say the words to my sister first, it'll be to Brynn. When she's ready to have that discussion, at least.

Kimberly laughs when she sees Rowan fall to the floor as if Layla "pulled" him down. "I don't even understand this type of play. I can't remember the last time Ryan got on a floor with his kids. Dad would never have considered it. It's just . . . this is really great to see, you know? She's getting to be the kid we dreamed of."

"I think we turned out okay," I say, trying to imagine my older brother rolling on the floor with his kids the way Rowan is doing with Layla.

"We turned out rich. I don't know that it's okay though. I'm almost thirty and have never been in a relationship because I was terrified I'd be forced to marry him. We don't have much fun because we were taught if we had time, we should use it to make more money. I think that we're great at business and terrible at life."

I know she's right in some regards. My life was work, so I think I was pretty good at it, but I was lonely. Marrying Jacqueline was what was expected and not what I wanted. All of those things brought me here to Brynn, though. If I took a different route, there's no guarantee that I'd have her now.

We were so young when we met, and not only in age, but in experience as well. Brynn and I probably would've fallen apart. She'd have seen the ugly side of coming into my family, the expectations I had on my shoulders, and the way I was required to be more.

"Life is about growing. It's about trying things, loving, laughing, and finding a way to handle your shit. My wife taught me how to do all those things in just a short time. Ten years ago, she showed me what love was and I walked away from it. Then, somehow, I got her back and with it came all the good things that I didn't think I'd have again. You'll find a guy who makes you want to walk away from your company, your work, your stresses because you're happy with them. Like I am with Brynn and Layla."

As though she heard us, Layla comes running over, a huge smile on her face. "I made Uncle Rowan fall down."

"I saw. You're very strong."

She giggles. "Just like you, Daddy."

"Well, my strong little niece, we better get out of here before you hurt someone," Kimberly says, getting to her feet.

"I want to stay with Daddy and see Brynn."

I take her hands in mine. "Brynn is going to be very sleepy and won't be able to see us, but as soon as she's better, she made me promise to let you come visit. Go with Aunt Kimberly and I'll be home to see you tomorrow." Her lip drops but she nods. "That's my ladybug. Give me a big hug."

She does, and much too soon I let her go, grateful for getting some time to think of anything other than the surgery.

After they leave, a nurse comes in to update us that both Brynn and Howie are doing well, and they should be getting ready to close them up within the next hour.

The four of us head down to get some food, and when I get back up to the waiting room, the doctor is walking down the hall. I call her name.

She stops and heads back to where we are.

"How is she?"

"She did great. Howie is still in surgery, but doing well. Everything went just as we hoped and Brynn will be back in the recovery room in about twenty minutes, and then one person can go back at a time for no more than ten minutes."

"I'm staying with her tonight."

Dr. Carr nods. "That's fine, but just one person and she's going to be very tired and out of it."

"I know, but she won't be alone."

She fills us in on some other things, explaining possible side effects and what will happen during the next week while she'll be here for observation.

"Mr. Knight, I just wanted to personally thank you for the donation you made to Guardian Angels. You have no idea how many people's lives you're helping."

I tense because I haven't told anyone other than Ford about the donation. "It was nothing."

"I don't think six million dollars is nothing. You've given families who were beyond stressed out about how to pay for surgery peace of mind," Dr. Carr says with a sigh. "I know you did it to fund your wife's surgery, but you donated so much more than was needed."

"Brynn's is being covered by insurance," I clarify.

"Well, whatever the reasons or the payment source, just know that my team is deeply grateful, and we appreciate the generosity you've shown."

"Thank you for taking care of my wife. I'd truly appreciate it if you didn't say anything to her about the donation. I wanted it to remain anonymous."

"Of course. I won't say anything," she promises.

"Thank you, Doctor." I shake her hand and turn to see Asher, Grady, and Rowan standing behind me.

"Not a word," I warn them.

"You want us to lie to Brynn and not tell her she didn't get some grant because of whatever crap she was fed?" Rowan asks.

"No, I want you to forget you heard any of that and not say a word to her. She doesn't want my money and technically, she didn't get it. She got money from the charity and insurance," I clarify.

Asher laughs once. "You think my sister is going to make the same distinction?"

"I think Brynn needs to focus on her recovery."

Rowan snorts. "My friend, you're in a world of trouble when my sister finds out and I can't wait. If you could have the fallout in Sugarloaf, that would be great, I'm sure we'd all like to watch."

I roll my eyes. "I'll see what I can do."

Rowan and Asher walk away, joking with each other, and Grady waits silently. "I would've done the same if I knew it mattered to Addison."

"I didn't want her to worry about anything. This made things . . . easier for her. The money came from a charity, instead of me."

Only I gave the charity the money to do that.

I knew that when she found out, if she did, this would be a fight, but everything I've done has been to make her life easier. My wife shouldn't have to worry about money when I have more than enough. I made the donation large enough because I want other people like Brynn to have the opportunity to help someone they love.

"She'll forgive you, no matter how mad she gets."

I laugh. "I know."

"She can't stay mad at anything for too long, just wait her out."

"I can do that."

Grady nods. "I know we have this strange relationship, you and Rowan too. You're our brother-in-law, but also our boss. I've done what I could to keep things professional when we're in that setting, and brotherly when we're in Sugarloaf, but I want you to know that we all respect you, Carson. We see the way you treat our sister, and while I thought you guys were out of your damn minds to get married in a week, I also respect it. I think this surgery was partially why you rushed."

"Partially," I confess. Grady is a smart guy, way smarter than others give him credit for. He was the one I always suspected knew that things weren't exactly how they seemed. "My feelings for her are real, Grady. I want to make that clear. I've loved her for ten years and there was an urgency that wasn't solely financial."

"You don't owe me an explanation. My relationship with Addison was unconventional, to say the least. My point is that I respect you. In the time you've been in her life, you've given her more than she's ever had. She's the most unselfish human I know, and never asks for anything, so you just do it and I know she sees it and so do we."

"All I want is to take care of her."

He smiles and bobs his head. "You're doing a great job so far."

"Mr. Knight?" A nurse calls my attention.

"Yes?"

"You can come back now."

"Thanks, Grady, I'll call you guys back once I'm done," I tell him and then follow the nurse back to see my wife.

Brynlee is recovering well. Dr. Carr says her age, healthy lifestyle, and desire to get back to her life are all playing a part.

We are now four days post-op and she's already becoming the worst patient ever.

Exhibit A is that she's arguing that she wants to do another walk.

"Brynn, you have to take it easy. You had major surgery."

"I also don't want to be laying around here. I feel better than yesterday."

I sigh heavily. "You need to listen to the doctors. They said tomorrow you can do another short walk. Today, you need to sit in the damn chair and eat."

"I'm not hungry," she says with defiance.

This has been her biggest hurdle so far. She has no appetite. Everything she eats has no taste or makes her nauseous. The dietitian explained this was thanks to the pain meds and can be normal after a long surgical procedure.

I roll over the cart that has toast, eggs, and a fruit cup. "If you eat, I'll have Kimberly bring Layla to visit and we can go visit your dad."

Brynn's eyes narrow. "That's a low blow."

I grin. "I'm using the bargaining chips I have."

Her father is doing well post-surgery. Once a day, we bring Brynn in to see him, which always seems to brighten his mood. He had a few small complications coming out of anesthesia, but overall, he's handling her liver well.

She grabs the toast, taking a small bite before making a face. "It tastes like cardboard."

"Try the eggs."

Brynn shakes her head quickly. "They smell bad."

"Bee, you have to eat something. Please. If you can't eat, they're not going to send you home."

Since the day after surgery, it's all she's talked about. The bed here is very uncomfortable and she misses our home. I hired a nurse who will come to the house four days a week to help her with anything that I can't. Celeste has done extensive research on what types of food will help her with recovery and has stocked the kitchen. Layla is going to spend the rest of the week with my sister since this is where I need to be.

"How is Layla?" she asks, clearly not wanting to talk about food.

"Eat and I'll talk."

She sighs and picks up the toast again. Once she takes a bite, I continue. "She's doing okay. Jacqueline entered·the rehab facility today and since all the paperwork is final and filed, I plan to tell Layla that she's going to live with us."

"As happy as she's going to be, she's still going to want her mother, just know that. Even after we left my dad, I would cry for him. It didn't make sense to others, especially my grandparents. They assumed after the hell he put me through, that I wouldn't want him around, but I did. I cried for him every night. Maybe we should tell her once we're both home?"

"Why?" I ask.

"So that she has her daddy home and she doesn't expect you to leave too."

She has a good point there. "I didn't even think about it that way."

Brynn grins a little. "Another reason you're lucky you have me."

"I have a lot of those, do I?"

"I'd say so."

This is the first time I see a bit of the woman I've known coming through. The doctors warned us about the psychological sides of her recovery. That things were going to be really hard for her as she can't do certain things, she may tire a lot faster, and just struggle from the stress she's been under.

Not to mention the stress we were under beforehand.

Which is why I wanted to relieve as much of it as I could.

"I think I might be the luckiest man in the world."

Brynn raises her brows. "Oh? Why is that?"

I walk over, brush my thumb against her cheek and look into her beautiful, brown eyes. "Because you're my wife." I kiss her lips tenderly. When I pull back, I grin. "Now eat or I won't tell you about the drama in Sugarloaf with Austin Arrowood."

twenty-nine

"Why do you look like you're ready to cry, love?" Crew asks as I'm leaning against the bathroom counter.

I'm really struggling since coming home. Everything feels … off. I'm tired, can't eat a lot, I feel gross, and showering is incredibly painful. All I want is to take a long bath, but I can't because of the wound. Don't even get me started on my hair.

"I'm gross!" I admit.

Suddenly, tears start to fall and Crew carefully moves me to face him. His strong hands frame my face, the callouses on his fingertips brush the soft skin under my cheek. "You are not gross. Don't cry, Bee."

"I just didn't expect it to be so hard," I admit.

"What?"

"The recovery. I mean, I heard all the warnings, read all the paperwork, and was well aware of it, but living it is so different."

He leans down and kisses my nose. "You're also incredibly stubborn and don't want help, which is making things harder."

I've never been any other way. I've always had to do it on my own or it didn't get done. I take care of others. I'm the one that fixes the broken things because there's a joy in doing that. I'm not sure I even know what it looks like to ask for help.

However, if there's any person in the world that I trust to take care of me, it's Crew.

I look up into his blue eyes and through the unshed tears, I allow my vulnerability to come through. "Will you help me?"

"I'll do anything for you. What do you need?"

I sniff, my hands holding onto his wrists. "I feel so greasy, and it hurts to lift my arms. Will you ... wash my hair?"

His lips find mine in the softest, most tender kiss and he brushes his nose against mine. "Just tell me how."

We stay like this for a beat and then he releases me. "I'll get in the tub then."

Crew helps me get undressed and covers the wound with the plastic to avoid it getting wet. Once I'm seated in the tub, he wraps a towel around me so I don't get too cold.

I sit here as he carefully pours warm water on my head, soaking the strands and then I hand him my shampoo.

Slowly he starts to massage the soap, rubbing in the most delicious circles against my scalp. I close my eyes, letting the sensation breathe life into me. It's like heaven and hell at the same time because it feels so damn good but I know I can only have this.

"Please don't stop," I beg.

His voice is deeper than before. "I'll do this everyday if I know it makes you feel good."

It feels good physically, but also to my soul. This is such a basic human need, to clean yourself, and to have someone do it for you. Crew literally rolled up his shirt sleeves to take care of me and those damn tears are back.

"It does, but it's more than that," I admit.

"More than what?"

"You didn't sign up for this and I appreciate that you're doing it no matter what."

He pauses for a second and then lets out a long sigh. "One day you'll stop fighting the truth that's in front of you." I go to ask what he means by that, but he speaks before I can. "Lean your head back, Bee."

I comply, because I'm a big chicken shit and he rinses the shampoo out before massaging the conditioner in.

"You know, if this billionaire thing doesn't work out, you could become a hairdresser," I say, wanting to change the subject.

Crew chuckles. "I'll keep that in mind as a backup. The bottle says to let it sit?"

I slowly turn my head to see him. "For just a minute."

"Lean back on me, love."

His arms reach around the front of me, around my belly and I rest my wet, soapy head on his shoulder. "I'm ruining your shirt."

"I don't give a damn. You could ruin me, and I let you— gladly."

I think he's already ruined me, but I don't say that. "I would never."

"I know, that's why I'd let you. Are you comfortable?"

My eyes close because I'm eternally exhausted and let out a mewling noise. I'm so damn comfortable and I could sleep like this. The security I have with his arms around me is the best place I could be right now.

He laughs softly against my hear. "Don't fall asleep, Bee, we need to wash this out."

I yawn. "Right. No sleeping."

Crew kisses the side of my face and then pulls back, forcing me to use my waning strength as he rinses the conditioner.

Much too soon, he's bundling me up in multiple towels and helping me out of the tub. "Stay right here," he commands as he sits me on the bench at the foot of the bed.

There's not a chance I could move anywhere without falling. "Okay."

He comes back in with three different hairbrushes, sprays, and oils. "What do I use?"

I seriously love this man. With my whole damn heart.

I want to say it. I should now, I know this, but my eyelids droop just a little and the exhaustion weighs even heavier on me. If I said it, it wouldn't be the right time. We have a lot to discuss after those words are put out there.

295

"The spray first, then oil," I manage to get out I'm fading fast.

There's a deep concern in his eyes as he moves to hold onto my shoulders as I teeter to the side. "Let's get you in pajamas and then I'll brush your hair."

He grabs the oversized shirt pulling it over my head and then helps me get the arms in. I'm so weak, and the pain killers I took before the bath are so strong that I can barely focus for a moment. We get to the chair that I slept in last night because I couldn't handle the bed after night one. I couldn't get up and I screamed in pain when I tried. It's so much easier from a sitting position.

As Crew runs the brush through my hair, I fall asleep, feeling so much hope that we'll talk soon, and I can tell him that I don't want our marriage to end.

I love you Carson Benjamin Knight and I want to keep you.

Recovery is like watching molasses drip.

It's terrible and takes forever.

I hate every damn second of it. One would think being waited on hand and foot would be great, it's not.

The one thing I've never been is idle. I want to get up, run, play with Layla, instead, I'm stuck in this apartment that once felt behemoth and now is like a cage.

"Rin, look what I have!" Layla says, running into the living room, where I basically live during the day.

"What is it?" I ask, pushing myself out of my funk.

"Animals!" She brings over a basket that's filled with little plastic petting zoo animals and I force a smile. I want to go home.

I want to be around *my* animals. I miss them so much and while I get twice a day reports on their status, I just . . . want so desperately to be near them. It's been ten days since the surgery. I came home after a week, no matter how much badgering I did, they wouldn't relent and let me out early.

"They're amazing, Layla."

She beams. "Can we play for a little bit?"

Layla and Crew are the only things that have kept me from falling apart. During the day, Layla comes to see me almost every hour. I'm sure she's driving the nanny absolutely crazy, but as soon as I see her beautiful blue eyes, my worries fade away.

At night, much earlier than a man who runs five companies ever should, Crew comes home and makes me smile until I have to go to sleep in this stupid recliner alone.

That's when I fall apart.

But right now, I need to push that away and spend time with my stepdaughter who I adore.

"I would love to play."

"Don't get too tired, Rin."

I fight back a laugh. "I'll try not to."

Layla hands me a cow. "Sometimes, when we play, you go to sleep."

That's another fun side effect that hasn't gotten any better. I tire so damn easily. Talking, going to the bathroom, eating, anything you can think of makes me extremely sleepy.

"I'm sorry."

She smiles brightly. "It's okay. I know you have a big boo-boo and you need to sleep."

"I do, but when we play, it makes me feel so much better."

"And here I thought I did that." Crew's deep voice echoes in the room and Layla drops the toys and runs to her daddy.

He scoops her up, kissing her cheek, and walks over to me. "You're home at lunch?" I ask, completely confused.

"I am."

Crew leans in and kisses me.

"Why?" I ask.

"Because I missed you both."

Sometimes, I don't know what I did to get so lucky to have found him again.

"I happy you're home, Daddy."

"I'm happy too." Layla giggles when he tickles her a little and then he puts her down.

Crew waves his hand and the nanny enters. "How about we head to the park, Layla?" she asks.

"I don't want to. I want to stay with Daddy and Rin."

I would like her to stay too, but Crew turns to his daughter and squats down. "Why don't we let Brynn rest a little? You head to the park with Jane and when you get back, we'll watch a movie?"

I'm a little confused, but I'm guessing my husband is home early for something that has nothing to do with missing us.

"Okay, Daddy."

She's seriously the sweetest kid ever. She gives him a big hug, then comes to me and does the same. "Have fun."

Layla and Jane head out and my phone alarm buzzes, reminding me it's time to take my afternoon medicine.

Crew walks over to the table, gathering the rather large number of pills and my drink. "How is the pain?"

"Well, painful." I swallow them in batches because that's seriously how many things they have me on and then extend my hands. "But better than Howie is."

"Did you talk to him today?" Crew asks, moving to refill my next medication dose bin. Yes, bin.

I sigh and feel as though there are knives in my back. "I did. He's very tired, but the rehab center is really nice, thank you for setting that up."

He looks at me with all innocence. "I did nothing."

"Liar."

I know it was him. Howie could never afford to be in a center like that with all the luxuries and comforts that he has now. Crew just does stuff like this, though. It's him taking care of me without having to ask. As much as I hate it, I also appreciate it more than I can ever say.

The pain is now moving down my legs. I can't sit here. "Can you help me up? I need to walk for a few."

"I think it's better if you remain in the chair." The way he won't meet my eyes and the strain in his voice sends a different kind of signal through me.

298

Well, now I'm pretty sure I need to stand even more. "I'm in pain, and it helps when I don't get too stiff. You're not home early because you miss us, are you?"

He helps me get to my feet and I could cry in relief. I slowly stretch my muscles, and Crew hovers close in case I'm woozy again. Between the pain killers and the actual pain, I'm a fall risk.

Earlier I was really cold, and my head was pounding, but that seems to have gone away.

The last two days I've been even more tired than before, having strange symptoms that disappear within a few hours. The doctor said it's completely normal and that I'm entering the next phase of recovery where there's so much healing going on and my body is still in a trauma state.

However, I'd do it all again tomorrow if it meant I could help my dad.

"No, I'm not."

"I knew it," I say as I move slowly. "Is it about Layla?"

He shakes his head. "No, Jacqueline entered the rehab center today. It's . . . fuck, Bee, I don't even know how to tell you this."

My stomach drops. "Please just say it because my head is making up a million ideas."

"Please sit."

"I'd rather not."

I don't know why, but I know sitting is not going to help. He runs his hand through his hair and sighs. "My PR team was contacted to comment on a story that was set to run tomorrow. Most of the time, they ignore them, but the writer called four times from a reputable publication. My team asked to see an advance on the article as well as a timeline, and requested to hold publishing it so we could review and comment."

I nod. All of that is what I would do if I was on his PR team. "Okay, is it about Layla? The custody? Oh God, did they find out about the drunk driving incident?"

"I wish it was any of that."

My eyes widen. "What?"

"It's about us."

What the hell could anyone write about us? "I'm not under-standing. We get things written about us daily."

Then I wonder if it's about my father and the surgery. What if they went through some of my past and found out about his drinking and the arrest when I was a kid? He can't endure that kind of pain and he shouldn't have to.

"Someone, and I don't know who, sold our story. Our whole story. At first the PR team didn't think anything of it, but there are specific details and dates. Things that only someone who is close to me or you would have access to."

"You're going to need to stop dancing around. I'm not feeling all that great right now and this anxiety is only making it worse."

He comes to me, taking my hands. "Brynn, someone told them that we got married for the custody arrangement and to get insurance for your father's surgery. They had specifics on how we found each other again and how my lawyer advised a marriage. Everything in the article is true and everything is going to be out there."

My jaw drops. "I never told anyone. Not a soul."

"I didn't either."

"Well, clearly you did if I didn't. Someone had to know some-thing. I lied to everyone, Crew. Everyone I love thinks that we've been madly in love since the day we found each other again!" I pull my hands away.

"Calm down," he says quickly. "Please. I didn't tell anyone, either."

"No one? Not your stupid friend, Ford? Not your brothers or sister? No one at work?"

"No! I promised I wouldn't," he says and then pulls his tie off. "I'm just as pissed off as you are. I lied to everyone too. I never wanted this to get out."

This really can't get any worse.

I struggle to breathe as my anxiety rises and then I force myself to get control. I'm a crisis management publicist. I think my fear is coming from my lack of knowledge and I need to break it all down.

"I want to see the article," I demand.

"Sure, I'll show you, but it doesn't change the fact that this is lingering, and we were only able to hold it for another three days. After that they'll be publishing."

I extend my hand. "Understood. Give it to me."

He walks over to his briefcase and grabs the paper, handing it to me.

I think I might be sick. All of it. Every single thing is true. It talks about how he came to my brother's wedding and I was blindsided by him being there. Details about us in college and how he married Jacqueline after lying to me about his real name. Line after line is filled with truths about our life and then the bombshell about how we married because his lawyer suggested it.

How we lied to everyone to avoid the scandal of the photo of us together and that I was in need of medical insurance and money to pay for my father's transplant.

"Brynn. You look pale, please sit."

My heart begins to race and I toss the papers down. "How could anyone know this?"

"I'm working incredibly hard to find out."

I can feel the panic I had pushed down start to rise and my breathing accelerates. "God, my brothers, my friends, everyone is going to know I lied and that you don't even love me!"

"I do love you!" he yells, coming closer. "I love you, Brynlee. I have since the moment I met you ten years ago. You didn't want to talk about this before and I let you have that space because you asked, but don't you dare assume I don't love you. Everything I've done is because I love you. Please, sit down and calm down. You can't get upset like this."

Every part of my head is warring with my heart. Every man I've trusted has betrayed me. Every man I've loved has left me. Even him.

Even the man standing before me that I love so much I ache for him.

He broke my heart.

He left me.

He lied to me.

And right now, I'm feeling so many emotions.

"If you wanted to end things, you could've just told me. You didn't have to do it this way!"

"End it? Are you insane? I don't want to end it."

I don't even know if that's true. After my surgery, I thought we'd have the talk because our agreement was that once he had Layla and he took care of me after my surgery, we'd walk away. When nothing was said, I just . . . I worried.

Sure, I could've brought it up, but honestly, I didn't want to hurt more than I was physically.

But I guess we'll have it out now.

I stand behind the chair, using it for support as I'm starting to tire and need to sleep. "And what happens from here with us? What do we tell everyone, because that article has made it impossible?"

"What do you mean?"

"I have spent my entire life waiting for someone to choose me. To make me their first choice. I've given my heart to men who have thrown me aside for whatever their reasons were. Jonathan used me for what he wanted, and I found a way through it. Howie always went for the drink, and I learned to accept it. You chose to leave me, without giving me a reason, and I got over it and here I am now, married to you and still not sure if you choose me." Tears stream down my face and I start to sway, but I hold on. "I'm going to say this next part, and I don't want you to respond right away. You say you love me now, and everything inside of me is screaming to believe you, but you said that last time too." I step toward him, my hand resting on his chest. "I love you. I have always chosen you. I have to pee, when I get back, we'll finish."

"Brynn," he calls me, but I shake my head because I need to get to the bathroom.

"I'll be right back. Just think about what I said. I need . . . I can't."

I walk to the bathroom slowly and the tears keep coming. I

use my hand against the wall to keep me up as I keep moving down the hall.

"Brynlee! Brynn!"

I hear him call, but God, everything hurts.

My breathing starts to become labored and I call for Crew, but I don't know if I get it out because everything goes black.

thirty

CARSON

I watch her go down, running as fast as I can to get to her, and just barely catch her head before it hits the marble floor.

"Brynn!" I yell, trying to get her to wake up, but her eyes don't move. "Celeste! Cliff!" I scream for help and Cliff is at my side first. "Call 9-1-1!" He pulls his phone out, but I can't wait for help. The closest hospital is two blocks away. "I'll take her. I'll get her there faster."

"Crew?" Cliff calls my name.

I pull her into my arms, cradling her like a baby, and Cliff steadies me when I'm on my feet. "I'm going to the hospital with her. She needs help."

"I'll go with you."

"Get my phone on the table," I tell him, and he runs to grab it. "Call the nanny and let her know what's happened!"

We get on the elevator, and I swear, I curse every fucking floor that we pass. I should've bought a first-floor unit. I could've already been there.

I curse everything. The sun. The moon. The fact that she had this surgery. Her father. Most of all myself. I should've told her everything. I should've told her before I got Layla. The day I saw her, married her, made love to her, I should've done so many damn things differently.

My whole life, I've messed things up with Brynlee and I'll never forgive myself.

The elevator door opens and I move through the streets, carrying her in my arms as Cliff moves people out of the way.

It's two blocks, but it feels like eternity. I start to talk to her. "Wake up, Bee. Wake up. Come on, baby, I need you."

"The nanny is bringing Layla home and she'll stay with her. The ER is aware we're coming and they're calling her surgeon to come as well," Cliff says as he's on the phone. "They're ready for her with a trauma team. Do you want me to take her for a minute?"

"No!" I move faster, somehow finding the strength to keep going.

The hospital comes into view and sure enough, there's a team of doctors and nurses outside of the entrance. As I get closer, they bring the stretcher to me, and I place her down. She's still not awake.

"What happened?" the doctor asks.

I fill him in on how we were talking, she was pale, and struggling to walk. I relive the entire moment of her calling my name, or trying to, but then her body just collapsing. Every detail plays in a loop as we rush into the trauma room, my hand wrapped around her cold one.

"Mr. Knight," the doctor calls my name and I look up. "You need to let us work on your wife."

My eyes go to her, so still, and my heart aches. "I can't leave her."

"You have to. We have to do our job."

"Come on, Crew," Cliff says, pulling me back out of the room.

People move in and out of her room, while I stand here, my hand over my mouth as the reality that I could lose her hits me.

Tears fall down my face as fear like I've never known takes hold. She's everything to me and I don't want to go back to a life without her. I can't. Not now that I've had months of this. Waking up with her wrapped around me, going to sleep with her in my arms, the laughs, the way her eyes brighten when something makes her happy.

I need that.

I need her.

Cliff places his hand on my shoulder. "I called Kimberly, she's on her way. I think you should call her brothers."

I nod. "Call the company I used for the helicopter in Pennsylvania, get them to Sugarloaf to pick them up. It's the fastest way."

He walks to the side to call them, and I dial Asher's number.

"Hey, Crew."

"Asher, your sister collapsed a few minutes ago. I'm sending a helicopter to you so you and your brothers can get here quickly."

"What happened?"

I exhale, hating that I'm what caused it. "We were discussing something, I kept trying to calm her down, but she said she had to go to the bathroom, then I saw her go down. I don't know. She's been recovering okay, and said she was off yesterday and today, but the doctor said it was normal."

I can hear shuffling around behind him. "Is she alert?"

"No, she's unconscious, I got here as soon as I could. They're working on her now." I look to Cliff and he gives me a thumbs up. "The helicopter is on its way to your farm. I'll keep you informed."

"We'll be there as soon as we can."

I hang up and Cliff hands me a bottle of water. "I called Ford as well. He's in the office and is also on his way here now."

"I can't lose her," I tell him. Needing to say the words aloud.

"She's young and healthy. Plus, you saw it and reacted quickly, keeping her from any further issues. Just let the doctors work and keep faith alive."

Dr. Carr comes running down the hallway and pushes into her room. It's been no more than ten minutes, but I'm losing my mind. People move in and out of her room and then the first doctor comes out.

"Your wife's heart rate was very high, we've been able to stabilize it, however there are some other issues that we're working to address. We're taking her down for a CT scan and from there, we'll determine the possible cause. I'm sorry I can't give you more information, but we're doing everything we can."

"Is she awake?" I ask quickly.

"Not at this time."

"But she's alive?" My voice cracks.

"Yes, her heart rate is back in a normal range and she's breathing on her own. Both of those are good signs. We'll update you as soon as we know more."

He leaves and I see her door open, and then she's wheeled past me and it's as though my heart is being ripped from my chest.

Cliff places a hand on my back, leading me to the waiting room. I sit, my head in my hands, trying to keep from falling apart.

Kimberly enters the room, her blond hair swaying as she rushes in. "Crew! Is she okay?"

I shake my head. "I don't know."

"Oh, God."

I tell my sister the story and she holds my hand, squeezing as she listens.

"What were you discussing?"

I'm not sure I want to tell her, but at the same time, I trust my sister with my life. "Brynlee and I have a complicated relationship, and someone sold our story."

Her eyes widen. "Sold what story?"

"It doesn't matter. What matters is someone betrayed us. Neither of us told anyone, so someone in my inner circle found out and sold it to a reporter at Metro NY. It's not even some trashy paper that I can laugh off. The things they know, it's all true, and she thinks I did this to end our marriage."

My sister rears back. "I'm sorry, what? Why the hell would you . . .?"

"I didn't. I didn't tell anyone. It's not their business and I love her. Take apart all the other reasons, I don't want our marriage to end. I want her for the rest of my life."

I get to my feet, feeling anxious. Kimberly asks, "Did you tell her that?"

"No," I confess. "Not in so many words. I hurt her, Kimberly. I broke her heart years ago and while we've found a way to mend things, there's an underlying mistrust that this just brought back up."

My sister stands and comes to nudge me with her elbow. "You are one of the smartest and most successful men in the world. You make some of the most risky and brilliant decisions I've ever seen, you're also a fucking idiot."

"Excuse me?"

"Brynlee, Layla, and life—they're not a business. You can't run things or make them go your way. Dad and Grandpa always tried to make us think it was that way. That we could just decide to be a certain thing and it happened. Look at how that model of thinking worked out. Grandpa died miserable, Dad and Mom can barely stand to be in the same room, and you were forced to marry Digger, and that went to shit. If you love Brynlee like I think you do, then you have to fight. Not just any fight, but one that matters. Every day, you have to give her a reason to believe you'll go to war for her."

"I would burn down the world for her."

My sister cocks her head to the side. "So what are you going to do?"

"I'm going to start with the paper that's trying to ruin our lives."

"I want the company under my control by the end of the day," I say to my lawyer.

"Mr. Knight, it's not that simple."

I laugh once. "Make it simple. I expect to own Metro NY by the close of business. I don't care how much money it takes. I pay you to make things happen, so do your goddamn job."

Ford huffs after telling me how absolutely ridiculous this idea is. He's on the call with me as well. "You can't do this. It's literally the most financially reckless decision you could make!"

I need to fix this. I need to make everything better for her so when she wakes up, there's nothing to worry about. I can do this for her.

I will do this for her.

"I don't fucking care!" I'm standing outside the hospital. We still haven't had an update on Brynn, and I needed some air. "Do whatever it takes. I want to be the owner and I want all employees rolled into the company payroll. Call me once it's done."

I hang up the phone and get a text from Asher that they're in the helicopter, on their way now and will be here in an hour.

Kimberly comes out. "Crew, the doctor. Come on."

We rush back in, and Dr. Carr is in the waiting room. "Hi, Mr. Knight. We went through all of Brynlee's tests, and it looks like she's bleeding internally. We're prepping her for surgery now so we can go in and try to stop the bleed. I don't know how long we'll be in, but I'll do my best to have someone come update you once we know more."

"Dr. Carr," I say, my voice trembling. "Do anything you can to bring my wife back to me. Anything."

She nods once. "I'll keep you updated."

And now I wait to find out if I still have a heart.

thirty-one
CARSON

"I'm not trying to get in your business, but you mentioned you were talking about something when this happened . . .?" Asher leaves the question off.

"We were discussing something that was brought to my attention, and I didn't want to keep it from her. I'm handling it, but I'd like to talk to you all about it."

Rowan and Grady look up, and my sister does as well. As much as I don't want to tell them the truth, if I do, then Brynlee won't have to do it. I'm going to be honest with her brothers and let them come at me, not at her.

"Brynlee and I didn't get married because we were madly in love. At least we weren't at the time. I have always loved her. I know that may sound ridiculous, but even after ten years, the feelings I had for her didn't diminish." I wait, watching their reactions, but no one moves. "I was in the early stages of a horrible custody battle for Layla. Her mother had me followed and they took photos of Brynn and I together. In the prior two weeks, I'd had a lot of photos published with different women, all the publications intent on painting me as a playboy. None of them were women I was even talking to. They were business dinners, but my ex-wife was building a false case to discredit me as a steady household. My lawyer was sure that we'd lose the case if I was seen with a single woman from that point forward. I knew about Brynn's surgery and that she wasn't sure how she was going to afford it. I came to her one night and proposed so that we could marry and fix both our problems."

I glance at the three of them, each with a varying expression. Asher's jaw is clenched and keeps shaking his head. Grady looks as though he's ready to laugh and then I look to Rowan.

He huffs and pinches the bridge of his nose. "Okay, so that explains a lot. How did we get to today?"

"The agreement we made was that we didn't tell anyone. Partially, because the less people who knew, the better chance we'd have of it staying a secret. The other was because I hoped, in my heart, that I could win her. I wanted her back. I love your sister. I love her more than anything."

Asher nods. "All right. I also know her, and she is clearly in love with you, but I'm going to assume something happened to cause a fight. Did you decide to leave her?"

"Fuck, no. Someone sold our story. I don't know why, since Layla is now ours. It makes no fucking sense other than money. Brynlee was upset and felt like I betrayed her. She knew she'd have to tell you the truth and was afraid because she'd lied to everyone."

"And our family hates liars," Grady says with a sigh. "Sometimes I forget just how much that girl has gone through and how deep her issues are."

Asher starts to pace. "It's my fault. I drilled that shit into her head and I'm a hothead at times."

Rowan scoffs. "At times. Right."

Asher flips him off. "My point is that she's probably afraid to come to us."

"I never should've asked her to lie," I admit, stopping the convo. "I did this. I brought this to her and now she's going to be hurt because someone thought to use me to make money. I'm going to find out who it was. I'm going to stop the story from being published. My reason for telling you is that what may have started out as an agreement became more. Every day I spend with her, I fall harder. Everything I did for her was to make her happy. Because she's what makes my life complete. Now, to think I could lose her . . ." My words crack at the end because it's too fucking much.

Asher grips my shoulder. "Don't think that way."

Rowan moves to come beside me. "I respect you being honest and being willing to take the hits. I won't lie, if we'd found this out another way, I wouldn't be as calm as I am now. Mostly because, in the grand scheme of this, it's fucking nothing compared to the fears we're all facing."

"She was never okay with lying," I tell the three of them. "Never. She hated it and then . . . it stopped being a lie for us." We're all quiet for a moment and I clear my throat. "If you want to be angry at anyone, let it be me. Your sister isn't at fault. I asked her to do this to save my daughter from her mother. I offered her a way to save her father and she took it, not to hurt anyone, but because she's incapable of not helping others who need her. I'm the selfish one. I'm the asshole."

Grady lets out a long sigh and stands in front of me, hand extended. "Any man who would come to us, tell us the truth, and explain is worthy of my sister."

I get to my feet and take his hand in mine. "I'm not worthy yet, but I'm trying and I'm going to fix this, no matter what."

"The doctor was able to find the bleed. They're in now and I'll be back as soon as we have another update, but it'll be at least an hour," the nurse explains and then rushes out.

"This is good," Kimberly says as she rubs my back. "They found it."

I nod because I'm not sure what I think right now.

My phone rings for the tenth time, Ford's name appearing this round. Kimberly spoke with him the last call, she came back with her tight smile and said she took care of it. Clearly not.

I know that talking to him isn't a good idea. There are some things that are becoming clearer as more time passes. I send him to voicemail and send an email to my security team and office manager, apprising them of a possibility they need to be aware of at the office.

Once again, Ford's name comes up on my screen.

"I'll go take this," I tell Kimberly and head outside of the hospital where I can have some privacy.

"Is the deal done?" I ask, my voice clipped because I have a feeling this phone call is going to change everything.

"Crew, do you even understand the money they're going to ask for? It's not even anything in the realm of what it's worth. Then you're going to shut it down? Literally costing you hundreds of millions of dollars? You can't do this."

I push my tongue to the roof of my mouth so I don't say something that ruins almost twenty-five years of friendship, and then decide I don't really give a shit. "You know, I keep going over in my head who would know the most intimate details of my life. I've sat here, while my wife fights for her life, with nothing to think about besides this story."

"What story?" he asks.

"The one I think you fucking sold. No one knew the details of North Carolina like you would. The story describes things we did on that trip, things that only you knew." The anger builds because I tried to come up with another possibility and failed.

"Crew . . ."

"Was it you?"

There's a pause and I don't need him to confirm it, he just did. "You had Layla. I waited until you had Layla."

"How could you ever betray me like this? After I bailed you out after your divorce? After I gave you a job you weren't even fully qualified for? You were my best man in my goddamn wedding!"

If he was here, I'd fucking kill him. It'd be a good thing we were at the hospital because he'd need it.

"I'm sorry. I know you won't understand, but you had custody. I didn't think it would matter since I figured you were going to walk away from her. I needed to do it. I couldn't hold them off anymore."

"Who?"

"The people I owed money to."

Unreal. "You sold me out. That matters. Your selfishness might cost me the woman I love. So spare me your reasons and lies. We're done. You're fired. Get the fuck out of my life."

I hang up, my anger boiling, and I want to throw something. Instead, I let out a roar, hating the world for putting Brynn through this. Hating that my fucking best friend is the one who did this. I trusted him and he might have taken everything away from me.

I can't think that way. Brynn will come back. She has to.

Once I have a little more control, I call my lawyer and the human resources department to have Ford escorted off the property immediately.

"We'll handle it, Mr. Knight."

"Thank you. Where are we with the purchase?" I ask again.

"We're still negotiating. Obviously, they were taken by surprise since they weren't interested in selling. However, your name carries a lot of weight and they've called for a closed-door emergency board meeting."

"How much did you offer?"

My lawyer clears his throat. "We asked what it would take to have it done by end of business. I thought it was the best route with the lack of preparation. Looking over the last press releases regarding a purchase of a publication, the prices ranged astronomically. We don't have time to go through their financials to get the best deal."

"I don't care about that."

He's silent for a minute. "Can you tell me why you're interested in purchasing this particular paper today?"

I inform him of the article that is being written and who is responsible for the information they were provided. "As you can understand, my wife will be hurt by this. Therefore, I want it done."

"I understand. We already have a preliminary contract drawn up, and while the final sale may not go through by the end of business, we'll have the employees under Knight Corporation by the end of the day."

"I want all editorial stories stopped and under the company umbrella of ownership."

"That won't be a problem. What if they ask for a number far beyond what the company is worth?"

"I'm sure they will. Do your best to negotiate and bring me the final offer options. You have my non-negotiables and I'll pay whatever it takes for those to be accepted."

"We'll be in touch with your options."

thirty-two
BRYNLEE

My eyes flutter open and close before the light blinds me.

I feel so tired, like I did when I woke from my surgery. There's constant beeping around me and I try to remember what happened.

Crew and I were fighting. We were discussing that horrible article that exposed everything about us and I was so emotional.

My heart felt like it was beating out of my chest, and I had to go to the bathroom so bad.

Then there was pain and . . . nothing.

Oh, God. Am I dead?

No. I think if I was dead, it would be quiet, and there's supposed to be a light. I definitely didn't see a light until I opened my eyes.

I wonder if that's it then. Maybe I can avoid it if I just keep them closed.

"Brynlee." I hear Crew calling my name softly. There's a light pressure on the top of my head and then I can feel his lips there. "Open your eyes, Bee."

This totally could be a trick. *Open your eyes, look at me, then you'll die.*

I'd rather not.

I have a lot more to say to my husband, so I'll just stay away from the light, thank you very much.

"I don't know if you can hear me, but I'm going to hope you can. I love you so much, Brynlee Knight. Come back to me, sweetheart. I choose you every day, every hour, every minute. I choose you forever, I just need you to wake up."

I'm starting to think I'm not dead or near a light, but when I go to open my eyes, I can't. I'm just so sleepy.

I do everything I can to get my muscles to cooperate, but I can't, so I let the exhaustion take me back to the abyss.

"And when do we start to worry?" Crew's voice wakes me a little.

"She's had a very traumatic surgery, then a complication. I expect her to rest as much as she can. She's breathing on her own, her heart rate is great. She's responsive to light and sound. She's not in a coma, Mr. Knight. I'm not concerned."

There's a silent pause. "It's been two days, Dr. Carr. Two days of resting, as you call it."

"She awoke once, and that was a great sign. I promise, she's being given the absolute best care."

Oh, he's not going to like that. Nothing is good enough for the people he loves.

"I'm not questioning your level of care. I'm questioning why my wife still hasn't opened her eyes. Why we're happy with the fact that she only twitched her hands when you asked her a question."

"If she didn't show any signs of response, we'd have cause to worry. Right now, I'm trusting the medicine. I know this is incredibly difficult for you. Believe me, I wish I could change it, but we found and stopped the bleed, and her vitals and labs show that she's doing much better. Give her some time to heal and get her strength back."

He sighs heavily and I hear footsteps leave the room. Then there's pressure on my hand and he laces our fingers together.

"I'll lend you all my strength." Crew brushes his lips against mine. "I'll give you the breath from my lungs, the beat of my heart, just . . . don't leave me, Bee. Don't let me go another day without telling you how much I love you and need you. I will fix everything, just come back to me."

The pain in his voice has me fighting even harder to wake up. I don't want him to be sad. I know he chooses me. He has since the day he came back into my life, whether I wanted to believe it or not.

I love him. I love him so much that it actually hurts to hear him in pain.

"Crew." I force my lips open and hope his name comes out.

It must, because I hear him jump to his feet. "Brynn? Baby, wake up."

I sigh, using whatever strength I can find to turn my head, hoping when I open my eyes this time, it won't be so bright.

His fingers tighten around mine. "That's it," he coaxes. "I just need to see those beautiful brown eyes."

I lift my lids, and the lights are low. It must be nighttime. "Crew," I rasp his name again and he brushes my hair back.

"I'm right here, my love. I'm right here."

His face comes into focus. He looks like shit. His normally trimmed scruff is almost a beard, there are deep circles under his eyes, and his hair is a mess. Crew lifts our entwined hands to his lips and kisses my knuckles.

"Hi," he says softly.

"Hi." His forehead drops to our hands, and his anguish is palpable. "What happened?" I ask, the details feeling a little foggy.

"You collapsed, you had a bleed at the incision site. They had to go back in and thank God they were able to stop it. You've been semi-conscious for two days, sort of coming in for a moment and then back out. Between all the medications you were on and the anesthesia, it was . . . terrifying."

I try to clear my throat a little, but it hurts. "Water?"

He nods, reaching over for the cup. I take a small sip and then he kisses my lips. "Brynn, I . . . I love you so much. I'm so sorry that I pushed you. I . . . there's a lot to say—"

I bring my hand to his lips. "Shh. I know. I love you too."

He looks down at me with tear-filled eyes. "You asked me to choose you. There's no one else in the world I would ever choose over you and Layla."

"I know."

And I do. I knew it all along. I think I was just so afraid. My insecurities were screaming at me, no matter what the evidence pointed to.

"I need to say all of this, Bee. I need to get it out."

"Okay," I say softly, feeling tired again, but forcing myself to stay awake as long as I can.

"You are my heart and soul. You are the reason that the world makes sense, and why it continues to turn. You're everything good and for some reason, I get to love you twice. You're my wife, but more than that, you're the reason I draw breath. I choose you, Brynn. I love you and I want you to be my wife in every way. I want you to marry me again, not because we both want something from each other, but because we want to give each other everything. Marry me? Marry me because you love me and want to spend the rest of your life with me."

I feel the tears fall and all the exhaustion fades for a moment. "Yes."

He smiles and takes my face in his hands. "Bee, steal my heart because ten years ago I gave it to you, and it's only ever been yours."

I laugh at what might be the cheesiest and sweetest line I've ever heard. "Why should I steal it?"

"Because then you're the only one who can decide if I ever get it back."

"I plan to keep it forever," I tell him.

"Good, because if you said no to marrying me again, you were going to be in for one hell of a contested divorce." I laugh and he kisses me softly. "Rest, my love, I'll be right beside you."

And without even thinking about it, my eyes close, and I sleep with my husband's hand wrapped around mine.

When I wake again, it's not only Crew beside me, but my brothers as well.

"This is never a good thing," I say when the four of them are looking at me.

Asher grins. "At least we didn't kill your husband for upsetting you so much that you required another surgery."

I roll my eyes. "I'd like to think that had nothing to do with it."

"Maybe," Rowan says with a smirk. "Still, we do like to at least threaten violence."

"Yes, I'm aware."

Grady moves to my side. "Everyone here was willing to fight for you, though. So we let him live another day."

"That's good."

He smiles. "It's still on a probationary status."

I look at my husband, who winks at me. "Your brothers would never do anything to hurt you, so I'm feeling pretty safe."

I sigh heavily, looking around the room, and Asher steps forward, always the serious one. "We know the truth, Brynn. Crew told us about how you met, found each other again, and the reasons you married. I want you to know that none of us are upset with you. I know that you wouldn't have lied to us unless you thought you had to. I also think you did that to save a little girl, and none of us could ever be upset for that." My heart races a little and Asher puts his hand on my shoulder. "Take a deep breath and calm yourself. I'm telling you this so you don't worry about it. None of us would ever turn our backs on you, even if you lied about something much worse than marrying the man you actually loved, no matter the reason."

I look at Crew. "Why did you tell them?"

He moves around to the other side of the bed. "So you didn't have to. If they wanted to be upset with anyone, it should be me. I asked this of you, it was my mess to clean up."

I shake my head. "I agreed to it." I pause a moment, then tentatively ask, "What about the article?" I barely get the words out, my breathing is a little labored.

Crew looks to the guys and back at me. "There won't be an article."

"What?"

"That paper and the journalist will not be printing anything about us."

I saw the article. It's been more than three days. I don't understand. "Why not?"

"Do you want them to?"

"No, of course not. I don't ever want Layla or our friends and family to know any of it."

"Then they won't." Okay, he really has me confused now. I know he's rich and powerful, but stopping a freaking article from running seems a little much, even for him. He looks to my brothers. "I need to talk to Brynn."

They take turns kissing my cheek and then leave us alone in the room. "Explain."

He sits on the edge of my bed, leaning on each of the rails. "I'll explain as long as you keep yourself calm. Deal?"

"Deal."

Crew kisses me briefly and then sits beside me on the bed.

"I found out who it was that sold the information to the paper. It was someone close to us. Well, me."

"Who would do that to you? To Layla?"

That was part of what hurt too. It would be damaging to her. She would have this out in the world where down the line, she'd have to someday read these things about her father.

I remember reading some of what was written, but honestly, my head was a mess that day and I don't recall everything. I know it said stuff about how we met, how he slept with me and left when we were young. It talked about how he and I saw each other again and then a few weeks later were engaged at the urging of his lawyer.

Other than that . . . I'm drawing a blank.

"Ford."

My jaw drops. "Ford, as in the best man at our wedding?"

"Yes."

"How? Why?" I feel a level of betrayal that makes no sense, but more for Crew than for myself. Ford was his best friend for years. I don't understand how he could do that to him.

"For money. He said he knew that Layla was safe now and he was in a dark place. He no longer works for me, and I doubt that there will ever be a way to repair our friendship. To sell me out is one thing, but he came after you and Layla too."

"I'm so sorry, Crew."

He takes my hand, bringing it to his lips. "I'm still not sure I know how I feel. He was my best friend for years and I don't understand how he could do this to me."

"I don't either."

As much as I disliked him, he seemed so important to Crew.

"Thankfully, I've had you to focus on."

But that will end and then he'll have to deal with the fact that his best friend betrayed him. "Still, he was important to you."

"Not only as my friend, but in the company too."

"You fired him?"

"Of course I did." Crew pulls back. "Fuck him and the fact that he came after my wife. You and Layla are my world and I'll destroy anyone who tries to fuck with that."

I bring my hand to his face. "Calm, remember?"

"You could've died, Brynlee. If you . . . if I wasn't home to see you . . . if . . . I can't even say it, but I would've killed him. I know you joke about Asher and how he went after the man who hurt you and Phoebe, but I would've done the same. There is nothing in this world I wouldn't do to keep you happy."

I bring my other hand to his cheek. "All I need is you."

"You have that." He laughs once. "You've always had that."

I smile softly and then recall he said the article wasn't going to run. "You mentioned they weren't going to print the article? How did you manage that?"

Crew shrugs. "I bought the paper."

"You bought what paper?"

"The newspaper that was planning to print the article. I own it, as well as all the articles past, current, and those in process. Knight Corporation has a very strict rule about defamation of the company, especially anything about me. The minute we signed the deal, that article became part of my company property, which means they couldn't print it."

I blink, my jaw is slack, and I stare at him. "You bought the paper. Like the whole thing?"

"Yes. On the day you collapsed."

"In a day?"

"Yes."

"Because?"

He sighs with a shake of his head. "Because they made you cry. They almost took you from me. They made you think I didn't love you or want you, and I was not going to let anything hurt you. I vowed, on that beach, in front of our family that I would honor and protect you. So, I bought the paper that threatened to hurt you and shut it down."

I gasp. "Wait. You shut it down?"

"Yup."

"Crew, you can't . . . no . . . you can't just buy a paper and shut it down. That had to cost a fortune!" My hand covers my mouth and then I ask the next most important question. "For how much?"

He just looks at me without emotion. "Well, I did buy it, and now it's my turn to remind you that you promised to stay calm."

Right. Calm. Like I can stay calm now. I focus on doing some breathing exercises because there's no way this conversation is over.

"Do you really want to know how much I paid?"

I'm not really sure I do, but . . .

"I think so."

"You get really uncomfortable when it comes to money."

Yes, because I really don't understand just how rich he is. It's *his* money and I never feel comfortable asking.

But he bought a damn company and shut it down. That couldn't be cheap, right? I mean, it was at least ten million I would guess.

"Can I ask a few questions first?"

He nods with a grin. "Anything."

"Okay . . . how rich are you?"

Crew laughs softly. "Took you long enough to ask that. I'm extremely wealthy. On top of what my companies are worth, I inherited a ridiculous amount of money when my grandfather died. I've sold three companies prior to the five I own now, and one sold for three billion dollars."

Oh. So, yeah, he's like . . . loaded-loaded.

"I'm starting to feel woozy," I admit.

"Do you understand that I would give it all up for you and Layla?" I have a feeling he took out a healthy chunk by buying this paper. He lifts my chin, so our eyes meet. "That the money means nothing without the two of you?"

I nod. "It was never about the money for me."

"I know, and me buying the paper wasn't about the money either. I did it because I love you and I refuse to let anything tarnish your name. I will stop at nothing to keep you from being hurt, Bee. Nothing."

Why does he have to be so damn sweet? "I didn't need you to buy the paper," I tell him, my hand moving to his cheek. "I would've weathered the storm beside you."

"I'm hoping you'll do that anyway."

"I will."

He smiles. "I'm going to take that as a vow."

"We've already said those."

"I want to marry you again."

"Uhh, what?" I ask, confused. "We're not divorced, unless you managed to buy the courthouse and change records while I was in surgery."

At this point I wouldn't put it past him.

His soft laugh is followed by a deep exhale. "I didn't, but that's not a bad idea."

I roll my eyes. "Anyway . . . we're already married."

Crew's smile makes my heart race. "I want to marry you for the right reasons. I want to stand up there with you knowing that I'm choosing you for the rest of my life, even if I already did. The first time, you thought it was just for Layla, and that was part of it, but I've always loved you, Bee. You've always been what I wanted."

"Kiss me," I request because I can't move to him.

He brings his lips to mine in the sweetest, most tender kiss I've ever had. When he breaks away, he rubs his thumb against my cheek. "I would marry you every day if that's what you needed to prove how much I love you."

"I don't need that. You've more than proven how much you love me. You bought a freaking newspaper to avoid a story." Which brings me to the whole reason we're having this discussion. "Okay, last question."

"Go ahead."

I'm not sure I want to know this, but if this marriage is now real, and we're a couple, we're merging our lives together. Which includes money, not that I have any.

"Exactly how much did your newspaper takeover cost?"

Crew laughs once. "Two hundred and fifty-six million."

thirty-three

CARSON

"Where the hell do you think you're going?" I ask my wife when I find her standing by the back door with her boots on.

She tilts her head to the side. "To see the animals."

I huff, crossing my arms over my chest. "I said we'd come to Sugarloaf for the next week as long as you promised not to overdo it."

Brynn shrugs with a smile, but I see through her little innocent act. "I'm not overdoing it. I'm going to pet a goat."

We arrived back in Sugarloaf last night. After a lot of arguing, I agreed to take the trip as long as she followed the rules. The last two weeks in New York have been calm. She's gone to her therapy, done great with her medications, and it's a very different experience than she had right after the liver donation.

The doctors told us at her last visit it would be okay to spend some time out of New York and might even help her spirits.

Like a lovesick fool, I couldn't say no when she asked me to please let her have some time at home.

I sigh. "Let me get my shoes."

Seems I'll never learn to say no.

Layla is at Grady's house because the three kids wanted to

have a playdate and she loves her new cousins. I *thought* my wife would take this time to rest, but I should've known that wouldn't happen.

I head back to our room, get my shoes on, and we head toward the barn. She wraps her arm around my back, and I drape mine over her shoulder. We walk in silence, and I take in the peace of being out here.

Brynn looks up at me, a soft smile on her face. "I love you."

"I love you."

"I know you weren't comfortable coming out here, but I needed it."

I kiss the top of her head. "I think Layla and I did too."

"She seems happy."

She is. Her life has been upended in the last month and Brynlee and I have worked hard to give her a sense of stability while nothing has felt stable.

"I wish everything didn't collapse at once," I say, pulling her a little closer.

"I wish nothing collapsed, but I feel like things worked out in the end."

"Especially for me."

Brynn laughs. "How so?"

"I have permanent custody of Layla. I have an amazing wife who loves me beyond reason."

"Beyond reason?" She cuts me off.

"Absolutely. I'm a catch, Bee. I don't know if you knew this, but I was once named one of New York's most eligible bachelors. You really should be impressed with that."

Her brown eyes find mine. "Oh. So. Impressed. I mean, you are like, top tier, baby."

I grin. "I'm glad you agree."

"Well, since you have all the things you want in the world and it seems to all be going your way, what has you so quiet lately?"

When a crisis happens, I tend to shut the world out. I focus on that single thing because it's what needs all my energy. That's what I did when Brynn collapsed, and the article was coming out.

All the other things sort of fell by the wayside while I worked through what I deemed most important.

Now, that crisis has passed, and all the other things are back to the forefront.

As angry as I am at Ford, a part of me is really fucking hurt. He was my best friend. At least I thought he was.

We haven't spoken since that day, and I don't have anything to say, but for years, he's been my right-hand man.

That's gone.

I promoted another person to that position, but it's not the same.

"I think it's the last few months just coming to a head. I went to call Ford a couple of days ago and then stopped myself. Layla asked about her mom too. We need to figure out how the hell to deal with that."

Brynn stops walking and faces me. "Can I offer my opinion?"

"Of course," I say quickly. "When the hell have I ever made you think I don't want your thoughts?"

"Never, but Layla is your daughter and I never want to overstep."

I cup her cheeks. "You are my wife, Bee. You aren't overstepping when we're raising her together."

There's caution in her eyes, but a smile on her lips. "You know that Layla and I share a lot of similarities. I was much older than her though, so I can only hope that Jacqueline gets sober and stays that way and Layla won't remember this part. I want to believe that somewhere deep, she wants what's best for her daughter. I kind of think Howie did, and that's why he signed over custody to Asher when my mom died. I know your marriage and how Layla came to be aren't happy memories, but Jacqueline's her mom. No matter what void I fill, she'll have that hole."

It's what bothers me so much. I know that Brynlee will be an amazing stepmother. She already is. Layla adores her and since she's young, she doesn't feel like Brynn stole me or whatever things my friends used to say when their parents divorced. Layla never grew up in a two-parent home.

"I won't keep Jacqueline from her daughter, regardless of how I feel about her, but she has to be sober, and it has to be supervised."

"I agree. I'm just telling you that from the child's perspective, it's incredibly difficult. Layla is going to need all the reassurance in the world that it wasn't her fault. My dad refused to get help. He didn't think he had a problem, which was the hardest part. My mother tried, even after we left, to help him, and he wouldn't even try. It took me a long time to forgive him and to understand that it wasn't because of me."

She never should've felt that, but all I can do is show her that she's everything to me and give Layla the home she deserves.

"Her lawyer reached out to mine, informing us of her progress. As of now, she has no visitation until treatment is completed, which is why I think they want to discuss that now."

Brynn nods. "As for the Ford thing, maybe you should talk to him."

My head jerks back as I gape at her. "Do you need me to remind you what the piece of shit did?"

"No," she says hesitantly. "I just think it would help if you had a conversation while my life isn't hanging in the balance, and you aren't trying to shut a publisher down. You know, since you're calm and I'm very much alive."

I love my wife. I love that she's a kind soul with a forgiving heart. It's what makes her everything good in this world.

I, however, don't share that with her.

"No."

She blinks twice. "No what?"

"No, I don't want to hear him out, see his face, or listen to whatever bullshit excuses he could come up with. He was paid, he can enjoy his twenty-grand and fuck right off."

Brynn sighs and shakes her head. "You men, you're all the same."

"You mean we're all right? Yes, I agree."

"Stubborn was the word I was going with."

I pull her just a little closer and kiss her gently. "I'm only stubborn when it comes to you."

She laughs at that. "You're stubborn with everything, but nice try on the flattery. Now, I want to see the animals and go back, lie on the couch, and snuggle with you until I pass out."

"Okay."

Just then, one of her cows comes close to the fence and Brynn sees her. "Hey there, Mootilda! I've missed you, girl. Look at how pretty you are."

She drops my hands and walks to the fence to pet her cow, forgetting I'm even here.

"Crew? What are you doing here? Is Brynn okay?" Asher asks.

"Yeah, she's fine. She's going over a new sheep pasture plan with the caretakers to make sure they're getting variety in their diet." I laugh because . . . of course she is.

"God, I'm so glad she's your problem now."

"I am too."

"Come in," he says, pushing the door open. "Phoebe is at the college apartment with Sienna. I'll head up there in a few hours to watch the baby while she goes to class tomorrow."

The way they make their relationship work is admirable because I know they make sacrifices to keep each other happy.

"I won't take long."

"Want something to drink?"

"No, actually, I'm here to ask you something."

Asher leans against the back of the chair and his posture shifts. "Okay, what is it?"

"I would like your permission to marry Brynlee again."

He looks at me, sort of like Brynn did when I told her I wanted to marry her again. I wasn't kidding. I want to give her the wedding of her dreams. Not a shotgun wedding on the beach when neither of us were doing it for the reasons we should've.

"I'm not really sure what to say since you're already married. Unless that wedding wasn't real?"

I laugh once. "No, we're actually married."

"Then . . ."

"I've always tried to be a man who earned respect. Not just because of my money or last name, but because of who I am. If things hadn't been so . . . stressful when we got married, I would've done it differently. You would've been asked, probably Howie too, since they're in communication. I would've proposed the right way, and I want to give all of that to her. If she wants another wedding, we can have that. If she wants a party, here in Sugarloaf, we'll do it. I never want to rob her of anything. So, this is me, as her husband, asking for your permission to ask her to marry me the right way. I plan to ask Grady and Rowan as well."

When I proposed to her the first time, I told her I wasn't going to rob her of the man she loved asking her in earnest. Now, it feels like I robbed her of it because I am that man. While a lot of this won't make sense to anyone, it's what I want to do for her.

Asher cracks a half grin and stands tall. "You know, all any of us have ever wanted for Brynn was to find a man worthy of her. I didn't think such a person existed. I'm still not sure, but if there was one, I think it would be you. I'd like to stand here, give you shit, make you sweat it out, but after everything you did for her, I can't. If you need my permission, you have it."

"Thank you," I say, extending my hand.

He shakes it and nods once. "I wish you luck with the other two. Well, Rowan more than Grady."

"I appreciate that."

I leave his house and head to Grady next, figuring it's probably easier to go down the list of Whitlocks in order. I'm met with the same confusion as I was with Asher.

"You want to marry your wife?"

"I do."

"I mean, what the hell does anyone say to that?" Grady asks with a laugh. "Carson, if you want to marry your wife, I say go for it. Besides, my permission isn't really necessary, it's up to Brynn.

Not that I think you have anything to worry about. She seems pretty head over heels for you."

I smile at that. "The feeling is mutual."

"I believe that."

"I appreciate you taking the time to hear me out."

Grady nods. "First of all, you're one of the key investors in my company, so of course, but besides that, you're family now. Plus, you clearly love my sister, and you came clean to three men who would risk jail time to protect their sister. I think that's pretty admirable."

"My investment in your company wouldn't change if things didn't work with Brynlee. I genuinely believe in your vision." I decided to invest a few months ago when Grady came to me with an expanded business plan. His other investor wasn't willing to give more to grow his fleet and I see value in it.

There are definite perks to having pilots and planes on call and reserved for the VIP clients who need it.

"You're a good man, Carson." Grady extends his hand to me, and I shake it.

"I'm glad you think so because that's all I want to be for your sister."

"Where to now, sir?" Cliff asks as I get back in the car.

"To Charlotte and Rowan's."

He gives me a brief nod and we take the five-minute drive. When I get there, Charlotte laughs once when I explain my reason for being there and grabs her walkie-talkie.

"Rowan, Crew is here to see you."

There's a touch of static then he comes in. "Understood, Angry Elf. Is he waiting or does he want me to come see him later? Over."

She sighs heavily. "He wants you to come here." Charlotte's eyes widen as she turns to me. "Right? You want to talk now?"

"If he can."

"He can," she replies without asking him.

"Angry Elf, do you read me? Over."

She mutters under her breath, but I can hear it. "He's going to see what the hell angry looks like." Then she brings the walkie-talkie to her mouth. "Rowan, come back to the house so Crew can talk."

"Angry Elf, this is Skittle Titties, do you copy? Over."

Her face turns a shade of red and she groans loudly. Then she forcibly grips the communication device. "Rowan! I swear to God! You are going to taste the rainbow of your teeth if you keep this up."

"Ten-four, Angry Elf. Message received. Over."

Very slowly, she places the walkie-talkie on the table and turns to me. "It's a good thing you're here, otherwise, I might have to kill him."

I laugh once, because what the hell do you say to that? "I could provide the bail money," I offer.

"Would you? I mean, that might be all the incentive I need."

"Although, I think Brynn would probably be angry if I helped her brother's murderer," I tack on, rethinking my strategy.

She shrugs. "She's lived with him, I'm sure she'd understand."

Rowan enters the house, a wide grin on his face. "Hey, Crew."

"Rowan."

He walks to his wife, pulls her in his arms, and kisses her. "Don't be too pissed, babe. It's my only fun now that I have double the work since merging."

Charlotte huffs and then shakes her head. "Talk to your brother-in-law while I think of ways you can make it up to me."

He slaps her ass as she passes and earns himself a middle finger.

When she's gone, he turns to me. "What's up?"

I launch into my speech about why I'm here and what I'm hoping for. I should've known the first two brothers were too easy.

While they were understanding and gracious, Rowan is . . . himself.

"Since I missed out on this the first time, I'd like to ask some questions before I consent."

I lean back in the chair and nod once. "Ask away."

Really, I can't be pissed, because if this was me, I'd probably do the same. At least, I'd make him sweat it out and enjoy myself.

"Do you love her?"

"Yes," I answer immediately.

"Will you always be faithful to her?" Rowan asks.

"Absolutely."

Rowan's eyes narrow. "Even when she's annoying? She can be a pain in the ass. Especially with those freaking animals."

"Even then," I vow.

"Okay, now to the really important questions . . ." He leans back. "Who is your favorite Whitlock?"

"Brynlee," I answer without pause.

"Yes, but she's actually Brynlee Knight so . . ."

I laugh. "I plead the fifth."

"I'm going to pretend that means me. I get it, I'm everyone's favorite." Rowan stands, and I do the same. "All kidding aside, it's very clear you love her. You bought that fucking company just to shut it down to avoid her being hurt. All any of us have ever wanted for Brynn was to find someone who would treat her right and love her."

I stare into his eyes, meaning every word that comes from my mouth. "I love her more than anything in this world, Rowan. I want to marry her again so she knows it."

"Then I can't wait to be there."

thirty-four

BRYNLEE

"Can we bring the chickens treats?" Layla asks as we're walking back from putting the animals in the barn.

It's getting late, and it's almost time for bed.

"What do you want to bring them?"

She loves coming out with her bucket of scraps. Although, I think the chickens love it even more, since this week, we had an egg, which was a huge shock since we haven't had any of the hens lay in months.

"Everything!" she yells and bounces up and down.

I smile and nod. "Okay, let's see what we have in the pail for them."

Layla rushes down the path, her pale blond hair flowing back and forth as she runs. We've spent almost all day outside, and as exhausted as I am, I also feel alive. Being back home has been exactly what I needed.

Addison has been amazing and takes Layla most mornings to come play with the kids until dinnertime. She says adding one more is no big deal, plus it keeps her two from fighting since Elodie has a girl to play girl stuff with.

Poor Jett is stuck doing what they want unless Grady takes him to the hangar and prays he doesn't break something.

CORINNE MICHAELS

When I get close to the house, Layla is already running back to me with the pail. "I have the treats!"

"You do? What's in there?"

She looks down and makes a face of disgust. "Green beans."

I fight back a laugh. "I thought you liked green beans." She doesn't. Last night was the first time I've really gotten to see her have a tantrum. She wouldn't eat them no matter what. Crew "allowed" me to cook since I went the entire day without a nap. I made pork chops, green beans, and corn bread. She loved the bread and the pork, but anything that's green or has the name in it, she says is disgusting.

"They're gross!"

I nod as though I agree. "Well, let's see if the chickens like them."

Layla takes my hand, and we walk back toward the chicken castle. "Here, girls," I call, clicking my tongue.

They run toward us and Layla giggles. "You wait, girls!" she tells them. "I give you one." She places a green bean down. "And you one." Another chicken gets it. "You can have one too!"

She continues doing that, giving treats out one at a time. "What about me?" a deep voice asks from behind me.

"Daddy!"

I smile as she dumps the pail and rushes to her hero. "Ladybug, are you feeding the chickens?" he asks as he lifts her into his arms. I close the coop door and walk over to where they're standing.

"I did, but now we have no more." She lifts both hands and shrugs.

"Well, that stinks. We need to find them some for tomorrow."

Layla looks at me. "Do we have more green beans?"

I burst out laughing. "Yes, sweetheart, we have more that we can give the chickens."

"Good, because they like them."

Crew comes closer, leaning down to give me a kiss. "You feeling okay?"

"Yes, honey."

He snorts. "Like you'd tell me anyway."

I ignore that one. "How did your meetings go?" I ask. He left early this morning saying he needed to take some meetings outside of the house.

"Good. Everything went as I hoped."

"That's good."

"Daddy, do we have to go back to the other house?" Layla takes his face in her hands, forcing him to look at her.

"Yes, we do, but we'll stay here for another night."

She pouts her lower lip, looking so damn cute. "Okay."

He sighs heavily. "It's late, Ladybug."

"I'm not tired."

He eyes her warily. "Still, it's bedtime."

"Can I run for just a minute? Please," Layla pleads.

He places her down. "You sure can, we'll be right behind you."

I love Layla. She's truly the most amazing little girl in the world. I'm so blessed I get to be her bonus mom and love her with my whole heart.

The two of us walk at a slow pace, I feel the weight of the day starting to come down on me. Once we're inside the house, Crew and I get Layla cleaned up and in bed.

I head into the kitchen to do the dishes. As I'm standing there, I feel Crew's arms snake around my stomach, his head on my shoulder. "I missed you all day today."

"You were gone three and a half hours."

"They were much too long."

I smile, turning my face to see him. "I missed you too. I never thought I'd say this, but I'm glad we're going back to the city tomorrow."

"You are?" he asks with surprise in his voice.

I turn the water off and face him. "Yeah, I have a lot of work to do, and Layla needs to get settled in the house. So far, since we've gotten custody, her life has been in upheaval. I want her to be comfortable."

While she seems to be thriving on the farm, it's not what she's used to. The back and forth isn't fair. The sooner we get her on a routine, the better. Plus, Jacqueline will start her visitation soon.

Crew kisses my nose. "What if we settled here?"

Now it's my turn to be shocked. "What?"

"What if we were in the city less than we were here?"

I truly can't do anything but gape at him. That makes no sense. He has his companies, family, friends. Well, maybe not that last one. Layla has her school there, that freaking insanely priced apartment that would just sit empty. Plus, my company is going to be based out of New York.

"Crew, there're a lot of reasons why New York works for us."

"And we can do most of it remotely," he tosses back. "We love it in Sugarloaf. We have a home, family, your friends are here, and Layla loves her cousins."

My heart melts at that. She really does love them. "Yes, but what about our companies?"

"Bee, you don't have to work. You know that, right?"

Yeah, I mean, now that I know a lot more about his net worth, I get that I don't have to work. Yet, I do.

My hands rest on his solid chest. "I want to work. I love what Thea and I are building, we just hired Aarabelle, and I'd like to have something of my own. Work makes me feel useful."

I hope he understands that.

"Okay." Crew accepts it without a fight. "I want you to know if there's a point where you don't want to work, you don't have to."

"I appreciate that."

"Like, maybe when we have kids?"

My brows rise and I gape at him. "Kids?"

"If you want."

I literally don't know what to say. "You want more kids?" I ask hesitantly.

He turns to face me, hands on my hips. "I never wanted kids, you know that. Then I had Layla and I learned how much love a father could have for his child. I figured she'd be my only child, and I've been completely fine with that. But . . . I want to have children with you, if that's what you want. I want to watch you grow heavy with our baby, knowing that he or she will come into a house filled with love." Crew sighs. "I'm fucking this up, but . . ."

"What do you mean?" He drops down on one knee, takes my hand, and looks up at me. "What are you doing?" I ask.

"Brynlee Knight, I married you, the woman I love, months ago. I stood in front of our family and friends and vowed to love you forever, only we agreed that forever wasn't in our cards. When I asked you to marry me, I didn't get to say the things I wanted, but I need to now."

Tears fill my eyes and I drop down onto my knees in my tiny kitchen. "Crew . . ."

"I love you more than I have ever loved anyone. I want to wake up next to you every morning. I want your nights to be in my arms. I want us to be a family, whatever that looks like. I want trips to Paris and kisses on the terrace. Every single day I choose you to be my wife, my lover, my fucking world. I asked you to be my wife to give us something, but I ended up getting everything." He reaches into his pocket, pulling out a box. "I spent today with your brothers and then visiting Howie. I asked each of them for permission to marry you again. I wish I could say that if I could go back in time, I would change things, but if I did that, I wouldn't have you."

He brushes the tears from my cheeks, and I take his face in my hands. "Yes."

Crew jerks back with a grin. "I didn't ask yet."

I let out a laugh and then sniff. "Sorry."

He opens the box and there is a diamond eternity band.

"So, I'm here, on my knees, asking if you will be my wife in every single way. Marry me. Marry me because you love me. Marry me because you know I love you with everything that I am. Marry me because we want to build a life together, a family. Be at my side—for eternity."

I rest my forehead to his. "Is there a question?"

He chuckles, framing my face and lifting my head. His crystal blue eyes are shimmering with unshed tears. "My darling Bee, will you do me the honor of being my wife for the rest of our lives?"

My fingers wrap around his wrists. "Yes."

He brings his lips to mine in the most tender kiss we've ever shared.

Slowly, the kiss becomes more passionate, and I'm desperate for him. It's been weeks we've gone without each other, and I need him.

So much.

"Crew," I whisper against his lips.

His tongue moves with mine and I could drown in him. We kiss deeper and I move my hand down his chest. Crew gentles the kiss, causing me to whimper.

"God, I want you so much," he confesses.

"Please. Please don't stop."

"Brynlee." My name sounds almost painful for him to say.

At my follow-up in a week, we should get the all clear, but I need something. I need to be close to him, to feel his body against mine. Not just cuddling, but . . . more.

"They never said we can't fool around," I remind him.

He smiles before kissing me again, and the hunger in his touch burns down to my toes. I push at his chest before taking his hand, leading him to our bedroom.

When we are inside, he kicks the door closed and then my face is cradled in his grasp, lips on mine again.

I move my hand back down his front, reaching for the waistband of his pants. I fumble at the button, but then it releases, and I slip my hand down, wrapping it around his erection as his pants fall to the floor. Crew breathes heavily, kissing me deeper as I start to stroke him.

He kicks the pants off and I work at pushing his underwear off. I want to feel him, all of him, without anything between us.

"I can't wait for you to be inside of me again," I tell him. "I miss us. I miss feeling you claim me."

He pants harder. "You have no idea how much I want that."

I'm pretty sure I do.

"Touch me, Crew."

"I don't think I could stop if I had to." His hands move from my face, down my neck and shoulders, before he reaches lower to the hem of my sundress. "This is convenient."

"Had I known this would've been the benefit, I would've worn one weeks ago."

Slowly, he lifts it up, my arms rising to allow him the ability to remove it. I stand in just my underwear since my bra wasn't necessary with the dress. "You are so damn beautiful."

I've always struggled with self-confidence. Most girls do, but for me, it was deeper. I felt unworthy, unloved, and stupid. Right now, I don't feel any of that, I just feel beautiful.

To him, my flaws don't exist, or if they do, he loves me because of them.

Crew steps back and tosses his shirt on the floor. "Climb on the bed, I don't want to hurt you."

"You could never hurt me. I don't think you would know how."

He shakes his head. "I've done it before, love, and I never want to feel that again."

I move around to the side, paying attention to my incision site, which is fully healed. When I'm sitting, he climbs in beside me. I move to him, knowing that he's never going to get on top, not when he worries about crushing me, moving me the wrong way. Hell, cuddling was an issue.

So, I'm going to have to lead this show.

Which is fine by me.

I straddle him and bring my lips to his. His fingers lace in my hair, holding me to him, as if I had any plans of moving.

His other hand moves to my breast, cupping it and rubbing his thumb back and forth against my nipple. I gasp and he groans when I rub myself against his erection, thankful I have my panties on or I would totally slip so he was inside me, where I want him most.

"Brynn," he groans my name when I move against him again. "Fuck, baby, we can't."

"No, but I can imagine. I can dream about how it would be if I was completely naked, and you were buried inside of me."

His fingers grip my ass, and he thrusts his hips up. "I'd torture you, going so slow, moving at a pace that would be just fast enough to make you close, but too slow to let you come. I'd make you crazy, make you beg for more of my cock, but only give it a little at a time."

I rock again. "Then what?"

"Then I'd slam into you so hard you felt it the next day." Oh, how much I wish that could be true. "Why don't I demonstrate another way?"

I look down at him in confusion. "What?"

"Take off your underwear, Bee."

I move and pull them down, praying he's going to ignore the doctor's orders and let me have what I want.

When I start to go back toward him, he grips my thigh. "Turn around." I do and he lifts one of my legs, shifting so he's under me, his mouth near my clit. "Now, I'm going to fuck you with my mouth while you suck my dick."

I am so turned on, I can't do anything other than moan. Crew pulls at my knees, so I lower to his face and his tongue swipes against my core. I don't have time to think or do anything before he's pulling me almost flat. My body is already tense and close. It's been so long, and I want this man so much.

Shifting forward, I maneuver myself so I can take him in my mouth. Crew moans against my clit and I feel the vibrations through my limbs. I try to focus on him, wanting him to lose it before me. My hand pumps at him as I suck him deeper, feeling him at the back of my throat. His fingers dig into my ass, and I keep going.

It feels so good and it's almost impossible to keep up my pace when my body begins to tremble. He moves one hand around and pushes inside, fingering me while his tongue assaults my clit.

Over and over he flicks and makes patterns that cause me to whimper. Then he takes over even more, shifting his hips so that he can control the pace of him fucking my mouth. God, this is too much.

I can't hold back.

I can't stop it.

I work harder, moving my hand faster as the two of us chase our releases. He slaps my ass and then pushes his face up more while pulling down.

When I feel his finger rim my ass, I nearly die. He plays just around the edge, not pushing in but letting me know he's there.

My orgasm rockets through me so intensely, I swear I might have blacked out. He licks and fingers me at the same time, pulling me through so many degrees of pleasure.

"Brynn, I'm going to, baby, move your mouth." I don't, though. I stay there, pumping him harder, and he groans. "Fuck, yes. That's it, good girl, let me come in your mouth."

He does and I take it all, loving that I brought him there.

I move to the side, curling up against him. "Are you okay?"

My eyes find his. "I'm very okay."

"I mean your incision. Does anything hurt?"

I smile at him, loving him so much. "Nothing hurts. Everything feels better."

"Everything is better with you, Bee. Everything."

And it is. Our lives, our hearts, our souls—our world is brighter, and I'm the happiest I've ever been.

I nestle in tighter, letting his warmth surround me. "Everything is better because we have each other."

thirty-five
BRYNLEE

~ONE YEAR LATER~

"Can I wear this dress to school tomorrow?" Layla asks as she twirls in her flower girl dress.

"I think it's a little fancy." I boop her nose. "But you can wear it around the house anytime you want."

"Are you going to wear your dress again?"

Of all the dresses I wish I could wear again, it would be this one. For my second wedding dress, I wore a strapless beaded gown that I'm obsessed with. The only reason I have it is thanks to the fact that the designer happens to be a client for Anchor Light.

When I told her we were having a second wedding, she demanded that I let her design my gown as a thank you for handling her social media crisis.

I couldn't really say no, and I'm so glad I didn't.

"You're only supposed to wear your wedding dress once," I tell her.

"I didn't get married, though."

I laugh. "That's true. So you can wear yours again."

She grins. "Can I wear it to see Mommy?"

"I don't see why not."

"And I get to see her in two days?"

"You sure do," I say with a smile.

Jacqueline has been doing really well. She's still sober, working on herself in therapy, and has been extremely consistent with Layla. While the relationship between Crew and Jacqueline may never be overly friendly, he will do anything required for Layla's sake.

Thankfully, Asher has been incredibly open about co-parenting and modeling what it can look like. Sara and Asher are friends more than anything, and Sara and Phoebe adore each other. It's the most incredibly functional relationship that should be dysfunctional.

After her first year of being sober, Jacqueline will be able to get one overnight visit unsupervised. After six months, Crew agreed to a dinner once a week, and that's been the pattern since.

"Are you and Daddy going to get married again?" she asks.

"Probably not. This was so that you could be here and get all dressed up."

At least that's what we're letting her believe.

"Layla! Come on! Let's go see the horses!" Elodie yells, waving her over.

She looks to me and I laugh once. "Go ahead, we already did pictures."

Layla doesn't hesitate, she's gone before I finish and off to harass Jett, if I know those two girls.

I look in through the big barn doors, taking in the scene and smiling. Everyone we love is here. My family, Crew's family, and the town of Sugarloaf.

My dad is talking to Phoebe's dad. The two of them, who I would think would be the most unlikely friends, have become besties. Howie comes to Sugarloaf once a month to spend time with our family. It was a bit awkward at first, but even my brothers have come around. While I don't push it, trying to bring him to family dinners, they were all nice to each other at Layla's birthday party.

The lights twinkle and the music changes again, and I see Crew being dragged out to dance by Mrs. Cooke. And I'm not even surprised she got her claws in him. Those ladies love him. Not that it's hard to find reasons to be completely enamored with him, but Crew can do no wrong in their eyes.

"Hello, Brynlee."

I turn to see Mrs. Symonds. Seriously, did she just appear here? For an elderly woman, she moves quickly.

"Oh, my. Hi, Mrs. Symonds. So great to see you."

"I came out here because it's so loud in there. You should've gone with a band, not that DJ, if you can call him that."

I smile because I'm not going to let anything ruin today. "I'll remember that for next time."

"Better not be a next time! You should thank your lucky stars a man like that came around. That Carson is just the most wonderful man we've ever known."

Every single time I come in contact with her or her two troublemaker best friends, they inform me on how lucky I am. As if I didn't already know that.

"He sure is."

She nods, agreeing with either herself or me. "I'll tell you, we worried about you for a long time."

"Oh?"

"You just had all those animals. You were the equivalent of an old lady with a hundred cats."

I fight back a laugh. "I don't think I was that bad. I wasn't even thirty."

"Yes, but who wants to take over a barn full of animals?" she tsks.

"Clearly, my husband."

Mrs. Symonds nods. "Yes, that Carson is a lovely man. Handsome too."

"That he is," I agree. Although, I think he's much more than handsome.

"Anyway, I just wanted to tell you the food is good, but the music is terrible."

I smile. "Thank you for the compliment on the food."

"I've watched you grow up, Brynlee. I've seen you endure some dark times and I know it was hard when you lost your mother. I just want you to know how proud I am. You've turned into an incredibly kind, beautiful, and caring woman. Your mother would be proud."

The tears I've held at bay almost all day come flooding forward. "I hope she would be."

Her paper-thin hands wrap around mine. "Any mother would." She smiles and releases me. "Now, go inside and make sure your brother isn't causing any issues."

"Which one?"

She shrugs. "They're all trouble."

I laugh and watch as she heads inside while I take a few more minutes out here.

Not even two minutes later, Charlotte peeks her head out. "Here you are!"

"I just needed a minute to breathe."

She closes the barn door and smiles. "I get it. Weddings are a lot and you've had more than one in just over a year."

"Both special in their own ways."

Both have given me the one thing I always wanted—Crew.

"If I had to pick between your weddings, I think this one is my favorite," Charlotte says as she hands me a glass of wine.

"I'm partial to the first one," I admit, taking the glass.

As amazing as this wedding is, being at the barn where Crew and I saw each other again—and truly, it is absolutely stunning—I really loved being where we met the first time.

Although, Crew likes to argue that this barn was where he found his life again, therefore it has more significance.

"This just feels full circle," Charlotte notes.

Since he wanted this wedding to be more for the town, we pretty much invited everyone we knew. All of our siblings were in the wedding party, Layla being the most stunning flower girl, alongside Elodie and Jett, and Olivia was my maid of honor.

Charlotte rests her hand on her protruding belly. "This baby is in a mood today."

I grin. "Well, it's half Rowan."

"Yes, and while I'll deny this if you ever repeat it, I'm not much better most days."

I bite back a laugh. "At least the sickness part is over."

She groans. "Please don't remind me."

Charlotte spent the better part of six months violently ill. I've never seen my brother so anxious before. Not that he's so much better now, but he's slightly less neurotic.

"Here you are," Crew says as he comes up behind me, wrapping his strong arms around my middle. "I was looking for you."

"Seems everyone is today." I smile, looking up at him from the side. "Charlotte and I were just talking."

He looks at my sister-in-law. "Your husband was searching for you as well."

"I'm sure he's convinced I'm giving birth in the bathroom. Let me go find him." Charlotte waddles off.

We stay like this for a minute and then he turns me to face him. "I think today went well."

"It did," he agrees. "The town seems extremely happy."

"That's because you gave them all gifts for coming," I remind him.

Instead of us getting wedding gifts, we decided to give them. Everyone who is attending received a tablet. I thought it was absolutely ridiculous, but Crew wasn't hearing it. He said he wanted to show love back to the people who have loved us.

"I find that bribery works because they're less likely to bring us more stray animals."

"Doubtful."

We've more than doubled Second Chances Animal Sanctuary since when we first married. I now have a full-time staff that runs it and when we're here, I get to love on the animals and watch them thrive.

"Yeah, I don't know what I was thinking."

I grin and grip his lapels. "I know what I'm thinking."

He raises one brow. "Oh?"

"I'm thinking that my husband is so incredibly perfect."

"And I hoped you were thinking something dirty," Crew tosses back.

"Sorry to disappoint."

"You never disappoint me, Bee."

I rise on my toes and kiss him. "Good."

I rock back and pull my lower lip between my teeth. I have to tell him something that I worry he won't react well to. Lord knows he has a tendency to overreact to everything when he's concerned about my safety.

Of course, my husband can read my face and his eyes narrow. "What's wrong?"

This isn't exactly how I wanted to discuss things, but I know better than to try to play it off like there's nothing wrong. He'll never believe me.

"I need you to not freak out, okay?"

His body tenses. Yeah, this is going to be great. Crew lets out a long breath through his nose. "I'll try."

I guess that's all I can ask for.

"I went to visit the transplant team two weeks ago for my routine visit."

"Yes, and you told me everything was great," he reminds me.

"I did. They ran a bunch of bloodwork and tests to make sure my liver function was back to normal, which it is. Mostly everything came back great."

"Mostly?"

"They found something in my bloodwork that was elevated, that normally isn't." Crew's arms drop, but I keep hold of his lapels. "Calm, baby. Please, stay calm."

His crystal blue eyes lock on mine. "What's wrong, Brynlee?"

Okay, well, here it goes.

"I'm pregnant." Crew doesn't blink, it's almost like a trance in a way. I move my head in front of his gaze. "Hello?"

"Pregnant?"

"I know we kind of talked about maybe having a baby at some

point. It really isn't the greatest timing with having the PR company going nuts."

We've signed so many new clients thanks to my husband's ridiculous contacts and the fact we signed a football team. Aarabelle is now running her own division dealing with social media crisis and has been absolutely amazing. Her team is signing more clients than we can handle, which is why we just hired two more publicists.

It's a lot.

It's amazing.

It's not the best time to have a baby, but here we are.

His hands move to my stomach. "Pregnant?"

I nod. "Yes. I'm maybe six weeks."

"How the hell didn't you notice?"

"I've been kind of busy with the company, planning a wedding, getting Layla enrolled in her new school, and us traveling back and forth. I honestly didn't register my period was late."

Crew just shakes his head, his eyes full of amazement. "Are you okay? Feeling good? What about your liver? The doctor told us to wait."

"Everything is fine. I'll be closely monitored. Dr. Carr isn't overly worried."

He cups my face. "I didn't know it was possible to love you any more than I already do. I didn't know that . . . Bee, we're going to have a baby."

A tear slips down my cheek. "I know."

"This makes my wedding gift of an office building in New York look lame."

I laugh. "You bought me a building?"

"It was supposed to be a surprise."

"I guess we both got surprises then."

Crew brings his lips to mine in a soft kiss, then he scoops me up in his arms and starts to walk away from the barn. "Crew! What are you doing?"

"You, my gorgeous, wonderful, pregnant wife, are going to your bed, where you will stay until you give birth."

I laugh, slapping his chest. "Put me down."

"Prepare, my love, I'm going to be overprotective and over-bearing."

I wrap my arms around his neck a little tighter. "So it'll be like normal?"

He snorts. "Not even close."

"Clearly since you're carrying me away from our wedding. People came to see us and how are we going to explain that my neanderthal husband needed to put me to bed?"

He looks back at the barn. "They'll survive and I don't care what they think. I most definitely need to take you to bed—immediately."

I roll my eyes and shake my head, grateful we thought ahead to have Layla stay at my brother's, because I'm going to enjoy this wedding night.

epilogue

BRYNLEE

~SEVEN MONTHS LATER~

"Brynlee! I swear to God you are the worst fucking patient that has ever lived!" Crew bellows as I'm sitting in my office with my phone to my ear.

I put my hand up, telling him to be quiet, and return to my call. "Killian, you need to calm down. We will handle it."

Killian Thorn is our biggest client. When he calls, we answer. "I don't know what to do, Brynn. This is blowing up. All because some woman made a claim on social media! There is press at my house, we had swarms of people outside the office. I need help. I need you to handle this."

"I understand. I really do, I would be there, but I just had a baby. I'm going to get our top person out there. Where are you now?"

"Ember Falls."

"Okay, send me an email with the address and I'll have Aarabelle get in touch. Just don't talk to anyone about this."

Crew enters my office, sitting in the chair in the corner, holding our son against his chest. I can't fight the smile on my face when I see him kiss the top of his head.

Jameson Crew Knight entered our world three days ago and I am under strict instructions to take it easy. I was in labor for thirty-three hours and it put a lot of strain on my body. I was literally minutes away from a c-section, but I was adamant I wanted to try it this way.

"This is a fucking nightmare, trust me I don't want to talk to anyone."

"We'll take care of it. If I were you, I'd be ready to spend some time in Ember Falls where you've evaded the press."

"That's my plan. I'll send that email now."

I hang up and my husband just sits there, Jameson asleep on his chest and one brow raised. "You promised, Bee."

He made me swear that I would listen to the doctors and rest, which I have done for the last two days. This was just . . . work. You'd think Crew, of all people, would understand. Although, he's cut back a lot. Kimberly now is the CEO of Knight Food Distribution. He handed that over to her a year ago. She's doing amazing things and he's able to spend a lot less time traveling now.

"I know, I know, but he called, and I needed to step in."

"You have Aarabelle," he reminds me.

"Yes, and she's going to be super happy that she needs to fly down there today to fix this."

I get up from my chair, wincing, because giving birth is not exactly comfortable, and walk over to my boys.

"Your entire freaking family is coming today to bring Layla back and see the baby. Could you please go back to bed and spend at least a few hours with your feet up? We all know once they get here, there will be no rest."

"Fine, but only if you both come with me," I acquiesce.

Crew gets up, cradling Jameson with one arm and pulling me to his side. "Let's go."

We get back to our bedroom and climb in bed, he places the baby between us, and I lie here, staring at my son. "He's so perfect."

"He came from you, of course he is."

I grin. "Layla asked if he could sleep in her room," I tell him.

"That would last one night."

"That's what I told her. She's just excited to have a brother." I also had to restrain myself from telling her how much brothers can suck.

Still, I hope they have the kind of love mine have with me. There's nothing in this world my brothers wouldn't do for me and vice versa.

"I honestly keep wondering how I got so lucky in life. I have two beautiful children and a wife I would lay down my life for."

Crew laces our fingers together and we rest them on Jameson. "I ask myself the same thing. You really are lucky."

We both laugh and Jameson fusses for a second. "Let's nap while he does because once the Whitlocks get here, there will be none of that."

I wish I could say I responded, but I'm pretty sure I was halfway asleep after the word nap.

~Carson~

"So, you marry our sister under duress, somehow convince her to marry you again, knock her up, and then make her go through hell for birth?" Rowan asks as he sits on the chair beside the baby, who is asleep in his stroller.

We're back in Sugarloaf and having one of our very long, very loud family barbecues.

"Pretty much."

He shrugs. "Sounds like the makings of a good marriage."

I grin. Her brothers, while being insanely annoying, are also a very welcome addition to my life. Since Rowan no longer works directly for me, our relationship has really changed. I've helped him and Charlotte with some business investments and her company has really taken off thanks to the social media virality she's had.

Rowan bought a failing farm a town over from Sugarloaf that

has nothing to do with cows, and he's been able to diversify and grow with Knight Food Distribution.

"And how is Maci doing?"

"Good. She's crawling all over the place, driving Charlotte nuts, which in turn, means I suffer."

"Please! You have never suffered a day in your life," Asher says handing us both a beer. "However, you really will when she starts dating."

"Says the man who is dating his daughter's nanny."

"Former nanny and married to," he corrects. "One day that joke will get old."

Rowan chuckles and looks to me. "Not until I'm dead."

"That can be arranged," Asher says with a smirk.

"You'll be the one who has to deal with dating before he does," I remind Asher. "Olivia is what? Thirteen?"

Rowan nods. "Yeah, that's right. Think of what we were doing at thirteen."

Asher's face falls. "Olivia has no interest in boys."

Just then my wife walks over with a tray of food. "What's going on here and why does Asher look close to homicide?"

I smile. "Just reminding Asher that Olivia is at that dating age."

Brynlee tilts her head. "Did she tell you about something?"

Asher's eyes snap to his sister. "Tell me about what?"

Brynn shrugs. "Nothing."

The way that came out tells all of us there's definitely something. Brynn's brother isn't stupid, he heard it too.

"Is she interested in some boy?" Asher asks.

"I wouldn't know, Ash." Then she winks at me. "Even if I did, I wouldn't tell you. That would be breaking the Auntie Code."

"What's going on?" Grady asks, rounding out the whole Whitlock crew.

I speak up because it's much too fun to stay out of. "We're all just telling Asher about a boy that Olivia may or may not like, that he may or may not have to worry about because you know . . . teenage boys."

Grady nods his head. "That would be why he looks like his head is going to explode."

He groans. "You know, you all are fucking assholes. Each and every one of you." He looks to Grady. "Elodie? Yeah, she's going to date." Then to me. "Oh, and Layla? Yeah . . . good luck with that." Then he turns to Rowan. "You think Maci is going to skip it? At least I will have survived once before you're all in the shit around the same time."

Brynlee clears her throat. "Excuse me, but you also have Sienna right on their heels."

He looks heavenward then reaches for his phone.

"What are you doing?" Rowan asks.

"Buying a chastity belt."

"See if there's a family discount," I say because there's no way I'm letting some little punk ass around Layla.

"Daddy, can Jameson stay in New York when we come to Sugarloaf?" Layla asks as we're sitting on the couch, trying to watch a movie while he wails in the bedroom with Brynn.

I fight back a laugh. "Jameson goes where we go, Ladybug."

"But he's very loud. I can't hear the movie."

Valid point. "He's still your brother and we love him."

"He just cries so much."

In all honesty, he really doesn't. She was a much fussier baby than he is. Once a day Jameson is beyond comfort and that's right after dinner. He screams and screams for at least forty minutes, then he falls asleep and it's easy sailing after that.

"You know, when you were a baby, I took you to the doctor thinking something was wrong because you cried all the time."

"You did?" Layla asks. "Maybe we should take Jameson because I think he's broken."

I pause on that one. "Broken?"

"Yeah, Uncle Rowan said he only cries when he breaks something. I think that Jameson has broken a lot of things."

I can't hold back a laugh this time. "I see. Jameson is a baby and he's tired, that's all. He'll stop soon." I look at my watch, it's been twenty minutes already. "How about I have Rin come out and hang with you. I'll take Jameson outside to see the stars."

She nods enthusiastically.

When I get in the room, Brynn is on the bed, Jameson in her arms, and she's got her reading glasses on with her eReader in her hand.

"You're reading?" I ask when he draws in a breath.

She glances up. "Might as well."

"You can think with his wailing?"

Just as I say that, Jameson whimpers, but it's not a complete scream. We both look down at him and Brynn smiles.

"Let's hope he's not just recharging for another round. Anyway, I'm reading this book about a Hollywood heartthrob named Dash, who comes back to his hometown, and he sees this girl whose family owns a diner in this small town *and* he's her best friend's brother. One thing leads to another, and they start hooking up, thinking it's short term, but he's totally in love with her and, ugh, it's going to break my heart when he has to leave her. I can't put it down."

"And people say our relationship sounds improbable."

"Well, you are the billionaire who fell for the small-town girl. Sort of unbelievable if you ask me."

I walk over, pulling the eReader out of her hand. "I fell in love with you before I was a billionaire. Also, anyone who spends two seconds with you understands how the only thing that would be unbelievable was if I let you go."

Brynn smiles softly. "Aww." Then her voice shifts and gone is the sweetness. "But. You did do that."

"I got you back."

"Yes," she sighs deeply. "I guess you did."

"I was coming in here to switch out with you. Layla wanted to watch a movie."

We both stare at our son who is now sleeping. Her eyes meet mine. "If we move him and he wakes . . ." Yeah, that's the worry each night. "Go get her."

"What?"

"Get Layla, we'll put the movie on in here, curl up together, and watch whatever she wants."

I kiss Brynn's forehead and head out to grab Layla.

"Rin, can we watch—" She stops when she sees it's me. "Hi, Daddy."

"How about we all lay in bed and watch a movie?"

"Jameson, too?" Layla asks.

I chuckle. "Jameson, too. He's nice and quiet, though."

Layla sighs heavily and gets up. "All right."

"That's my girl."

We head into the room where Brynn moved to the other side of the bed so we can all be comfortable and she can put Jameson in the side sleeper that attaches to the bed.

"What movie are we watching?" Brynn asks as Layla jumps up on the bed.

Layla heads right to her, sitting on her other side. Brynn wraps her other arm around Layla and kisses the top of her head. "*Cinderella*. I love it when the prince brings her shoe, and she dances with him. I hope one day I have a prince like that."

Brynn smiles and her eyes find mine. "I hope you do too and I'm glad I found mine."

"I'm pretty sure I found you."

She shrugs. "We found each other."

I climb into the bed with my wife and our two kids, push play on the movie, and smile, because there's nothing else in the world I need other than this.

I wasn't ready to let Crew and Brynlee go just yet. Swipe to the next page for access to an EXCLUSIVE Bonus Scene!

Next we're heading to Ember Falls! Who knows who we might run into there!

Preorder: All Too Well

Have you read all of the Whitlock Farm books?

Forbidden Hearts (Age Gap/Single Dad)
Broken Dreams (Fake Dating/Single Parents)
Tempting Promises (Enemies to Lovers/Forced Proximity)
Forgotten Desires (Billionaire/Single Dad)

Dear Reader,

I hope you enjoyed Forgotten Desires! I had a hard time saying goodbye to Crew & Brynlee. I wanted to give just a little more of a glimpse into their lives, so ... I wrote a super fun scene.

Since giving you a link would be a pain in the ... you know what ... I have an easy QR code you can scan, sign up, and you'll get and email giving you access! Or you can always type in the URL!

https://geni.us/FD_signup

If you'd like to just keep up with my sales and new releases, you can follow me on BookBub or sign up for text alerts!
BookBub: https://www.bookbub.com/authors/corinne-michaels

Join my Facebook group!
https://www.facebook.com/groups/corinnemichaelsbooks

books by corinne michaels

Want a downloadable reading order?

https://geni.us/CM_ReadingGuide

The Salvation Series

Beloved

Beholden

Consolation

Conviction

Defenseless

Evermore: A 1001 Dark Night Novella

Indefinite

Infinite

The Hennington Brothers

Say You'll Stay

Say You Want Me

Say I'm Yours

Say You Won't Let Go: A Return to Me/Masters and Mercenaries Novella

Second Time Around Series

We Own Tonight

One Last Time

Not Until You

If I Only Knew

The Arrowood Brothers

Come Back for Me

Fight for Me

The One for Me

Stay for Me

Destined for Me: An Arrowood/Hennington Brothers Crossover Novella

Willow Creek Valley Series

Return to Us

Could Have Been Us

A Moment for Us

A Chance for Us

Rose Canyon Series

Help Me Remember

Give Me Love

Keep This Promise

Whitlock Family Series

Forbidden Hearts

Broken Dreams

Tempting Promises

Forgotten Desires

Ember Falls Series

(Coming 2024-2025)

All Too Well

Against All Odds

Here and Now

Come What May

Co-Written with Melanie Harlow

Hold You Close

Imperfect Match

Standalone Novels

You Loved Me Once

acknowledgments

My husband and children. I love you all so much. Your love and support is why I get to even have an acknowledgment section.

My assistant, Christy Peckham, you always have my back and I can't imagine working with anyone else. I love your face.

Melanie Harlow, you have no idea how much I cherish our friendship. You are truly one of my best friends in the world and I don't know what I would do without you.

My publicist, Nina Grinstead, you're stuck with me forever at this point. You are more than a publicist, you're a friend, a cheerleader, a shoulder to lean on, and so much more.

The entire team at Valentine PR who support me, rally behind me, and keep me smiling.

Nancy Smay, my editor for taking such great care with my story. My cover designer who deals with my craziness, Sommer Stein. My proofreaders: Julia, and Michele.

Samaiya, thank you for drawing that lock so perfectly! You've become such an important part of my team.

Every influencer who picked this book up, made a post, video, phoned a friend … whatever it was. Thank you for making the book world a better place.

about the author

Corinne Michaels is a *New York Times, USA Today, and Wall Street Journal* bestselling author of romance novels. Her stories are chock full of emotion, humor, and unrelenting love, and she enjoys putting her characters through intense heartbreak before finding a way to heal them through their struggles.

Corinne is a former Navy wife and happily married to the man of her dreams. She began her writing career after spending months away from her husband while he was deployed—reading and writing were her escape from the loneliness. Corinne now lives in Virginia with her husband and is the emotional, witty, sarcastic, and fun-loving mom of two beautiful children.